**monsoon**books

OPERATION FOUR RING

Lt. Col. JP Cross is a retired British officer who served with Gurkha units for nearly forty years. He has been an Indian frontier soldier, jungle fighter, policeman, military attaché, Gurkha recruitment officer and a linguist researcher, and he is the author of twenty books. He has fought in Burma, Indo-China, Malaya and Borneo and served in India, Pakistan, Hong Kong, Laos and Nepal where he now lives. Well into his nineties, he still walks four hours daily.

Operation Four Rings is the fifth in a series of historical military novels set in Southeast Asia comprising, in chronological order, *Operation Black Rose*, *Operation Janus*, *Operation Blind Spot*, *Operation Stealth* and *Operation Four Rings*. The first three books may be read in any order; the final two are sequential. The series features Gurkha military units, and the author draws on real events he witnessed and real people he fought alongside in various theatres of war in Southeast Asia and India.

'Nobody in the world is better qualified to tell this story of the Gurkhas' deadly jungle battles against Communist insurgency in Malaya in the 1950s. Cross spins his tale with the eye of incomparable experience.'

John le Carré, on *Operation Janus*

'... a gripping adventure story ...
learn the ins and outs of jungle warfare from a true expert'

The Oldie, on *Operation Janus*

Also by JP Cross

OPERATION FOUR RINGS

JP CROSS

monsoon

monsoonbooks

First published in 2021
by Monsoon Books Ltd
www.monsoonbooks.co.uk

No.1 The Lodge, Burrough Court,
Burrough on the Hill, Leicestershire LE14 2QS, UK

ISBN (paperback): 9781912049509
ISBN (ebook): 9781912049516

Cover design by Cover Kitchen.

A Cataloguing-in-Publication data record is available from the British
Library.

Printed and bound in Great Britain by Clays Ltd, Elcograf S.p.A.
23 22 21   1 2 3

List of Characters

[Note: except for those with a * in front of their name, all the others were born in the author's imagination]

Anthony Crosland, Major, British Assistant Military Attaché, Laos, and embassy Beaver pilot

Bill Hodges, Secret Intelligence Service official, London

Bounphong Sunthorn, a senior Lao communist. Ring B

Charlie Law, English name of Thai surrogate son of David Law

David Law, Sir, Lieutenant General, KCB, CBE, DSO, MC, Director of Military Intelligence, Ministry of Defence, London

Ed Murray, Central Intelligence Agency, listed as Cultural Attaché in the Bangkok embassy

Etam Singvongsa, Brigadier General, Director of Intelligence, Royal Lao Army

François Lafouasse, of Veha Akad, a private aircraft maintenance concern, Vientiane, Laos

Gordon Parks, Secret Intelligence Service representative in British embassy, Vientiane, Laos

*Hồ Chí Minh, first Vietnamese leader

Inkham Hatsady, a.k.a. Princess Golden Fairy, Third Secretary, Royal Lao Embassy, London

Jason Percival Vere Rance, Lieutenant Colonel, Commandant, British Army Jungle Warfare School, Malaysia, later British Defence Attaché, Laos

Jay V. Gurganus, Colonel, US Army Attaché, Laos

John (J L B) Chambers, Indo-China desk officer in the Secret Intelligence Service, London

Joseph, Mr, supporting clerk for British Defence Attaché, Vientiane, Laos

Kaysorn Bouapha, Lao language teacher, Vientiane, Laos

Khian An, British Defence Attaché's house boy, Vientiane, Laos

Lanouk na Champassac, Prince, Defence Minister, Laos

Le Dâng Khoã, Major, Army of the Republic of Vietnam Guiding Officer, British Army Jungle Warfare School. A senior Vietnamese communist. Ring A

Leuam Sunthorn, British Defence Attaché's driver, Vientiane, Laos

Mana Varamit, Major, a.k.a. Major Chok Di when in Thai Secret Army

'Mango', code name for Head of Station, CIA, Vientiane

Maurice Richard Burke, Central Intelligence Agency representative in London

Nga Sô Lựu, a Vietnamese political commissar

Phannyana Maha Thera, abbot of Sam Neua, later Chief Bonze of Laos in Luang Prabang

Phoun Kaysorn, Lao barber, Vientiane, Laos

Prachan Pimparyon, Sergeant Major, Thai Frontier Police

*Savang Vatthana, King of Laos from 1959

*Soth Petrasy, head of Lao Patriotic Front delegation in Vientiane, Laos

*Souvanna Phouma, Prince, the Neutralist Prime Minister of Laos

Tâ Tran Quán, a.k.a. Tanh Bên Lòng, a senior Lao communist. Ring C

Thong Damdouane, a senior Lao communist. Ring D

Tom Higgins, Central Intelligence Agency contract Case Officer, Vientiane, Laos

*Vang Pao, Major General, Commander, Royal Lao Army, Military Region 2

Vladimir Gretchanine, Third Secretary, USSR embassy in Paris, later Defence Attaché in Laos

Vong, Major, a Tai Dam, Royal Lao Army

William Rogers, Head of Chancery and First Secretary, British embassy, Vientiane, Laos

Xutiati Xuto, a.k.a. Charlie Law

Yvonne Grambert, French language teacher, London

Abbreviations

AMA	Assistant Military Attaché
ARVN	Army of the Republic of Vietnam, South Vietnamese Army
BBC	British Broadcasting Corporation
BE	Buddhist Era
C-in-C	Commander-in-Chief
CIA	Central Intelligence Agency, USA
CPLA	Chinese People's Liberation Army
CTC	Central Training Command, Saigon
DA	Defence Attaché
DI	Defence Intelligence, Ministry of Defence, London
DMI	Director of Military Intelligence, Ministry of Defence, London
FCO	Foreign and Commonwealth Office, London
GHQ	General Headquarters
GI	'General issue', a US army private soldier
GR	Gurkha Rifles, British Army
GRU	Soviet Military Intelligence Agency
HE	His Excellency, used for ambassadors, etc
ICSC	International Control and Supervision Commission

LBJ	Lyndon (Baines) Johnson, 1908-73, 36th USA President, 1963-9
LP	Luang Prabang, the Lao royal capital
LPF	Lao Patriotic Front, political wing of anti-royalist faction in Laos
LPLA	Lao People's Liberation Army, more commonly known as PL
LS	Landing Site
MMF	Mission Militaire Français, a low-level training establishment for the Royal Lao Army
MOD	Ministry of Defence
MR	Military Region, Royal Lao Army
NVA	North Vietnamese Army. Its official name was The People's Army of the Democratic Republic of Vietnam but it was always alluded to as NVA
PA	personal assistant
PGNU	Provisional Government of National Union: joint Royal Lao Government and Lao Patriotic Front administration after Pathet Lao military victory
PL	Pathet Lao, military wing of Lao Patriotic Front
PLA	(Chinese) Peoples' Liberation Army
RLA	Royal Lao Army
RLAF	Royal Lao Air Force
RLG	Royal Lao Government
SDECE	French external intelligence service
SIS	Special Intelligence Service, United Kingdom, a.k.a. MI 6

| USAF | United States Air Force |
| USAID | United States Agency for International Development |

Lao Terms

baçi	ceremony of prayer and good wishes
ban	village, house
bor	a question suffix
bor pen nyang	it doesn't matter
Chao Ban	village headman
Meo	Lao ethnic tribe, now known as Mhong
phee	thirty-two spirits that inhabit a Lao's body
sabai di	how do you do
Tan	Mr
thud	attaché
Tu Nong	Your Highness, to a princess
wai	alutation, hands joined in front of face
wat	Buddhist temple

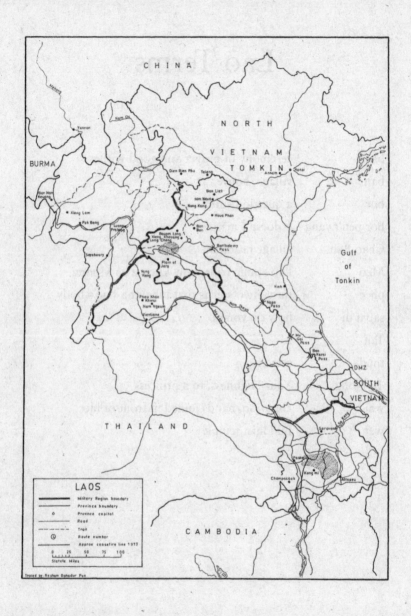

LAOS

- Military Region boundary
- Province boundary
- ○ Province capital
- Road
- Trail
- Ⓝ Route number
- Approx ceasefire line 1973

0   25   50   75   100
Statute Miles

Traced by Rashem Bahadur Pun

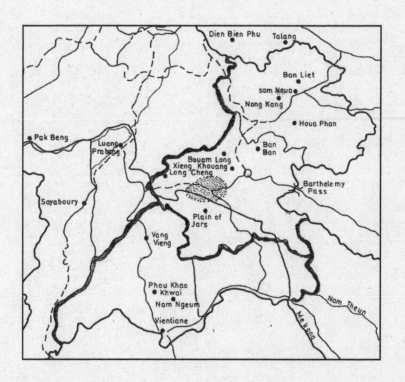

Preface

From pre-war days the Vietnamese Communists had wanted to emulate the French and take over, by influence if not by government, both Laos and Cambodia. Ruthlessly continuing their way soon after the end of World War Two, they were secretly countered by four dedicated Lao 'moles', all given a special ring, who tried to thwart these aims as well as avenge their parents' killing. A Thai secret agent of the Vietnamese actively tried to thwart them.

After being commissioned into the Gurkhas during World War Two Jason Rance unwittingly became the target to be killed a number of times. Most unusually his enemies chose a codeword for their operations that were also chosen by Jason's 'home team'. In his twenties it was *Operation Black Rose* mostly in India and Burma, in his thirties *Operation Janus* and *Operation Red Tidings* in Malaya, in his forties *Operation Blind Spot* in Peninsular Malaysia and Borneo.

In his fifties he was the last Commandant of the British Army's Jungle Warfare School near Johor Bahru in Peninsular Malaysia. In April 1972, during the last ever jungle warfare course comprising both Thai and Vietnamese students, the Thai Guiding Officer was the secret agent and the Vietnamese Guiding

Officer one of the 'moles'.

The Commandant was unwittingly dragged into their quarrel and the 'mole' gave him his ring for saving him from being killed by the Thai.

Rance was then posted to Laos as the Defence Attaché and even before he left England was a target of the Soviet KGB. As he had had Lao lessons with the King's niece when still in London, it was thought there was a very slim, one-off chance of stealthily persuading the uncrowned King of Laos to be crowned. It was even given its own codeword, *Operation Stealth*.

At the same time the Vietnamese Communists felt they had a good chance of taking over the country, slowly and stealthily, so they gave their proceedings a similar name, *Operation Stealth*.

Colonel Rance was made known to the King when the new ambassador presented his credentials and, by that time, he had met two of the four moles.

The Provisional Government of National Union in Laos was announced on 19 September 1973 and on 12 October London heavily ordained that any contact that Rance might make with the King would only be ceremonial, according to protocol if at all, so *Operation Stealth* became a dead letter. In its stead the General in MOD responsible for planning a continuation of Rance's quest, to be named *Operation Four Rings*, mandated that any contacts the secret world had for contact with any of the 'moles', would only be based using the Defence Attaché 'unconsciously', within the bounds of official constraints.

1

January-February 1974: Northwest Laos: The pornographic film flickered on the bare end wall of the mess room in an expanded United States Army Type C Special Forces camp at Xieng Lom in northwest Laos. As a particularly scabrous scene came to an erotic climax, the young Lao Captain sitting on the right of the British Defence Attaché, Colonel Jason Rance, could contain himself no longer. He half turned, squeezed the Englishman's knee and moaned. Rance recoiled in revulsion, hating to be touched. Also at the show were a Lao Staff Colonel, there for protocol reasons, selected officers from the five Lao Irregular and the two Thai Unity Force of the Thai secret army battalions under training and, unexpectedly, an excellent English-speaking Thai Captain – 'Call me Charlie,' he had said to Rance when introduced – the British Embassy Beaver aircraft pilot, Major Anthony Crosland, and, of course, the American host.

Colonel Rance had arrived mid-afternoon and had had a session with both Lao officers in their part of the camp. He had found the Colonel to be burnt out – *used to be a ball of fire but the fire has burnt out and left the balls so we call him Clinker Bill* was his private comment – so he had decided to try and work on the English-speaking Thai Captain, Charlie, hence getting a seat next to him at the appallingly bad film show. In any case, not to have attended would have been a grave breach of etiquette.

The meal earlier on had been a convivial affair, unusual in that camp which otherwise was a lonely place for the sole American, Tom Higgins, the young, Thai-speaking CIA contract Case Officer. Having had prior warning of his visitors, he had decided to throw a party and had ordered a turkey and some wine from his base in Udorn, in Thailand. The double X film, with the unedifying title of 'Fay and Gay', was a bonus. Tom Higgins had as an unquenchable an appetite for the salacious as had any woman-starved member of the forces in his camp.

Even after the ceasefire had been signed on 23 February 1973 the war had grumbled on in the rest of Laos, indeed in the rest of Indo-China, sometimes dying down as the Communists manoeuvred for tactical advantage and occasionally flaring up as they gobbled up more real estate before the other side could react. However, where the camp was, not far from the Golden Triangle, it was quiet. Calm, however, was illusory: to the north flowed the brown-watered Mekong, the property of the Pathet Lao for a long stretch. Away to the northwest was Route 46, off limits because it was secretly occupied by the Chinese People's Liberation Army.

Frequently the area was clouded over. Fly above the weather and risk getting into Burmese airspace: fly under it, dodging the mountain peaks, and risk being a target for hostile ground forces. Fly direct from Vientiane and over Thai airspace, even with clearance, and the T-28s of the Royal Thai Air Force on anti-guerrilla patrols were trigger-happily eager to take on something unarmed and slower than themselves.

It was Anthony Crosland's first flight along this testing corridor into Xieng Lom so he was both relieved and relaxed during the meal. Conversation was mostly in English, the wine making the Asians more fluent than normal – except for the Thai Captain whose English was superb in any event, having been fully educated in England. He had been introduced as Captain Xutiati Xuto, which had so utterly floored the British pilot, unused to the Lao and Thai tongue-twisting names, that they settled for his English nickname – Charlie. It was Charlie who sat on Rance's left at the film show.

Rance, of course, had no idea that Lieutenant General Sir David Law, KCB, CBE, DSO, MC, Director of Military Intelligence, was Charlie's foster father. Charlie had never intruded into his foster father's official life. Never, that is, till recently. Even before the heart-searching that went on in the arcane counsels of the shadowy intelligence world after the abortive meeting of the previous 12 October that prevented Rance from being used operationally, even though he had stumbled on two of four 'moles', now known as the Four Rings, even though one of them, named Le Dâng Khoã, had given his ring to Jason in the final exercise of the Jungle Warfare course. The General's covert plan, dubbed 'Operation Four Rings', was to be withheld from Rance for security reasons, meant he needed Rance to stay on in Vientiane after his original 'end of tour' date. So he had written to him, the burden of the letter being that they were having trouble in finding a suitable replacement for him. 'Therefore I am asking the Military Secretary's branch to consider your extension by at least eight months in the first instance. Think it over and let us know your answer, preferably within a month. It will also give you a chance to continue work on your almost impossible quest to get the king to announce his date for his coronation, through your Lao teacher, who is, I believe, the King's niece and elder sister of your teacher in London. We were unduly dramatic in calling it "Operation Stealth".'

Rance, not unhappy with the idea, recalled his driver Leuam's words soon after he got to Vientiane. He had been most upset by a nasty trick the Popovs, as he privately dubbed all Russians, had tried to play on him on his first ever visit to their embassy. *What was it? Yes, something about thirty-two months needed to placate his thirty-two body spirit* phees. *Almost as though he had known in advance!* He had sent his reply by return – yes, he would stay on.

After the General had formulated his plan, he invited Charlie home from a course he was attending at, as it so happened, the army Intelligence school at Ashford in Kent. Charlie was, in fact, a member of the Thai Intelligence Service seconded to the Royal Thai Army. He had developed into somebody different from other Thais. Small of stature and with pleasing features, he radiated a quiet purposefulness with a presence that impressed his seniors and subdued his juniors. After dinner on the Saturday, the General took him into his study and worked his way around to what had been on his mind for some time.

'Charlie, you are well on your way to becoming a success in your own particular line. I gather that the British are quietly popular with the Thai government although overshadowed at the present time by the Americans. English girls as wives of rich and influential Thais are not unheard of and are accepted in society. Thus your excellent English and your British connections are not a disadvantage.'

Charlie had made a noncommittal reply. *This is not what the Old Man usually speaks about. What's coming?* He would not have to wait long to find out.

'I have often wondered about the day your mother ran out into the road and my Jeep killed her so, by Thai law, made me your foster father. You can't remember her. I never knew her. As for your real father, the only rumour I ever heard was that he'd been a soldier, taken his elder son somewhere to the northeast and had never returned. But to come back to us: our relationship is a special one. I have never tried to claim any allegiance from you over and above normal family connections. Tonight,' and a harshness crept into his voice and a bitter look simmered in his eyes, 'I am going to change that. I myself have no higher to go in this man's army. You can still rise high in yours. But that is no use to you if your country is overtaken by events now simmering in Indo-China. I need help – your help – to contact certain people in Laos or for them to contact you. I warn you here and now that what I am asking may be dangerous. I am not asking you to divulge any state secrets but cooperation may be needed. Those bridges can be crossed later. What I really want to say is I can offer you a situation you can exploit, that, for reasons of British Government policy, I cannot process myself but, under certain circumstances, I can support – so can the SIS and, obviously, the

CIA can be relied on, that is if we don't touch their temporary contract men. If you want more, tell me. If you want no more, also tell me and we'll both forget it.'

The Thai nodded his agreement. 'Carry on, father. If it weren't of paramount importance you wouldn't be talking like this'

'Right. I thank you most sincerely.' The two men shook hands and regarded each other with affection and respect. 'Listen to this: the man at the centre of this is a certain Colonel Jason Rance, now our Attaché to Laos …'

… now squirming, on Charlie's right-hand side, as a particularly loathsome scene of a young boy fondling his elder sister's breasts kept the rest of the audience riveted with further expectation.

As the Lao Captain's attention was fully drawn to the film, now showing a scene of incest and sodomy taking place in a bath, Rance could see he would get nothing out of him. He made himself as comfortable as possible and shut his eyes. Scarcely had he done that when he heard a quiet, insistent voice in his left ear, 'Colonel, Colonel.' He turned towards the voice and there was Charlie looking at him intensely. 'This is a bloody awful film but we can't leave or our absence will be noted. Listen. If there is anything I can tell you about our secret army, for your ears only, please, as to source, anything at all, past, present or future, ask me now and I'll tell you what I can.'

Rance could scarcely credit what he heard. For months he had waited, wondering how to penetrate this particular organisation. The Thais were naturally always silent about their secret Unity Forces, the faked documentation, the volunteers with altered names and their dependence on the Americans. And yet, here was someone he did not know offering it to him, unasked for, on a plate. Suspiciously he asked, 'How come you trust me enough to offer this to me?'

'Don't underestimate yourself, Colonel. Your reputation among some of the people I deal with is that you must have three eyes to cope with all you see. No confidence that you have been given has ever come to the ears of another. Just take it that I am ready and willing to talk – nor am I asking for anything in return.'

Before Rance had a chance of replying the reel came to an end and the lights were turned on. He glanced at Charlie: *Who does he remind me of?* 'Pretty good, eh?' asked Tom Higgins to everyone in general. '*Di ti sut loeui*' – the best there is, and set about changing the reel. Lights were switched off and the dreadful movie continued.

Rance turned to Charlie, having made up his mind to squeeze this unexpected lemon as dry as he could. 'Tell me about your relations with General Vang Pao in Military Region 2.'

Charlie was scathing about the setup. 'In MR 2 it's all right for our artillerymen but hard on our infantry deployed away from base on the hill tops. The General pinches our supply planes when we're short of rations to fly girls into that enclave at Bouam Long, know which I mean?'

'Yes, I do.' He hadn't been there yet but he was determined to get there. An enclave, halfway between Luang Prabang, the royal capital, and Sam Neua, the Lao Patriotic Front capital, that was, in effect, a group of fortified Meo villages, above Ban Ban on Route 6. Ban Ban, a strange-sounding name, meant, he knew,

'Home Village'.

They continued talking intermittently until there was another pause as the last reel was made ready. When once again their voices would be drowned by the sound track, Charlie said, 'You are obviously puzzled by my openness. This is to your credit. I expected it. You may report what I have told you to your Defence Intelligence – don't be surprised! I know your terminology but, once again, please don't use my name. When you get back to Vientiane, write a private letter to General Sir David Law. In it say you've met Charlie and have had a chat but you wish to check on his credentials. Just that. Nothing more. Then sit back and await the answer. It will be positive. After that, put me out of your mind until sometime in the future when we'll meet again. I'll make the running, not you. You can get hold of me only through Gordon Parks – again don't be surprised I know who your intelligence man is. Don't use my name. Let our association be code-named "Perseverance". Do you know the Thai for that? It is an easy word – *Mana*. And the omens are good: your name is the same without the Jason – Percival, shortened to Percy Vere Rance: same difference!'

On hearing the word Mana, Jason's mind flashed back to when he was commanding the last ever two jungle courses, one for the Royal Thai Army and the other for the Army of the Republic of Vietnam, ARVN, at the Jungle Warfare School in Malaysia. The 'exercise-enemy' Gurkhas had been withdrawn and he had had to use Thais v Viets and Viets v Thais. The Guiding Officer of the Thais, Major Mana Varamit and that of the Viets, Major Le Dâng

Khoã, had had a fight, which he had managed to settle. Almost as a reward, the Vietnamese Major had given him a ring which, he had eventually found out, belonged to one of the yet to be traced four 'moles', almost, working in the Communist cause. Later, even before he had taken over as attaché, he had met one of his ex-Thai students, now in the Thai secret army, at MR 2 HQ who had told him that Major Mana Varamit, calling himself Chok Di, had just left to attack a North Vietnamese Army position.

What Rance did not then know was that another 'ring', Tâ Tran Quán, working with the NVA, was wounded by Mana as he tried to kill him on defecting to the NVA. Mana was wounded in the head and Tâ Tran Quán was also wounded. He had taken off his ring before being captured by the Thai secret army and swallowed it to hide it. What he had unexpectedly found out the first time he had visited the LPF HQ was that their latest arrival from the Communist HQ in Sam Neua in northeast Lao, was also a ring wearer. His name was Bounphong Sunthorn; Jason and Gordon Parks knew him as Ring B. Jason had, in fact, met two of the four.

On the morrow the two Englishmen, after a cup of coffee, were airborne and Rance sat in the copilot's seat with his notebook in front of him, racking his brain for what Charlie had said that he knew still evaded him. Anthony Crosland concentrated on his job of getting back safely. Rance scarcely noticed the flight, engrossed in this new dimension of his Attaché's life. He had been so stunned by learning that his and Mana's name were the same, 'perseverance', that he had no answer for Charlie, which was just as well as the projector broke down at that moment.

He was still deep in thought when they arrived on schedule at 10.30 at Wattay. On the way back to the villa for a wash and change, he called in at the embassy to see if there was any mail. While waiting for the brew, Mr Joseph his clerk had started preparing for him, he went and asked Gordon Parks if he could spare some time for him that afternoon. Back in his own office, sipping his cup of coffee, he opened an unsealed envelope that he found was an invitation to a film in the Lao Patriotic Front compound near the Morning Market on the morrow, starting at 7 p.m. The title of the film translated as 'Culture and Acrobatics' and, with a sick grin, he realised that could have also been the title of the previous night's film.

'Mr Joseph. Get the operator to ring the LPF and tell them I'll be delighted to attend but don't add that I could have been happier without it. Thanks for the brew. I'll be back this afternoon and will deal with anything else you've got for me then.'

He had a long session with Gordon Parks who admitted that he had been warned by London to expect a move from the Thai named Charlie with an unpronounceable name and that London had said he could indoctrinate Rance only after Charlie had made the first move. He gave the impression that the whole affair was a touch unorthodox.

'What does it mean, Gordon? Things are happening behind my back. I'm puzzled at this unexpected dimension, or should I say intrusion, into my life.'

'I'm not so sure myself. I have been told to expect him and use him on any "need to know" work that comes my way, not yours.' The SIS man was in a quandary. He had been told about General Law's plan to extend Jason Rance in post to use him as an 'unconscious agent' only for 'Operation Four Rings'. He had also been told not to tell Rance about the operation. But not to help him out with genuine advice was impossible. He sighed inwardly and, against his better nature, temporised. 'Keep him in the back of your mind but, my advice for what it is worth, do not tell him about your Four Rings or other sources until there is no other solution but that he might provide it. As we don't know what sort of problem needs that sort of solution, we are no further forward. What else did you learn on your trip?' and he listened, not interrupting once, as Rance told him as much as he could recall of the previous night's conversation.

'Yes, send your report as any other but don't reveal your source as it would be wrong in any case to mention the Thai by either name. If London wants to know who was the "officer in the Thai Unity Forces" with whom you spoke, your best answer is to say you did not ask him his name as, apart from being embarrassed, it would only have been an alias.'

'OK, Gordon. One other thing. I've been invited to the LPF compound tomorrow night to watch a movie. If I get the chance, I'll hint heavily that the British Co-Chairman and his military representative should pay the Red Prince and his gang a visit in Sam Neua – the Popovs crew were recently there in a Co-Chairman's guise.'

And before the close of play, Rance wrote his acceptance letter to the General.

Rance felt a thrill of expectancy as he was driven down the Avenue Lane Xang to the Lao Patriotic Front compound opposite the southern end of the Morning Market. He had the ring that Major Le Dâng Khoã had given to him that day in the jungle on the little finger of his right hand – *just in case*. Doubtless most of the guests would be Communists, complete with bear-hugging, treble-kissing and heavy handshakes. But it was probable that Bounphong Sunthorn, Ring B, would be there and just a chance that Le Dâng Khoã, 'Ring A without the ring', might show up though he was not banking on it. If his ex-colleague was there, he would play it cool and hope for an opportunity for contact.

The car turned through the gates, checking momentarily as Leuam showed the sentry Rance's invitation card. They were directed to an area to one side of the main building, only Heads of Mission being allowed to drive up to the front door. Rance walked over to the line of guests that was slowly filing forward towards the main entrance. At the door were Soth Petrasy and Bounphong Sunthorn. Rance smiled at them both. They both smiled back at him as they shook hands.

'Good evening, gentlemen. It is a pleasure to be asked to your cultural evening and a privilege to attend. I am much looking forward to it.'

'I'm so glad you could spare the time to come,' said Soth, with no trace of irony in his voice. 'We haven't seen you around much lately.'

'Yes,' chimed Sunthorn as Rance reached him, moving steadily forward so as not to block the door or slow down the queue. 'I haven't seen you since our men flew in three months ago. I wanted to thank you for coming down to the airport.' He was referring to when, after the ceasefire accords had been signed the Pathet Lao forces arrived in Vientiane.

'Please think nothing of it,' said Rance lightly, passing on into the main reception room. He took a soft drink from a tray and mingled with the crowd. He spied Le Dâng Khoã talking to a Czech diplomat. His former student looked up and saw him and looked away again with a flickered warning, unseen by anyone else. Presently people were herded into an open courtyard the other side of the reception room. Rance hung back, being deliberately slow, hoping to get a seat at the back. He was rewarded by this tactic. Le Dâng Khoã came over to him, introduced himself in Lao, not Vietnamese, English or Thai and shook his hand.

'*Sabai di, Tan*. I am Le Dâng Khoã, a northerner from near Sam Neua. I am in command of the LPF troops here in Vientiane. Who are you?'

'I am Colonel Rance, the British Defence Attaché. How nice to make your acquaintance. I hope you are well and are not having too many problems.'

They wandered out of the room together, like any other host and guest. Le Dâng Khoã found him a seat, one from the end of the back row. 'Keep this for me,' he whispered. 'I'll be back.'

The lights went out and the film began with hill people from the 'Liberated Zone', as the occupied zone was called, dancing traditionally in tribal dress. It was mellow, dexterous, colourful and realistic. It was such a contrast to the show of two nights before that Rance was prepared to enjoy it. Someone came and sat on his left. It was Le Dâng Khoã who said nothing as he cautiously moved his chair a fraction nearer to Rance.

'I'm delighted to see you,' he breathed in Rance's ear. 'I can't tell you what has happened since we last met. You're safe enough right now and for the foreseeable future but nearer the time ...' and he let the sentence hang in the air. 'I trust you and you trust me, otherwise you would not have behaved as you have done with Bounphong. What I am more worried about is Mana Varamit. I hear he is in a camp somewhere near the Black River, probably near Office 95 and working for the Viets. Is it true he killed Tâ Tran Quán? I only got garbled reports and no feedback from Thai sources was picked up.'

The South Vietnamese attaché had told Jason that Tâ Tran Quán, dubbed Ring C, had been captured and was being held by the RLA. Jason had had permission from the Deputy C-in-C to visit him. 'No, Tâ Tran Quán's alive and well and not far away. He was wounded but is better. I have met him and he knows that I know about you three others.'

'Oh, how wonderful. HQ are not quite convinced he's dead although they have announced him as such. They don't understand certain mysterious circumstances, that is to say, how did he come to be away to a flank just at a crucial time.' This last allusion was lost on Rance but he was wise enough not to comment. 'But it's Mana who can spoil everything planned for us. You see, he was in the wat with us after Ban Liet was burnt' – Rance remembered his driver Leuam's story about the genesis of the 'ring' story, way back in 1945 – 'then he disappeared. His father was a deserter from the Thai army. I gather he was killed soon after by the same Communist gang. Mana indeed knows about us and the rings so he will try his best to prevent us from doing what we have to do. I was never more surprised to see him at the Jungle Warfare School and I don't know what would have happened that day had you not intervened. After I gave you the ring – I still don't let myself wear one – I felt dreadful as I had, in fact, broken our boyhood oath. But so much of what we were looking for was in you that I just had to. I did steal time with His Holiness and explain matters to him. He forgave me, even said it would have been wrong not to have done what I did. Without you wearing it we may fail: in good time I will wear it once more. So please, regard it as yours now.'

Rance was flabbergasted by so outright an explanation? warning? request? *What more?* The reel was coming to an end with a crescendo of patriotic fervour and his companion slipped away.

The next film was entirely devoted to the LPF acrobatic team, giving open air shows to many villages and schools. The standard was high and the two clowns extremely clever. Rance chuckled as he watched it. After a while, Le Dâng Khoã returned.

'We must meet when the time is ripe. I'll let you know somehow or other but please do not try to contact me. As a guide, remember this: plans are being made to take this country over territorially within two months of the fall of Saigon. Agitation will start the day after Saigon falls – and it will fall sooner than you think. I must leave you now but just one more point; when you go to Luang Prabang you must contact Thong Damdouane. He's the fourth of our team. He knows about you and is waiting for you. He may have news of Mana's exact whereabouts. I'm so glad I've made contact. I feel I have found an old friend after many years. *La korn*,' and with that 'goodbye', he melted away, leaving Rance's eyes on the film but his mind playing back everything he had been told.

The show finished. The audience applauded heartily and moved back to the central room. As Rance said his farewells to Soth and Bounphong, he asked them when the Central Committee was going to invite the British up to Sam Neua. He got the totally unexpected reply that arrangements were, in fact, being finalised before an official invitation was extended. In other words, quite soon.

February 1974: Sam Neua, Northeast Laos: Sam Neua is in the northeast of Laos near the border with Vietnam. Apart from being a provincial capital and on the French-built Route 6, it had been a quiet and sleepy place for many years. The war of 1939-1945 passed it by and only when French armoured columns probed into the area from Hanoi, which they did infrequently between 1949 and 1954, was the tranquility of the region shattered. Even the cataclysmic upheaval at Dien Bien Phu that culminated in the octave of Easter 1954 only sent ripples not waves that, on the surface at any rate, soon petered out as the last vestige of the French army dismally concentrated in Hanoi. The only French vestiges that remained were an indifferent infrastructure, an educational system of sorts and an embryo civil service.

Apart from being within easy enough striking distance of Hanoi, another reason for Sam Neua being eminently suitable was that communications with, so therefore disturbances from, Luang

Prabang and Vientiane, would be tenuous. So, not only was Sam Neua remote, it had the further tremendous advantage of being in limestone cliff country that meant it was riddled with deep caves wherein life, although tedious, uncomfortable and cheerless, could continue despite the massive American air attacks that laid waste acres of surrounding forests but did little real damage to the LPF cause. Indeed, it often enhanced it. Eastern Europeans, subservient to the Communist Cause, meddling Cubans and fence-sitting Swedes saw the many surrounding bomb craters, some of which were later used as fish farms, and the shattered remains of Sam Neua town, with only the wat unscathed, as a sure and encouraging sign of little people being bullied by a vicious and wicked super-power, and emerging triumphant. Although basically the Lao and the Viets are antipathetic on one another, an understanding can always be found for political opportunism.

The Protocol Officer in Sam Neua rehearsed the details in his mind after the Politburo decision. Clearance would be given for four British diplomats to fly in their Beaver aircraft. They would be His Excellency the Ambassador, Mr Cameron; the First Secretary and Head of Chancery, Mr William Rogers – both of whom spoke good French; the Defence Attaché, Colonel Rance, who spoke good Lao; and the pilot, Major Anthony Crosland, who spoke only English. As far as the Vientiane comrades were concerned, the British Attaché was no menace: he never asked them awkward questions, never tried to make them do things – oh, how hard they had tried to get the Polish Major on the International Control and Supervision Commission to get the Soviets in turn to lay off them, but to no avail: nag, nag, nag, thought the Protocol Officer, involuntarily grimacing, and also he kept himself to himself except when amusing the children. What was it that Comrade Nga Sô Lưu had said though? Playboy? Something about sightseeing like a tourist, visiting the wats in Luang Prabang with his driver. Nothing wrong with that, surely? It was common knowledge that Comrade Bounphong was the driver's brother: Leuam Sunthorn. Was Leuam better as the driver to the DA or working with his younger brother? It would be an interesting decision, whichever way it went. So much depended on the comrades in Vientiane and their struggle. Even though the American imperialists had won military victories, the Saigon clique was no political match for the Hanoi government. It was a question of time, stealth and perseverance.

The aircraft would be seen off at Vientiane by Comrades Soth Petrasy and Bounphong Sunthorn, and met in Luang Prabang by Comrade Thong Damdouane who, as the LPF political representative there, would be the obvious man for the job. There would have to be another comrade with him. Thong could choose which one, probably the local Neutralisation troops' military commander. It was hoped that the British aircraft would be able to use its six seats so that the two comrades could travel with the British delegation. This would obviate calling on the bigger, though slower AN-2, so save the humiliation of the British seeing the Soviet plane being refuelled by non-Soviet petrol, Shell. Furthermore, they could act as guardians if anything were to go wrong when the plane landed. Clearance would be given for the nearer of the two strips, Nong Kang, but weather might make the strip at Sam Neua safer. In that case, reception would be needed there.

He stood up and looked around his work cave. Cold as death in winter. Even in summer precious little warmth penetrated so far down. Prints and slogans covered much of the walls to hide the damp and take away the dullness as much as anything else. The Red Prince's cave, where they had their Politburo meetings, was nearer the surface, but it was no warmer there. He walked along a passage. Over the years an electricity generating system had been installed but it was temperamental. Alternative sources of light were candle and hurricane lamp but, earlier on, especially during the intense bombing, supplies from Hanoi were often held up. He reached the outside and stood blinking in the bright sunlight, sighing with pleasure as he felt the warmth. Being January, it was a clear, bright and cool day compared with conditions down in Vientiane but after the cold dampness of the caves, it was pleasantly warm. Across the small valley was another precipitous limestone mountain, similar to that which he had emerged from. It, too, was riddled with caves. One complex was where guests were put, or rather, where the British foursome would go, not to the wooden huts where Socialist country comrades were put. The complex was self-contained, that was to say it had toilet facilities, a place to sleep where booths had been partitioned off for some semblance of privacy, a small cave for eating in and a recess where most of the preliminary talking would take place. In front of the entrance a vast stone baffle had been erected against the bombing. The aircraft, those cursed B-52s, that dropped bombs so accurately on the bridges over the Red River thus isolating Hanoi from the rest of the country, had also tried to drop bombs actually on the cave entrance. Near successes had been frightening. Shot-down US flyers, severely interrogated as they had been escorted through Sam Neua, had agreed that television camera aiming techniques helped to do the trick. Not that he understood how – not his line.

He passed the sentry at the opening through the barbed wire that guarded the sensitive cave. Not more than seventeen years of age, he was dressed in baggy green uniform with a Chinese-style cap. The only difference in dress between the two was that the Protocol Officer, being a civilian, wore the same style uniform but in blue. The sentry said nothing, his doe-like eyes watched him pass. In the western armies and in other comrades' military forces, soldiers were paid. Not these, though. Tokens, instead of money, were given when anyone performed particularly meritoriously. The only place to change those tokens for goods was deep down in yet another cave, not far from the generator. He continued towards the visitors' cave, crossing a rough gravel track. A powerful, Soviet-made vehicle drove past, full of soldiers. Probably came from one of the eight static pickets that ringed the cave complex and airfields. Each had a force of up to two hundred men, constantly on the alert for infiltrators. On the left was a hut, used for a school. Children of the few married functionaries and some local peasants had classes there. He walked up a path, wound his way through another barbed-wire entanglement, skirted the vast baffle and went inside the visitors' cave, shivering as he left the warmth behind. Inside, he came across a fatigue party. 'Everything under control?' he asked, knowing it would be. They never left their visitors alone except when they were safely together in their cave. The small microphones would have to be activated, then tested. The Cubans had helped to put them in. Hiding them had been a problem but, from what was known of the British, they were not inquisitive enough to search for such things. Three places would be live, the conference recess, the sleeping booths and the eating area. They might pick something up. That Rance fellow: pity he was on the other side. Comrades said that the Englishman was in revolutionary mould, walked everywhere, had strict self-discipline and set an example of correct behaviour yet mixing with the children. The Politburo received periodical reports about him: what was it that had pleased them? *Not my quarrel, not my business. I represent the British in Laos as a whole.* With Comrade Thong Damdouane monitoring the party, the Committee was bound to get a good report on the true feelings of the British delegation. Good man, Comrade Thong, trusted by everyone ...

He left the visitors' cave, still deep in thought. As he stood blinking in the sunlight, he took off his cap. The doe-eyed sentry looked at him standing there, an elderly, balding man, slightly stooped with a perpetually worried look on his face. As a cadre, he was entirely devoted to the Cause, if only because he had never known any other. He was like millions of similar featureless functionaries throughout the world, doomed to the treadmill-like monotony of constantly coping with trivia, despite the grandiose eloquence of superiority every system aired.

By the next mail bag Rance got a reply from General Sir David Law. In it was confirmation that Charlie was no more and no less than what he claimed to be. Rance should treat this information with even more circumspection than ever, if indeed this were possible. 'We are working more in the dark than normal. I stress that in no way will I order you or expect you to exceed your powers or alter the constraints on your appointment which have been settled by international protocol. However, an Attaché can accept points of view from others, can help them analyse their problems, can respect their confidences and can shield their contacts and sources. No move in this direction is too small not to pay some dividend, be that also ever so small, sometime or other. You must have realised this by now. On the other hand, the possibilities of future benefit that careful handling can produce are inestimable. I am one hundred percent behind you but, and I am afraid this is cold comfort, unofficially. Officially, you know the answer. You have worked yourself, unwittingly, into a unique position, some would say preordained. God go with you.'

That struck Rance as most unlike the awesome Whitehall Warrior as he had shown himself at his initial briefing in London. Good wishes and an order to shred the letter finished off the text, so he did just that.

The invitation for the British delegation to pay a fraternal visit to the Lao Patriotic Front base at Sam Neua was received at the end of January 1974 for 12 to 14 February. The Foreign and Commonwealth Office had already been warned and guidance had been given so an acceptance could be sent almost by return. Preparations had to be made: the Ambassador had certain points he knew he would have to make such as how long did the LPF want a Co-Chairmanship, of which the United Kingdom was the right-wing representative, to stay in force and, until it was disbanded, on what scale was its powers and writ envisaged? For instance, were the Soviet and British DAs to help monitor any infringement of the ceasefire or the placing of boundary markers between the two zones? He also knew that the LPF would represent to him that the Vientiane side had abused protocol and had harassed some of their functionaries. Aid would also be mentioned in the context of rehabilitating bombed areas and the Ambassador felt that an attempt would be made to portray the British as lackeys of the Americans. Accordingly, he had his First Secretary delve into the archives for instances when there had been a divergence of opinion between the two.

As far as Rance was concerned, he knew that he had to keep his ears and eyes open as he would be asked many questions on his return: numbers and types of equipment, vehicles, weapons; state of bridges, roads and runways; state of alertness, morale and training of the soldiers and officers; any storage capacity for fuel; any medical and hospital facilities and what, if any, generating capacity there was for a start, as well as any and everything else that might be of conceivable interest. He knew already that there had been much speculation as to whether certain models and marks of fighting vehicles were purely Soviet or made in China under licence but he doubted his ability to glean such esoteric knowledge. With regard to the pilot, his flight plan occupied his time; frequencies, zonal boundaries; altitudes of both airfields, approach angles, call signs and local hazards; fuel availability, local protection at night and by day; alternative airfields for diversion purposes in case of bad weather. One problem exercised his mind – if bad weather at Sam Neua and Nong Kang prevented any landing there and it was impossible to return to Luang Prabang, would he be able to fly to Hanoi? The mere possession of passports would not obviate many problems were this to happen, the hardest of which would probably be getting back again quickly. He found out that Sam Neua was some three-quarters of an hour's drive from the cave complex where they would be staying whereas the other and smaller strip was much closer – would both places be alerted? He had to work out a time and space equation: so many gallons of fuel would allow so much luggage to be carried but would leave too little in the tank for a safety margin. In the end Rance made the pilot's mind up for him.

'Anthony. Tell our two civilians they are allowed one suitcase each. A small one at that. The Ambassador and the First Secretary will sit in the two middle seats. I'll go at the back. Get your maintenance man, François Lafouasse' to rig up two headsets that can be used to talk to each other but to nobody else. Put those for the two rear passengers. I will sit in one of those two seats and hope that my neighbour can be induced to talk to me. The other man who travels can go in front with you. Err on the heavy side for fuel and, if needs be, we'll only have one escort with us – and he'll sit beside me.'

2

11-14 February 1974: Sam Neua, Northeast Laos: Since the last Frenchman had left Sam Neua on 3 April, 1953, nearly twenty-one years before, there had been only one occasion when the non-communist world had been invited there and that was the British, some ten years previously. Rance was down at the hanger first thing that morning as he wanted to be quite sure that Lafouasse, an ardent hater of *Les Popovs*, had rigged up the rear pair of headsets to be mutually compatible and on their own private circuit – *just in case*. He asked Crosland and Lafouasse to talk into them while he listened on the main channel. Only then did he profess himself satisfied. He thanked Lafouasse who grinned a happy, appreciative and conspiratorial smile in silent answer.

At twenty past nine, two LPF men turned up, driven and escorted by a pair of hard-faced PL soldiers. 'I am indeed looking forward to these next few days, *Tan* Soth, *Tan* Bounphong. I am conscious of the honour of the occasion and its importance. I would like to think that I can act, even ever so slightly, as a bridge between the two sides. Quite how, I don't know but I believe your people in the other zone,' – Rance could never get himself to call it the Liberated Zone – 'have to get used to non-communists and representatives of the western world, meeting them and talking to them, using a different dialectic from that which has been their staple for so long. It will be hard work prising themselves from their caves and harder work facing the world. I remember first meeting you, Tan Soth. You are now as you were then but you, *Tan* Bounphong, were different when we first met. As the English expression has it, "people could run rings round you" as far as talking with my sort of person was concerned but now,' and Rance's eyes met the others' unflinchingly, 'you have acclimatised.' He broke off, apologetically. 'Sorry! I am overstepping the mark. I'm really not a diplomat, only a soldier so I shouldn't talk like this.'

'Not at all, *Tan Colonen*. You have an uncanny knack of touching on matters many foreigners never notice or, if they do notice them, take them for granted. I agree with you entirely,' said Soth. 'What do you think, Comrade?'

Bounphong Sunthorn was spared an answer as the noise of a car distracted them. Soth Petrasy turned round, saw the British flagged car approaching them and moved away from the Beaver to greet the Ambassador and the First Secretary. The two escorts were with the car that was parked to a flank. Bounphong Sunthorn moved close to Rance and, in an undertone and not looking at him, said, 'I wish you a good, safe journey. I am not sure what you will learn in Sam Neua but I hope you can get a chance to talk with Thong Damdouane. Try and find out about Mana. He is the big, main and dangerous worry.'

'Tango Papa Charlie,' called the Tower. 'Clear for take-off'

'Tango Papa Charlie. Roger. Rolling,' crooned the pilot into his headset, letting the brakes off as he did. The Beaver surged forward, slowly at first then accelerated and, as it drew level with the two LPF officials waving to is passengers, lifted into the air, banked and, making a slow turn north, headed for Luang Prabang. The two men on the ground glanced at their watch. 'Got away dead on schedule, 10 o'clock. These British are sticklers for time,' said the elder.

'Indeed, Comrade Soth. I have noticed that. Compared with the French, they are harder to get to know but much less insincere. They never give the impression of racial superiority as the French do when they shrug and puff. Look how much larger the French embassy is than the British, even than the Americans, yet not one of them speaks our language.' Bounphong Sunthorn sounded severe as he answered the elder man. What he thought but dared not say was that the Soviets had no Lao speaker in their embassy either and were, in fact, rabidly racist. Criticism of Big Brother, however much it was merited, was forbidden.

'I hope they have an interesting time while they are in Sam Neua. The comrades there will make them welcome. The extra food for the group went up from here by AN-2 on Friday, not that the British will know that, but to send the biplane up twice in such a short time would have been an extravagance. Besides which, our Soviet comrades are touchy on the refuelling problem. Ah well.' A pause, as though to make his mind up about something. 'Come. We must be on our way back and get a message off that the British have left Vientiane at 10 o'clock as planned. These next few days are a good opportunity to try and teach your brother how to help us. It would be a point of honour to have two men like you in one family.'

As Bounphong Sunthorn only smiled to himself, Soth Petrasy did not notice it.

The journey was uneventful and an hour and twenty minutes later, after circling Luang Prabang, the aircraft landed and taxied to a halt. The noisy engine was switched off and the comparative silence was a welcome relief. The pilot took his helmet off, undid his harness, turned to the others, Said, 'We've made it spot on. I suggest you go and get settled and leave me to finish off. It will take me quite some time to get refuelled, do the paperwork and put her to bed. Any idea what time we're leaving tomorrow?'

By then Rance was on the ground and had opened the two doors of the plane so that the other passengers could climb down. He had slipped on the ring, feeling a surge of excitement as he had glanced at two LPF officials, come to welcome them.

'Mr Cameron. May I suggest you take your time, just a shade longer than normal, in getting out. I'll go and introduce myself to those two as your spokesman and bring them over, if you agree.'

'Right you are. Won't take long, will it?'

'No, sir. I'll be right back with them.'

Rance walked over to the LPF group which was standing on the edge of the runway. A few paces away from them he stopped, made the *wai* salutation and introduced himself.

'*Sabai di, Tan. Sabai di, bor?*'

Yes, they were well, they answered. He told them who he was and held out his right hand as he took a step nearer. His eyes were riveted on the one he had seen with a ring on the little finger of his right hand, without appearing to stare or be discourteous. He was, in fact, a shade nearer them than normal but so purposeful and genuine was he that no offence could be taken. 'Are you Comrade Thong Damdouane?' he asked. *If so, he'll be Ring D.*

'Yes, I am.' Hands were clasped and, as Asian handshakes are more protracted than European ones generally, there was enough time for Rance's to be tightly squeezed after Thong's little finger had unobtrusively explored where the ring was, almost as though he had not believed the evidence of his eyes. 'May I introduce my companion, the military commander of the Neutralisation Force?'

The second introduction was made and Rance suggested they walk over to the Beaver. By now Mr Cameron and Bill Rogers had emerged from the plane, stamped their cramped legs, tucked in their shirt, put their coat on, smoothed their hair and felt representational enough to do their duty. More introductions followed.

'If possible, Excellency, we should like to accompany you in the aeroplane tomorrow,' said the military commander. 'It would not only be a pleasure but also a precaution in that it is not often such an aircraft flies over our territory and, in the eventuality of having to land other than in Nong Kang, we would be of as much benefit to you as any documentation you carry.'

'H'm. What about the fuel stakes and weight, Anthony? Can you accommodate two more passengers and still have enough fuel for emergencies?' the Ambassador asked.

'I may have, sir. I want to check the diversionary strips once more as I was not able to get a clear enough answer in Vientiane. I don't relish the idea of having to make for Hanoi or Vinh. Our answer would have to be back here or as far away as Sayaboury.'

'All right, all right. I've got the idea.' Mr Cameron tried to keep the edge out of his voice. It were almost as if the pilot was trying to read him a lesson. He turned to the two Lao. 'If we can take you, we will. If we can't, could one of you come along with us, leaving the other behind?'

It was time for the Lao to reflect. 'Like you, Excellency, we will make up our minds tomorrow. We will both come prepared.'

Rance then said, 'If either or both do come with us, please bring minimum luggage. We have hardly any ourselves but every bit extra soon adds up. We will do our sums. If two of you travel, one can sit in front with the pilot and use the second headset to talk to the air traffic controller. The other would sit at the back, next to me, with hardly any view but a comfortable bucket seat,' and his glance fell momentarily on Thong as he finished speaking. It was obvious that the message was understood.

After the official welcome was over, the party, less the pilot, walked over to the entrance where two cars were parked, one the welcoming LPF delegation had come in and the other for the British. As there were two PL soldiers, driver and escort, in each vehicle, it was agreed that Rance should travel in the LPF car as it was the bigger. He had a Union Jack car flag with him that he affixed to the car in which the Ambassador was travelling then jumped into the other.

'You speak our language well, *Tan Colonen*. Where did you learn it and how long have you been in our country?' Thong spoke slowly and shyly. 'It is not often we have foreigners who have such an aptitude.'

'Oh, I learnt the basic requirements in London before coming out here and in the fifteen months I have been here I have taken every opportunity of studying and practising. Your accent is not unlike the one they use here but is not quite the same. Where are you from?'

'I'm from Sam Neua province. In our zone, one of the problems that faces us is that, leaving accents out of it, we have over fifty different languages to contend with and many of those speakers do not know Lao so have to be taught. Here in Luang Prabang the two accents are not dissimilar so conversation is no problem.'

Talk was kept on this dull and mild topic until as they reached the town.

'Where is your office? I would like to come and pay a return courtesy call on you some time if that is in order? I understand you are the senior political cadre in the area.'

'Yes, I am. My office is ...' and he pointed to a turning off the main road as they drove by. 'My companion, as the senior military commander, has his HQ off the back road that runs to the south of the town. The troops live under canvas.'

At their overnight hotel there was a short conference on the next day's timings. It had been planned that the British group would arrive at Nong Kang airstrip at 1400 hours. That was when the reception committee, aircraft sentries and transport would be ready and waiting. 'Meet tomorrow at noon at the aircraft?' 'All right, see you then,' and the two cars drove off.

'What did you talk about on the way here, Jason?' Mr Cameron smilingly asked his DA who was folding up the flag with a far away look in his eyes.

'Tribal dialects in their zone and the difficulties encountered in running an administration with over fifty languages.'

'A similar problem with us in the UK these days,' remarked the Ambassador, half to himself.

'Leuam Sunthorn. We have called you here tonight for a special purpose. Before much longer, a year or two at the most, everything will be different. What is happening now is a passing phase, a page of history being turned. Do you want to live peaceably with your large family?' Soth Petrasy's silken tones were menacingly obvious. The question hung heavily.

Leuam stood before a table at which five comrades sat, one of them his younger brother. The other three were members of the Neutralisation Force. Ten pairs of eyes stared at the luckless Leuam, who licked his lips and nodded.

'You are only the British Defence Attaché's driver because we let you be. It is time you started really working for your living. From today you have joined our Cause. When we give the order, you will come over to us and operate from here. Until then we regard you as a front-line soldier in the enemy's camp. You had better get used to the idea. Any time of the day or night we want something we think you can get for us, we will let you know.'

Leuam said nothing. He was not a great talker. 'If Colonel Rance gets wind of this, you're finished. Go.'

Shortly before noon the next day, 12 February, the four Britons and the two Lao met up at the airport. The pilot greeted them with the news that he was not entirely happy to take both Lao but the met forecast, at least for the first part of the journey, was fair with some haze but as there would be a tailwind until the air corridor jinked from east to east-north-east he was willing to try the hardest part of the flight which was take off out of Luang Prabang valley, 931 feet high. Anthony Crosland warned that he would not attempt to bring the two Lao back as the aircraft could not lift such a weight from the height of the Sam Neua area, 3346 feet. 'What is your answer?'

The military commander was clearly unhappy about the situation when it was explained to him. He did not feel that it was right for one man to accompany the group and yet maybe two men were too heavy. Comrade Thong Damdouane, though, was made of sterner stuff and opted for going. It seemed as though an impasse had been reached. Rance then asked the pilot how much weight could he allow the two men, body and baggage. 'Two hundred and twenty pounds only.'

'Both of you are small and slight. If together you're not more than a hundred kilos, we'll take you. Go and weigh yourselves.'

They were just inside the limit, the military commander the heavier. Back at the plane, Rance looked hard at the pilot. 'Anthony, the limit had not been breached. The military commander is the heavier so can balance up with you so should sit in front. That means the other man will sit behind with me. Our two will occupy the middle seats. The added advantage is that the military man can talk to the ground forces once their territory was being overflown.'

That was agreed and the two diplomats were checked into

their seat belts by the pilot while Rance helped the military commander into the copilot's seat, adjusted his harness for him and explained how he operated the headset. So that the other Lao could hear, he also explained how it operated and that only passengers could hear what was being said, not the outside world, but please to say as little as possible so that the pilot was not distracted.

Checks, contact with control, taxi to the edge of the strip, switch to tower, clearance for the 040° take-off, more taxiing, this time to the western end of the strip. 'Tango Papa Charlie. Ready for take-off.'

'Tango Papa Charlie. Clear for take-off.'

'Roger. Rolling,' and a long, long drive forward then, only just in time, the wheels left the ground and they were airborne. Both Crosland and Rance breathed a sigh of relief, but for different reasons.

Safe in the knowledge that they could not be overheard, Rance leant over to Thong's headset and switched it on. Thong looked enquiringly at him, then ahead at the others, then back to Rance.

'Don't worry, *Tan* Thong. These two headsets are for us only. The others cannot hear us. Watch,' and he called up the other four passengers by name. With no visible reaction, Thong relaxed. He turned to the Englishman and smiled.

'So you are the one. You've been a long time coming but there's time enough left. It was clever of you to fix this. I have been waiting to talk with you for some time. Now we've an ideal opportunity.'

'I have had a long talk with the Chief Bonze. I have also got through to the King.' That had unobtrusively occurred during the Presentation of Credentials of the present ambassador. 'I have got contact to Bounphong Sunthorn, Le Dâng Khoã and Tâ Tran Quán ...'

Thong interrupted him excitedly. 'With Tâ Tran Quán, did you say? But surely he's dead? Don't tell me isn't, that he's still alive?'

'Yes, he's alive. He was wounded not far from Long Cheng, on 18 November, 1972, fifteen months ago. That was the day Mana disappeared.' *Mana – Perseverance.* 'So I know all of you. I call you the Four Rings.'

'What wonderful news about Tâ. I'm so glad he's still alive. Is he well? Where is he? Does he know about you? Please tell me.'

One of the hardest contortions to go through in the front seat of a Beaver is to turn round and see what is happening at the back. The harness prevents it for a start, the headset with its cable reduces easy movement and the passengers in this middle obscure what little there might be to look at in the unlikely event of a concerted effort being made. Also portholes rather than windows in the back make people sitting the two rear seats dim and difficult to see clearly. So it was in the security of the back of an aeroplane that Rance had the first long talk with any of the Four Rings.

'You say you know the background to us four,' continued Thong as he settled back in his seat. 'What I want to do is try and formulate a plan, or rather a course of action, that can stand us in good stead when the opportunity arises, as arise it will. We four have been living our lives in hope, prisoners of hope you might say, waiting for a sign. We were taught where the sign would come from and today's meeting is of the highest importance. It is through you that success or failure to our lifelong aim and ambition can be realised. Next year is crucial; BE 2518, AD 1975. Some time during that year, we four will be able to reap our vengeance on what we have suffered.' His face took on a firm, fierce look as it suffused with anger, zeal and hatred, the opposite of the softer, calmer aspect presented under normal conditions. 'None of us yet know how the chance will be presented but we firmly believe that, with your help, that chance will be recognised and taken. This will be hard for you but we are relying on you more than you realise. In fact, we may yet fail even with you but, without you, we have no chance whatsoever of success.'

Rance sat is a stunned daze. Never in a month of Sundays, a year of Sundays, a decade of the wretched days, had he ever imagined he was pivotal to any chances that the Four Rings might have. Help in some modest way, perhaps, but for everything to depend on him, a foreigner, a part-time diplomat, a soldier even though he had some knowledge of matters Asian and was anti-communist: *I – one man.*

'How and what do you envisage? I accept you have put your trust in me but my resources are nil, my influence trivial and my contacts hemmed in with protocol.'

'Who have you contact with? You've already given me a hint. You must have a number of people that none of us four have. If you can get a safe channel through to us we have our own ways and means. Not that we are members of the Politburo, we're still too young for that. Who are your contacts?'

The plane droned steadily on. The two civilians had entered

their own dream world of time passing. The pilot was completely engulfed in concentrating on flying and navigation. He had to make two changes of direction, each having recognised a place on the ground before course correction. His companion, initially having taken much interest in the layout of the dial panel, was now soporifically slouching in his seat.

'My contacts are the Royal Lao Army Generals and the Military Region commanders, the Defence Minister, along with his future wife and her sister, through to the King's brother and the King himself; the Chief Bonze, through Leuam Sunthorn; the other Attachés though which of them I trust is another matter – and of courses my own people.'

'Indeed, that is an impressive list. When you contact the King, what is your message? What can you tell him others can't?'

'It's not so much a question of what I can tell him that others can't but the perspective in which I tell it, the scenario I build into it and the conclusions I can draw from it. As you know, it is almost impossible to keep secrets in Laos. Let the Communists get a whiff of a plan and they counter it. Let the toadies and the robber barons get a whiff of it and they're twisting it for their own means. Say too much and you're taken for a meddler, too little and your point doesn't get across. Then there's the age-old philosophy among Asians: behave well to your enemies of today as they may be your friends of tomorrow and be wary of your friends of today as they may be your enemies of tomorrow. Bend and you survive: break and you die.'

'So where does this leave us?'

'If a thing is worth dying for, of course you can afford to be rigid. But if a thing is worth living for, maybe you can't afford to be rigid.'

'And in this connection, how do you see your relationship with the King? Will he take a message? Anyway, what is your message?'

Rance told Thong Damdouane the thread of what he had told the King's brother, wife and the Chief Bonze in the wat, then added. 'It is my firm belief therefore that were the King to be crowned, there is a chance for a happy-go-lucky Laotian Laos, a gain for mankind in itself, let alone to the other countries of the region. And yet, I fear that the Communists will thwart him and the country thereby be doomed for at least another generation, probably longer.'

'You will already know that every year there is a date set by the Vientiane side for the coronation, regardless of any other consideration. I fear the situation will be seen as not ready enough in 1974: by 1975 the 30-year wait for us could coincide with just that. But, however right you are, and I believe you are right, it will be a race against time. The odds are against him and you with the task. Nevertheless, if it could, somehow, be joined to our endeavour, double purpose will be served.'

The plane titled its starboard wing slightly as the first course correction was made. 'But I am worried, *Tan Colonen*, as I think you know we all are, about Mana, the Thai, who has known about us since the killings in Ban Liet. You may not have heard: he had been groomed as a long-term agent and was being run by Office 95. He had come into contact with Le Dâng Khoã in South Vietnam and later in Malaysia. Office 95 wants to use him, wants to debrief him not only in what he has discovered about the Thais, the Lao Irregulars, the Americans but chiefly because, somehow or other, our bosses have wind of us. I've heard a codename I don't understand – Four Days – but our bosses don't know who, where, how many or what we are but something that took place in South Vietnam between Le Dâng Khoã and Mana has made them suspicious. They believe Mana can provide the clues to their suspicions. Mana, as you know, went over to them. Tâ Tran Quán's military commander found him lying in a pool of blood with a head wound. I think Mana tried to kill Tâ Tran Quán. Tâ's body was never found as the operation was mounted just to bring Mana over and the counter-attack that was mounted by the Thais, presumably because Mana gave them the slip, was too fierce to allow a search.'

'But hasn't Mana told Office 95 and others also all he knows?'

'No. The wound to his head has badly affected his memory. Most of the time he only remembers odd incidents since his childhood. They've had a neurologist to see him and who has told them to wait. Events elsewhere in Indo-China are going well for them, that's the Communists I am talking about, except that the Americans in Cambodia with their concentrated bombing. No, they are waiting for Mana to remember who he is. He believes he is Le Dâng Khoã. They dare not bring the real Le Dâng Khoã yet awhile as they fear that the shock may be too much for him – not that they won't try if all else fails. Nobody knows how long his condition will last. What worries me is how much he'll remember when eventually he comes round and recalls who he is.'

Then Rance had a brainwave. Casually he asked if Thong

knew where Mana was. Yes, at a Pathet Lao training camp at Ban Ban, a name meaning 'House Village' so easy to remember. Is he heavily guarded? No, and he is well looked after. There was a small military hospital there and some defence troops. Would rescue be possible? Well, would it? Just, just possible with a special man I know. Who is he? Tâ Tran Quán.

After the second correction for course, the haze thinned and the scenery became more majestic as the little-seen hinterland of northeast Laos came into view. Rance saw an ugly patch of sere ground, acres across, victim of a napalm attack. He saw limestone cliffs and precipices ahead. Glancing at his watch, he saw they must be near their destination. Thong once more spoke into the rigged headset.

'We're not far away. It will be difficult for us to have so much privacy again. I like your idea about Mana. It won't be easy but Tâ Tran Quán is the man for the job. Tell him from me when you next meet him. When I last heard, and this was recently, Mana had only just been moved to the hospital at Ban Ban. You probably know it is on the junctions of Routes 6 and 7. It's not so remote. The hospital is not in a cave, like the one at Sam Neua, which will make it easier for Tâ. Mana is allowed to walk around as the brain specialist thinks that contact with soldiers might jog his memory.

'When we're on the ground again, we'll have to revert to officialdom. You understand. I have heard how you play your role in Vientiane and no one is any the wiser. Bounphong's brother, Leuam, will be under pressure, if I know how their minds work, either to defect or to spy on you. There'll be more pressure still after Liberation Day. Plans are being laid for a cultural revolution – the masses' wish being made known to the government without the masses realising they're being manipulated. Don't know how I've stuck it for so long. Can't give it up now. No way. Look, before we separate, I want you to be under no illusion of how grateful we are or how dangerous it is.'

And with that cold comfort, Rance felt that anything he said would be inadequate. So he just wished Thong good luck and stared moodily out the porthole as they came in to land at the Sam Neua stronghold.

After being official for three days and not achieving much the British delegation returned. Back in Vientiane, before the weekend, Rance wrote as full a report as he could for London. Looking back at the time spent in the Sam Neua area, it was more of impressions and feelings than hard, usable, military intelligence. Many of the questions he had asked himself remained unanswered as he feared would be the case. They, the visitors, had been circumscribed as to their movements. It was more an object lesson in survival than anything else. Nevertheless, even without the conversation in the aircraft, it was an achievement, something to add to the sum of his knowledge. But with the conversation in the aircraft, it was the breakthrough they had been waiting for. Rance discussed it with Gordon Parks.

'So, to recapitulate: all Four Rings are now known to us and I to them. Each one is more or less contactable but even limited access is never easy to come by. They are not near enough the top echelon to influence policy nor so junior as to be without influence. Then there's Mana. If we could neutralise, eliminate or dispose of him there is much less risk. He is in the hospital at Ban Ban training camp.' He got up to look at the map. 'It's well inside their zone. See Bouam Long? Make a note of the grid reference – UG 2628. That's the enclave. Look east. See Route 67? Follow that down. Make another note: UG 4971. That's Ban Ban. It strikes me,' continued Rance as he returned to his chair, 'that we ought to take advantage of the enclave. It is the nearest launching pad for Ban Ban. Any other overland route is a long, long hike. Thinking it over out loud, how many do we need to the party? Is this where Charlie comes in? Somehow I feel not. There are the ralliers who have drifted in from the other side over the years. I'd have to learn more about them before we could find suitable men from amongst them. To use them we would have to put pressure on the Minister or the Commander-in-Chief and they would want to know the whole story. No mileage in that.'

'I think I could get the Americans to lean on GHQ and lend us Tâ Tran Quán, Ring C, – the one that was captured. But he cannot go by himself. He'd have to keep hidden by day and would need considerable help. Besides, how many people think he is dead? You'll have to go and talk to him, Jason, and see what he thinks. Whatever the difficulties to be overcome there'll be nothing we can't sort out. We can't just sit back and let it work itself out.'

'Gordon, I'll talk to him but I must do it by myself. He is a man who knows enough Lao to cope although I didn't realise that at our first meeting. However, to get him out from wherever he is might need some ingenuity. His wounds must have healed by now. How about an American doctor examining him, say in the Silver

City medical centre, with a view to passing him fit for active duty? Can I leave details with you?'

Next Monday morning the long telegram that John Chambers read contained a précis of the aeroplane conversation, an allusion to the LPF answers to the question of the coronation and an outline of how the British DA suggested Mana be recovered. He contacted Bill Hodges and Maurice Burke, CIA representative in London, who, in turn, contacted Ed Murray, the CIA man in Bangkok. General Law was not brought into the matter: it was felt that any required denial would be more easily believed if it were completely genuine. It was decided that, under the circumstances, Head of Station, Vientiane, needed to be alerted, through London if not through Langley, to give his British counterpart *carte blanche* with Tâ Tran Quán. A bit of bait might have to be offered such as the USA offering political asylum for the man in question and a speeding up of quota restrictions for one or two others to immigrate also to be offered at the same time. No real difficulty need be expected.

Those at the meeting were obviously curious as to details but wisely refrained from suggesting any course that might prevent them from developing at their own speed. There was an air of suppressed expectancy that made all four men cheerful.

Just as the British compiled a report about their visit to Sam Neua, so did those Lao officials concerned compile one about the British and put on record those aspects of the discussions that would be of particular interest to Officer 95, Hanoi, Beijing and Moscow. They noted that the English were unswayed about some of the reports of right-wing behaviour in Vientiane, that the hospital visit had to be aborted – the report did not include the reason, namely that the Cuban doctors would have been seen at work – that the English were taken to the shop and on the way the DA had stopped to talk to some soldiers. The soldiers had been closely questioned afterwards and had not deviated from their original version that the Englishman asked them if they were married and how long they had been in uniform; that the English had good appetites, were not highly motivated politically, were victims of imperialist propaganda in that they raised the point of there being foreign fraternal troops in the country, that they alleged they were not under the influence of the imperialist Americans but offered no details about the feudalist troops from Thailand and the imperialist Americans posing as Assistant Attachés, that culturally they were well motivated. They finished up with a character assessment of each one: the Ambassador was sensible though pro-American yet independently minded to a degree but reasonable; the First Secretary was earnest, had done much research into the origins of the present situation which made him hard-working but probably not an academic; the pilot was a non-entity. That left the enigma, the Attaché. Part of the opinion mooted at the after-visit conference thought him devious, deep and dangerous, one to be watched and thwarted. No real reason could be given for such thoughts and certainly the tapes from the caves had only revealed comments about how cold it was – so the British had, to an extent, been punished – but from midday on the second day hardly anything had been said by the

British. Curious, almost as though they had found out about the bugs: in fact Rance had silently pointed out their possibility. The other school of thought admitted he was deep but felt he was neither devious nor dangerous. Indeed, probably the opposite. He was sincere, fair and flexible and should be cultivated so as to help the image of the emergent government whenever it was formed by his understanding of some of its problems. He was neutral, disinterested, did not meddle nor offer gratuitous advice. He should be left alone. This point of view was accepted. Its main proponent was Thong Damdouane

'Jason,' said Gordon Parks, 'I have arranged for you to see Tâ Tran Quán on Monday next, the 25th, at 10 o'clock. Our American friends have fixed a "return to fitness" medical examination. He will be taken to the Silver City medical centre in an ambulance and he will have a thorough medical check. After that's over you'll be taken in to see him. Have as long as you like. The way they'll play him is, unless you specify to the contrary, he won't know you're there. His Tai Dam Major will be available if, and only if, you want him. I gather he is reliable.'

'That sounds just the hammer. At the hospital who shall I contact?'

'Go to the waiting room and you'll be called. When you've finished with him, tell me what emerged and I'll steer it thereon.'

At the hospital, a white-coated man invited Rance to follow him up a passage to a door which he opened for him, revealing a simply furnished office containing a table and two easy chairs in front of a normal desk and its chair. 'Ring the bell when you've finished,' he said and left. Rance made his way over to greet the other man sitting in one of the chairs. They appraised each other cordially.

It was several months since they had last met. Whilst Rance's life had been active, Tâ's had been restricted by his wound and by the constraints on his freedom. It was not obvious that he had fully recovered although as he arose to welcome Rance, there was no hesitation in his movements.

'How are you, *Tan* Tâ?' he asked, using the Lao for 'mister', not the Vietnamese *Ông*. 'You certainly look much better. Are you fully recovered?'

'Yes. I have indeed recovered from the wounds, both in my leg and chest, but my enforced sedentary life hasn't made me actively fit. The doctors have been giving me an examination for the last two hours although they had not taken much notice of me over the last six months.'

'We'll talk about your health in a moment. You presumably want to know why I am here today and why you have been brought here. What have they told you?'

'That it was time for a USA-based check. I gather there is some sort of scheme that allows people like me to be resettled in the USA with a view to being granted American citizenship. I didn't say I wasn't interested in American citizenship. Oh, I know they mean it kindly, and I could be of use to them, but I have my life's work to complete before I think of such things.'

'I can give you some details that the others cannot. Ready? Point one: Bounphong Sunthorn and Le Dâng Khoã are here in Vientiane. I have managed to talk with both of them and am waiting until they can make the next move. Point two: I have had a long conversation with Thong Damdouane, who is the Political Commissar in Luang Prabang. I travelled with him to Sam Neua where I've just come from. Incidentally, he sent you the most cordial greetings. Point three: they are now aware that I know you, you know me, know where you are, know how you are and are overjoyed you are well. Pont four: Mana in now in the PL camp in Ban Ban, recuperating after the head wound he got when he went over to the Communists, the same day that you were wounded. You must tell me about that later, there's obviously a connection that I'm unaware of. Mana has lost his memory, thinks he is Le Dâng Khoã and was originally taken to a hospital not so far from Office 95. He has been visited and examined by an eminent neurologist and is now convalescing in Ban Ban. The idea is to treat him kindly, keep him near soldiers and hope he recovers his memory that way. Point five: our other three friends are most worried that Mana will regain his memory and jeopardise whatever chances there are for you four, yes, you included, to carry out your life's ambition. This they believe will be next year by when the Vietnam war will be over, although western opinion doesn't go along with that, and that conditions will be ripe for the Communists to gain mastery over Laos for the next generation unless something drastic is done. It is also my contention that the LPF are only paying lip service to the idea of retaining a King and that His Majesty, King Savang Vatthana, should be crowned before then. Are you following me?'

Tâ's large eyes had been unblinkingly fixed on Rance, almost in a thousand-yard stare. He lifted his palms about an inch and a half from his knees indicating acceptance but said nothing. 'So we come to point six,' continued Rance, ticking if off on his fingers. 'Mana has got to be taken away from Ban Ban just as soon as that can be arranged and brought, initially, to Vientiane for interrogation and safe keeping. And point seven is that you are the best man to entice him away so that others can ensure he doesn't escape. Before I go any further, I think it only fair to give you point eight and that is Thong says that the Nga Sô Lựự is suspicious of what you Four Rings, as I call you, are doing. He has heard something about Four Days. He doesn't know you exist as such, he doesn't know who you are or even if you are. Merely that there is something that he and possibly others higher up still can't put their fingers on. Were Mana to regain his memory then you four are finished.'

He paused to let his long list sink in. Tâ Tran Quán nodded but said nothing.

Rance continued: 'Quite why Mana hasn't given the game away yet, I don't know. Maybe none of us ever will. Right now that doesn't matter. What does matter is that he's got to be retrieved as soon as possible. There is one more point, which I'll make number nine: I gather that Office 95 and the Central Committee are not convinced you're dead, if only because your body was never recovered. It is that fact that has made me believe that you are the one with the best chance of success. With travel documents in a forged name, you too could pretend that you had lost your memory were it ever to come to the crunch that indeed it is you and you could assume the identification for real if, as Thong himself believes, Office 95's records are ever to show that you are dead. So, using this new name and your natural authority, you'd be able to gain access at Ban Ban hospital and do what is needed to be done before contact with Sam Neua or Office 95 was made. We can talk about who will go with you later. We would launch you from Bouam Long. If you like I would go as far as the enclave with you. You would have to travel dressed as a civilian and carry Pathet Lao uniform with you. So would your companions, I expect.'

Tâ Tran Quán's eyes had not left the speaker's face during this long exposition. He looked away now and considered the proposition. Never a coward, never one to shirk a task, this would not be one he'd have chosen himself for. Yet it was clear from the English Colonel's talk that he had already been picked as the key man. In that case, yes, of course he'd do it. 'Do you really want Mana brought back alive?'

'Dead men don't talk and, always provided no permanent damage has been done to his brain, the government and its allies could use him as a source of great value to say nothing of his own government wanting him back on spying charges. The background to personalities and events could forestall more people like him from causing disruption to the Free World. Yes, alive is the answer, with killing him only as a last resort. If it were you or he to die, for instances, the choice is obvious.'

'I'll need a travel document made out in a name other than mine. Similar documents will be needed for as many as go with me. I think it best if we go as a group of soldiers returning from a mission. I can cover that reasonably well. I'll need to be briefed on the current situation. Dependent on that, I'll make my cover plan. Money. It would be nice to have some Pathet Lao kip on me but money is not so much of a problem as you might think. Barter is widely practised. We ought to go armed, preferably with Kalashnikovs, Shpagins or Sudayevs, not American type carbines. I'll take a pistol as I'll be a political man. A Tokarev or a Makarev, I don't mind which, depending on the type of ammunition you can get. Let me think this out for a few days. For planning purposes, let us say I'll need six people. An overall commander who knows the area and is able to arrange a snatch: of the other five, a protection group consisting of a noncom and four soldiers to carry Mana on a stretcher if it comes to that. Where'll you get my companions from? They'll have to be strong and completely trustworthy. Cover story? As I said, let me think on this for a bit. It's all so sudden.'

'What happened at Skyline Ridge above Long Cheng on the Saturday, 18 November, 1972?'

'It dates back to when the Thai Black Cobra Division, or was it the Queen's Division? was in South Vietnam. I had infiltrated South Vietnamese Intelligence. By various ways and means, I learnt about a certain Thai; you can guess it was Mana, whom I'd first set eyes on when still a boy at Ban Liet, although I couldn't be sure it was the same person even though I did have a photo of him. I had not seen him for such a long time. Simple desertions are simple but this wasn't a simple one. Sorry, I'm not telling this story well. This Thai was clearly up to something he should not have been as an ordinary regimental officer. I put out feelers to contact him and found out that he had something of great importance. By then I suspected it might just be the boy I'd known when I was a boy but I couldn't be sure. Do you understand me now?'

It was Rance's turn to nod, not completely understanding what Tâ was getting at but not wishing to break the thread of a complicated story. 'He was a long-term North Vietnamese spy and I gave him the impression, not by direct contact, that I was in the same game. He wanted to get across and report to his bosses but in the chaos and difficulties of war, it was decided that transfer to the north that way was dodgy. He had come across Le Dâng Khoã and had surmised something wasn't as he thought it ought to be. Might even have been Le Dâng Khoã's ring or the mark on his finger.' Tâ pointed to his own as he spoke. 'I got hold of my people in the north, took a long time as I was officially in the southern army, ARVN. By the time I got my message back, the Thai had received forewarning of return to Thailand and, apart from a course of instruction, a posting to the Thai Unity Forces. As I was his contact, we only met once at night so I never got a really good view of him. I was told to disappear from that job – there was someone else who could look after the post I had had. He was not slanted as I was so I dropped a hint in the right quarters and got him removed. Shot later as a spy! I was told to reappear, after a time, with 335 Regiment. It was felt that, as I had had the contact with Mana in South Vietnam, I should try and get him across to the north after his course of instruction and posting to Laos. There was a risk that he would go to Pakse or to Xieng Lom but 335 was central enough for him to make plans to defect through them. You can guess the rest, in fact you know more about some of it that do I. By one of these coincidences, Mana Varamit and Le Dâng Khoã went to Malaysia where you were the

Commandant of the school that ran the training both happened to be sent on. Mana and Le Dâng Khoã had a quarrel, yes? That much I heard. What an extraordinary coincidence, really. First Mana and me and Le Dâng Khoã in South Vietnam, then the two of them in Malaysia. But to get back to November 1972. By then Mana must have realised who I was or might be. I had an inkling, more than an inkling, from reports from Long Cheng that my man was Mana. I had a desperate plan that I could kill him before he came over, or as he came over, and then surrendering. I knew the dangers but I am under a special oath and I felt this was one occasion where my life was worth forfeit. Just before I managed to get away to a flank, when a Jet Ranger was circling around above us and the RLAF T-28s were bombing and strafing us, I was reminded that Mana might see my ring and recognise me too soon. So I decided to take no chances. Not that I knew for sure he knew who I was. Unless he saw or felt the ring when we jumped into a trench to avoid the T-28s. On the spur of the moment I slipped my ring off and swallowed it. Only place to hide it and keep it. If you monitor yourself you should pick it up later. Being in prison and in hospital, the chances are you yourself can get it back. It is not the sort of thing most people would be suspected of doing.'

It was now Jason's turn to fill in details: 'Another coincidence is that I was circling in that Jet Ranger on the day you came over! I also learnt that Mana's name in the Thai Unity Forces is Chok Di. But let me recapitulate: you and Le Dâng Khoã were both in South Vietnam up to no good and so was Mana. He met Le Dâng Khoã and thought he was up to no good. Could even have thought

74

it was one of the four boys from Ban Liet. He also thought the same of you, probably. That was the information he wanted to get back to the Politburo or Office 95. The course of instruction in Malaysia was a bonus but the Thai Unity Force posting was cleverly contrived. Office 95 was a bit greedy so allowed him to get to them via Thailand. If the planners had insisted on his reaching them direct from the south he could have done it. It was only because Office 95 was that bit too greedy that I ever came into it. Correct?'

'Yes. If you reconstruct it in that light, that is correct. But had it not been like that, you would never have come into our lives. Office 95's greed is a good omen for us.'

There was a long silence as Rance digested what had been revealed to him. He conjured up memories of the initial jungle scene, then with Princess Golden Fairy, the first meeting with Bounphong ... Tâ waited patiently. Rance dragged himself back to the present with a wrench.

'You have been talking as though you were dead set on going on this venture. Will your health stand it?'

'After the exhaustive medical examination I've just had, I'm not the person to ask! Get the report from the doctor. Personally I feel fit and that is what matters. This talk we've been having has whetted my appetite.'

'Right you are! I have to go to Luang Prabang for a wedding tomorrow or the next day. I'll arrange for your return now and see what can be done to fix you up correctly so that this mission has as good a chance of success as humanly possible. I'd like to see it start within ten days at the latest. Even if you don't see me again during this phase, it won't be lack of interest, I can assure you, just expediency. May I wish you the very, very best of luck. Oh yes. Any choice of another name?'

Tâ Tran Quán thought for a minute and then said, 'Tanh Bên Lòng.'

'Tanh Bên Lòng? Does it have any significance?'

'Yes. It is a nickname I am fond of.'

Rance got up and shook hands then, going over to the door, rang the bell and almost immediately was ushered away by the doctor. As he was shutting the door he put his head round and asked what Tanh Ben Long meant.

'It is the Vietnamese for 'Perseverance'.'

'So it was a successful meeting? Tell me every little bit of it. Leave nothing out. There may be things that were better done by me than by you and even better still by others than by me.'

In the greatest detail, Rance recapitulated what he and Tâ Tran Quán had discussed. Gordon Parks made meticulous notes. 'As I see it, I have to work fast. We may be too late, of course, but that is a risk we'll have to take. I wonder if there is any merit in your going to Bouam Long, except as an Attaché, invited by General Vang Pao, so escorted by the CIA as it is still their sole concern. In might, in fact, be a good wheeze as your presence could take the attention off the other activity. Of course, sentries, observation posts and patrols will have to be alerted as well as having to find out if there are any minefields. I think a good ploy would be to say we've heard that one of the captured American flyers is reported to be held in Ban Ban or is expected to be passing through. You won't have forgotten that fellow who baled out when he ran out of fuel after the cease-fire.' Rance indeed did remember it. It was one of the points the American embassy had asked the British delegation to try and find out when there were in Sam Neua. 'Although everyone is pretty sure that this guy is in Sam Neua, there's no proof. He was captured quite close to Ban Ban. What's your immediate programme?'

'Tomorrow, Tuesday 26, fly up to Luang Prabang for the wedding of the Defence Minister to Princess Jasmine. 27 and 28, Wednesday and Thursday, bun fights and bean feasts and, fingers crossed, I'll be back down here on the Friday or Saturday.'

Only towards the end of the wedding ceremony, as the crowd was thinning out, did Jason manage to talk to Golden Fairy, Inkham Hatsady, his first Lao teacher, out from London, till then fully involved with the proceedings. She had taken off her ceremonial gear and was wearing normal Lao clothes. 'Oh, Jason, Jason. How lovely to see you again. I've heard so much about you. You are renowned and respected, Colonel Three Eyes,' and she laughed delightedly. 'I knew I had a good pupil but never dreamt how good.'

He answered banter with banter. 'And you, *Tu Nong*, you look as beautiful as ever, more so in your Lao clothes and in your own royal capital. It is lovely, lovely to see you again.'

'I have been worried, Jason, about that business.' She lowered her voice. 'The ring. What happened?' Before he had time to make up his mind what to tell her, she said, 'Oh bother. I must go now. Look, this evening. We'll have much more time to talk. I want to hear everything. Everything, you understand?'

'Just before you go, Inkham, I must ask you one thing. This could be vital. You have met your uncle, His Majesty? You will meet him again soon? Could you pass a message through your father to him? Don't look like that,' he implored. 'I mean it. I most sincerely request you somehow to pass this to His Majesty from me – "Next year it may be too late." Got it? Thank you a thousand times. And if humanly possible, could you tell me the reaction when we meet later on this evening? That, too, is important.'

The guests assembled at 7 p.m. in the same place. Princess Golden Fairy came up to Rance, who was dressed in his black regimental mess kit. 'Oh, you look so handsome,' she trilled. She then became serious. 'Come with me, Jason. Stay close!'

They went through a gate at the back of the garden, unseen by anyone, so they thought. Down an ally, across the main road and in at the palace gates. The sentries did not try to stop them. They walked towards the palace but turned off before they reached the throne room and the large room where he had waited before being presented. They skirted the building and, on the far side, came to a door. She opened it. 'Wait here.'

Two minutes later, she reappeared and led him in. 'Don't be afraid. Use French or common Lao though French might be better.'

Down a corridor and, stopping outside a door, she nodded to the palace guard on duty. The guard knocked softly on the door. A voice bade them enter. There, on a chair at a desk, sat His

Majesty, the King. Princess Golden Fairy curtsied and Rance, who had his hat in his hand, bowed from the waist, as the King, having risen from his chair, came over. Rance straightened and looked into the calm, steady, peaceful face. They shook hands.

'Come along and sit down. It is not often that a meeting like this can be arranged. Let us make the most of it. Tell me your message in full.'

His Majesty was a good listener and nodded gravely during Rance's dissertation as each point was made. There was no one else in the room. Princess Golden Fairy listened fascinated as Rance rehearsed the salient points concerning the Four Rings and Mana's treachery. 'So you see, Your Majesty,' Rance wound up, 'every omen points to next year, the Year of the Tiger, as being the last chance. The following year, the Year of the Hare, may well be too late.'

The King viewed Rance, earnest and dedicated, with a grave look. *If only more of my subjects were as perspicacious and thorough in what they did and believed as this Englishman in front of me.*

'Colonel. I sincerely thank you for the concern you have shown for me and the risks I know you are taking. You have met and talked with the Chief Bonze, my brother and sister-in-law. They are convinced that you are correct. Nevertheless, I, as both Head of State and of the Buddhist Church, must stand by the tenets of my faith. For, if I deviate from them, how can I keep them? Indeed some omens do point to the Year of the Hare for my coronation but other pointers in the astrological calendar show omens of dread. Take but one example: the wedding today, admirable from so many points of view, not the least being the uniting of the Houses of Luang Prabang and of Champassak after many, many years of estrangement, did not take place during the time it should have. Instead, it being the eleventh month of Mina, I cannot attend it, so it cannot be held here. These matters are beyond you, dear Colonel. You look worried, disappointed, frustrated. That is how I feel. I either stick to what I stand for or I don't. *You* understand that. Fain would I waste your time explaining why: the *Theung Sok*, the *Suthin*, the *Somphut Athit*, the *Ken* ... look, you who know so much and whom I admire, are lost already! Believe me, Colonel, the crux of the matter you dilate upon, lies solely and heavily on my shoulders.'

As he heard what the King was saying, the bottom fell out of Rance's world. Ever since that far-off day in the office of General Sir David Law he had had it firmly in his mind that the only way to save Laos from the Communists was by getting the King crowned. It was an impossible task, almost an impertinence, to think he could in any way influence the course of events to that extent. Asia was too subtle and too old for an upstart like him ever to affect its history. He looked at the King and rose to leave, regardless of the protocol for such occasions.

'Sire. I thank you for being so graciously considerate. I never wanted to intrude on matters that were not mine. I hope I do not have the name of a meddler.' He slipped his hand into the breast pocket of his black monkey-jacket and produced the ring. 'But this has come across my path and its influence enmeshed me.'

He put the ring back in his pocket and glanced at the King, who was watching him with compassion and pity. 'You, who like our proverbs, make note of this one: "When one acts, one should act with all one's heart and soul and not turn round even if the loved one tickles the ribs a thousand times". Go now. Put me out of your mind. You have done enough for me already. Take my niece and go back to the party. Before the tickling of ribs tonight, they have to cut their wedding cake.' He glanced at a clock on the wall. 'It is due to be cut in ten minutes' time.'

Outside, in the dark, on their way back to the party, Inkham turned to Rance and asked, in a low voice, 'Is it as bad that?'

'I'm afraid so. Maybe even worse.'

'But, surely, if it is as bad as you say, why aren't the others doing anything about it? Why are we left on our own?'

Rance thought of the many, many sacrifices that the Free World had made since the end of the war: Lord knows what blood and treasure had been spent, and in good measure, by a number of governments who also hated Communism. And yet how could she say that the others were doing nothing? He felt too tired and dispirited to argue any more, so he simply said, 'Because too many people are too comfortable.'

He then turned and, before she could resist, took her in his arms and kissed her, tenderly at first, then with a mounting hunger. She gasped but responded as though, that also, had been her wish from a long time past.

They finally separated. 'Jason. Thank you. It's done you good, also!'

'Come,' he said, taking her by the hand. 'Let's go and have a piece of somebody else's wedding cake.'

The combined 'Brass' in London were saddened but not surprised at the failure of 'Operation Stealth' 'We never really expected it to work but it was amazing just far Colonel Rance did manage to get,' was the general verdict.

'However, our efforts don't end there. I will now work on the Attaché turning his attention to ... what shall we call it this time?' General Sir David Law thought for a moment. 'Got it: "Operation Four Rings".'

3

February-March 1974: near Dien Bien Phu, North Vietnam: In the remote, jungle-covered hills some eighty kilometres from the Laos-Tonkin border, near Diện Bien Phu was a small, heavily guarded camp. It contained the highly secret Office 95, staffed by dedicated Political Commissars and civilian functionaries. The significance of '95' was merely that the chief Vietnamese representative worked in room number 9 while his Lao counterpart in room number 5. Planning, coordinating and directing clandestine activities, such as subversion, sabotage, the running of intelligence and counter-intelligence networks, disinformation and brazen strong-arm tactics designed to further the revolution by exerting political pressure wherever necessary was its responsibility. Its teaching was based on Marxist-Leninist principles as dilated and modelled on the KGB Training School No 311 in Novosibirsk, Siberia's largest town. Various courses and seminars were also run in the camp, as was now the case.

On Wednesday, 27 February, an important meeting, chaired by the Political Commissar, Nga Sô Lựu, had lasted some time. There were only two more points for discussion: 'The last but one item needs careful consideration; in fact both these last two points do. One we can't do anything about and one we can. First, then, the one we have to live with: the royal wedding.' The sneer in the speaker's voice and the glare from his soulless, vacant-pitted, black eyes, were so malevolent that the others, used though they were to the never-to-be-used nicknamed Black-eyed Butcher's bile, looked at him in surprise. Even the Communists recognised marriages, albeit hemmed in with man-made constraints. 'The royal wedding is nothing but an imperialist-feudalist plot to perpetuate the corrupt regimes of the puppet Princes of Champassak and the decaying relics of Luang Prabang. What reports have we had in about any populist reaction against it?'

The general consensus was that among the foreign community, the upper and middle class Lao, the wedding was seen as a welcome and steadying influence for unity, while among the peasantry, hardly any feelings would be generated. It was felt that the wedding might possibly bespeak an early coronation and it seemed that the Vientiane-side propaganda was making efforts to swing opinion in that direction. Nga Sô Lựu thought for a while then continued:

'I believe that the down-trodden masses of the Occupied Zone have an unhealthy fixation about the coronation. That will serve our immediate purpose. I will recommend that the invitation to Savang Vatthana to visit Sam Neua be processed to coincide with New Year, 2518 in their calendar, the Year of the Hare. I rather like these long-range ploys. In this case, we cannot ignore the situation. As I have said before, this is one aspect of that corrupt society we must put right. We fixed that fat French puppet Bao Dai, now Savang Vatthana and Norodom Sihanouk I Cambodia must be disposed with.' The Black-eyed Butcher had rubbed his hands in glee when he mentioned getting rid of the former emperor whom the French had installed in Vietnam soon after the end of the war. On mentioning the other two names, his gestures once more became tautly hostile.

'So regarding the royal wedding' – again with heavy sarcasm – 'I will issue some instructions about informing the masses of our attitude to it. And now onto my last point: a long-range ploy I do not like: Mana Varamit, our comrade returning to the fold. It is more than fifteen months since he was wounded, a sad day for him and us. Recovered in body but not in mind, we have had the neurologist to see him two or three times. On the last occasion he said that Mana should be given another three months at Ban Ban, attached to the hospital but free to wander around contacting soldiers. The hope was that he might realise that he was not Le Dâng Khoã by an association of ideas. The latest reports from Ban Ban indicate no change in his condition. The two doctors in charge of the case believe they should now take certain corrective action, if possible with a second opinion beforehand. The Politburo feels such is justified as, despite the positive outcome of our heroic struggle, it is ever vital that the body politic of our movement remains Marxist-Leninist pure. They have a feeling that Comrade Mana can help consolidate any devious thinking or tendencies amongst a miniscule handful of us – I leave it at that,' and he leant forward in his chair, looking hard at everyone there in turn as if to say, 'If it is you …'

'Back then to specifics,' he continued after taking a sip of water from a glass on his table. 'In Mana Varamit's case, mid-March is the deadline for natural recovery. Then a team, probably comprising two doctors, a Political Commissar, an Intelligence officer and two escorts, will go to Ban Ban and, having interviewed him there, bring him back here to decide on whether lobotomy is the answer. You, Comrade,' pointing to one of the men sitting opposite him, 'will go to Ban Ban and warn the hospital to expect a delegation arriving on the ...' and he searched through some papers on his desk. 'Yes, here we are; 15 March. Travel details have yet to be finalised.'

The date was duly noted and after some ritual haranguing and extolling of even greater vigilance to safeguard themselves against the wicked tricks of the imperialists and reactionaries, the meeting broke up. As an afterthought, Nga Sô Lựu turned to the man going to Ban Ban and said, almost conspiratorially, 'Tell them we're persevering with Mana. 'Perseverance' is the watchword.'

At about the same time as the Office 95 meeting drew to a close and Rance was having an impromptu audience with the King, yet another meeting was under way in Vientiane. This was a two-man affair being held in the house of the Director of Intelligence of the Royal Lao Army, one Brigadier General Etam Singvongsa. The Director was an interesting man: a native of Sam Neua, he had remained loyal to his French oath from pre-1954. He had an innate astuteness above the average of his brother officers so, although not from any of the hereditary landed families, he had risen to the rank of 2-Star General. Most of the top brass had gone to the wedding but not General Etam. This was not out of any disrespect to the royal couple or to the throne but merely that his name had come out of the hat for the one man of any executive power to stay back in Vientiane. He was not to know that there had only been one name in the hat to start with.

The British intelligence fraternity could be of use to their American counterparts when the attitude of the locals, or those in opposition to the locals, was xenophobic in their opposition to the USA. Such places were North Vietnam, Cuba and Mother Russia. Conversely, where locals were engaged in trying to keep the Baddies at bay, for example in Laos, the Khmer Republic, South Vietnam and South Korea, they were more than likely to be prepared to listen to what the Americans had to say and, at times, even to help them out. This was the case in Vientiane so perforce the Americans had to be brought in. The person needed was the CIA Head of Station, a man so code-word crazy that he was only ever known as 'Mango'. The name confused the Lao who came into contact with him and made an added mystery out of the English language but so many things the Americans did confused them one more detail did not matter. The meeting had been initiated by Gordon Parks who had persuaded Mango to fix one with General Etam 'today as ever is'. Late evening was the only time the General was free.

Gordon Parks had liked the idea of Tâ Tran Quán being the man to try and recover Mana and had further agreed that Charlie, a Thai, not a Lao, was therefore the best bet in not breaking the ceasefire protocols and only involving the Lao minimally. He had therefore sent an urgent signal to his opposite number in Bangkok asking that Charlie be made available to come and see him, Gordon Parks, and be his guest for about a fortnight. The answer had come on the morning of the 27th saying that regrettably Charlie could not be immediately contacted and anyway a period of fourteen days needed considerable notice to arrange. This added a further dimension in the planning and the only man Parks could think of to solve this new problem was General Etam.

So it was that over supper prior to the meeting Gordon Parks brought Mango up-to-date with what Rance had reported from his talk with Tâ and the outline operational requirements. 'The question is,' Gordon Parks was saying as his servant had put some bean-curd mousse in front of them both and retired, 'Who do we have, now, instead of Charlie?'

'I believe it has to be someone who knows Tâ, can get on with him and whom Tâ trusts. I've been around the "rallier" set-up as they like it known and my guess is that the Tai Dam Major Vong who looks after Tâ is the cookie we're looking for – hates the Gooks' guts and if he was a Christian he'd say "kill a Communist and Christ smiles". He has probably already operated in the target area and maybe he knows Ban Ban personally. If I were a betting man, I'd put my money on him.'

'Sounds just right. Do you think Etam will bite? If not, can he suggest A N Other and, if so, what do you think his price will be and, even if we can pay, what will Tâ say to him?'

'I think he'll bite but let me talk to him nicely. The other points we need his agreement on are tacit approval of what we are doing, provision of another four men, help in providing documents and radio, clearance to fly the party into the Irregular enclave at Bouam Long and requirements therefrom – local protection, emergency procedures and the like.'

'And cover story?'

'The truth, as near as we can. Tell him one of the Thai Unity Forces is our agent, was on his way over to us after completing a particularly hazardous mission and is detained in Ban Ban hospital. No need to tell him how we know that. Once we've gotten him out, Etam can use him or, at least, be privy to our debrief. Our team will be six: Tâ as a visiting doctor, the Tai Dam as overall commander and we will need an Intelligence man, one who has had some minor sabotage training and two others. Time frame? To be at Ban Ban by the 13th or 14th of the coming month. Neat? Neat! I'm on my way now. I'll call in tomorrow with the answers. By the way, what was that we've just eaten?'

'Bean-curd mousse. Change from mango chutney. On your way or you'll be late!'

Mango grinned, thanked Gordon Parks for the meal and drove away to the General's house. He was only semi-confident he would succeed. Etam's price might be too high.

The General greeted him affectionately. 'Come in, Mr Mango. What would you like to drink? I've got some Singha whisky, some Thai brandy, a spot of Bourbon.'

'Bourbon on the rocks please, General, if you've got any rocks.'

They made themselves comfortable and Mango gave Etam a Camel cigarette and lit it for him. He lifted his glass. 'Cheers, General. Here's to our health, an easy conscience, a quick victory and a lasting peace.'

They clinked glasses and drank. Etam looked at his guest quizzically, lower lip stretched slightly, creasing the corners of his mouth. 'Out with it, Mango, but keep it simple. My English is not so good. Better than your French, though!' A smile robbed the remark of any offence.

'General, it's like this. It's a sensitive matter I want to discuss with you and only you. It is one that could do Laos a lot of good. I say "could" not "will" because there's always the chance of failure. It concerns one of our Thai Unity Forces, someone we had groomed for a dangerous mission. Using the cover of the secret army, he slipped across to the other side and became involved in matters not normally the prerogative of a soldier. Sorry, not normally the concern, the business, of a soldier.' He had seen a look on Etam's face that showed he had not fully followed what had been said. 'He bugged out before it was too hot for him and got sick. Somehow he found that he could get admitted to Ban Ban hospital, where he is now. I want him rescued before the Baddies catch up with him. Now there are snags to this: one is the ceasefire and the protocols and another is who goes and fetches him, always provided he can't get away under his own steam. My info is that he needs rescuing. Yet another problem is where does the rescue team launch itself from? I have one possibility in mind. I'm not going too fast for you, am I, General?'

Etam's shrewd eyes gave none of his feelings away. He was a past master at concealing them. 'So far I understand you perfectly, Mango. You want us to get our hands dirty at our expense and your convenience. Please continue.'

'Put like that, it sounds a bit raw, General,' said Mango, smiling deprecatingly. 'Let me tell you some more. This man, Mana Varamit, got friendly with Tâ Tran Quán and, under the circumstances, I guess, Tâ is the best man to go and rescue him. I have every reason to believe he would be prepared to cooperate. He used to be a Political Commissar and knew our man when they were both in Nam.' Etam remembered the recent medical examination in the American hospital that Tâ had undergone and he knew that the British Attaché had secretly gone there to talk to him. He had known it would not stop there. Mango continued, 'He knows enough to bluff his way into the Ban Ban hospital. For a friend to go with him I have thought your arch Gook-hater, the Tai Dam Major, would be ideal. Go disguised as a doctor and be ready with the treatment if necessary, for our man or for anyone else in need of it.' He emphasised the word "treatment", gave a sick grin which Etam, noticing, replied in similar vein. 'The party would be small, just those two and a close escort of, say, four men. They would fly into Bouam Long on the milk run and be launched for Ban Ban the same day. We have it in mind, provided we can get your agreement, to rescue our man on March 13 or 14. Once that is agreed in outline, we need to consider such details as documents, uniform, rations and so forth.'

'H'm. You seem pretty keen to get him. You're not saying he's a prisoner of war? If so, no deal. The protocols of POWs will be seen to have been broken.'

'No, General. I can assure you that he's not in that category. He's an agent on the run who's gotten into difficulties. The information he may well be in possession of is difficult to assess but we firmly believe he had a lead into Office 95. If that is the case, it would be mighty useful to us and to you. Might forestall a whole heap of trouble and forewarn us of their long-range plans.'

'Yes, I can see that it's important. I'd be happier if we could make it …' he searched for a word. 'What do you call it in English? Un … Unat …'

'Unattributable.'

'That's it. Unattributable.'

'It'll be the next best thing the way we've got it so far.'

There was a silence. General Etam filled up Mango's glass and took another cigarette. He had his own reasons for wanting to know what was going on in Ban Ban but the American need not know that. He would have to talk with Tâ and Vong. If they were willing, well and good. If not, he would have to say no. It was a tricky one. If all went well, it would redound greatly in his favour, certainly among some of the more senior members of the Vientiane side. If not, he'd be in stook. He glanced up at the American. Was there more to it than met the eye? There usually was when dealing with Americans. He broke the silence.

'How many others know about this?'

'On my net, General, only myself and two others, on the need-to-know basis. As far as my embassy staff is concerned, nobody, not even the Ambassador.'

'So the Thais in Bangkok know about this man?'

'This is the tricky aspect of the whole affair. It was not from their sources I got the news about our man so, as far as that is concerned, no. In that he is one of their men, he will be recorded either under his real name or his secret one.'

'And you say Tâ is a volunteer? That he will accept, has accepted, this mission?'

'Yes, General, that is what I am saying.'

'That *is* interesting, Mango. I know you can't speak Lao, Vietnamese or French. I also know that Tâ cannot speak English. Who did you use as your interpreter?'

There was an uneasy pause. Better to come clean. 'I never spoke to Tâ myself so I never used an interpreter. It was the British Defence Attaché, Colonel Rance, who spoke to him and he told Gordon Parks, whom you know well, and Gordon told me. They are the other two who know.'

This was not the breach of trust that might have been committed had Parks' name not been already declared to the General, so he did not look surprised on hearing his name. He digested the news gravely, measuring the significance.

'As you say in English, "the plot thickens". From what I know of Colonel Three Eyes, the man who doesn't miss a trick, it'll be genuine and worthwhile to mount as an operation. I remember the Deputy C-in-C giving clearance for the medical examination – I wonder if he knows the full story?' Mango took this last as more of a statement than a question, so remained silent. 'I'll let you know definitely in a day or two,' and with that Mango had to be satisfied.

Mana Varamit, blissfully ignorant of the urgent concern about his memory, lay on his back in a small isolation ward in Ban Ban hospital, staring at the ceiling. His head felt muzzy, as it often did these days. He was given drugs and they cleared his head for a while but made him feel sleepy. He found it difficult to concentrate. They had asked him so many questions, so many times. He remembered his name, Le Dâng Khoã, and could talk about some aspects of his earlier days in Vietnam. But they said his name was Mana ... what was it? ... Varamit. He could speak Lao, Thai and Vietnamese, had done for as long as he could remember. English, which he never used now, also came into his mind often, so did some French. Came and went. Better some days than others. He was not lonely in this Ban Ban place. It had been fun when he first got to this new place. Could wander around and see what was going on. Could ask questions and understand some of the answers. But it was the nights that troubled him. Nightmares. People creeping up behind him, people moving forwards towards him. Sometimes a large black tadpole that made a loud noise flew round and round overhead. Never had any wings. And then a face looking at his with strange, staring eyes. He'd never forget that face. He often looked for it but he'd never seen it again. He was sure he'd recognise it if ever he did see it. He dozed. There was a knock on the door and a nurse entered. Pretty young thing. She always came at this time of evening. Stopped for a short chat. Always said something different but he could never remember clearly what she had said from one day to another. She took his temperature, felt his pulse, gave him his pills and started talking about rice planting. He could keep pace with most of it but some of it didn't mean much. The nurse looked at her watch. *Keep at it for fifteen minutes*, they had said. Gave her a topic. She didn't know what was in their minds but she liked this man: strong, sometimes that glint in his eyes made her shudder with something she dare not tell her comrades. Maybe one day she would be able to make an unofficial approach to him – should be easy enough especially as the doctor lived out. She put those thoughts out of her mind and once more glanced at her watch. 'Time to leave. Good luck.' She left him. Said in Thai, '*Chok di.*' She had turned her head back to the door so she did not see a spurt of interest flicker in his eyes. She left him. He lay back on his bed, staring at the ceiling. A nag was at the back of his mind. *Chok Di ... Chok Di ...* No, he couldn't get it. He fell into an uneasy sleep.

Ban Ban camp consisted of a headquarters, a 34-man garrison of security troops, a few sappers for road maintenance, clerks, cooks and bottle-washers. There were a 30-bed hospital and, just out of sight of the main camp road, a communication centre. Part of the camp nestled up against a river that formed a protective arc deemed sufficiently secure not to need reinforcement. This was where the senior cadres slept and ate and where visitors were housed. An underground shelter had been dug nearby. The junior cadres were housed halfway between there and the camp entrance. The rest of the camp had a barbed wire fence around it. A road neatly divided the camp in two. At the entrance was a ceremonial arch on which the Pathet Lao flag was unfurled during the day and, close by, a guardroom manned day and night. The hospital was in the centre of the camp, to the north of the road, opposite the cookhouse and not far from the offices, stores and accommodation for lesser-ranked functionaries, for while all Communists were equal in the eyes of Lenin's ghost, until the Day of Red Awakening as the Propaganda Department had it, the humble were to remain humble. The corollary was never stated nor hinted at – merely accepted with bored indifference.

The hospital consisted of an office block, a medical store and a pathological laboratory, where rudimentary tests could be carried out, a small operating theatre, a smaller mortuary, three wards for ten patients each and an isolation ward in the middle of the hospital complex, easily visible from the other buildings. The staff quarters had accommodation for a resident doctor although, since the ceasefire, he had been allowed to sleep out in the village of Ban Ban, to run the local clinic.

There was electricity of sorts available in the camp, supplied by a charging engine that was fitful in performance and wasteful of fuel. Apart from a daily communications schedule, it was only used on rare occasions such as an emergency. Otherwise messages of a routine nature were sent over the landline. For lighting, hurricane lanterns were used. Cooking was done by firewood.

The enclave at Bouam Long, three days' slow walk away, gave no trouble. Before the ceasefire, the NVA had tried to capture it but had always been repulsed by massive B-52 strikes. At the end of February 1974, all was quiet, with a tacit agreement of non-interference. Both sides liked it that way.

Before flying back to Vientiane from the royal wedding and his late-night meeting with the King, Jason called on the Neutralisation Forces and had a formal, stiff meeting, hemmed in, orally by platitudes, physically by henchmen. After the routine ritual was over, Rance thanked them formally. Thong said he would escort him to the gate. When out of earshot of the others Thong said, 'I hate it like this but we must be patient. Tell Tâ from me to try and swap with Mana. I'll get to see him at Sam Neua or Office 95.' He stopped, put out his hand, turned his head slightly so that anyone watching might read disdain in the motion and bade

Rance farewell. 'Go carefully,' he whispered.

Rance nodded gently and walked slowly back to the hotel. He spent the evening reading quietly but found he could not concentrate.

His Majesty the King of Laos and the Chief Bonze were having an informal chat in the same room where the King had spoken to Rance and Princess Golden Fairy the previous night. The two men, wise and highly respected, felt a deep empathy with and affection for each other. They had known one another for many years and, despite informality, had never deviated from the correct titles and dignities that society and rank had accorded them. Both were dressed casually, the King wearing a loose jacket over a homespun shirt, with a draped skirt-like garment over his lower limbs and the monk a plain saffron robe. Both were bare footed.

'I am worried, Your Holiness, as I expect you are. We seem to be living in a world that is foreign and different in character from what we knew before. Oh, I know we've had wars and feuds since the beginning of time but I find it hard to imagine when any period was quite so universally nasty, so degrading and so unnecessary. Almost wherever one turns there's violence. I tell you I'm troubled.'

'Your Majesty. We have good reason to be troubled. I have spent a lifetime in search of dharma but can in no way reconcile my life's efforts to the current situation.'

'When my father was on the throne, we thought we were living through troubled times, as indeed we were, but we hoped that after the Japanese had gone, peace would return. Instead of which our beloved Luang Prabang is surrounded by my subjects who have been led down the wrong path for so long that they know no other way of life.'

'Your Majesty. We were at a crossroads in history after the Japanese war and, next year, we will be at yet another, certainly as far as our beloved land is concerned. After the war we took the wrong turning. Or put it this way: the world needed a purge but, instead of voiding only the dross, voided its heart and soul at the same time. I pray that we take the correct path at the crossroads next year.' He paused, collected his thoughts and continued. 'Maybe we were too young or too tired after the war, or too blind to see where to go twenty-nine years ago. For me the crisis was revealed at Ban Liet in ...' And he paused again, this time for longer.

'I never knew quite what happened, Your Holiness,' the King gently intervened. 'You have always been reticent about it yet involved you were. Can you enlighten me? It might somehow bear some relevance to my present worries.'

The Chief Bonze collected his thoughts and told him the whole story. His memory was faultless: a massacre outside his wat by Communist fanatics in late 1945, five young boys, one a Thai named Mana Varamit who disappeared, and his prophesy. My words come back to me: "I see right not left, blue not red, white not brown as being essential to and in sympathy with the quest for salvation. But above all I see delusion, pain, suffering and great hardship. Thirty agonising years will elapse before the time is ripe for anything that I have read in the divinations to be pronounced true. Patience and stealth will be the watchwords.

Much is still obscure and, hate to say it though I do, one amongst you will betray the others. But salvation will be reached: however, the sixty-year cycle will have to run its course before true and lasting salvation is obtained because, in the first thirty years, evil will be in the ascendancy."'

Silence reigned for a while before the King asked 'Who did you see as a probable bringer of redemption? How did you envisage the white not brown, the blue not red, west not east? Of course, divinations are, to a great extent, symbolic. How did you see your prophesy actually working out, or couldn't you see so far ahead all that clearly?'

'I accept your implications, Your Majesty. To be truthful, I would have to say I didn't but I have enough faith to say I'd recognise the portents when revealed.'

'H'm, but the four little boys and the fifth who ran away. Where are they now?'

'The four are in the guise of working for the opposition, if I can use that phrase. They seek the moment of retribution before their redemption. As for the fifth, the wayward, he has taken the worst path possible – to betray those who feel betrayed. He, too, as far as I know, is somewhere in the other part of your realm.'

'Your Holiness. As we know each other so well, I accepted the message given to you, my brother and sister-in-law from the English Colonel. It is not in my nature to dispute anything that you say but the ring the Englishman showed me last night, can you give me your version of how that ties up with those far-off days? I talked with him and he told me much that was new to me but I'd like to have some background to his story to corroborate it.'

So the Chief Bonze told the King that part of the story that concerned Leuam Sunthorn, his relationship with the British and, as best he remembered it, the incident in the Malaysian jungle when Rance, Mana Varamit and Le Dâng Khoã were involved, even the bit about Le Dâng Khoã giving Colonel Rance his ring.

The King nodded in understanding. 'The Englishman, so that's how he fits in. In the modern idiom, I can see how it can be he, the colours referring to his skin and his politics, with the direction referring to the non-communist world. And, Your Holiness, the thirty-year and the sixty-year cycle is fully understood by him also.'

'Indeed, it is, Your Majesty. It is that one crucial point that has concerned him since he has met all of, shall I coin a phrase, the Four Rings, since he has been here.'

There was a long, long pause and, with a look of ineffable sadness, His Majesty, King Savang Vatthana, said, 'Now I understand. He has got himself enmeshed with our problems in a way I would never have credited. Let us hope he emerges from them unscathed … What a story! Indeed, truth is stranger than fiction.'

Brigadier General Etam had given Mango's report and request a great deal of thought. He had arranged that Major Vong bring Tâ Tran Quán to his house the following evening, after dark. He had sat them down and made them comfortable. Little by little he had let them know how much he knew.

'I hear, *Tan* Tâ, that the Englishman, Colonel Rance, had a long conversation with you.' As it was not a question there was no need for an answer. Tâ started impassively at the General, who continued, 'It seems that somehow he convinced you to go to Ban Ban to recapture somebody. How was this?' The question had to be answered. It was one he had been expecting.

'*Tan* General. You must understand my position. I am your guest,' he stressed the word "guest". 'It is incumbent on me to talk to any and everybody I am ordered to. It was some time ago that the English Colonel came to see me in Phone Kheng. Major Vong was there the whole time.' Vong nodded agreement. 'We talked about tactics but I could not help him much. The next time I saw him was the other day. No one ever sees me without clearance from your staff, General. I have no idea why you chose him to talk to me rather than so many of the others who have been sent to see me since I was wounded. The English Colonel gave me a proposition. I presumed it was yours to start with but, for reasons yet known to me, you chose Colonel Rance to put it to me. The proposition came as a veiled order and put in a way I could scarcely refuse. Perhaps, General, you would pardon the impertinence and let me know why you sent the Englishman to talk to me in the first place?'

It was neatly done and General Etam knew it, as indeed did Tâ. Major Vong was obviously mystified. It was then for the General to take the conversational initiative, the upshot of which Mango got his telephone call of agreement the next morning and Gordon Parks his only a few minutes later.

'Sit down, Jason. I've news for you and I expect you haven't come empty-handed to me. You never seem to so why start now?' Gordon Parks told Rance the latest situation as regards recovering Mana: Tâ and Vong, the Tai Dam Major, and four men, a total of six, would fly to Bouam Long and be launched on the 9th. They and an escort from Bouam Long would veer east and approach Ban Ban from the Sam Neua side but that part of the business was being left to them. Back-up, in the shape of operational and administrative requirements, was being jacked up by the CIA and the Lao Intelligence Chief. The security aspect had been more rigorously stressed and the cover story was Mana was a returning US agent, on the run, who had become somehow enmeshed and detained at Ban Ban. It was thought that he was ill but unsuspected.

'Gordon, I interrupt here. I have a message from Thong to Tâ.' Gordon Parks hid his surprise. The British DA had an extraordinary habit of successfully trawling in opposition waters with seemingly little effort and no pre-planning. Rance then told him of his latest LPF encounter.

'But this is suicide, Jason. Wouldn't Tâ be more useful with us, being interrogated in depth and used for his expert knowledge and understanding of opposition personalities? It seems such a pity to waste both him and what you can do with him.'

'This is a most difficult problem, Gordon. I doubt we'll ever get such a man on our side again but how willing has he been in interrogations et cetera to date? Don't forget it is only my particular relationship with him that has made him appear so willing. I have no doubt that he is a genuinely dedicated mole. If we can get him back into the guts of the opposition and, always provided he is accepted back, he can get into a position of being used by them against us, against the Vientiane side that is, and has lines open through the other three Rings who can still contact us – isn't that a situation that could pay greater dividends? Here external influences will play less and less of a role and, if ever Communism is to be beaten, it can only be really and properly beaten by internal implosion, the edifice collapsing on itself, rather than by any other means. The Vietnamese are the master Indo-China race, always have been, always will be. Geography will win out because it can't be changed. History can do things neither geography nor we do-gooders can. My gut feeling is to take the risk of getting him back in, great though the risks for him are.'

Gordon Parks nodded slowly. 'You'll have to talk to him, Jason. I'll fix that. Now that I've knowledge of the party's composition and General Etam is in on it, you may have a larger audience than you had before.'

'H'm. I'd prefer Tâ on his own if you can arrange it. In any case the smaller the audience the happier I am and the fewer people to spill the beans through careless talk or bloody mindedness.'

'I'll see what I can do. What else have you, Jason? I can't believe you've picked up nothing else.' Gordon Parks was not really being sarcastic but even he was scarcely able to credit that Rance had had an audience with the King. Rance spelled it out in great detail, only omitting his brief entanglement with Princess Golden Fairy. The stenographer took both reports down, the secret audience with the King and the contact with Thong Damdouane: they made as full and interesting a report as John

Chambers and Maurice Burke had received in a long time.

Rance was able to see Tâ Tran Quán only once more before his departure for Ban Ban. It had been felt by General Etam, who vetted Attachés' movements to sensitive areas and who under normal circumstances would have welcomed Rance's presence in Bouam Long, that it were better to allow nothing of a coincidental nature during the sensitive stage. A meeting, less secretive than the last time, was arranged at the same office in Phone Kheng as the first time Rance had met Tâ. Major Vong was present. He somehow sensed Rance and Tâ had more between them than would normally be the case but also being on the fringe of the twilight intelligence world, understood there were many things he could never understand. This was one of them. He himself was pining for action, being of war-like stock and, having no hope of ever returning to his beloved natal place, was more than content to prevent as many of the other side from ever returning to theirs. He was one of the school who thought that, while being glorious to die for your country, it was far more glorious to make the other man die for his – a sentiment fully shared by Rance.

After greetings, Rance asked Tâ how matters had developed since their last meeting. 'Are you still of like mind?'

'Indeed I am,' answered Tâ gravely. 'I am also glad that I have Major Vong here to be with me. I have developed a healthy respect for him since we were thrown together.'

'It's just as well I don't know what you are doing in detail as it means I can give nothing away by any indication but,' pointing to a map of Laos hanging at the far end of the wall, 'could you, Major, show me in outline how you propose to tackle this problem? It is purely for professional interest only.'

As the Major walked over to the wall map, Rance whispered, 'I met Thong six days ago. He knows of the plan. He gave you this mes ...' Major Vong had reached the map and, picking up a pointer, was about to begin his delivery.

'We fly into Bouam Long of Saturday, the 9th. That's D-Day. We go in as civilians. We propose to leave that afternoon and two or possibly three days later approach Ban Ban from the Sam Neua direction by Route 6, to be exact it is numbered 61 there. My thoughts are that we arrive on foot at last light. I know Ban Ban from old but there may be differences that I have yet to learn about so I have asked for an overflight for an up-to-date aerial photograph. I may be able to pick up some tips on our way there. Mana may be anywhere but, using bluff, I propose we get escorted to where he is. If the authorities cavil at our unusual timings, Tâ will pull rank and explain our vehicle has broken down a few kilometres up the road about here,' and he turned and peered at the map, looking for area intently. As he did, Rance continued speaking to Tâ, urgently.

'The message was to swap with Mana.'

'Just about here,' said Major Vong, turning back to face them.

'I'm so sorry,' said Rance, 'but I didn't quite see. Please show me again.'

Major Vong turned, thinking his pointer might have slipped, as Rance said, 'and he'll meet you in Sam Neua or Office 95 when he can.'

'I beg your pardon,' said Major Vong, turning back. 'Did you say Sam Neua or Office 95?'

'Yes, I did. I merely said to Tan Tâ here that maybe the authorities would try and get in touch with one or both of those locations.'

'From what I know of them, I can't see them trying anything at night. It may be that the generator will be started for emergency communications. One of my group will have, among his other toys, plastic explosive and will either try to talk to the operators in Sam Neua or blow the thing up. I'm looking at that side of the business and will decided on what to do once we are there. It may be difficult getting Mana out of the camp with seven men, not six but ...'

He broke off as Tâ interrupted him. 'I'll swap with Mana. I'm blown anyway. I can do to them what they're trying to do to us, hoodwink and seduce. Let me pretend that you are a party of like-minded men who have found out who I am, that I had lost my mind, forgotten my identity – my new papers will prove that – and wandered into Bouam Long. There you, pro-LPF agents, hoodwinked the Irregulars and got me back to Ban Ban. I already know when and how to deflect Communist tactics. No, wait one, please,' he held up a restraining hand to Vong. 'You have proof of my intentions and integrity in my accepting this mission. I now know the other side of the story.' His face was intense with pleading. 'If I were still a stooge, I could so easily ditch you there, couldn't I?' Not waiting for an answer, 'Of course I could. Even now, I could be putting my head on a platter. Doesn't that prove how sincere I am? If you don't believe that, I'll refuse to go and that won't be popular now.'

He paused, more for breath than because he had run out of things to say. He turned to Rance and, as Vong could not see him, winked. 'You believe me, *Tan Colonen*, don't you?'

'Ye-es, Yes, I do, *Tan* Tâ. It is a brave thing you're doing and I believe you are a hero.'

'Hero.' Tâ spat the word out. 'Believe what you like. There are no medals in this game. And, Major Vong, I need you cooperation. During the snatch of Mana, you'll have to make certain sure that the others, the LPF, are not there. You'll have to keep them quiet. You'll also need to take some dope, I've heard mention of Scopolamine I think it is, and give me a jab. That'll put me out and take time to wear off. That's my cover plan for re-entry into their rotten system, on my terms.' He shifted in his chair and then, 'Oh yes. One more thought. I need to learn some medical terms to make the Political Commissar in Ban Ban think I am genuine.'

Bouam Long was an enclave deep inside Communist-dominated territory, a series of Meo villages joined into one fortified base and garrisoned by Irregular troops. There was a small landing strip of red gravel but, being 4000 feet up in the mountains, certain weather problems of turbulence made its use tricky. Surrounding the enclave were thick strands of wire and a series of observation posts and defensive positions. Gruesome relics of the last determined NVA attack still draped the wire in some places; skeletons, tattered bits of clothing and old pieces of equipment, awesome travesties of scarecrows. Beyond the wire, outside the enclave but reaching almost up to the rim of the defensive positions, were countless large bomb craters that bore mute testimony of the efficacy of aerial power used with pin-point precision. No troops in the world could stand firm against such an onslaught and the peasants of Uncle Ho's army were no exception.

Around the centrally-situated airstrip the ground rose steeply. Dug deep inside one of the hills were headquarters of the military unit commanding the enclave, the place whence strict orders for the two Irregular battalions emanated and wherein records were maintained and plans prepared both for their own military activities and, as far as possible, those of their enemies. On the morning of Saturday, 9 March, a balding, hard-faced Meo Major of Irregulars was in conference with his subordinates. He was the overall Garrison Commander.

'We've got a Continental Airways Twin Otter coming in later on. I gather it has a strange cargo, or rather the cargo is normal men but they're shrouded in secrecy – not that anyone can keep a secret here. They say that they are a party going on a hush-hush mission to Ban Ban to meet some LPF officials. It might have something to do with the status of this enclave after the next stage of political wrangling but the area of Bouam Long is so well known that I can only presume it is to stop the LPF from using their nibbling tactics, but that's pure guesswork. It may be that they're going to meet up with a party of LPF from Sam Neua or even Hanoi. I know nothing except that it is none of our business.

'Apart from the crew, the party consists of six men. There will be some stores on the plane for us as well as for them. I gather that the party will be away for anything up to two weeks. They will take an escort from here and may need helping out during their return. To this end, the camp will be on first-stage alert during the time they are away. My orders, that came in by the last courier, stress that the garrison is to be told that we can expect retaliatory action by LPF but we are to initiate no activity ourselves that could be construed as being counter to the ceasefire protocols – though what they,' and he gestured with his head towards the east as he said it, 'have been doing these last few months has hardly been conducive to peaceful relations. In fact, we have been quiet recently so I'm not going to mention anything about retaliation in any orders I subsequently give. Neither will you.

'When the plane arrives, action normal. Sentries will be out. I will meet the party and bring them here. I will establish any particular requirements they may have and then let them carry on with their task.'

He looked around the crude table, made from packing cases, at the hardy, tough, expectant faces. Apart from the two Battalion Commanders, a staff officer, a logistics expert, the escort commander and a communications man were present, every one of them campaign-tested and two of them had been on courses in the States. 'Any questions?'

'Will they need escorting all or only part of the way?' asked the escort commander. 'I have given provisional orders for a platoon to be ready for ten days.'

'A squad, not a platoon. Go yourself and have with you any of your men who have relatives in the Ban Ban area.'

'Will they bring a radio with them and have to be netted into our frequencies?' asked the communicator.

'Nothing about it in my orders. Apart from that, be prepared to give them any help they may need.' He turned to the escort commander. 'Unless you are in an emergency, you will observe radio silence. We are still not sure how much monitoring the Cubans are doing for our fellow countrymen.'

There were no more questions. 'They'll be flying in along the normal circuitous route so expect nothing,' he glanced at this watch, 'for another couple of hours.'

With that, they departed.

Shortly after noon the Twin Otter arrived. It taxied to the dispersal area and cut its engines. Six men got out and a crewman helped them with some sacks. A folding stretcher was among the kit. The Garrison Commander went up to the group, who were dressed in plain clothes. 'Welcome to Bouam Long. I am the Garrison Commander here. Is there anything I can do for you right now before we go and have a talk?'

A thick-set, burly thug answered. 'Thanks. I am Major Vong and this is my gang.' He made no attempt to introduce his team who looked equally tough except for one who was a paler, non-military type and less fit-looking man who could have been a Vietnamese. This man seemed totally withdrawn into himself. *A meeting with the LPF?* the Garrison Commander mused. *On whose terms, I wonder?*

He took them off to his underground command post and produced coffee for them. After they had settled themselves comfortably, he rehearsed what orders he had had. Major Vong nodded his agreement. 'That's about the sum of it. It'll be plain sailing going out but could be rough on the way back if they lose their tempers! You have our outline programme? Leave today and hopefully be back on the 17th or 18th. If we abort, it may be before then. It may even be later. We're wearing plain clothes now and we'll change into our other clothes nearer the time. Which one of you is the escort commander? Please make sure you have a couple of men who know Ban Ban. Better still if they have relatives in the village or neighbouring hamlets. I want them to be dressed as though they had been out hunting or something similar that will not arouse suspicions. You've already got them detailed?' in answer to a gesture from the escort commander. 'The rest of the escort will have to lie up while we're negotiating. I'll give orders for what we need nearer the time. I don't expect anything drastic but, to be on the safe side, I hope you've got some tough cookies lined up!'

The Garrison Commander listened impassively. 'Do you need any intercom facility?'

'We have our own and will net in with you before we leave. I propose radio silence to start with.' The escort commander nodded agreement. 'Apart from that, my only need is the way out clear of any patrol or minefield and an exact knowledge of how to get back in – just in case we get separated. On our way back we may make contact with you before dark,' this to the Garrison Commander, 'and ask for the rest of the party to be allowed in after nightfall. I'm sorry to be a nuisance if that is against your Standing Operational Procedures but the people in Vientiane told me to fix those details directly with you.'

They talked for a while longer and then Major Vong looked at his watch. 'Time to be on our way. Let us start six zero minutes from now.'

'One last point: password and countersign?'

'Something easy to remember and innocuous. Something your soldiers will find comes naturally to them.'

'In that case, let us say that the password is 'One more forest' and the countersign is 'One less tree'.

In any army, certain set types of man will be found and the most rare is probably the professional killer. Some join because the life attracts them, a life of no responsibility, merely taking orders and being fed, clothed and paid. Some join out of a sense of adventure and travel, some even because they have been ordered to by hard-up parents, others, especially in Communist-inspired guerilla armies, out of fear of reprisals to their family if they do not throw their lot in with the bully boys in uniform. There is another rare class of man who joins because he finds solace in bugle and camp as indeed others similarly disposed find peace in bell and cloister. In every army, the bully and barrack-room lawyer will be found as well as the one in every twenty or thirty who wishes he had never joined and cannot find a way out. Of the six men who were on this mission, Major Vong could be described as the professional's professional. Combat-seasoned, highly trained and dedicated to a remarkable degree, he was a natural. Tâ Tran Quán was a soldier of faith, a man with a lifetime mission, a crusader. If what he had to do, however unpleasant, helped his Cause, then so be it. The other four were tough, battle-inoculated men who knew there would never be any peace for them if the Communists came to power. They were good at close-combat work, adept with knife and rope, and had a knowledge of demolitions. They were physically fit.

They were not volunteers for this particular mission; they were volunteers for any such mission. They had one thing in common; their homes had been overrun by the Communists and they could never return to their nearest and dearest – '180 degrees' different from the sad, press-ganged peasants that made up the army of those venal robber-barons posing as Generals in the Royal Lao Army. Vong had collected his team with intelligence and skill. He knew that his mission was tight-rope fraught.

The journey to Ban Ban was a cautious affair. Not only was there the imperative necessity to remain completely hidden but also any traces that the group made had either to be eradicated or made to seem as though locals had been responsible for them. Initially, the men were virtually on home ground, certainly until the first evening, and this gave them a chance to practise their jungle movement without much fear of being discovered. Major Vong was a tower of strength. He was obviously no stranger to jungle conditions and he had the happy knack of impressing his personality on the escort to the extent that they accepted his strictures when they moved clumsily.

Once over the high ground surrounding Bouam Long, their track led them downhill. That first night they made camp near a stream. They scouted around to see if there was any NVA or LPF movement before tying groundsheets to stakes to keep off the dew. They collected firewood and cooked themselves a modest meal before dusk. After washing up their cooking pots and mess tins, they held a council of war before turning in for the night.

'Up in the fortress one of your men said he had recently

travelled to Ban Ban. Which one is he?' Vong asked the escort commander.

The man was sent for and Vong questioned him carefully. Their main worry was unexpectedly meeting a group of people from the other side. To obviate against any danger that might arise, it was decided to move in two groups, some fifty or so metres apart when visibility allowed. If the group in front did stumble across any enemy, they could explain their presence as best they could. To this end, three men were detailed to wear plain clothes and to carry weapons – not an uncommon phenomenon in a country where boredom, banditry and shortage of rations resulted in a number of strangely dressed people to be found in areas outside villages as they looked for something to do, someone to rob or something to eat. The special clothes, LPF-style uniform, of the leading group, would be carried by the rest of the team, whose other task would be to try and obviate any telltale marks.

They spent a comfortable enough night, Tâ sleeping on the stretcher, reasonably free from insects. Sentries were not posted as, so Vong's reasoning went, they would not keep awake with no immediate danger and, if it were too difficult for their group to move at night, it would probably be too difficult for anyone else to.

The second day was a repetition of the first, only longer, more tiring and getting warmer as their route took them from the mountains to the plains. Vong realised that Tâ was tiring but he did not dare let up. By 4 o'clock that evening, everybody had walked far enough. They decided to make camp near the first running water they found. As the squad was checking the area and preparing camp, Tâ took his footwear off and bathed his sore feet.

'How are you, Tâ?' Vong asked solicitously. 'Bearing up?'

'I've got to. I must,' Tâ answered gravely. 'Today has been hard. Tell me how you see us progressing from here.'

'Tomorrow is the 11th of March. We will hit an old French-built road in the morning and follow that. Depending on our speed, obviously, I will make up my mind where to lie up. I'd like to reach here,' and he showed Tâ where he referred to on his map. 'Sometime in the small hours of Tuesday morning we should have reached Route 61, the Sam Neua-Muong Peon-Ban Ban road. Near to where I expect we'll hit the road is our guide's village, still more or less intact. He has a pretty good idea of where we can hide up. All Wednesday he and a friend will patrol from there to Ban Ban, trying to find out any info that could help us at the last minute. You, my friend, will lie up and rest. We'll get your shirt and underpants laundered and dried so that, when we eventually get into Ban Ban, there are no traces of what we've been through.

'Then, on the Thursday, timings later but towards evening we move. By then, my friend, we will have rested up, have had the latest news – hopefully – and will be ready to meet our challenge.'

'You're a good man, Vong. Under different circumstances there's no telling what we wouldn't have done together. Have you got a pin? I need to prick a blister.'

They moved off shortly after dawn and, by 10 o'clock, reached the outer edge of the cultivated land that from the now on would be a constant feature up to Ban Ban. Soon after, they met the road that was more a wide, overgrown trail than a motor road. They decided to risk walking along it as the going was so much easier. They kept their eyes skinned for signs of others in the area.

Towards evening, they rested up for a couple of hours in a small hut used, during the rice harvest, for accommodating the harvesters so saving them a journey to and from their main settlement. Before moving off, they cooked themselves another meal. Vong had taken the precaution of providing enough string to tie themselves together so, with torches that had a thin green leaf tucked behind the glass, they could walk during the night. These preparations were obvious ones, although the risk of dogs barking and so alerting people had to be taken.

Some three hours' walk from Ban Ban, the guide took them due east, away from the road, and after crossing a tributary of the River Nam, brought them, in the small hours, to Route 61, the road that would take them to Ban Ban. The guide told them to wait while he went to reconnoitre. He faded into the night and the others, except Vong, thankfully sank to the ground and dropped off to sleep.

Tâ was woken by Vong. 'Up you get, we're off again,' he said softly.

Tâ clambered slowly and stiffly to his feet. He finished off the contents of his water bottle and followed the shadowy figure in front of him. There was no need for the string to be tied as there was now enough residual starlight to see by. Thankfully, twenty minutes later, the leading scout stopped and the others bumped together. 'We're here,' Vong whispered to Tâ. The place was an old dwelling, scarcely a house, built on stilts, set in a clump of custard apple trees, the result of some pre-war French attempt to encourage orchards for cash crops. Even had it been light enough to see them, they were of no interest to Tâ who, in a short time after the group reached the hide-out, was blissfully asleep on the stretcher.

Next morning the two men with relatives in the Ban Ban area left and returned late that evening. It so happened that the mother-in-law of the elder lived not far from the clinic run by the camp doctor and his wife. The sister-in-law's cousin also happened to have a bad stomach and had been to the clinic for treatment. Whilst waiting his turn, he had overheard the doctor telling his wife that he would have to cancel the Friday clinic as doctors from Hanoi were coming to see, and here he had tapped his head, in the camp. After getting his tablets, the man called in to see his cousin. The two-man team, having a meal in the kitchen, also overheard the conversation and, at an appropriate moment, left for their temporary base as fast as they could. They told Vong to tell Tâ. They then went into a huddle to try and solve what was essentially a time and space problem.

The six men had prepared themselves before leaving the escort party. Three of them had green PL uniform and the other three blue. A casual observer would have noticed no difference in Tâ's mien but Vong sensed an inner tension and an inner fortitude. Despite trusting Tâ not going to double cross them, he was ever suspicious, had his own plans for that eventuality. He patted his pistol unconsciously as he stole a glance at the others who looked the part they had to play.

The two scouts had done their work well and saved the group much bother. Due to set off at half past 5 in the evening of Thursday, 14 March, they had eaten before they left but, tense with excitement, forced the food down. Even if their presence was noticed, the villagers paid no attention to yet another group of uniformed men walking down the road. Darkness fell. At one point, Major Vong, ears sharper than the others', pulled them into the undergrowth as a patrol of soldiers came from the other direction. Back on the road, they continued their journey, having first cached the stretcher.

The camp came into sight. They automatically stopped. Vong briefly told the others what to expect then he and Tâ shook hands. 'Thank you, Vong, for being a friend as well as an escort. You have done much to restore my faith in humankind.'

'Goodbye, Tâ. You're a brave man. I hope we meet again.'

At the camp entrance, the sentry challenged them. He had not been alerted for anybody at this time of night. He called the Guard Commander.

'Listen, my good man,' said Tâ, when the first sign of stubbornness was obvious, 'I am Doctor Tanh Bên Lòng. I have been sent on a delicate medical mission. We should have been here hours ago but our transport broke down some distance away, about five kilometres. I'll need a mechanic tomorrow or else send for an aeroplane. Go and send someone immediately to the Commanding Officer and tell him I am here. Have you got the name? No? How dare you forget it so quickly! Listen – Dr. Tanh

Bên Lòng. Say it back to me ... once more,' commanded Tâ, in a virtuoso performance. The other five members of the team were listening to a Tâ they had not previously met.

At this display of authority, the Guard Commander had adopted the position of attention. 'Well, Comrade,' continued Tâ, 'off you go and carry out my orders – send a soldier if you must stay here yourself.' The Guard Commander moved away but was roughly called back by Tâ. 'Aren't you going to let us sit down until the Commanding Officer comes to fetch us?'

A shame-faced and cowed Guard Commander invited them into the guardroom and offered them a bench, the only one there was, to sit on. A soldier was sent at full speed and the group waited, feigning impatience. As they waited, they studied the layout. 'How many men do you have on duty here?' Vong asked casually.

'Myself and six soldiers, Comrade,' answered the Guard Commander, glancing up at Vong who smiled in appreciation. Feeling encouraged and wishing to eradicate, as far as possible, any adverse opinion he might have let himself for, he started telling Vong about his duties in great detail.

At about the same time that evening, there was one more report left to be read by Nga Sô Lựu. Normally communications were slow but the date on each, as he glanced at the franking stamp on the envelope, was recent. He was in a hurry to go across to talk with the team that was flying in to Ban Ban on the morrow but they would have to wait a little longer.

The report was compulsive reading and his black eyes glinted more glassily than usual. It was sent from Luang Prabang where Comrade Thong Damdouane had unearthed something of great importance. He read it through twice, slowly and carefully. During the festivities over the period of the royal wedding – a shudder ran through the reader – some of the GHQ hierarchy had been too talkative. It appeared that Comrade Tâ Tran Quán, once thought to be dead, was alive but in dubious health. He had been in the hands of the right-wing clique but had never given up hope of returning to his beloved party. He had contrived, quite how had yet to be established, to get some papers, personal documents, but probably not in his own name. It looked as though he had forgotten his real name. He could even be mentally ill. He had escaped, again the details were exceedingly vague – or just that the garrulous General Staff had not bothered to expose their lack of vigilance – he had been so intent on rejoining the Movement, he had wandered, by himself, into the Liberated Zone. The writer was sorry not to have more facts but he believed that Tâ had made his bid for escape a few weeks previously. What concerned him about Comrade Tâ was that he might do himself a damage or be mistakenly thought of as an imposter by anyone who picked him up. His mental state was probably caused by worry, not wounds. It was rumoured that he believed himself to be a doctor but, on that score, no one was certain. If, Thong Damdouane finished, Comrade Tâ Tran Quán was found, as an old friend, he hoped that they would be allowed to meet. It would be therapeutic.

How wonderful, thought Nga Sô Lưu, showing a rare smile, *if the lost comrade did return.*

The member of the guard who had been detailed to go and tell his superiors about the unexpected visitors, hurried down the centre road that divided the camp. On his left was the hospital where that strange, wandering comrade was billeted. Some said he was fey, other that he was crazed. He himself doubted it. Fed up with the war and of being in the army and not allowed to go back home. Enough to send a fellow off his rocker. His steps led him past the main office and to the small accommodation area where the Vietnamese 'elder brothers' would take their ease and prepare their daily indoctrination lectures. Now they *were* boring. Endlessly repetitious but one simply dare not listen. On to you like a ton of bricks. Only sometimes was there something new, like when this crazed comrade, the fellow who was working his ticket, was brought in. Suffered at the hands of the imperialists, feudalists and fascists, so they were told. He shuddered. Any one of those three was bad enough but all three at once was enough to send a bloke bonkers. Worse than this lot, he thought derogatorily. He had reached the hut where his Commanding Officer lived and knocked on the door. He rehearsed the name he had been given. He was but a simple Lao peasant, not cut out for the subtleties and complexities of the situation, like many other simple Lao peasants who only asked to be left in peace at home.

'Who's that outside? What do you want?'

'Comrade Commanding Officer. I am a camp sentry. The Guard Commander has sent me with a message. Shall I come in and deliver it or will you come outside?'

He was called inside the simply furnished room which boasted a wooden bed, a table, two chairs and a wardrobe. The

Commanding Officer sighed. 'Well, what is it?'

The sentry saluted in the open doorway. 'Six men are at the guardroom. Come from Sam Neua on some medical job. Car broken down. Walked the last bit.'

'Six men ... Say that again, Comrade.' Such a message was most unusual and needed time for reflection. It was repeated, with the sentry adding, 'The comrade said he was Dr. Tanh Bên Lòng.' Gosh, but he'd nearly forgotten that bit. 'He said you had to be told about it, immediately. He seemed angry.'

The CO was not at his brightest. 'Dr. Who?' he demanded querulously. The sentry repeated it, proud that he'd got it right twice running. 'Go and call the Political Commissar. He's in the hut nearest the river, then come back.'

Doing as bid, the sentry walked the twenty paces to the end hut, one similar to that of the CO. He again knocked on the door and called out, 'Comrade Political Commissar. Excuse me but the Comrade CO has told me to ask would you go and see him here and now.'

'Tell him I'm on my way.' The Political Commissar also sighed as he put his shirt on, slipped his feet into his flip-flops and hurried out into the night. He knocked on the CO's door and went straight in, unbidden, the knock only a formality. 'What do you want me for?'

The CO stood up. 'I'm so sorry to disturb you but this is important. You know, as indeed do I, that we are expecting a couple of high-ranking doctors with an escort to come tomorrow as ever is, 15 March, Friday, to look at Comrade Mana. I have just been told by the sentry that a party of six men, just as we are expecting, have arrived at the main gate. They are there now. Why, I wonder, are they so early? Their vehicle has broken down somewhere a few kilometres up the road and they walked in here. But they were due to come by air.' The CO sounded aggrieved. 'We must look after them, yet, I ask you again, why the change in programme without our being told?'

'Well, I've certainly heard nothing different. What are their names? Did the sentry check their documents?'

'Did you check their documents, lad?' the CO asked gruffly, wishing that he had remembered to ask that question himself.

The young sentry shook his head. 'I was merely given this message. I'm not on duty and was inside.'

'The name of the doctor, according to the sentry, is Tanh Bên Lòng. I have never heard of him, have you?'

And then it struck the Political Commissar that the neurologist was operating under the code name he had been told about when he was at that meeting in Office 95. 'Yes, I've had forewarning that they might present themselves like this,' he answered, embroidering slightly on what he had been told but confident that the CO would be none the wiser. Nevertheless, it was vexing not to know about this change of timings.

'We'd better get dressed and go and welcome them. They'll be in need of a meal and a wash, I expect. They won't want to start work tonight. Meet you here in five minutes. There's no need to alert the cooks until we know more about their wants.'

That evening the pretty nurse visited Mana Varamit. She took his temperature and talked a while. As she left him she said, '*Chok*

Di,' for his good luck for the examination in the morning.

Mana lay back on his bed. Why were those words so familiar? And then his mind gave a jump and he remembered a large place with hills all round, and an airstrip, and some medium artillery. Where was it? Why was it trying to ring a bell? There was a hurricane lantern on the table near his bed. A large black insect, attracted by the light, flew into the room and buzzed angrily and noisily around it. In his mind's eye the room grew lighter and lighter, and the beetle flew higher and higher and made more and more of a whining note and there was the black Jet Ranger flying round and round over him as he went forward along Skyline Ridge, leading his troops, he Major Chok Di of the Thai Unity Forces. *That* was it. She was calling him by a name he had had. But why had he had it? That lamp hurt his eyes. He got off his bed and blew it out. He shut his eyes and shook his head. The insect, deprived of its magnet, flew away. He heard footsteps outside on the road that ran through the middle of the camp. Someone was going towards the officers' quarters. He felt lonely. Chok Di. Not Le Dâng Khoã …

… there were trees on Skyline Ridge, thick trees but how could he see the Jet Ranger if there were trees? His head whirled. Here were no trees and yet it was dark, like it was now, almost. He hears a voice call him, 'I cannot accept your behaviour. Whatever you did in Vietnam is over and done with. I'm not interested in who started this, only that it ends peaceably. Offer your hand,' and he felt a great weakness as the machete someone was holding ready to chop him was taken away. 'Sergeant Major Pracham.' Who said that? Not Le Dâng Khoã. He was crouching there with his back to that big tree, a look in his eyes. Or was it near Pleku, or Danang, or Nha Trang? Or was it …? But there were no trees on Skyline Ridge. And then there was someone coming towards him, and he was going towards someone, faster and faster, nearer and nearer. He grabbed the side of the bed and the vision faded. He heard the footsteps going up the road. Movement: who was going where? Someone was coming towards him, he could almost see the face. 'I'll get you, you treacherous sod. I'll make sure you don't get away this time.' Where's my weapon, was it pistol or carbine? He searched frantically for it under his pillow, weeping with frustration as he groped in vain.

In the guardroom, the CO and the Political Commissar looked at the six men. The latter took the initiative and after introducing himself and the CO said, primly, 'We were not expecting you until tomorrow. Can you explain why you have not kept to the programme? I find this highly irregular.'

The man who called himself Dr. Tanh Bên Lòng drew himself up stiffly and, in an icy tone of voice, said, 'It is not up to you to doubt my orders. I'll have you know I am a busy man. I have been given this assignment and I am late. I am used to having fraternal civilities extended to me, not this carping effrontery. I should have examined Comrade Mana Varamit this afternoon. Those were my instructions: the afternoon of Thursday, 14 March. I want, and will have, an inspection now. Show me where he is. I have his records here with me. After my inspection, I will come and join you in some refreshment – coffee is my preference. My team will remain with me until I meet you wherever your eating place happens to be. I'll then have a wash and spend the night here, only returning tomorrow. We will discuss those details later. Is that understood?'

There was something vaguely familiar about the speaker that the Political Commissar could not place. There was no doubting his authority. Only the most favoured were as sure of themselves as that.

'Yes, Comrade Doctor. As you wish, as you wish. Any irregularities in the programme can, I am sure, be explained. If there is anything else I can do for you, please do not hesitate to tell me.'

Comrade Doctor Tanh Bên Lòng looked at his watch. 'In a way I am glad we are here only at this time.' The unexpected doctor started telling them about his treatment, leaving the two senior comrades gasping: *Lobus occipitalis and temporalis ... the cortex and connecting fibres of the corpus callosum ... the hippocampus and mammillary bodies and fornix are damaged so amnesia stagnate so causing mental aphasia ...* until both were utterly lost and bewildered. There was no doubting the Comrade Doctor's unrivalled knowledge.

'The new therapy works better at night. It is now 1955 hours. You will take me to where Mana is. You will not come in with me. You will give orders that your generator will operate from, say, 2050 to 2015. You will then turn it off. I will have no further use for it. You can expect us to join you soon afterwards. Part of Comrade Mana's shock therapy must be done in the dark. The rest we will do tomorrow before we go. I hope that is clear.'

There were unusual orders, but again, some of these specialists were divas. 'I'll point out where we'll be as we escort you down the road. If you want the lights on as stated then I must quickly give executive orders. Everything shall be as you have ordered.' Then, as an afterthought, the CO added, 'Do you want us to fetch the camp doctor?'

As they went in a bunch towards the isolation ward of the hospital and there was no answer, the Political Commissar could only presume that the neurologist had not heard the question.

Mana Varamit had found his weapon. It was on his belt. Why had he looked for it under his pillow? And then he saw the man who was coming to meet him, the man he was going to kill because he had been a treacherous sod. It was Tâ Tran Quán who was looking at him in a hurt and a surprised way so he saw Mana Varamit take aim and fire ...

... there was an enormous flash and there, in front of him, Mana Varamit as he now knew himself to be, was Tâ Tran Quán looking at him with murder in his eyes. The Thai opened his mouth to scream and scream and scream but a hand was put over it and smothered any noise there might have been. He passed out in a dead faint.

'Good work, Vong. Strip him. Then jab me,' and, so saying, Tâ started to undress.

4

March 1974: Northeast Laos: Major Vong gave a quick set of orders: a man to stand outside the door to prevent anyone from entering; a man to prepare the hypodermic syringe; two men to undress Mana. He himself sat on the chair and thought out his next move. So far, so good. The element of surprise and bluff, along with superb confidence, had got them into the camp. Now they had to get out, with Mana, leaving Tâ behind. He had already considered several courses of action but the solution had to depend on the circumstances of the moment. One method was kill both the Commanding Officer and the Political Commissar, Commil and Compol as he thought of them; one was to overpower them and, gagged and bound, leave them to be found; one was to make them insensible with poison; and one was to walk out as they had walked in. He himself was ready for any one of them. Speed was essential but, for the sake of a clean break, he was prepared to sacrifice a couple of hours. The dose he had for Tâ should last twenty-four hours and find him slightly disorientated when he awoke. That was how Tâ had said he could cope with the situation so that's how it had to be. He watched the others carry out their tasks. He made up his mind: he would take care of the two senior men by giving them some doped coffee and isolate the camp by burning down the communications centre: for both tasks he was fully prepared.

'Listen: the man outside the door will stay until he sees the communication centre, the comcen, burning. You and you will find the comcen, you know roughly where it is already, and set it alight, at, say, as near 9 o'clock as possible. You,' to the fourth, 'will stay with Mana. Bind him and gag him but, with the guy outside, walk him to near the guardroom as soon as the blaze has caused the general alarm. That's Plan A.'

By now Tâ and Mana were dressed in what the other had been wearing. 'If anything goes wrong, Plan B will be to wait until I return from having disposed of the two boss men. The two who should have burnt the comcen will report here at 10 p.m. If we get separated outside the camp, the two bodyguards will make their own way with Mana to where we left the escort. That's the first fall-back position. If that's compromised, the second fall-back position will be the clump of trees where we crossed Route 61. Same recognition signals as before. Any questions? No? Good! So, get to it! Goodbye Tâ,' he said as the needle was being inserted. Tâ didn't reply. Vong left the room, having a word with the man guarding the door as he went. The whole business had taken five and a half long minutes.

He had a shrewd idea of the layout of Ban Ban camp from aerial photographs, debriefings and interrogations to update his own personal knowledge. As he walked down the road to where the senior officers and important visitors were housed, he patted his pockets and shrugged his shoulders to make his pack sit squarely. He whistled a revolutionary tune.

'Over here. Over here,' he thought it was Commil. 'Come in and tell us what's what.'

Vong entered and, with a cheery smile, took his pack off and put it in a corner. He took the chair he was offered and said, 'My, my! What a business. First orders were for tomorrow and then we were needed for another investigation rather quicker than expected.' His brow furrowed. 'Don't tell me you weren't informed of the change.' Both Commil and Compol shook their head. 'You weren't? Then I must apologise for what must seem infernal cheek.'

The other two men seemed mollified and visibly relaxed. 'This new treatment that we have got from our colleagues in Moscow is most interesting and a radical departure from what is known as "western medicine". Some of it is delicate, some of it relies on shock. The reason for our getting here in the afternoon – had we not been delayed – was to introduce ourselves and settle in before tonight's session. As it is, nothing has been wasted by our late arrival. Dr. Tanh Bên Lòng explained why to you.'

As he was talking, he was taking in every detail of the room. 'I haven't been here for some time. I was last here, when was it now, soon after it became part of the Liberated Zone. You've had a lot done to it since. The hospital, for instance. We used to have the comcen there. Cooking was done centrally not far from the stream that circles this part of the camp.'

'Yes, we have changed things around since then. The comcen is where the offices used to be – over there,' and Commil automatically pointed the direction.

'You may be interested in watching Dr. Tanh Bên Lòng

treating Mana. We've given him a jab and the Doctor is sitting with him in the dark. Boring but essential. Nice man, the Doctor. Haven't known him long. Terribly absent-minded. Apt to forget his own name at times! Gave me quite a turn at first. Would you care to participate later? We'd like you to. Be of help in filling in details of recent behavioural trends. In any case, I've got to stay awake. I'll tell you what, I've got some fresh Bolovens coffee with me. Get some hot water could you and we'll have a brew, shall we? I'm dying for a cup after my walk.'

'Yes, we'd like to join you. Won't take long to get some water heated up.' Commil got up and went into another room. Vong heard him pottering about and, from the noises, presumed he was kindling a fire. Left alone with Compol, he tried to steer the conversation into topics that could confirm some of the rumours and speculations that General Etam had been making, but nothing much productive ensued.

'Kettle's boiling,' came Commil's voice. 'Do you want to percolate the stuff or what? Percolating it takes time.'

'No. I have had this prepared like the instant stuff you can buy,' called back Vong, hoping that the two men had heard of instant coffee. 'I suggest you bring cups and kettle in here while I get the coffee out of my pack.'

'Good idea!' Commil brought cups and kettle in and put them on the table. Vong went over to his pack and rummaged around for the coffee container. It was made of plastic and, from the outside, looked normal. Inside, however, it had been especially prepared, thanks to Mango. It was in two sections and the lid was attached to a lever that, depending on how much pressure was applied, could allow one or other section to be covered. In the container normal coffee had been put into one of the sections but, in the other, it had been doctored with the barbiturate Phenobarbitone. Vong, unscrewing the lid as he came back to the table, asked for a spoon. He was lucky in that the change over from one section to the other was masked to an extent as the two hurricane lamps only gave a subdued and slightly flickering light. He took the three cups and lined them up in front of him, then, looking at Compol, asked, 'Weak or strong? One spoonful or two?'

'Oh, so-so, thanks. One and a bit,' and Vong carefully carried out his instructions, secure in the knowledge that the dope was strong enough to act for half a spoonful. 'There you are, Comrade,' he said, passing the cup over. 'And you, Comrade?' he asked Commil.

'Much the same, please, but maybe a bit stronger.' His was also doled out and the cup handed to him. As they were adding water to their brew, Vong switched the inner lid over. 'I'll have two spoonfuls to keep me awake after my walk,' he said conversationally and ladled himself out a couple of them. 'Be a kind fellow and put some water in for me. Thanks.'

Coffee in front of them, they continued to talk and sip. 'The processing of the coffee beans not to need percolating makes just a tiny difference to the flavour. I rather like it myself.'

'So that's what it is,' said Compol. 'I thought for a moment that my palate had changed. Yes, the flavour is agreeable, isn't it?'

Ten minutes later, they had emptied their cups. They chatted inconsequentially for a while then Vong asked them if they'd like any more before he put the coffee away? He could have saved himself the trouble. The two officials were already unconscious, as he knew they would be. He had only said it for form's sake, just in case anybody was in earshot. He went into the other room and had a good look around. He fetched the kettle and the three cups, washed them and put one away. In both the other two he put a trace of unadulterated coffee powder and a spot of water. He swilled them both around, made them seem as though they had been drunk from by putting them to his lips and returned to the table. He put the coffee container back into his pack, withdrew a small bottle and, opening it, put it under the nose of each sleeping man for at least a minute, being careful not to inhale any himself. *That really should fix them*. He glanced at his watch. 8 p.m. Good timing. He quickly, yet thoroughly, searched the quarter for any papers, collecting what he found. He took a piece of paper from his own pocket, paper that was unattributable as it had no watermark, tore it in two and wrote something on both pieces. He put one piece into the pocket of each man, put his pack on, blew out the hurricane lanterns and stepped outside, having quietly shut the door. He listened intently. He made his way to the other quarter, Compol's, searched it by torchlight for any documents, then made his way towards the comcen.

He made a noise like a frog croaking, three times. An answering three croaks came from the darkness. Vong made three more and two shadows emerged. 'Ready?' he whispered. 'Yes,' the answer was hissed. 'Everything is set and ready.'

'Good. I've fixed my targets. As soon as you've destroyed the comcen come to the isolation ward. Not heard anyone walking around? Most people in this camp go to bed early. I'm off to Mana now.'

Soundlessly, the three men parted. The two detailed to burn down the comcen went to the far side of the building and put the final touches to a sodium-filled device into which they put a primer and connected two leads therein. By then it was nearly 9 o'clock and, on the hour, they joined the leads to a positive and negative terminal on a small 1.5 volt battery to set the sodium alight. Using long forceps, they applied the blaze, like that of a blow lamp, to the wooden uprights. When satisfied that the uprights were burning, they did the same to the roof, in several places. They were, by then, confident that their handiwork would be successful so, going the twenty paces to the river, they threw away the device which sank with a loud hiss and a nasty smell. They then made their unhurried way to the hospital's isolation ward.

At the isolation ward, Vong checked with the door sentry that no one had tried to enter and went inside. Tâ was in the bed that Mana had been in, breathing deeply. Vong felt his pulse and decided he was safe. He gently turned Tâ's face to the wall, pulled the sheet up and tucked in the mosquito net. Mana, dressed in Tâ's blue uniform, was bound and gagged, conscious, eyes wild and rolling, completely mystified. Vong said to Mana's guard, 'When I say so, untie his hands and feet. You and the man on the door will put yourselves one on each side of him and walk him to near the guardroom. I'll be with you. Be ready to make a dash for it if we can't get him or ourselves out of the camp peaceably.'

At 9.12 p.m. the two men arrived from the now-blazing comcen and reported what they had done. 'On our way! Follow me,' Vong ordered and they reached the central road, crossed it, skirted round the back of the central cookhouse and watched the guardroom, surprised that no alarm of the fire had yet been given. Almost directly they did hear shouting as the burning building showered sparks high into the air. There was a commotion at the guardroom.

'Stay here for a moment,' said Vong as he ran forward to the sentry in front of the building. 'Every one of you to the scene of the fire. The whole lot, do you understand? Those are the orders the Commissar has given and sent me to tell you. Quick. Go and see if there's any danger elsewhere. Grief but you're slow. Hurry up!' he ordered, infusing them with an urgency that eventually got them moving. 'I'm going back to the fire. Follow me.'

In the confusion, he once more slipped into the shadows, rejoined his men and, unobserved by anyone, they left the camp.

One of the characteristics of the Communist-orientated armies is inflexibility. All orders and initiatives stem from the political bosses who reign supreme, so it seems, even to the extent of forcing decisions that override tactical requirements on the field of battle. Once a course of action was planned and embarked upon, it was sacrosanct. In matters of the purest routine, the well-worn ruts were slavishly followed. In emergencies everybody waited for the political Supremo. When, in this case, neither the Political Commissar nor the CO appeared, astoundingly no one reacted positively to try and put the fire out. Thus the comcen, which contained the radio sets and the land line terminal, was burnt to the ground.

Little bunches of men, attracted like moths to a bright light, stood around gawping, until eventually the next senior military man, the Deputy, announced in a loud voice that he would go and report to the officers' quarters and tell the two superiors that the fire had burnt itself out, meanwhile the guardroom men were to return to their post and the in-lying picket was to patrol the camp to check any untoward discrepancy. The Deputy was an earnest, bespectacled man in his early thirties and, although on the military side, was a candidate for the political stewardship. He knew the Standing Orders for Alarms but none of these maestros had prepared him for what he saw by the light of his torch having repeatedly knocked on his superior's door in vain. The two leaders sat at the table, their heads touching it, apparently fast asleep, with an empty coffee cup in front of each man. He coughed nervously. No reaction. He found some matches and lit one of the hurricane lanterns the better to have his hands free. He then shook first one man then the other. They both slumped farther forward. Something was horribly wrong. He had a modicum of first-aid training so he felt each man's pulse. Both were sluggish though regular. His next thought was to get them to the hospital so he returned to the main part of the camp to find some fatigue men. He detailed the first four men he found to go and fetch two stretchers from the hospital and to report to him at the officers' quarters. It took them nearly half an hour to bring them. The Deputy led the four soldiers to the CO's quarter and told them to lift the stricken men, gently, ever so gently, one by one, and lay them on a stretcher. The soldiers, goggle-eyed at such an unexpected sight, were so careful in carrying out the

Deputy's instructions that they moved like men in a slow-motion film. Finally, the Deputy's patience snapped. He scolded them for their slowness and, like soldiers everywhere, marvelling at an officer's cussedness, completed the task in their own time. Once loaded, the cortege moved off towards the hospital, the Deputy following on behind, wondering how best to react to this totally unexpected situation. The camp doctor lived out but the senior medical orderly could tell if there was so grave an emergency that the medical officer would have to be sent for. If the two men were really seriously ill, the specialists coming from Hanoi in the morning would be of great, and possibly life-saving, value. What *had* happened to these two could, he fretted, also happen to him.

They reached the hospital complex. 'Stretcher bearers, put your load down carefully and you,' the Deputy detailed one of the soldiers, 'go and fetch the duty medical orderly.'

'What a time you've taken,' remonstrated the Deputy when the duty medical orderly eventually appeared. 'Listen to me. I found the two comrades unconscious and immediately had them brought in. You now take charge of them.'

No one had thought to start the generator so there was no electricity. Hurricane lamps and torches gave enough light to get the two unconscious men into bed, in separate rooms. The orderly checked the other patient and found him fast asleep, presumably not having been awoken either by the stretcher bearers or the commotion of the comcen burning.

The blaze was seen for many miles around, reddening the night sky spectacularly. Those units that saw it tried to find out where it was and by the process of elimination, presumed it was in or near Ban Ban camp. However, even then that was not certain as they could get no response from their land line. Duty men reasoned that, as nothing came from Ban Ban, the fire was not there so why report it higher?

Major Vong looked at his watch. Its luminous hands pointed to ten past ten. They were not far from where they had cached the stretcher. Mana was faltering and in distress. He had been able to walk reasonably quickly for the first short distance but, although his gag had been loosened, he was being too slow. He would have to be carried. Vong could not risk ungagging him completely until they were away from local, so sensitive, habitations. A hornets' nest had been stirred and maybe long before daylight, despite the precautions he had taken, search parties would be out in force. Speed was vital. They reached the cache. The stretcher was there. Vong breathed a long sigh of relief. The group moved off the road, prepared the stretcher and put Mana on it, tying him securely. So far he had not spoken, nor had he tried to resist them. They continued on their way. Vong reckoned they should meet the escort within the hour, certainly well this side of where he had left them. Their orders had been explicit: no move if no blaze was seen. If a blaze was seen, move towards the camp, either until meeting up with Vong's group or until the road junction was reached. If they got that far, to wait until 3 a.m. then return to their original hiding place if nobody turned up.

With four men taking it in turns to carry the stretcher, Vong moved ahead, keeping in earshot but sufficiently distant to take what evasive action might be needed, depending on whom he met. He felt elated. This is what he enjoyed: challenge, danger and the thrill of the illegal, especially when directed against his enemies.

There was a scuff in front of him. He stiffened momentarily, then made a noise like a young water buffalo heifer. It was answered in kind, twice. Two more similar grunts from Vong confirmed their recognition.

'Anything to report? All well?'

'Yes. Hell of a blaze but it didn't last for long. No reaction from the locals but I didn't expect any. What now?'

Vong quickly and quietly gave his orders. 'Take Mana's gag off. All of you take the sacking from your pack and tie it round your shoes. We will move on up the road until short of the first fall-back position. Get ready now.' A few minutes later, he said, 'Off we go, at best quiet speed.'

By midnight they had reached the place Vong had pre-selected. A small track led off west. This the escort group would take. Another, larger track, led off east, to a village. 'Take the stretcher over there,' said Vong, pointing west to a clump of tress visible in the moonlight. 'Undo Mana and give him some water. Let him flex his muscles, have a pee, regain his circulation but no noise, no noise whatsoever.'

Once under the trees, with shielded torches, the next part of Vong's plan was revealed. Turning to the escort commander, he said, 'You are responsible for taking Mana to our next fall-back position. You should get there by first light. Once there, hide up, taking defensive precautions. You should be safe but be prepared to bug out in an emergency. If you have to leave in a hurry, try and move back to our second night camp. Personally, I don't think it will come to that and anyway, I hope to join you before then. Don't forget, he,' pointing to Mana with his foot, 'is your overriding priority and concern. Here's a sleeping pill for him. Make him swallow it with some water. It'll keep him quiet so there'll be no need to put that gag back on but keep it handy just in case. You'll obviously have to carry him but you'd have to with or without him sleeping.' He continued his briefing. 'I will stay behind for a bit longer with three of my squad to lay a false trail. My fourth man, my tame executioner, will stay with you and kill Mana rather than letting the Viets recapture him. I and the three men I am taking with me will take the sacking off our shoes. You others keep it on.' Vong then inspected their shoes for wrapping and torches to see that they had either some of the green paper he had earlier issued or a thin leaf. He glanced at his watch again. 'I'll try and catch up with you as soon I can. Hopefully by dawn. Right. Any last questions? No? Then good luck to you. Move no later than in five minutes.'

As soon as they had gone, Vong said, 'Now for our false trail. Follow me. Only talk when spoken to. Take the green paper out of your torches first.'

They crossed over the road and walked up the track towards the village, flashing their torches and making no attempt at walking silently. Dogs started barking. Vong raised his voice and cursed them loudly, shining his torch at the first house they saw. It obviously belonged to a poor man as it was not built on stilts. He led his men up to it and knocked loudly on the door. 'Open up. Open up, in the name of the Party. We are on urgent business.

Hurry and open up!'

There was a noise inside but no one opened the door. Vong knocked again, this time with a stick he had picked up. 'Don't worry. I am from Ban Ban camp. This is an emergency. Open up, open up, immediately.'

At last a tremulous voice answered from within. 'How do I know you're not bandits? You might be bandits. I'm afraid.'

'Fools,' spat Vong. 'Look outside. I'll show you who we are,' and he shone his torch at the other men. The door then opened. An elderly man stood there, obviously terrified.

'Don't be afraid, Granddad. Just take me to the *Chau Ban*, the headman. Go and put some more clothes on. Quickly!'

The man disappeared and, a short while later, reappeared, dressed. 'Follow me, please.'

They walked back down the path, reached the road and turned left, southwards, in the direction of Ban Ban. Some distance down the road, they again turned up a track and soon reached some more houses. The villager pointed out one larger than the rest that loomed up in front of them. 'That is it. The *Chao Ban* lives here. May I go now? I've done enough for you, haven't I?'

'No! Wait.' Vong then raised his voice and called loudly, 'O-é, *Chao Ban*. Wake up and come down. I am a cadre from Ban Ban. I want help urgently.'

A torch shone from above and a voice demanded, 'What's the trouble? Who are you? What do you want at this time of night?'

In answer, Vong shone his torch on himself and his men. 'Come down and I'll tell you. Hurry please. This is an emergency.'

The *Chao Ban* quickly dressed and came down. He introduced

himself and asked how he could help the Comrade Commissar.

'Did you see the fire lighting up the sky earlier on tonight?' The *Chao Ban* nodded. 'It was in the camp and is the work, so far as we can tell, of a demented man who has probably run away. I have a search party up the road and I'm convinced that the man has not come as far as this. He is reputed to be heading for Sam Neua, not that anyone knows for certain, but that's why I'm here so soon. *I* think he'll be found near the camp when it's light. What I'm going to do is to ask you to put out a roadblock, now, and keep it going till noon and then, if there hasn't been any contact, raise it. After that come down to us at Ban Ban camp and report your negative result.' Vong paused. 'No, sorry. I think that's probably unnecessary. They'll be up here in their own good time. Now, there is one more point. Come over here, please. It's confidential.' He led the Headman out of earshot of the others and continued, most earnestly, 'This man is a true Lao patriot and somehow he's offended the "elder brothers". You understand? I'm sure you do. I'm on his side. I want to save him and I don't want the "elder brothers" to get their hands on him. To this end, please, when other comrades come, be circumspect. If the "elder brothers" know I've told you about this, it will go badly against me although,' with a bitter laugh, 'I'm as much as, if not more of, a Lao patriot than are many others, especially them. So, these aren't orders, only a patriotic comrade's request to a man of responsibility. You understand my dilemma? I now move east, see if the man's in any of those villages I can get to in the next few hours. I want to get back to Ban Ban by dawn before "elder brother" discovers I've been on this mission. To this end, my request is twofold: one, the road block to be put out and maintained on your own initiative because you saw the fire; and second, please, please don't mention my search party. Can you manage that?'

'Yes, I can,' said the *Chao Ban*, suitably impressed. 'I understand entirely. I wish there were more like you. Don't be afraid. I'd like to know you better. Can we meet again after this has died down?'

'Yes, I'm sure we can. Let's leave names out of this, shall we? What is not known cannot be divulged. In this day and age that's a safe motto. Goodbye and a thousand thanks. I must hurry. For your information, I'm going back down the road, see that this man, my guide, gets back safely, move off east, then south from there.' He put out his hand, shook the other's and, together, joined the waiting man.

'Goodbye,' said the *Chao Ban*. 'Go safely. I'll keep this man here and give him orders for his part of the village. There's no need for you to escort him back to his house. Thanks for the offer.'

'Goodbye and again thank you,' said Vong and, followed by his men, vanished into the night. A little later Vong said, 'Put the green paper back into your torch and bind your feet. If we're lucky we'll pick up the others well before dawn.'

They moved swiftly and quietly westward.

The fire in the camp earlier on in the night scared many of the inmates. So suddenly had the comcen burnt down and so intense was the blaze that those who did gather at the spot could do nothing about it. The Guard Commander, suddenly realising that the guardroom was unmanned, cursed and sent two men back there. The Deputy eventually returned to the burnt shell of the comcen and sent the mawkish onlookers away. There was nothing that anyone could do.

Next morning, one of the first people to be about her duty was the Lao nurse who looked after Mana. She had been frightened stiff the previous night, not so much by the unexpected arrival of the inspecting doctors' team but why then she could not fathom. but rather by that terrible blaze. She had seen it from her window. But the doctors obviously had not needed her. It had not been her turn for duty so when the Deputy had brought the CO and the Political Commissar along, overcome by the smoke of the fire, no doubt, and the Senior Medical Orderly, who was on duty, had looked after them. She had stayed in her room and as there had been no more activity, she had gone to sleep, though not very quickly.

Now, slightly guiltily, she went into the little annex to see how her man, as she referred to Mana privately, had survived the night. He had seemed, if anything, more withdrawn than normal when she had left him. Maybe he would have got out of bed the right side this morning. She knocked on the door. No response. She tried again and, getting no answer, went inside, calling him endearingly and softly. He lay in bed, face turned to the wall, not moving. Under the mosquito net, he had pulled the sheet almost over his face. She stared at him, fascinated, puzzled and a bit scared. She strained her ears and heard his regular breathing. *Shall I wake him or let him sleep on?* she mused. She decided to go and see the senior medic in the duty room.

The senior medic stood up as she entered and, before she could open her mouth, he said, 'Come with me, Comrade. We've got to see the two men who came in last night, the Political Commissar and the CO. Brought in, I should say. Can't think what hit them unless it was the smoke from that fire. Now, wasn't that dreadful? Can't think how it happened. Something to do with the batteries, I expect,' he said vaguely. 'Did you go and watch it, Comrade? I certainly didn't see you there.' She shook her head but he was in front of her so did not see her gesture. He took her silence as her answer that she had not gone to see the fire. 'Quite right. Can't have everybody rubbernecking, can we? Here we are. Wouldn't be surprised if the two bosses hadn't had a better night than either of us or in their own beds. Always did think how damp it was over there by the river. Bad for ageing bones.'

The garrulous man and silent woman went into the quarantine block. It was simply designed, two rooms left and two right of the entrance, with one toilet and shower.

They knocked on the first door and, having had no answer, pushed it open. They saw the CO, lying on his back, fast asleep. The senior medic cleared his throat noisily then, with no sign of the sleeping man stirring, coughed even louder. A puzzled look came over his usually bland face. He approached the bed, stared hard at the recumbent figure, leant over him and shook him, tentatively at first, then more vigorously. There was no reaction whatsoever. The CO was still just as limply unconscious as he had been when brought in.

'I don't like this one little bit,' muttered the senior medic.

'Not one little bit.'

He bent down and sniffed the sleeping man's breath. He straightened up and made a grimace. 'If I didn't know how impossible it would be, I'd say he's been drugged. No, I don't like this one little bit.' A cold fear gripped him as he realised that maybe he should have sent for the doctor straightaway or at least examined the CO during the night. 'Come, Comrade,' he said, trying to keep his voice steady, 'Let us see how the other patient is.'

The other man was a carbon copy of the first. Little beads of sweat broke out on the senior medic's forehead. The nurse looked at him apprehensively. He opened his mouth, closed it, cleared his throat. 'Some terrible jinx is on us, Comrade, and I cannot understand it. Let us go and see if Mana is ready for his inspection.'

The two entered the third room, went up to the bed, pulled away the mosquito net, horrified at Mana's inertness. They gently took the sheet from his face and stared down, unnerved at the sight of somebody neither of them recognised. He, too, was out cold. It was the nurse's turn to open then close her mouth in silent agony.

'Who is this?' queried the senior medic in an odd, strangled tone of voice. 'When did he come here? Why wasn't I told? Did you put Mana in the next room?' He turned on the nurse with a spurt of hope. 'Maybe he went next door himself. Go and see how he is.'

The nurse made slowly for the door, as though her feet were made of lead. The senior medic watched her as she left the room and saw her turn the handle of the fourth and last door of the quarantine block. He saw her put her hand up to her mouth in horror, shut the door with a bang and almost totter back to him. A cold worm of fear turned in his belly.

'No trouble is there?' he called out, not believing his own optimistic tone of voice.

'The room's empty. No one has been in it. Oh, what can have happened?' and she started to weep, covering her face in her hands as she stood there.

The senior medic sat down on a chair to steady himself. The three unconscious men were three problems, the stranger was an enigma, while no Mana was a disaster.

Early that Friday morning, the Deputy felt distinctly perturbed: the fire and his two bosses were playing on his conscious mind in the same way as they had plagued his dreams as he slept, shallowly and fitfully. He fervently hoped that they were now well on the way to recovery if not already completely better from whatever it was that had struck them. Food poisoning, he presumed, as he dressed. He had half convinced himself that matters would be back to normal by the time he was ready to leave his quarter. His bosses would want to know about the fire just as soon as possible. On his way to hospital he glumly reviewed the blackened remains of the comcen and whatever had been inside: the manual telephone exchange and every single bit of kit irrevocably damaged and completely unsalvageable. He shook his head at the thought of the reports and inquiries it would result in. The thought had worried him greatly for, although responsibility of the camp was not his, he was responsible to his bosses for it. While his future did not look so rosy, it could not be as black as that charred mess. Sunk in gloom, he moved over to the hospital, calling in at the duty room where he was told that the senior medic was visiting the patients. The Deputy felt he ought to go and see for himself how the others were and, on reaching the isolation ward, saw the senior medic sitting on a chair with his head in his hands, the nurse standing nearby with her head in her hands, weeping softly. It was a macabre scene and it filled him with alarm.

'Good morning, Comrade Senior Medical Orderly and Comrade Nurse,' he said with exaggerated politeness. 'I hope I'm not intruding.'

The senior medic lifted his head, saw who was addressing him, and stood up. 'Good morning, Comrade Deputy. I was on my way to report to you but, not being quite sure in which order my report should be given, I was considering the problem.'

'Problem? Problem? I'm not a doctor so why come to me? Nurse, stop crying.'

'It will concern you, be you a doctor or no. The CO and the Political Commissar are as unconscious as when they were brought in last night, there is an unconscious stranger in Mana's bed and, apart from that, Comrade Mana has vanished. That is why it concerns you, Comrade Deputy.'

There was an arid silence while the Deputy assimilated this startling and totally unexpected news. The senior medic prepared himself the better to ward off the Deputy's wrath, while the girl was too cowed to say anything coherent.

'Well, what have you done about it and what will you do

about it? Whatever else you do, you can't do nothing,' said the Deputy, peevishly, his mind already on the many departmental horrors now even more manifestly waiting for him. The two men looked at each other in veiled hostility, both wondering how they could shift as much blame as possible onto the other.

'At least we will have our own doctor with us soon, not to mention the two specialists. I can go and warn our doctor. If you let me have use of a vehicle, I can get to his house probably before he goes to the airstrip to meet the plane,' said the senior medic.

There were two vehicles in the camp. The Deputy felt he needed one to go and report the burnt-out comcen to the nearest unit with radio contact with higher formation. The PL units along Route 61 did not have radio and the NVA units, which did, were not on any of the recently constructed feeder roads. This meant sending out a couple of runners some of the way by vehicle and then their hoofing it.

'Did the Comrade Doctor say he was coming here before the specialists arrived or that he'd meet them on the airstrip?'

'He said he'd go to the airstrip and bring them in. I was to get the patient ready. That was meant to ensure he hadn't gone walkabout.'

The Deputy mulled this over. 'Right. You have a search of the camp and see where Mana has gone. One vehicle will go to the airstrip when confirmation of take-off is received. I'll go and arrange for someone to go and report the loss of the communication centre in the other one. You'd better hurry as the plane will leave as soon as the mist clears. Mana can't be far away.'

'Fine, Comrade Deputy.' The senior medic could see that the

orders to go and fetch the doctors were in the process of becoming snarled up. 'Please will you confirm exactly what has been done for the visitors' transport.'

The Deputy tried to control his temper. 'Go and do what I have told you, Comrade. I will do what needs to be done about the visitors being met.'

The senior medic shrugged his shoulders and the Deputy, wanting to ensure that Mana was in camp, went to the guardroom instead of going directly to the vehicle park. He called the Guard Commander who came running outside. 'Comrade, have you seen Comrade Mana this morning?'

'No, Comrade Deputy. He most certainly hasn't been out of the camp since we've been on duty and that is since 4 o'clock last evening.'

Greatly relieved that at last there was a break in the run of bad luck, the Deputy relaxed a little. 'Then, in that case, he must be in the camp somewhere. If he does happen to try and leave, turn him back. The doctors have got to look at him. They are due in any time after 9 o'clock.'

The Guard Commander looked blankly at his Deputy Commander. 'The doctors due at 9 o'clock did you say, Comrade?' he asked disbelievingly.

The brief ray of bonhomie disappeared as the Deputy's temper snapped. 'Yes, fool. Didn't you hear what I said? I will repeat myself slowly so that there can be no mistake this time,' he continued, exaggerating the syllable content of each word. 'They, the doc-tors, are due an-y time af-ter 9 o'clock this morn-ing.'

The Guard Commander shuffled his feet uneasily. 'Then there

will be two sets of doctors in the camp, Comrade?' he asked ingenuously.

The Deputy stared harshly as the Guard Commander, thinking, with a certain amount of relish, of what re-education this man needed. 'If you're trying to be funny and count our own doctor separately, the answer is "yes". Does this answer your question?' he asked sarcastically.

The Guard Commander was not to be deflated. 'In that case, Comrade, there will be three sets of doctors.'

The Deputy lost control of himself and rudely upbraided the Guard Commander, using most intemperate language, for his stupidity, misplaced sense of humour and a general lack of discipline. Finishing his diatribe by calling the Guard Commander a lot of uncomradely names, the Deputy took a grip of himself and asked, with withering scorn, whether he had gone off his rocker, was trying to be funny or what? Would the Comrade Guard Commander explain himself exactly and fully?

The Guard Commander resolutely stood his ground, realising that, somehow or other, the Deputy had not been told of the doctors' change of programme and that the visitors had been welcomed by the CO and the Political Commissar. However, he was not in the mood for long explanations so he stolidly said, 'Since the doctors and their team arrived after dark last night, have not yet left the camp and so are still here, I am only trying to confirm whether this is, if fact, yet another lot of doctors coming this morning.'

He could have said a lot more but prudence forbade it.

The Deputy was completely taken aback by this bolt from

the blue. 'Wh ... wh ... what do you mean?' he stammered, trying to collect his thoughts but with little success. 'I d ... d ... don't understand you. Ex ... explain yourself.'

'The group of six men whom we expected this morning showed up last night after dark. I had the CO and the Political Commissar fetched and they came here, welcomed the visitors and took them away.'

The Deputy, utterly deflated, stood there as he digested this shattering piece of news. His own sleeping accommodation was not in the senior officers' compound, a bone of contention, but set back some distance away. It was most unlikely that he would have heard anything even had it been noisier than was the case. He turned and made his way to the visitors' quarters. Finding no trace of anyone, he was at a complete loss to know who or what to believe. How could the Guard Commander say such a thing? At least he would find Mana who had, for some unknown reason, hidden himself. He'd find him, even if it took till dusk. With a single-mindedness only found in the most pig-headed, most zealous or most stupid of men, trusting no one but himself, off he went, unmindful of everything else. While he was in the underground air-raid shelter a member of the roving security picket pulled the open door shut and wedged it tight so it would not open of itself again, so trapping the hapless Deputy.

The radio operators in Sam Neua and attached to Office 95 were puzzled by Ban Ban camp's radio silence. Communications were a problem, it was generally accepted, but normally contact by radio or land line was made at 0800 hours daily. The network was complicated by the NVA units having their own net conventionally linking units of lower formation with higher formation and on up to Army Command in Hanoi. It was therefore only later in the morning that units near Ban Ban, having reported a major fire the previous night and none having admitted to it being in their location, that a suspicious Duty Officer in Army HQ contacted Sam Neua on another net. Sam Neua contacted Office 95 and it was then presumed that the fire had taken place in Ban Ban camp. By that time, the visitors' AN-2 on loan from Aeroflot had left the strip at Office 95. A high-ranking group that included Comrade Nga Sô Lưu, who was especially interested in the outcome of their mission, had seen the plane off.

The Ban Ban airstrip was an hour's walk from the camp doctor's house. It was a fine morning, Friday 15 March, and the doctor felt he would like some exercise. As he could also visit a case of his own on the way, he set off earlier than he would otherwise have done. His route took him over the road that had, unusually, a roadblock with unarmed villagers manning it. Intrigued, he asked why and received a garbled reply that there had been a fire somewhere in the direction of the camp and the *Chao Ban* had ordered it just in case it was arson and the Comrades wanted any local screening to be done. Rather far-fetched, thought the doctor who kept away from the political aspect of life as much as it was possible under normal circumstances. His remarks to that effect were echoed by the men on the roadblock. The doctor, a popular figure in the neighbourhood, got a cheery smile as he left and soon put the incident out of his mind and, in due course, having had a session with the patient, reached the airstrip.

He had faith that the senior medic would have Mana ready and he also felt that the visiting doctors would be favourably impressed by his role of 'travelling doctor'. He had tried his best with Mana. The nurse was a good girl and her reports, although disappointing clinically, were based on astute observation and considerable personal involvement: shock, of love or the opposite, she had said. He himself merely had a watching brief, so to speak, on Mana. He found it hard to understand such high-level interest but he was wise enough not to poke his nose into non-medical business. He settled down to await the plane's arrival.

The senior medic was having an argument with the Comrade in charge of the two vehicles. The Deputy' orders were that one vehicle was to take a squad as close to the nearest "elder brother" unit to make a report of last night's damage and the other was on stand-by to go to the airstrip to meet the Hanoi delegates. 'How is it?' demanded the harassed functionary, 'that the Comrade Senior Medical Assistant needs yet a third and nonexistent vehicle to go and see the doctor? Hasn't the Comrade got a bicycle like the doctor has?'

'If there is no communication with the outside world,' countered a nettled senior medic, 'how do you think you can tell when your stand-by vehicle is needed?'

This blindingly obvious point had been overlooked by the transport functionary and the Deputy who was the only person who could resolve such a thorny problem. Before the man in charge of the vehicles could go and clear up this matter for the senior medic, he had to ensure that the squad going to report the fire and the driver had been briefed on where to go and how long they could stay away from camp. Once that was over and done with, the senior medic and the 'transport administrator', as he liked to be called when standing on his dignity, could go in search of the Deputy.

Once that vehicle was on its way, the two men went to the Deputy's office, then his quarter, but met with no success in either place. They went round the camp, drawing a blank. 'Let us go and ask the sentry on the gate and see if he has left the camp,' one of them suggested, so off they went to the guardroom.

The sentry said, no, the Comrade Deputy had not left the camp during his stint but he'd call the Guard Commander, which he obligingly did. The Guard Commander shook his head. 'I don't know what's happening around here. One mighty jinx! First the Deputy comes and questions me about Comrade Mana. Then he balls me out because I tell him the doctors arrived last night and now …'

The senior medic interrupted him. 'Say that again. The doctors came last night, did you say? How many of them, what time and when did they leave?'

The Guard Commander patiently explained to the two unbelieving men exactly what he knew, finishing up with the statement that the doctors had not left the camp and if the two men did not believe him, why, for Lenin's sake, didn't they clear the matter with the CO and the Political Commissar instead of worrying him?

This information surprised the senior medic more than the

other man who merely said that since the doctors had arrived, there was no need to send any transport to meet them and, certainly, until he was specifically ordered by the CO, the Political Commissar or the Deputy, he would not be able to allow the senior medic to take that one remaining vehicle.

There was nothing that the senior medic could do other than start a dreary trudge to the camp doctor's house. He knew that there was no bicycle he could borrow.

The AN-2 circled the Ban Ban airstrip and made a perfect landing. The Cuban pilot cut the engine and a crew man opened the door and put the small steps ready for the group of six in blue uniform to clamber down. *A strange bunch*, the pilot thought to himself; *two elderly doctors. Look out of place here - more at home in a hospital.. The other four look different –they had all looked the same when I first arrived in Hanoi from Havana – two of them strong-arm merchants if ever there were any and the other couple have that stamp associated with inquisitors. A strange bunch indeed. Ah well, not my job to bother who they are.*

The camp doctor went forward to greet them. 'Good morning, Comrades. Welcome to Ban Ban. I am the camp doctor and have walked across from my village clinic. The two senior comrades will be here to meet you directly. We will then go to the camp. My Senior Medical Assistant, a devoted comrade, has Comrade Mana Varamit happily waiting for your arrival.'

The men from Hanoi introduced themselves to the camp doctor and then collected their individual baggage from the grass where the crew man had put it, easing their cramped legs.

The crew joined them. Cigarettes were offered and lit. Glances were shot at watches with that careless ease that is a busy man's prerogative.

'You think the camp got our message about a slightly earlier than forecast arrival? The quicker we get there, the quicker we can start work.'

'I am sure they did, Comrade. Our communications centre is as efficient as any other. They'll have been alerted and orders for the vehicle to pick you up will, doubtless, already have been given. As soon as we get to the camp, we'll send a message telling higher formation of your safe arrival.'

'The pilot will have already reported a safe landing,' said the senior doctor, a trifle huffily, once more looking at his watch, rather more obviously this time.

The crew finished their cigarettes. The Cuban pilot looked at his watch and announced it was time he should be getting back for his next mission. 'Tomorrow morning at about the same time, Comrades,' he said in passable French. 'Until then, farewell and good luck.'

The crew boarded the aircraft and the engine soon crackled into life. Ban Ban airstrip was just that and nothing else; no tower, no ground staff, no facilities. When the plane had taken off and the noise of its engine had disappeared, bird song and a dog barking made the emptiness of the place even more noticeable.

'No transport. Can't think what has happened. Don't suppose there has been anything worse than a puncture on the way. I propose, Comrades, that not to waste any more of you valuable time than necessary, we start walking. I'm sure we'll meet up with the camp vehicle in a minute or so,' said a worried camp doctor, trying not to sound so. 'It's still quite cool.'

This suggestion was debated and reluctantly accepted. None of them wanted to risk leaving any of their baggage behind so, carrying it as best they could, they set off down the road towards Ban Ban. It was an angry and sweaty group of men who, two hours later, saw the camp entrance in front of them.

At the gate, the camp doctor, not for the first time, apologised profusely for the perplexing and embarrassing absence of any vehicle. The sentry, recognising the camp doctor, entered the newcomers' name in the registry and let them into the camp. Since no one asked the Guard Commander about the lack of transport or the whereabouts of the senior staff, he said nothing. 'Let us go straight away to the mess compound, find your accommodation, dump the kit and have some refreshment,' suggested the camp doctor.

They were met by an orderly who took them and showed them their rooms. 'While you are getting yourselves ready, I'll go and tell them we've arrived,' said the camp doctor, trying to sound happier than he felt. 'If you would like to wait for us in that building over there,' he pointed out the communal mess building, 'I'll be back with the Commanding Officer and the Political Commissar.'

He peeked into their sleeping quarters, not really expecting to find them there and went on to their offices. No one there, either. No one knew where they were. The camp doctor was dismayed. *I'll pop over and see if they're with Mana*, he thought, as he hurried over to the hospital. He reached the duty room and saw the nurse. One look at her face and his heart sank. *Been crying*, he saw. *Moony about Mana?* Outwardly he tried to appear calm but inwardly he was in turmoil. 'Where is Comrade Senior Medical Assistant?' he asked.

'Comrade Doctor. I don't know. I believe he went to fetch you but, since the fire last night, everything has gone wrong,' and, unable to control herself any longer, she burst into floods of tears.

'Fire? What fire?' He then remembered the roadblock. 'What was the fire to do with us? Really, Comrade, control yourself. It can't be that bad.'

She tried to muffle her sobs but was only partially successful. Her words came flooding out like an uncontrollable torrent, each convulsive rush bringing worse and worse news: 'The Comrade Commanding Officer and the Comrade Political Commissar ... both in hospital ... still unconscious ...fire burnt down the comcen ... Deputy missing ... Mana Varamit missing ... stranger in his bed ...'

A cold hand gripped the camp doctor's heart. Indeed, something had gone terribly, terribly wrong. He felt he had to know the worst. He pushed past her, asking her where the two officials had been put. The first room held the CO. He leant over him. Regular breathing, lips slightly dry, one day's growth of stubble on his chin. He felt his pulse: a touch slow. He lifted an eyelid. Nothing untoward. He sniffed his breath. Certainly garlic, a trace, perhaps, of coffee. Something else, but what? He went into the next room and performed the same routine on the Political Commissar. He then went into the last room and, on reaching the bed, stared hard and long at the sleeping figure before he examined him. He stood up and unconsciously shook his head. Yes, things were about as wrong as they ever could be – or ever had been. He turned to the nurse and posed a question.

'Have you any idea who this man is, how and when he came here?' His voice hardly sounded like his own.

'He was not here last night.' He had to strain to hear what she said. 'Mana was here last night. This morning Mana was not here. He,' indicating the sleeping man with her head, 'was.'

Curtly he told her to stay around and returned to the mess compound by way of the burnt-down comcen. No wonder no message of an earlier arrival. What on earth had caused such chaos? He forced his unwilling footsteps back to the mess room and went inside. They had finished a light meal and had coffee cups in front of them. He had been longer than he had realised. They looked up as he came in, impatient and fretful, and saw, from his expression, that something was amiss, more amiss than no transport and no welcome. He stood in front of them, hanging his head slightly and, in a confessional monotone, told them what he had just found out.

'Comrades, please heed what I have to say before deciding your next step. I can explain, but only in part, some of what seems to be an inexplicable disaster. First, the two senior comrades, the Commanding Officer and the Political Commissar, are both lying unconscious in hospital.' There was a quick intake of breath from the visitors who were paying him every attention. 'They have been, so it seems, there since last night. I was not called and that is why they were not at the airstrip to meet you. Second, a stranger, similarly unconscious, is lying in Mana's bed. I deduced no specific reason for this state of affairs from my cursory inspection. Third, Mana is missing. Fourth, the communication centre has been burnt to the ground. Fifth, the Deputy is missing. He was last seen earlier on this morning.'

There was a horrified hush as the audience grappled with the enormity of the situation. In the silence a thin voice, far away and faint, was heard in hoarse ululation. It was so faint that no one recognised it as human.

By dawn on the morning of 15 March, Major Vong caught up with the escort group. He came across them, as ordered, at RV 1, a short way from the road trace that would lead them north, if he decided to follow it, before reaching the comparative safety of the jungle area to the south of Bouam Long. Mana's escorts were in the clump of trees they had rested under on the way down. They looked tired. Mana was asleep on the stretcher. Vong looked disdainfully at the escort and, saying nothing, went and sniffed their breath, one at a time. He yanked one man up to a standing position by his hair and slapped his face hard. The man screamed and glowered back, hurt and mystified. He could see that Vong was furious.

'I could have found this hiding place by the smell of your cigarette smoke. It's not the normal local stuff but the same as what the Viets smoke. You must have got a packet from when you visited your relatives. What I can smell, so can our enemies – and they can tell the difference so work out where the smoker came from. Only your breath stinks of tobacco. I had several whiffs of it on the way up.' He let go of the man who sat down, rubbing his head, muttering. He was wrong, and he knew it. So did the others.

The scream had woken Mana. Vong saw him lick his lips and, taking his water bottle, went to him and gave him a drink.

'How are you? Not too sore-footed, I hope. We could never have saved you any other way. You'll be completely safe soon. We still have a long way to go but we'll look after you. We had to bug out in a hurry. That's why your clothes are strange. There's no need to be scared of any of us.'

The kind, reassuring words soothed Mana who answered in a tone of voice that, to the listening men, sounded perfectly normal. 'Tell me what has happened.' He waved his hand at the group and his clothes. 'I can't remember much. I had a dreadful nightmare. I tried to wake up and thought I had. You know that sort of dream, don't you? Think you're awake from a dream but really you've gone into another dream. I'm awake now,' and he smiled.

'Can you remember any of your dream?' Vong asked casually, sitting down beside him.

Mana rucked his brow and looked speculatively at Vong. 'If I didn't know you were real and sitting beside me, I'd swear I saw you.' He laughed apologetically. 'I saw someone else who funnily enough is familiar. Not here, by any chance, is he?' He looked around, grinning slightly shamefacedly as though he had made a bad joke. 'Gosh, but my mouth feels like the proverbial sawdust. No, he's not here. Shame. I'd like to have met him in real life. Wait.' Again he puckered his brow. 'I saw, wait … I saw … I've got it,' and he almost shouted with relief. 'Tâ Tran Quán. It was Tâ, wasn't it? Do say "yes",' he implored. He had got up from the stretcher, a rapturous look on his face. 'I've got it at last,' he said to their surprise. 'I've got it at last. I'm Mana Varamit and there were four others.' He beamed expansively, looking at his escort. 'Now I've reached you, it's come back to me. You have come to take me to Sam Neua, haven't you? Sent me to Skyline Ridge as I've got to give my report about the Four Rings.'

They searched for some water to cook their meal. The river running along the other side of the trace and the jungle fringe beyond it made them move over the trace into the shade where they would have kindling as well as shielding any smoke their fire made. Rice, the sticky kind so beloved of all Lao and Thai, and some dried meat heavily impregnated with curry powder, was what they cooked. As they washed up, they heard the sound of an aeroplane flying from north to south. Vong listened attentively and moved to a spot where he could see it. An AN-2, he saw, but was unable to pick out whether it carried USSR or LPF markings as the sun was in his eyes. He did notice, however, that it was descending. As far as he remembered, Ban Ban was the only strip in the area that comfortably took the AN-2. He rejoined the group and asked the two men who knew the area well whether an AN-2 was a common occurrence. Only one man bothered to answer. No, they didn't often fly this way but when they did they normally carried important people. The other man did not answer as he was still upset by having his hair pulled and his face slapped, both publicly. One answer was good enough as Vong had, by this time, presumed that the passengers were the doctors mentioned by the two scouts, but he kept his counsel. He wondered what range and speed of flight he could expect from the hornets whose nest he had so recently stirred up.

He turned back to Mana. 'Comrade Mana. I owe you an apology for the rough handling you have received.' He looked most grave. 'You have been the target of a filthy imperialist kidnap plot. I cannot explain now, much as I'd like to, and as indeed I will, because your presence is urgently needed in Sam Neua. We had to bring you out this way otherwise I can't think what would have happened to you. As it is, we are well on the way to finding out who is responsible for the frantic act of sabotage. The reason why Sam Neua has ordered us to do things in this fashion is not fully understood but, on the way, we are going to meet the traitorous lackeys who wanted to stop our report from reaching Sam Neua and the Politburo. They will in turn, be ambushed and, being caught red-handed, they will not fail to divulge who the other traitors are.' Mana Varamit nodded understandingly. 'For that reason we must press on, quickly, cautiously and cleverly. Are you ready?'

The six visitors were dumbfounded. The magnitude and suddenness of such a situation utterly shocked them. The senior doctor recovered first.

'Take me to the hospital now.' He got up and made for the door. One of the inquisitors interrupted him.

'Comrade Doctor. I doubt you want me and my fellow comrades to accompany you under these circumstances. I suggest that I try, we try that is, and find out as best we can just what has been happening. We will most certainly talk to the hospital staff when you let us. It is now a little after 2 o'clock. We have just over four hours of daylight left. Do you agree? Shall we try and meet here at, say, 6 p.m.?'

There was no dissent. They went about their separate ways, the camp doctor taking the two specialist doctors to the hospital. The inquisitors were perfectly capable of finding their own way about – that is why they were inquisitors.

At the hospital, the two specialists took one look at the CO and, as indeed the camp doctor had thought to himself, declared him drugged and in no immediate harm. One asked the camp doctor if there was any Phenobarbitone in the dangerous drugs store and looked serious when the reply was that none had ever yet been issued to the hospital.

They made the same judgement on the Political Commissar. They then came to the unknown man.

'You say you don't know who this man is?'

'No, Comrade, I don't. I have no idea who he is, who brought him here, how he was found or anything about him. Neither have I any theories.'

A thorough examination was made of the two camp inmates before the third man was looked at in detail and it was during this last examination that they were joined by a dishevelled and tired senior medical orderly. He looked despairingly at the camp doctor, who put his finger to his lips. Only when the two specialists had finished was he invited to explain his case. His audience listened attentively.

'You say that the Guard Commander reported that the medical team came last night? That their vehicle broke down somewhere up the road and they walked in? What is this nonsense?' Before the senior medic had time to answer, the senior doctor continued. 'We'll have to keep a strict watch on these three and hope they come to before much longer. There'll be quite a load of us going back tomorrow. If they are still unconscious by, say, last light, we'll fix up a saline drip in each case.'

He made as to leave the isolation ward, the camp doctor wondering if the allusion to the plane load referred to the patients being evacuated or to his going back under arrest. Halfway to the door, the neurologist turned back, re-entered the CO's room and turned out the unconscious man's pockets. A note fluttered out and was seized upon. It was written in Vietnamese on cheap paper. He read it through and whistled. 'Grief! Listen to this! 'This man, because of his evil nature, his devotion to a Cause that is also evil, his repression of those who are not evil, is being punished. We, the people of Laos, do not want to be ruled by and ruined by the Vietnamese bully-boys. We, the punishers, are many. You, the tainted, are, regrettably, even more: be warned – "The pitcher goes so often to the well that at last it breaks".' It is signed by "A devotee of the rain drop". What fool's nonsense it this? Go, Comrade, and see what the Political Commissar has on him.'

There was a replica of that which had already been found. 'And now, let us even more thoroughly examine the third man, his clothes and his body. We may be able to establish his identity or, at least, see if there are any clues.'

But there was nothing either as spectacular or as vitriolic in this case. Under the pillow were his papers. They showed that his name was Tanh Bên Lòng. 'Don't know the name, do you?'

'No,' answered his companion, shaking his head. 'Doesn't look to be a strong person. Been walking hard. Look at his feet.'

They opened up his clothes. 'Been wounded, too. Quite badly. Close range. Healed up well. Must have knocked the stuffing out of him. And in the leg!'

They continued their examination. 'See this? Surely not a mosquito bite? Pajamas too thick for that, and a net. Who jabbed him, I wonder? Blasted body snatchers.'

At the end, they put his arms and legs back into normal positions. 'That's a strange tattoo mark,' one of them observed, looking at the inside of the little finger of the man's right hand. 'Looks like the roman numeral 9.'

After his meal halt, Vong debated whether to lie up there and then or continue with daylight movement. He had, in any case, ordered them to relax for half an hour after the meal and to freshen up in the river. As they were relaxing, he again heard the engine of the returning AN-2. That cleared his mind: he calculated that, given luck, he had slightly more than a head start on the inevitable search parties but he could not count on more than four hours of daylight walking in safety up the road trace, immeasurably quicker than walking through secondary or primary jungle. Were they to meet anybody or even a unit patrolling, he could explain his presence by saying that he was on an extended patrol from Ban Ban, checking on any movement of suspicious people in connection with the mysterious fire. They might get away with such a story for a short while yet but even that was a risk. Much could depend on how effective his false trail and careful movement would prove and how soon 'the opposition' took the initiative – both imponderables. He looked at his men and saw they were more tired then he was. He decided, even so, to take the risk, for at least another four hours. 'On your feet,' he ordered. 'Straight up the road trace. Keep alert and leave the talking to me.'

It was just as well for his peace of mind that he did not know the resentment the aggrieved man was feeling.

The AN-2 had to refuel in Sam Neua before proceeding to Office 95 on another mission. Before take off from Ban Ban, the Cuban pilot and his Vietnamese co-pilot briefly chatted about the poor arrangements. Speaking in French, they both agreed how strange it was that nobody had met the delegation. Once they had climbed to their cruising height and levelled off, control was contacted and told that the plane was airborne once more and was in-bound for Sam Neua. A voice crackled back at them, asking if they had either seen any trace of or been told about a fire in the district? Negative. Had Ban Ban contacted them? Not by radio. Control relapsed into momentary silence. 'There's something wrong somewhere,' observed the Cuban but as the man on the strip who had been introduced as the camp doctor had not seemed unduly worried nor said anything, the pilot did not consider it worth his while to return and circle Ban Ban, although he did have enough fuel.

During the afternoon, the inquisitors had solved some of the mysteries but had found new ones. They had examined, with the greatest care, the wreckage of the comcen but had found nothing in the rubble to show any evidence of arson however strong the suspicion; they had cross-examined the guard and had established that a party of six had indeed entered the camp after nightfall and that they were not expected, that the sentry had challenged them, the Guard Commander had made them wait at the gate, an off-duty man had been sent to inform the CO and the Political Commissar with the doctor's name – and they also understood from the messenger that the two commanders were equally nonplussed – at the doctor's insistence and that the two leaders had come personally to the guardroom and allowed them in, the doctor wanting to go directly to the hospital; that none of the six nor Mana – everybody knew him nor the Deputy had been seen to leave the camp; that the living quarters of the Deputy and the Commissar were untampered with and, to corroborate the story of the soldier sent to the mess compound, two unwashed cups of coffee were on the table but nothing else. The coffee would have to be examined to see if it had been doctored. Some coffee beans were found in the back room but they were reckoned as safe. The four men, two inquisitors and two thugs, had made a thorough inspection of the wire surrounding the camp and had found nothing amiss. They had spoken to many people, most of whom had no idea of anything wrong except the previous night's fire. The man in charge of the vehicles told them what little he knew, which was not much. Before they foregathered in the mess, there was just time to get hold of the Guard Commander for one last point to be clarified. 'Come with us to the hospital and see if you can recognise the stranger,' one of the inquisitors had commanded.

'Stranger?' queried the Guard Commander, by now

thoroughly bemused.

'Yes, stranger,' was the rough reply.

The Guard Commander, recognising the stranger as Dr. Tanh Bên Lòng, was really the only positive clue.

That had taken them to early evening. They went over to the mess compound and joined the two specialists who were already there. They held a council of war and agreed that one of the four should stand guard inside the hospital and look at the three men inside every so often. The senior medic would act as runner in the event of consciousness being regained. The news that the third man had come in with the group the previous evening had not been greeted with much joy. His name meant nothing to them. It was further felt that superior authority could well have news of the fire by then but it were better that the camp was sealed off, as best it could be, until either outside help arrived or the AN-2 returned. This disappearance of eight people was a complete mystery.

They contemplated, in silence, the gravity of the situation. A faint noise again assailed their ears. 'That's the second or third time I've heard that noise,' remarked one of the inquisitors. 'I don't like it. It's not far off.'

He got up and went outside. He cocked his head. He heard it again, this time a hoarse moan. 'I'm off to have a look,' he called and moved off in the direction of the noise and soon saw the old air-raid shelter. He saw steps leading down to a door and, forcing it open, a half-demented man rushed out. The Deputy, crazed by incarceration, maddened by thirst, tortured by fear of punishment for the shambles in the camp, not knowing who had shut him in nor who was trying to plague him yet more and not knowing about the search party, made a terrific lunge at the shadowy figure he saw in the doorway. He took one enormous swipe at his imaginary oppressor, missed, tripped, hit his head a resounding whack and passed out cold as he fell to the ground.

'Careful,' called one of the doctors from above. 'Even this light may damage his eyes.' The inquisitor fumbled around in the gloom, found the unconscious, limp body and, with it over his shoulder, emerged in the open.

'Who on earth is this?' chorused the astonished onlookers.

'Doesn't matter who he is. Get him to the hospital immediately,' ordered the doctor, then, with no trace of irony, said 'How lucky we've still got an empty bed'

Vong was a successful soldier because, although he did not believe in luck, he recognised its existence. To date, they had been lucky and, as far as he could tell, their quick getaway from the camp had been unobserved but the rest of his measures were unknown qualities. He had made no outward sign that Mana's announcement meant anything to him. Certainly he in no way associated any ring with Tâ Tran Quán. He did remember when Rance came in to see Tâ the first time that the Englishman was wearing some ring or other. Or was he? He normally noticed such things and he was sure there was no ring on his finger when they shook hands – or was there? Not that it mattered here and now, however intriguing the problem was. Men had lost their life for not noticing such details. He was wandering. He jerked his mind back to the present. They needed a rest. It would be unnecessarily rash to bank on a continued avoidance of trouble, certainly after today. The trace they had been following led, eventually, to not far from Bouam Long, on a northwesterly axis. Any troops that were ferried from anywhere else by road would have to go to Ban Ban as there was no other road junction. It was, therefore, still a safe gamble to use the trace that night. He further reckoned that, when his watch showed 4 o'clock, they would find a place to have a rest until after dark. He decided he would get the signaller to open the set and see if he could pick up an NVA frequency. He would then move slightly off net and send a spoof message. He would talk in Vietnamese, pretend he was sender and receiver, and, as his rescue team had not made contact with him yet, he would go south until he met a river junction and wait there. He would add, plaintively, radio silence until tomorrow 1600 hours. It might buy more time. After that, they would prepare a meal, rest and move up the trail all night. But they would have to rest up the next day, Saturday the 16th. '4 o'clock. Time for a halt.' His men sank wearily to the ground, delighted to be able to rest.

Late that Friday afternoon a message reached Office 95 saying that a report had at last been received from Ban Ban, by runner, to a neighbouring battalion to the effect that there had been a fire the night before and that the comcen had been destroyed. There were no other reports of further damage or any casualties. Nga Sô Lưu, eyes sultry and inscrutable, mobilised a team to go down to Ban Ban in the AN-2 on the morrow, Saturday, to investigate. So, until their report was received or until the other party returned, he had to bide his time and rest content.

Content was not a word that could be used about anybody in Ban Ban just then. Not really knowing where to turn, the inquisitors had again interrogated the guard who steadfastly maintained that they had seen no one leave the camp during their spell of duty. They described the six men who came in as best they could but it was after dark and a Lao peasant was not renowned for his powers of description. Afraid to say that there was a period when the gate was unmanned, they were correct in their assertion that they had seen no one leave. Doubtless, when the inquisitors got round to recording individual statements, a discrepancy would be found but they might get away with it. The nurse's statement was so incoherent as to be virtually useless and the senior medic had not deviated from his original statement, which did not make happy reading. The search party that had been sent out to see if there were any signs of the missing men having left the camp by the river had reported no trace of any untoward movement. It was the consensus that until contact was made with the outside world – the AN-2 on the morrow or the sleeping men awoke – there was not a lot else that could be done.

At 8 o'clock that evening, their patience was rewarded. News was brought that the CO had come round but was still groggy. He had been given water and indicated he wanted a meal. Would the doctors please go and have a look at him. Would they? Whilst looking at the CO, the Political Commissar groaned and stirred. He, too, was groggy and demanded water. And then the third man awoke but his awakening was not immediately noticed. He heard voices next door and he kept his eyes tight shut as he recalled where, *Ban Ban camp hospital*, and who he was. *I am Tâ Tran*

Quán inside but, until I feel the time ripe, I am Dr. Tanh Bên Lòng. He felt lethargic and opened one eye slightly and saw that he was in a ward with the door open and a blue-uniformed man standing with his back towards him. He twitched his legs. Stiff. *Yes, that had been a long walk and I turned myself into Dr. Tanh Bên Lòng on the way. Vong. Dear Vong. Mana. Had they got away safely or had they been caught and were even now being held just to trap him?* He would have to be cautious but he had a raging thirst. *Ready? Why not?* He composed himself, counting ten. He then let out a long sigh, stretched himself and raised himself onto his elbows. The effect was gratifyingly instantaneous. The man on the door wheeled round and came over to him. Tâ was glad to see no hostility in his face, only concern. 'Comrade, how do you feel? Are you hurt or not?'

The sound of his voice brought the neurologist into the room. Tâ slipped his legs over the side of the bed and tried to stand up. He sat down abruptly. 'Where the hell am I?' he asked crossly, 'and who would you lot be?'

The neurologist eyed him keenly. 'Comrade Tanh Bên Lòng. I am glad to see you have regained consciousness. You are in Ban Ban camp. I am a doctor from Hanoi and my colleague is next door. Don't get up for a few minutes. You have been asleep for a long time. Do you hurt or ache anywhere?

'I am stiff. I must go and have a pee. I am also very thirsty.'

The neurologist directed one of the staff to help him and, while that was being done, a hoarse cry came from another room. The Deputy had also regained consciousness. It was his turn for solicitous attention. Tâ came back from the toilet and lay on his bed, still wobbly in the legs. He was left alone for a while, to his relief. On his way to the toilet he had noticed the activity in the place and wanted to clear his thoughts which were more sluggish than usual.

The neurologist and his fellow doctor decided that the three camp inmates should spend the rest of that night in the hospital, having first been given a light meal. It had not been forgotten that, had it not been for those who had come into the camp with this mysterious Tanh Bên Lòng, things would not have reached this parlous state they had, though the recovery of four out of four was, as one of the inquisitors who had service with the French put it, 'a full house in more than one way'. A guard was detailed with the strictest instructions not to let anybody other than the hospital staff in and, at the same time, the camp security was trebled in case the unknown tried either to get in, always presuming they had got out, or get out, always presuming they were still inside.

But however frustrated, afraid, angry or bemused people were, none could have guessed that the fortunes of little Laos had, by the efforts of men with other matters on their mind, been changed for longer than a generation, maybe even for longer, as a result of the previous twenty-four hours' events.

5

March 1974: Northeast Laos: Shortly after midnight on Saturday, 16 March, the Tai Dam Major noticed that his men were straggling. He called a halt and ordered them to take out of their packs the string they had used on the way down to Ban Ban and to tie it onto their neighbour's rear pack strap. The man behind could catch hold of the piece hanging from the man in front of him as they continued their walk in the dark. It was only when he was inspecting them that he found out that one man was missing. He called out softly, hoping to attract the missing man's attention: asleep or relieving nature perhaps. He shone his torch on the side of the road where they had rested, but to no avail. The missing man was none other than he who had felt the brunt of Vong's rage soon after dawn the day before. On questioning the rest of the men, no one knew when or where he had given them the slip. He had certainly been with them during the earlier part of the night.

Basic doctrine in armies modelled on French traditions is short of sympathy with both minor and major offenders against military discipline. Even in non-Christian forces, there is the equivalent of the Eleventh Commandment, 'Thou shalt not be found out'. It was hardly surprising that Vong's violent outburst had had no further attention paid to it by anybody, including the escort commander. Only the aggrieved man brooded. In his case, as a proud and mercurial Meo, his dignity had been hurt. He had risked his life for someone he did not know by going into country dominated by those filthy Viets, endangered his in-laws, and the only thanks he got was being insulted in front of the others by someone who was virtually a Viet himself, to say nothing of the unknown man from the camp. Sulking, but with no fixed purpose than to get his own back on Vong, he had decided to return to his relatives. He was fed up with the discomfort and danger. He had slipped off at a wayside hut and had decided to lie up there for the rest of the night. The others, lost in the rhythmic trudge of wearied march, had failed to notice.

Vong could only do one of three things: retrace his footsteps looking for the man, stay where he was in the hope that the man caught up with them or continue. Whichever way he reacted, there were disadvantages. *My top priority, the whole purpose of this demanding mission, is to get Mana back. Which course of action will least put my aim at risk?*, he asked himself. The missing man knew his way back to Bouam Long and to his relatives. His presence in the group, though of use, was not now essential as it had undoubtedly been on the way out. Were any follow-up party to meet him, it could prove most unhealthy for them.

'We'll continue without him,' Vong decided. 'Let's get moving. Probably catch us up before long. Knows where we're heading for.'

If, Vong bleakly thought, the man had not appeared by dawn, he'd have to reconsider the return route. They trudged on in the dark.

For the doctors and inquisitors in Ban Ban, Saturday, 16 March, started before dawn. The four patients had been given mild medication and some light food to settle them down for the rest of the night and an armed sentry had sat on a chair in the passage of the isolation ward. Unusually, the generator had also been kept running. Nothing abnormal happened, much to everyone's relief.

The men from Hanoi had decided that a soft approach was better than a hard one at this stage of the proceedings. Being heavy-handed was not something that either doctor liked and, until a full medical check could be made, was deemed out of the question.

One group went to Tâ's room, woke him, briefly looked at him and told him to go and freshen himself up by washing his face under the tap. This he did. On his return, an orderly brought some tea and the questioning began, the doctor talking and the inquisitor taking notes.

'Comrade Dr. Tanh Bên Lòng. How did you get here?'

'Comrade. You tell me. I don't know where I am. You live here. I don't. I go and see people all over the place. I could be anywhere.'

The doctor told him that he was in Ban Ban but the information did not have any visible effect, so he reverted to the previous line. 'People? What sort of people do you go and see? Can you tell me a little more about them?' and he re-filled Tâ's cup.

'Well, people who want to see me.' The doctor and the inquisitor's glances met. 'I've met so many of them. I try to give them advice on their health.'

'Are you a doctor, then? Have you studied medicine?'

'Maybe. I have a great interest in that subject, especially in people who lose their minds. I keep on asking who did this to me,' and he pulled his clothes up and showed them his chest-wound scar. 'I got a bullet here and bumped my head at the same time. I felt that other people too could have pains and, when mine hurt no longer, perhaps I could help them with theirs.'

'When did this happen to you? It looks more than a year old.'

'I expect it is. It seems a long time ago but it hasn't always been there.'

The neurologist changed the subject. 'Who brought you here? I can't imagine you came on your own. Can you remember who came with you?'

'You brought me here, didn't you? Some kind man, or were there more, brought me to the camp. Said that there was a hospital and a doctor. I suppose that this is the hospital and you two are doctors?'

The doctor from Hanoi again changed tack. The man spoke lucidly and yet he could be shamming. 'Tell me, do you know anyone by the name of Mana Varamit?'

'Mana Varamit? That sounds like a Thai name. Has he been hurt also?'

'Yes, he was hurt looking for someone called Tâ Tran Quán. We're looking for Mana. We came here expecting to find him but found you here instead.'

So he had got away, it seemed. 'I can't say that I can put a face to the name but somehow the other name you mentioned is familiar. Were they both hurt? Like this?' and he pointed first to his chest, then to his leg.

'No. We know that he was hit in the head and was suffering from a loss of memory. That was over a year ago also. Strange if yours happened at the same time.'

That was too near the mark for comfort. 'Oh, that is unfortunate. I find I sometimes lose mine. Wake up sometimes and wonder where I got my sore feet from.' He laughed. 'I've never woken up quite like this before,' and waved his hand around him.

'Not even when you were wounded? You must have been looked after and treated by somebody somewhere.'

'Not in such a small place as this. No, I can't remember. I seem to recollect it was on a hill. I'll tell you when my mind clears.' He bent forward to examine his blistered feet. 'Need a thorough wash. I'd like a shower and some more clothes. Feel itchy.' He grimaced and straightened up.

'Do you know Le Dâng Khoã?'

It was lucky that his face was in an unnatural scowl and his body was moving as the question was asked. Gave him just enough time to hide his surprise.

'What's that, Comrade? Who? Le who was it?'

'I said 'Le Dâng Khoã'.'

'H'm. Like the other man you asked about, could well be but right now I can't put a face to the name. I'm sorry if I appear bemused. If I do it's because I am.'

While this conversation was being held, the CO and the Political Commissar had been called together into the room opposite to where Tâ was and they were explaining what had happened on the evening of the 14th. The CO, recovered almost completely, was relating how he had been called by the sentry and told that a Dr. Tanh Bên Lòng was waiting to see him. The doctor interrupted by saying that was the name of the man in the ward opposite. 'Wait a sec while I check with my colleague and see if it is in order for you to meet him.'

He got up, leaving the inquisitor with them and went and tapped on the door opposite. It was opened and he said, 'Excuse me, Comrade, but is your patient well enough to be spoken to by the CO and the Political Commissar?'

'Yes. Why not? It could prove interesting. Bring them in and come yourself.'

The three of them came into the room and the CO and the Political Commissar stared at Tâ. The Political Commissar broke the silence that had temporarily descended. 'Doctor, what on earth are you doing here? What did you do with Mana?' The four men from Hanoi stiffened perceptibly. This was something new, something significant. Tâ felt this quickening of interest. 'What happened to the other group? That man who said he left you undergoing your tests. The man who gave us that funny-tasting coffee. Don't tell me that he laid you low too?'

Tâ looked happily around. 'I don't know anything about coffee but otherwise I've got it. Or rather some of it. I was walking down the road. Someone came and asked me if I would look at Mana Varamit and I went with him. You were at the gate, weren't you? It was dark and nothing was distinct in the poor light of the hurricane lamps. Thank you for jogging my memory.'

'But you said that your vehicle had broken down somewhere on the road,' protested the Political Commissar, 'and that you had walked the rest of the way, that you were a busy man, should have examined Mana earlier in the afternoon and I don't know what else. You were most insistent and spoke with great authority, giving a whole lot of medical terms about the brain.'

Tâ again smiled. 'That would certainly explain these blisters but doesn't ring any bell otherwise,' he said, but a little voice warned him that he was treading on dangerous ground. The less he could commit himself now, the easier it would be later.

'Try hard and remember who was with you,' interrupted one of the inquisitors. 'Your memory is coming back even as you talk.'

'I seem to remember hearing that before,' Tâ observed sadly. 'If I caused you any trouble, I'm terribly sorry. Maybe you weren't hit in the chest. May I have my shower, please?'

The doctor conducting the interview was not anxious to allow him to go far on his own but a stand-up wash in the block would do no harm, besides which, he wanted to talk to the Deputy, so he gave Tâ permission and asked the staff for some clean kit to be produced.

With Tâ out of the room, the Political Commissar looked at the four men from Hanoi and said, 'You know, I've seen him before. Long ago and probably in Sam Neua but it could have been in Hanoi. He talks Vietnamese like a Viet and a Hanoi Viet at that. I guess he's one of those harmless shell-shocked fellows who are such a bore. I *do* wonder how he got muddled up in this nasty incident.'

None of the others felt it necessary to cap that remark so they went to see the Deputy, who had a large bump on his forehead and was hoarse but otherwise, apart from a headache, seemed physically well. There was no doubting his worry. When he saw his two superiors, he burst out with, 'Oh Comrades. I did try and tell you about the fire after you didn't come and help put it out. I feel to blame in not calling you earlier but I didn't know you were ill.'

'What fire?' both asked, almost in unison. 'What fire? Please explain yourself.'

What with the anxieties of the situation and the subsequent relief at finding the unconscious men seemingly better, no one had thought to mention the business of the fire and the damaged comcen. It clearly shook the two senior men rigid, making them speechless with chagrin and dismay. Even when Tâ came back from his wash, there was no denying his genuine astonishment at the information.

It was decided that the four men who had been admitted to the hospital should get ready to fly back north in the AN-2, provided there was room. The inquisitors were senior enough to take charge of affairs at Ban Ban temporarily. So the three camp officials were allowed back to their quarters to collect what kit they thought they would need. On rejoining the group in the mess room, the CO and the Political Commissar both mentioned that some of their papers were missing. Knowing the tight security regulations in force about not keeping sensitive material in places other than their office, they hastened to say that the papers were not of anything but a private nature. One of the doctors waited till his mouth was empty and said, 'Oh yes. Let me show you what was taken from your pockets,' and produced the two identical notes. 'Don't recognise the handwriting by any chance, do you?'

The documents were read through, the readers pursing their

lips. 'This is heresy,' breathed the Political Commissar. 'How dare anyone write this?' Fury and hatred creased his face into an ugly mask. He automatically held it up to the light to see if there was an attributable watermark on it, but there was none.

The CO was equally hostile but more down-to-earth. 'Bloody nonsense. Work of a nut-case.' He looked at the offending bit of paper once more. 'And what does "devotee of the rain drop" mean? How I'd like to get my hands on him!' Injury plus insult had resulted in more than indignation.

Dawn on the old French road trace saw an exhausted group of men shuffling along in a westerly direction. As daylight seeped over the eastern mountains, Vong looked at the haggard faces and saw that they simply had to have a decent long and uninterrupted rest, preferably for twenty-four hours. It would mean that he could no longer afford to go back to Bouam Long by the easier, quicker way up the trace and so would have to use a harder, more circuitous route than he would have liked but he knew he had no alternative if he were to rest his men, and rest them he had to. He halted them.

'Gather round and listen,' he said. 'You have done better than I ever expected and are indeed knackered. We are going to hide and lie up for the rest of today and tonight. It will need unusually careful preparation if we are going to do that in safety but it will not only save a sentry on full time but will also prevent follow-up parties from finding out where we are. After we've made camp and had a meal we'll bed down. Provided no one has nightmares and yells in his sleep, we'll be safe. Now, in order to achieve this, follow my directions in every, but every, detail. The safety or otherwise of this whole venture depends on everybody, every single body, making no mistakes.'

They had been walking parallel with a river that had swung into line with the trace at the top of the Ban Ban valley where it flowed down from a 7247-foot high mountain to their west. To its north was a saddle, about ten crow-flying miles from Bouam Long but, in broken country with dense jungle, was about twenty walking hours if, and it was a big if, they were not harassed and could conceal their tracks. Of course, they could force the pace but that would increase the risks. Vong had made his calculations: stay where the river debouched, lie up and on the following day, the 17th, reach the saddle and, fingers crossed as he had heard the Americans say, reach Bouam Long on the 19th. He would not alert them until he was sure that he had a reasonable chance of reaching them as stated. He had said that it would be the 17th or 18th when he would probably regain the enclave. One more day would make no difference. They'd be ready for them.

Vong made his men walk on the right of the road for fifty metres and cut an obvious path wide enough for a stretcher through some undergrowth as though they were a group moving north. They then walked backwards across the road to the edge of the undergrowth on the left of the road. There they moved forwards and parted the long grass with infinite care, treading delicately over it. The last man then teased it back, as best he could, into its original position. They reached the river, which was knee-deep, treading into the water from a large stone. This the last man washed with river water to erase any telltale marks. They waded upstream for a quarter of an hour when Vong decided to make camp just out of sight of the river on their left. Before leaving the river, Vong ordered all water bottles to be filled and then, treading on another conveniently placed stone, they got out of the water, the last man again washing the stone. The undergrowth was less dense, there being a thick jungle canopy above. In single file, they moved into the jungle where they would make a sheltered, overnight camp. Vong ordered two of his own men, not the escort, to collect the water bottles, empty their contents into a waterproof container, empty their packs, put the empty water bottles in them, return to the river, refill them and bring them back in their packs. On their way back towards the river they were to uproot any small saplings they came across, up to as many as either man could carry and, on the return journey, treading on exactly the same ground as the main group had trodden on, plant, as living camouflage, the saplings they had uprooted. This should have the effect of making the camp site invisible from that direction. Whilst this was being carried out, Vong beckoned to the escort commander and told him to start preparing camp. Rudimentary shelters only were to be put up and great care was to be exercised in his group not moving out of the small area chosen. Cooking could begin but, for goodness sake, try to keep smoke to a minimum. He also ordered the radio operator to prepare his radio. Mana watched what was going on with intense interest. When the dipole had been erected, the set being the kind that had to be netted in, Vong put on the earphones, told the signaller to take out the Morse key and go through the motions of sending a tuning call. Vong wrote on a page of his note book, 'Don't open up. Only pretend to.' Vong took his headset off, gave a wink to the 'executioner' who, unbeknownst to Mana had been his shadow since Ban Ban, and went and sat down by the Thai.

'You may wonder at these precautions,' he remarked chattily. 'I didn't say so earlier on but when I made contact with Sam Neua, they told me to lie low here and contact them at about this time. I'll let you know what messages they pass back.'

After ten minutes Vong went over to the radio operator, made as though he had read a message and came back to Mana as the two men returned from planting the living camouflage and with more water. 'Done just what you wanted,' they said. Vong nodded back.

'Sam Neua has sent a message saying that there is reason to believe that the imperialists are once more breaking the ceasefire protocols. The AN-2 yesterday reported suspicious movement to our north and whilst headquarters are sending some comrades to investigate, they want us to keep well clear of any action they may take and to avoid leaving any trails that the mercenary feudalists could follow up, however remote and fanciful that possibility be. To that end, I have reported our position. Sam Neua is happy to know we are on our way and safe, albeit tired, sends you fraternal greetings and hopes to see you in three days' time. The message sender trusts that you have the stamina, devotion and fortitude to emerge victorious. I said that you had. I have now been told to close down.'

Mana Varamit, exhausted by his night-long exertions, slowly took it in as he stared at Vong. Lucid, though bemused by so much unusual activity, he said, 'Comrade, I am proud to belong to such an organisation. I am scared lest the imperialists drag me back, however remote the possibility is, as you say. We are only a small group. What do we do if we are attacked during our stay here?'

'Don't worry, Mana,' Vong replied gravely. 'This comrade here will be tied to you all the time to give you comfort. He will guide you to safety under every difficulty,' silently adding, *and may the Lord have mercy on your soul.*

On Saturday morning the AN-2, pre-positioned overnight at Office 95, had an early getaway as there was little mist. It carried a full load of technicians, advisers, inquisitors and a new radio set. These men were to stay in Ban Ban until further notice, take over various camp duties, examine any and everything that came their way. The mystery *had* to be solved. The plane flew low, at about 500 feet above the ground, following the line of Route 61.

Down on the ground and walking down the old French road trace, the man who had decided to go back to his relatives rather than stay with Vong, heard an aeroplane coming his way before he saw it over to his left, low down and heading south. It somehow annoyed him. Gesticulating wildly at it like a frustrated child would wave its arms in fury when something it wanted was removed, he spent some of his pent-up fury and frustration as it flew on out of sight.

In the plane the two advisers had a pair of binoculars and a map, and they probed the countryside as they flew over it. Still some way from the Ban Ban strip, over to the starboard side, one of them saw a man waving his arms vigorously, almost abnormally so. He looked at his map, made a note of the place and time, and checked that the other adviser, sitting behind him, had also noticed it. The place noted would be given to the pilot after landing and the pilot told to fly back up, part of the way at least, over the old French trace. Might pick up something. The plane droned on.

The AN-2 this time flew as far as Ban Ban camp and circled around it. The ugly black patch where the comcen had been was highly visible.

Figures came running out and the pilot, with a message already written and put into the highly-coloured, lead-weighted cloth streamer, threw it out of the window as he made a lower than normal circuit over the mess compound near the bend in the river. The long streamer fluttered prettily as it quickly fell and was equally quickly retrieved by willing hands. The message merely said, 'Send any man you believe needs sending, along with the Hanoi doctors, up to a total of ten non-stretcher cases, to the airstrip now. We will be waiting for you.'

The AN-2 flew off, made its landing and waited. Those destined for Ban Ban got out and the men who had noticed the person waving in the distance told the pilot to fly back that way, certainly to the top of the valley where the trace and river joined, keeping a good look out for anything unusual.

Surprisingly quickly a vehicle arrived from the camp bearing a different-looking lot of men. Apart from the two doctors, there were four others, three looking most upset and worried, especially the one with a large swelling on his forehead. The fourth looked blank.

The pilot asked for, and was given, a list of names. Once airborne, he flew almost at tree level along the trace until he came to the point where the river debouched from the jungle-clad hills and ran parallel with the old road. As he pulled his plane sharply to the right, he thought he saw a fresh cutting on the north side of the road. He made a mental note as he regained height and, seconds later, started sending a message to control. 'Item one: CO, Political Commissar, Deputy, of Ban Ban camp, on board, all suffering from shock. Mana Varamit not, repeat not, on plane. Tanh Bên Lòng, also suffering from shock, on board. Doctors request four beds made available, separated. Item two: suspicious person seen on French trace at UG 4476 and new cutting observed on road side at UG 4278. Suggest investigate. Inform Comrade Nga. Message ends.'

Down on the ground, Vong and his men were thankfully making themselves comfortable for a long sleep. They had had their meal and, with enough water in the container, washed up in the camp site. They had arranged their weapons and packs near them so they could bug out with their basic essentials if necessary. Similarly the radio had been packed up. A little north of their camp, an aircraft, with devastating suddenness, roared along at tree-top level. As one man, they sat up, utterly stunned. They looked through the trees up at the sky as though expecting to see the plane still overhead malevolently glaring down at them like some giant bird, then at each other, then at Vong.

As the noise receded, Vong answered their unspoken thoughts. 'It may just be a coincidence. Our absent friend won't have had time to make any mischief for us yet. That plane was on a recon but it was flying too fast to see us. We could almost have predicted it but not quite. I am confident that we shall be safe enough here until early tomorrow morning. We have taken every possible precaution. What we need now is to regain our strength. So go to sleep and stop worrying.' He hoped that he had been enigmatic enough to have allayed any doubts Mana might have had.

To show the others that he meant what he said, he lay back, closed his eyes and, Asian-fashion, pulled the light piece of cloth that did for a sheet up over his head.

Before the AN-2 had gone much farther, the crackling voice

of control came over the headset. 'Go back and alert Ban Ban camp of your observations, order a search party out up as far as northern grid reference and similar distance up Route 61. To use unit transport. Order set taken this morning open to confirm orders received. Revert to own task after recon mission complete.'

The pilot leaned forwards and turned his compass dial 180°, acknowledging his orders as he did. The passengers looked at each other wonderingly as the plane suddenly turned sharply back on its tracks. *They've seen something of great importance*, thought Tâ. *I hope to goodness Mana hasn't given Vong the slip or something equally disastrous has happened.* He tried not to imagine the worst.

The pilot ordered the copilot to prepare another streamer as he wrote the new message. Back over Ban Ban camp he brought his machine into as tight a turn as he dared and, when he saw people were looking up at him, dropped the second streamer. Once more round and they waved to him that they had picked it up. He readjusted his compass bearing on a course that would take him to Office 95 and reported 'mission complete and message passed'. 'Don't usually act as fast as this,' he said to his copilot. 'Must be something big they're after. Pity the poor bastards when they catch them. I wonder if it's anything to with the jokers we've got with us.'

In Ban Ban, the senior inquisitor read the message. 'This could mean we are in business,' he said, giving out warning orders to have two squads of men, Group A and Group B, prepared and the two drivers alerted. 'Be ready to move at 1130 hours. Squad commanders to meet me at the camp entrance. Each squad to carry three days' rations.' He looked at the map in the CO's office which he had taken over. 'Looks like Bouam Long,' he remarked to his colleague. 'If so, they are playing for high stakes. What sort of game is worth such an effort?'

The AN-2 landed at the strip near Office 95. A small group was there to meet it, a senior cadre of the Office 95 staff to escort the doctors to Comrade Nga Sô Lựu and staff from the hospital to take charge of the four from Ban Ban camp. The two Hanoi doctors overrode the urgency of the cadre's pleas and insisted on personally handing the four over to the hospital staff there, with specific orders as to what needed doing and details of what had been done so far. Then and only then did they leave for Comrade Nga Sô Lựu's office where they were closeted with him for a long time. At the end, the Political Commissar thanked them for what they had done, apologised for having put them into such an uncomfortable and inexplicable situation, ordered the AN-2 to fly them back to Hanoi and entertained them with light refreshments until their departure. He even went to the airstrip to bid them farewell. Inside he was fuming.

He returned to his office deep in thought and sat there, several questions churning through his head: how? who? why? whence? There were no obvious clues to the identity of the masqueraders. The name Tanh Bên Lòng was unknown to him but even so, a tiny bell chimed – where had he heard the name before? According to the report the inquisitors had prepared the day before and which he had read with great attention, they certainly seemed to be genuine members of the Lao Patriotic Front or the 'elder brothers' attached to it; dress, language, no document gave any cause for concern. But why, just then, kidnap

Mana? – he presumed that Mana had been absconded. The timing; was it pure coincidence? The notes found in the two men's pocket; identical, revealed a faint clue. He knew it referred to a South Vietnamese pop song, anti-war and banned by the Saigon regime. Although he would never admit it, he knew the words and he recalled them now, squirming as he did, eyes flashing blacker than normal:

The rain on the leaves is the tears of joy of the girl whose
  boy returns from the war;
Is the bitter tears when the mother hears her son is no
  more …[1]

and fifteen more poppycock verses. Was the writer trying to blame the north for the war? If the writer's group was from the north would they have known the song in the first place? Just suppose that they were from central Vietnam, from the Highlands, west of Hué, they'd have had one hell of a long walk. No, highly unlikely. If they were from the south, could they have come up from the enclave at Kong Mi? Far too far. The nearest enclave was Bouam Long: that was much more likely from an infiltrator's point of view. Was the waving man a clue there? But the stranger: according to the CO and the Political Commissar's statements, he originally said he was a doctor but this was neither substantiated nor properly denied in the neurologist's report. Time for a break.

---

1 When the author was Commandant of the Jungle Warfare School he sang this song to the Vietnamese students on the one major picnic the school hosted for them – until he learnt that it was banned!

Time for a stroll to stretch his legs. Time to visit the hospital. He'd have a look at the stranger without his knowing. He went across and asked where Dr. Tanh Bên Lòng was. His mind reeled when he recognised Tâ Tran Quán – back from the dead.

One group of soldiers with an inquisitor, Group A, moved up the bumpy, grassy trace, weapons at the ready, and the other lot, Group B, also with an inquisitor, moved up Route 61. About the time they moved off, the new radio had been erected, communications re-established and news of the search parties' moves was passed.

Group A's move up the trace was slow and uneventful. Relations between the enclave and farther south had been completely disrupted during the fighting and had not improved much since the ceasefire. The Meo, with an admirable disregard for political niceties, had kept some contact between the two communities but strictly on a personal basis. This was tolerated by Authority in that they could not prevent it.

The man in the front seat with the driver kept the map open on his knees and glanced at it from time to time. Navigation was no problem; he had to observe where the river and the trace started running in parallel and tell the driver when to stop. They would then debus and start searching. The lads in the back of the vehicle were excited and anxious to get to grips with whoever was responsible for the attack against their camp, as they saw it.

When the navigator judged they were about to reach their debussing point, he told the driver to drive more slowly. 'Driver, halt here. Out you get, lads. Remember what I've told you. Shake out. Don't bunch so present a target. Eyes skinned. Come on,' and, staying on the right of the road, they moved slowly forward.

'Comrades! Have a look at this!' A bright young lad who was leading scout pointed at some undergrowth that had recently been cut. They forgot their commander's words and bunched around to have a good look thus effectively erasing any other telltale marks that there might have been. The young lad put his right forefinger on a piece of the cut foliage and felt it. 'Almost dry but there is not much loss of colour. That'll be this morning's work. Movement going north, I'd say.'

'Well done,' praised the inquisitor. 'That's a great find. Any more traces? Continue east for just a bit, lads, and see if you can pick anything up.'

They searched around but found nothing suspicious. Disappointed, they gathered by the road side. Their find had given their search an added impetus.

'Don't think that was a false trail, do you?' one of the soldiers asked. 'Would it be worth looking on the left of the road as well?'

They crossed over and viewed the undergrowth, behind which was thick jungle, alive with insect noises yet mightily still.

'Not much chance, I'd have thought in that lot,' observed another man. 'Nothing looks as though it has been disturbed, let along cut.'

'Well, there's time enough to go and see,' retorted the inquisitor tartly who, despite his inquisitorial skill, was not hot on jungle lore but did not want to show it. 'We'll divide ourselves in two, go to the river and, keeping in sight, move up each side of it. That'll pick 'em up if they've been that way. Up for about twenty minutes and then straight back to the vehicle if we've found nothing. If we come across them, we'll try and capture them. If we find tracks, we'll try and follow them.'

It was not much of a plan but it did show some initiative. They deployed and moved up both sides of the river.

Vong woke up. He looked at his watch. 4 o'clock. He stretched and looked around him. The others were dead to the world. Time to raise them, get some more water, cook a meal and then get settled before dark. No noise, except for the faint eternal background threnody of a myriad insects. Suddenly a long-tailed tit flew by, followed by another, darting between the trees from the direction of the river. He glanced at them curiously. A woodpecker flew by, also from the river, followed by smaller birds. A sixth sense of danger alerted him. Something was putting the birds into a state of alarm. Man or animal? Bird life was one of the things a person lying in ambush always heeded. He picked up his weapon and cautiously moved back down the line of approach to the camp from the river until he could see the water. He gasped as he saw a PL soldier, then a second, third and a fourth. They came along the river bank from the direction of the road. He froze and held his breath as he saw first one then the next look at the undergrowth where he had his two men plant living camouflage. They continued upstream and he breathed out in silent relief as the last man passed out of sight. *Stay here a bit longer. Don't move yet. Keep still.* He merged even closer into some shadow, obscured by a small bush.

A few minutes later, he heard a shout, answered by one slightly fainter. He tensed and braced himself to get back to the others like greased lightening should he have to. He saw the four men return, moving quicker and less carefully this time. The rear man stopped opposite Vong and shouted something that sounded like, '*Bor mi khon chon thi ni*,' reporting, in Lao, that there were no bandits there to someone on the other side of the river, before passing out of sight. Even then, Vong did not move until he just heard the noise of a vehicle revving up.

He rejoined the others, most of whom were stirring. Mana was still asleep so, before arousing him, Vong got the rest together and told them what had happened. 'Next time, don't grumble. Have you never heard that "sweat saves blood"?'

Cutting the undergrowth on the right of the road might have been an act of folly: camouflaging their tracks so well on the left of the road was the mark of a truly experienced craftsman. Vong would never know how safe he would have been had he not done as he had, yet the joker in the pack, the aggrieved man, was still a threat.

Group B had not had such an exciting time but it was more positive. They had driven to the village clinic, gone inside and, after a few minutes' questioning, discovered that on the night of the fire someone had alerted the village to put a roadblock some distance farther up the road. It was thought that the *Chao Ban* could give them specific details so the squad jumped into their vehicle and drove up the road, taking a local man with them, until they were at a point nearest where the *Chao Ban* lived. Half of them debussed and moved down the track till they reached his house and the other half were ordered to continue to drive up the road, beyond the airstrip, to make sure there was no broken-down vehicle on the road.

The man who went into the village called to the headman who appeared on the verandah. 'Come on down, *Chao Ban*,' the inquisitor said. 'I was expecting you,' answered the headman, ill-concealing his contempt at the peremptory command.

He slowly came down the notched tree trunk that served as a ladder into his house and introduced himself. As he did, he noticed that the soldiers were Lao youths, but that the leader was an 'elder brother'.

'You say you were expecting me, Comrade?'

'Yes, indeed. After the fire on Thursday night, I felt that something had gone wrong but there were no means of telling. I still don't know the ins and outs of it. It seems that some poor demented fellow put a match to one of the buildings.'

'Have you been to the camp to tell them what you found out?'

'No, Comrade. There was no need to.'

'But why on earth not? Surely a man in your position must know that you have to report everything suspicious? You don't often neglect your duties like this, I hope.'

The Lao headman gave the inquisitor a withering look then answered with cold disdain. 'If you would only let me finish giving my answer instead of interrupting, there would have been no need to have accused me falsely. Listen. After I had put the roadblock in position, I was visited by a cadre. Dressed like you are as far as I could tell in the dark – no, it wasn't you, was it?' the headman asked with a wicked grin of mockery.

'No, no. Of course it wasn't, otherwise I wouldn't be asking you these questions.'

'Well, this comrade told me I had done well in erecting a roadblock. He was almost sure that the crazed man who was the arsonist was lurking nearer the camp than as far afield as here, so, if nobody came by noon on the 15th, that's yesterday,' he said, rather proudly using the only calendar that the 'elder brother' easily understood, 'then there'd be no need to mention it further. Do you see my point?'

Ignoring that last question, the inquisitor asked, 'What else did he tell you?'

'He thought that the crazed man would try to get to Sam Neua. Got a grudge, I gather. The cadre took his men away. Said he was going to search to the east and alert the villagers. That's the last I saw of him.'

'How many men were with him?'

'Let me see. He himself, then there was a guide who'd brought him to see me and two was it or one other. I'm sorry but I've been running around a bit and had my mind on other matters.'

'You can't tell me anything else about him? Did he wear a pack, was he armed, did he speak with any regional accent?'

'Comrade. You don't seem to understand that I have told you everything I know. Unless otherwise briefed, I'll have forgotten what you looked like by this time tomorrow.'

And with that, the inquisitor had to be satisfied. By the time they got back to the road, their vehicle had just returned from its search for any broken-down transport. No, there was nothing they could find. Repaired and returned to its base was the general verdict. They returned to Ban Ban camp.

That evening a suitable message was sent to Office 95 concerning the day's activities. What little there was pointed eastwards but there was nothing conclusive.

Nga Sô Lưu came to his decision deliberately and methodically. Being in a position of great trust and influence, he wielded equally great power, both directly and indirectly. He had remembered Thong Damdouane's report, he had taken the message passed to him by the pilot to the inquisitors and now the result of the pilot's own observations – nothing definite enough to be acted on but much too much to be ignored. Certainly there were straws in the wind but, as yet, the wind was a bit too variable for exact diagnosis. He had chosen to ignore an intercepted message about moving south because there was a PL unit on the river junction to the south of and near Ban Ban and they had certainly made no report, and the river junction that, time and space-wise could have been the one referred to, was to the east, not south. He doubted if there would be any more from that direction. Despite nothing definite, everything pointed to Bouam Long as the base for launching the operation but yet, if it were a straightforward case of kidnapping Mana – and that was how he was treating it – whoever thought of it had to be sure enough of his facts and desperate enough to mount such an adventure. His top priority now was to get a large search operation under way immediately. The area requiring investigating was, initially, from Ban Ban up the axis of the old French trace, then north to the saddle north of point 7247, east until Route 61 was met, then due south to the River Man. Duration? Certainly no less than four days. He sent a top priority request to the military headquarters at Sam Neua and Hanoi for such deployment giving a brief justification. Accordingly, 31 Division and 588 Transportation Regiment, NVA, and some PL units were alerted for a move, details later, as soon as possible after first light the next day, 17 March.

Nga Sô Lưu then turned his mind to the extraordinary reappearance of Tâ Tran Quán. That needed much thought and research before the whole story could be laid bare. He would send a report that Comrade Tâ Tran Quán had been retrieved and was currently under medical observation and that Comrade Mana Varamit was missing, believed escaped during the fire in Ban Ban camp. He called for the personal dossiers of the four men who had so strangely been stricken down that night in the camp to see if there was a common thread.

He did not waste much time on the three permanents. He refreshed his memory and sent for an inquisitor to comb through them for any deviation, not that he expected any to be found. He then turned to Tâ Tran Quán's: everything normal until that day, 18 November 1972, when there was that attempt to bring Mana Varamit over. He made a note of the NVA company commander and, having rung his table bell for an orderly, sent as urgent message to try and locate him and get him to report to Officer 95 as quickly as possible.

That done, he asked for Mana Varamit's file. There had always been something in it that had troubled him, something that did not ring true, or, if it did, he could not understand it. The file was a thick one and it took him a while to find what he was looking for. Once he located it, he glanced at his watch and started to read. It was, initially, routine reporting, low level stuff and then the bit he had never understood: '... there are four days that are a potential danger ... four days could be enough to play havoc with our Cause ... it will be easy for these four days to pass by unnoticed unless they are previously identified...when we meet I will tell you which four days need to be guarded against ...' Nga Sô Lưu was not a man who held any belief in zodiacs, horoscopes or almanacs nor was he a man who liked to get himself in a position to be mocked and so he had accepted the reports at face value and had been getting more and more impatient to have Mana reveal what to him meant something, meant a lot, but to the Political Commissar in Office 95 meant nothing. And now, on the eve of hearing if Mana Varamit could be made to remember what he had meant, he was lost. He closed the file with a long sigh. These now surely weren't the four days Mana had referred to? Wait till he got his hands on those responsible ... Although he knew his nickname was 'the Black-eyed Butcher' – which he loathed – he knew that he had not earned it in vain.

Vong roused his group at dawn on Sunday, the 17th, and struck camp as soon as it was fully light. The men were refreshed but stiff, thankful that they had escaped detection. They had used up considerable reserves of strength and were sluggish.

Before moving off certain precautions had to be taken. Some signs of temporary occupation could not be hidden but where saplings had been cut to make poles for shelters, he made one of the men responsible for cutting the sapling stumps at ground level then covering the visible remains with earth. The cut part of the saplings could be disposed of later. Earth from under fallen leaves was carefully gathered and sprinkled over the ashes of the fire. By the time that was completed, the area looked as though only a couple or so men had been there several days previously. Certainly nobody could have tracked them to their night stop from the river nor, even had anybody stumbled on their camp site, connected the Ban Ban snatch party with the remains. Vong's final command was for the sackcloth his men still carried to be bound around their footwear and the two rear men of the column to walk backwards barefooted for a short while. Vong knew that an expert tracker could easily tell from any footprint whether the person being tracked was laden or unladen, moved backwards or forwards, or was man, woman or child but the risk of discovery in this instance was minimal.

It suddenly dawned on Mana who was watching everything with great interest and thinking of what had gone on the previous day, that he had seen nothing so professional as this since his days at the Jungle Warfare School. During the first part of that long, tedious, tiring walk up the trace, memories of Colonel Rance and Le Dâng Khoã came flooding back. He had pretended not to understand Vietnamese during the time he was on the course at the School. It had taken considerable self-control not to give away his secrets: that, and the fact that he knew about Le Dâng Khoã in greater depth than Le Dâng Khoã knew about him. He recalled the tense scene in the jungle when he was so full of rage and impatience that he was so nearly killed by Le Dâng Khoã but was interrupted by the English Colonel. He had tiptoed back and waited in earshot long enough to hear what the Viet had told the Commandant about saving his life and to see him, the Viet, find the ring in the cut leaves used for bedding and give it to him. Self-satisfied, smug fellow, that Rance. Thought he knew all the answers. Those lectures about Communism, indeed! Well, he didn't know them although it would have been embarrassing if he, Mana, had disarmed the Viet and killed him, there and then. It would keep. He, Mana Varamit, would cheerfully kill Le Dâng Khoã whenever he met him again and, however remote the possibility was of ever meeting Rance again, he would cheerfully kill him too. In a way, now he felt so much better in his mind, it was really rather a pity he was going to Sam Neua. As a daydream, to keep him mind occupied, he imagined how he would have reacted were he to have been in the hands of his ideological enemies and was on his way to, say, Bouam Long instead of Sam Neua.

Considering everything, the deployment of the troops engaged in the search operation was efficiently carried out but it was not until after midday on the 27th that they were ready to leave their unit lines. Certain local patrols had to be brought in, various camp duties reallocated and special administrative requirements, such as the issue of ammunition and rations, needed to be carried out. These processes were put into action by a warning order early on the Sunday morning by land line. Time was also needed for planning the command and control structure of the operation. Despite their reputation as dogged fighters, the NVA, like every other Communist army, was slow to react to the unexpected and the need to have political clearance for military planning prohibited any quicker start. In fact, the plan had been hammered out during the night and it took most of the morning to be passed down to various commanders. Most of the details unit and formation commanders needed concerned co-ordination of areas, boundaries, axes of advance and direction of approach. In such a large area, despite the probable destination of the miscreants, nothing could be left to chance, so such a mass of detail was essential.

By last light on Sunday forces had been deployed. Some were making more house-to-house searches up Route 61, others had been given sectors of the old trace leading to Bouam Long to scour, looking for clues. Yet others were poised to search the terrain between the old trace and Route 61. Farther afield, troops were detailed to fly by giant Soviet-built 'Hook' helicopters, normally based in Hanoi and with the capacity easily to take more than a platoon of armed men at a time, to land at the head of the Ban Ban valley, to lay a cordon to the north of point 7247, stretching from the road trace to the western slopes of the mountain. They were not expected to reach their final positions until some time on Monday, 19 March.

As part of the overall plan, a curfew was imposed and strict orders were given to enforce it. In fact, any night movement in the 'Liberated Zone' was suspect and people rash enough to move away from their homes at night were liable to be questioned severely. However, since the ceasefire, the lack of activity had dulled the Communist authorities' vigilance to the extent that the restrictions on night movement had become virtually meaningless.

It had already been established that no patrol had been sent by any local unit on the night of the previous Thursday nor in the early hours of the Friday but the village roadblock had been lifted with nothing to report. It was decided to compile a register of strangers and of travellers from afar who had visited the area recently. This was thought not to prove too difficult as travel documents were required to be shown on demand and, without such local authority, nobody was allowed more than three kilometres from his home without this written approval.

Vong and his men reached the saddle that evening, having made good time. They were exhausted. Dirty, sweaty, smelly, scratched, leech-bitten and hungry, they were in no state to do anything else but make crude shelters near the first running water they found to the north of the pass. During the day they had not heard the faint but persistent rumble of the heavily laden 'Hook' helicopters ferrying in troops to their north. Movement through jungle tends to drown extraneous noises, especially when movement is of a pace that does not allow the movers to stop and listen. It was because they had been so painstaking that no follow-up party went anywhere near their previous overnight camp near the river. Circumstances this time were not nearly so kind to them: despite efforts to hide themselves, not even the tired but fresher, cordon troops could fail to pick up their telltale signs when they reached the saddle the next day.

At dusk that Sunday, the man who had been yanked to his feet by Vong approached the house he had visited only a few days before when on the recon with his friend. He had no clear intention of what he wanted to do. He had blown off a considerable amount of pent-up steam but he still felt aggrieved enough not to make his way back to his family in Bouam Long, at least for a few days. As was normal, PL tactics decreed that a small group of soldiers would be billeted in houses, one house in ten being the average ratio, when any operation of this nature was mounted. It so happened that the house that the disgruntled man was making for had PL soldiers in it. The soldier on duty saw a man approaching furtively. He noticed that the man was not dressed in PL uniform, carried a US-made M-16 rifle – *captured or issued?* – and wore a pack. The soldier waited until he was almost at the door before challenging him. The man fired a round at his challenger, missed hitting him by a fraction and turned to make his escape. The PL man shot him, knocking him over. The noise of the two shots rang out deafeningly in the stillness, alerting everybody and soon there was a crowd of people peering at a travel-stained man, lying, wounded and bleeding, on the ground. The soldier's commander ran up and ordered that the wounded man be carried to the local clinic. On arrival he was unconscious. He died soon afterwards but did utter three indistinct words beforehand. Some who heard him thought he said *Vong* three times, others though *Long* was what he had tried to say. The doctor, a Vietnamese, thought he had either heard *Ông*, Vietnamese for 'mister' or *không*, Vietnamese for 'no'. Inmates of the house the dead man was trying to visit were so frightened that they admitted they knew he came from Bouam Long and that he had been in that area since 13 March. Luckily for the relatives, the man had not deviated from his story that he had come across with a hunting party which had stayed up in the mountains and allowed him and his friend to come down and visit those he had not seen for a long time. Not even some nasty heavy-handed stuff shook them from this story that had everything going against it.

When the report reached Office 95, Nga Sô Lưu felt it was odds on that the dead man was the person who had waved to the AN-2. *Such* a pity he was dead. Vong, Vong, Vong made no sense, neither did three Longs, three Ôngs nor, really, three Khôngs. He called for the file containing names of known operators working for the Vientiane side and, after some research, wondered whether the dying man had tried to say 'Ông Vong, Bouam Long' rather than 'Không Ông Vong,' 'No, not Mr. Vong.' In the event he plumped for 'Ông Vong, Bouam Long'; it would make real sense if there was someone named Vong, even if the word 'Bouam' was not mentioned.

In Bouam Long, the Garrison Commander was suffering from 'that Monday morning' feeling. He was getting worried. It was now nine days since he had sent his escort with that strange crew from Vientiane and there had been no radio contact. They could well be running short of food but he had less reason to be worried about that. They had only started out carrying seven days' rations but Major Vong had said that he had enough money to buy what was needed, although food in March was not all that plentiful. Two of the escort group had contacts in the general area of Ban Ban so he did not envisage any great problem there. No, he was far more worried about reports he had received about large helicopters flying near the pass in the high ground to his east. They could only mean one thing: whatever that secretive group had gone to do had turned sour. Just what he did not want. He had held great hopes that, if Bouam Long enclave was not targeted as hostile by the NVA high command or whoever it was who did not want to live in peace under their own system, methods and arrangements could be worked out, as they had been since time immemorial, with there being a better chance of preserving their society intact when this present uncertain phase finished. If the soldiers ferried in by these helicopters were going to invest the Bouam Long enclave, he would have to let Long Cheng know right away. General Vang Pao would be hopping mad. Could be though that they were cordon troops only intent on sealing off an area quickly. He shrugged and went into the warm radio room just in case and, looking over the operator's shoulder, saw him taking down a message from Vong.

Vong, that morning of Monday, 18 March, decided that it was time to send a message to Bouam Long. He reckoned that he was near enough to safety to break radio silence. He had heard that the Soviet Union had interceptor stations placed around parts of North Vietnam which could tune in on any particular frequency and, by some method or other that was, in practical terms, taking back bearings, the coordinates of the sender's position could be determined.

His men were, by now, reaching the end of their tether. Cajoling, exhorting, playing them along, Vong himself was finding the going hard. He told the executioner to take Mana on one side on some pretext or other and he gathered the others around him. They did not look an inspiring crew but, to date, they had done him proud.

'We're not far away now,' he told them. 'Should be back in base, home and dry, by tomorrow evening. Stick it out till then, fellows.'

He then told the radio operator to prepare his set while he drafted a message: 'ETA your location 1200 hours 19 March. Request arrangements for immediate evacuation of personnel. Hostile forces being infiltrated into general area. Request patrols alerted to help recover group'.

After sending his message, Vong urged more speed. Unluckily Mana Varamit, weary beyond belief, slipped and sprained his ankle. He had to be put on the stretcher and carried. Thus it was that, when the cordon troops reached the saddle at midday and spotted tracks leading towards the enclave, instead of being a day behind Vong's men, they were only five hours, although neither group knew it.

Brigadier General Etam had an impish sense of humour. He liked to repay people in the same coin as they had, so he thought, used against him. At 10 o'clock that Monday morning, he had received a message from Bouam Long, relayed by Long Cheng, requesting an aircraft the following day. The General put a call through to Mango and gave him the news contained in the message. Mango was delighted and, when he was also asked for a suitable plane – 'maybe a Beechcraft, you know, one of our small jobs' – not only said he could confirm it ASP – 'as soon as possible, General' – but that he would take the opportunity to go to Bouam Long himself as he owed the place a visit.

Mango got a call through to Udorn and a Pilatus Pilot was detailed but, with a fuel problem, it could only take four passengers out of Bouam Long. Any fifth passenger who flew in would have to wait for the 'milk run' on Thursday. Mango rang Etam and told him. Etam thanked Mango. Three passengers on the way out would be Tâ Tran Quán, Vong and the rescued agent– names in code already agreed on so that the more than insecure telephone line should not give away secrets – and the fourth would be Mango. Etam had not been told by Vong of Tâ's crazy decision and was, therefore, still in ignorance on that score. Etam grinned to himself and asked Mango if he didn't think that the British DA should be sent in as well? 'I'll offer him a seat, seeing that he knows the principal characters. You'd escort him, wouldn't you?'

'Sure thing, General. I'll pose for him as I'll pose for the rest of them.' This was an obvious precaution, in Mango's eyes, not to blow his cover which he fondly believed was still extant. 'Shall you or shall I tell him?'

'I'll tell him,' said the General. 'Comes better that way. What time?'

'Tell him to be at Wattay, Continental Airways counter, by 0730 hours sharp.'

General Etam put a phone call through to the British embassy and asked for the DA. '*Sabai di bor, Tan Colonen*?' he purred down the line. 'Are you free tomorrow to fly into Landing Site 32, being at Wattay Continental Airways at 0730 hours?'

Rance answered the greeting and said, 'Stand by one, if you will, General. I'll have to check my map and see where LS 32 is.' He left the phone on the table and had a look to see where the Landing Site was. 'Sorry to keep you waiting, General. Yes, indeed, I certainly would. Nice of you to think of asking me.'

'My pleasure, my dear *Colonen*. I'll ensure that there'll be a ticket waiting for you as well as an escort. I hope it won't prove to be a one-way journey.'

'I'm sure it won't, General. I'll feel safe with the escort you have arranged. Will it be a night stop? Plain clothes or uniform?'

'As a good soldier, *Tan Thud*, I am sure you always carry an overnight bag, and as your country's accredited representative, plain clothes would not be suitable.'

After thanking General Etam, Rance rang off. *Even though it is not normal to wear a ring with uniform, I'll wear it as a talisman. I may need a lot of luck*, he said to himself.

It was fortunate that the military commander who had been with the Political Commissar Tâ Tran Quán that fateful day in November 1972 was not far away in Sam Neua when the call came through asking for details of his whereabouts. He was sent for by runner and told to report to Defence Control without delay, with overnight kit. Anxious yet expectant, he went back with the runner. He was dressed ready for transfer anywhere, wearing battle equipment and carrying his weapon. Defence Control briefed him.

'You have been sent for by a senior comrade and a vehicle will take you to your destination, Office 95. You should be prepared to stay for as long as you are required though probably only one session will be necessary.'

'Comrade, do you know why I have been sent for?' the man asked.

'No, but I am sure it is nothing to be worried about. I don't know why you have been sent for except it is obviously more important for them rather than for you.'

The military man saluted, relieved to learn that it was not something heinous that he had done, got into the vehicle and drove away. At least it made a change!

At his destination, he reported in, told he was sent for by Nga Sô Lưu and straightaway was taken in front of the senior comrade.

'Thank you for coming so quickly, Comrade. I hope you weren't inconvenienced at the short notice.'

Such honeyed words from the hierarchy, and that particular man, were uncommon but not necessarily designed to disarm.

'Comrade Political Commissar, in no way is it an inconvenience. It is a pleasure to be of help to the Cause.'

Nga Sô Lưu drew an open folder on his desk closer to him and invited the soldier to be seated. 'Listen carefully, Comrade. I want you to try and remember every single detail that happened on Skyline Ridge on 18 November, 1972, when Comrade Tâ Tran Quán was killed although his body was never found to prove it.'

The military man nodded.

'First, tell me what you can remember of the Saturday,' continued the Political Commissar. 'No detail, however unimportant it might strike you, is to be omitted. Think carefully and, in your own time, recount the day's events. There is no hurry.'

The one-time company commander thought back to that

day, sixteen months ago exactly. The events and course of the battle were not easy to forget. He had been debriefed on them a number of times. If he was surprised that he was asked yet again, he hid his feelings. So, without too long a pause, he recounted everything that had happened, the Political Commissar nodding in agreement as he kept pace with events in the written report. *No, nothing new*, Nga Sô Lựu sadly thought.

He suddenly felt tired and, stifling a yawn, asked, more as routine than by conviction, if there was nothing else to mention? He could no longer control his yawn. He lifted his right hand to his mouth and tilted his head back slightly. Click: in the military man's mind, he focused on an event that had seemed so trivial, albeit bizarre, that he had never mentioned it, never considered it worthwhile.

'Yes, Comrade Political Commissar, I do remember something that I never reported as it seemed so insignificant and unconnected with the other events of that day. I hesitate to mention it now but since you've asked and since I remember it, mention it I will. It was during the T-28 strafing. Comrade Tâ Tran Quán and I both fell to the ground and got spattered with dirt. When we stood up, he looked thoughtfully at a large rìng on the little finger of his right hand, took it off, wiped it clean, but, instead of putting it back on, swallowed it.'

Vong heard the noise of soldiers behind him during the afternoon of the 18th. Handicapped as they were with Mana on the stretcher, they had made slow progress, despite the relays of men used to carry the crippled man. Vong made a lightening decision.

He called to the executioner and told him that the situation was desperate.

'We have only one hope: bluff. You and half the team will continue just as fast as you can towards Bouam Long. Myself and the other half will remain and try and bluff, or shoot, our way out. You need not worry too much about any noise you make, carrying or cutting. I emphasise two points – speed and, in the last resort, do not let Mana fall into their hands alive. That means that if he goes the way of all flesh, so do you.'

The executioner looked troubled but knew Vong well enough not to argue. Vong caught up the stretcher bearers and called to Mana, almost endearingly. 'Mana, Comrade Mana. How are you? Could you walk if you really tried? I hear the imperialist lackeys coming up behind us. I'll stay back with half our group and beat them off, one way or another. There won't be many of them. You and the others make best speed. I'll catch up with you before long. I'm sure we'll be able to manage.'

He rattled off some orders and, within seconds, they had formed two groups. Vong saw Mana's group move off then disappear in the undergrowth. The escort commander was with that group and, provided they met no other enemy, had a chance, a slim chance, of reaching Bouam Long by noon the next day. Vong's own group looked at him expectantly.

'Listen. Remember 335 Brigade and 886 Brigade. Likewise 135 Independent Battalion: the men on our tail are, I expect, 335 or 86 NVA. If so, we are of 135.'

He turned and strained his ears. 'They'll come down into view any moment now.' He had not been surprised at hearing the troops long before seeing them. Jungle craft was not a skill that was a high priority in either the NVA or PL forces.

'O-hé. O-hé. Are you comrades of 335 or 886? Steady as you come. We're in front of you, standing still on the track.'

An answering shout: '886. Wait, we're coming.'

Heads, then bodies, came into view. NVA soldiers, armed and wearing PL uniform. They approached warily but seeing that Vong was dressed as a cadre, stood by respectfully.

'Lucky I heard you in time. Listen. How many are you and how is it you are on my patch?'

This question disquieted them. As far as they were concerned, they were doing what was required of them – following up suspicious signs, signs that they had been alerted to expect, yet, when they caught up with the group they had been tracking, they were, in effect, told that they should not be there. They stared at each other.

'We are part of the force that was detailed to cordon this large feature. We reached the saddle last night and saw tracks. This morning we were told to follow them up and investigate. Our cadre felt that they could have been made by those who broke into and out of Ban Ban camp and burnt the comcen.'

'Then it is lucky that we met.' Vong gave a great sigh of relief. 'We are from 135 Independent and we moved up to this part of the jungle the day before yesterday. Have you met any more of us? No? I wonder why not. Could be because we're farther south than you. Not that that matters. My group also saw these tracks and, like you, followed them. Just caught them up when we heard you. Don't look so surprised. They are some of our oppressed comrades from the imperialist enclave at Bouam Long. I should have thought of it myself but I still hoped to catch those other bastards. If these people were the group we are all looking for, do you really think they would have been so careless to have walked like this, leaving so many signs? Gosh, I feel sorry for them but Liberation Day is not quite yet. I'll bet they can't wait to shake off the feudalists who are the imperialists' lackeys.'

The soldiers nodded agreement. 'Luckily for them,' continued Vong glibly, 'I checked them before opening fire. Never have done to have shot our comrades, eh? So oppressed are they that the villagers have to search for game and jungle produce to eat. This was a hunting expedition. One of them had twisted his ankle and was being helped back by his friends. You wouldn't think, as I said earlier, that any soldiers of any army, even those poor misguided fools of American stooges, would operate so clumsily. That's why I didn't fire. Just as well, as I'm sure you'll agree.'

The soldiers agreed. 'But,' continue Vong, keeping the conversational initiative so preventing any continued follow up after the other group, 'I am worried about that Ban Ban gang. Now I know they are definitely not on this ridge I'm going back to my unit. They'll be wondering what on earth has happened to us. As for you, how far back is your base?'

He breathed an inward sigh of relief when he learnt that there was a small HQ not far from the saddle at least two to three hours' walk away. 'Look, not that I can counter any orders you have been given but what I'm going to do is go back and send a radio message saying I've met you, report the village hunting party, tell them that the rest of this ridge is clear and ask for more instructions. I believe we'll find we've outstripped those traitors, whoever they are, and, from what I've picked up from our civilian comrades on the way up along the same trace as you presumably came up, we'll meet them tomorrow, bumping into them from the south. They'll have tried to outflank us by coming over point 7274 rather than round, like we've done. That surmise would only be true *if* you credit that this gang has even come this way. Personally, I rather doubt it.'

He paused to let that sink in. As there seemed to be no reaction against his surmise, he continued, 'Right? Understood? You go back. Tell your cadre you have had orders, no, let us say, suggestions, from' and here Vong had a brainwave, 'Comrade Nga Sô Lựu. Got it? Ask your cadre just how well he knows that name. Off you go, now. I'll have a fag and a rest then follow along later. If you don't see us, it's because I want to check that nobody has made a detour to our west. Warn your people to expect us when they see us but not to shoot.'

The NVA men were on the point of going back when one of them said, 'No. I don't believe you. We were given explicit orders that we would capture, or kill, anybody we met to our front. I am not convinced of the truth of your statement.'

Vong looked him up and down with imperious disdain. 'My man. You exceed your authority. I cannot accept what you say.'

'I cannot accept what you say either.' It seemed that an impasse had been reached. The last thing Vong wanted was for his bluff to turn sour. 'Let us sit down and talk this over. We've got to sort this out,' he said, turning to his group. 'Take your packs off, lads, and relax. We'll soon clear this up. Let's rest while we can.'

He looked at the man he knew best and winked at him. 'We have far enough to go to return to our units not to take advantage of this opportunity.' He turned back to the Viets. 'I'll write a letter to your commander and explain the situation.'

He sat down and, having taken his notebook out of his pocket, started to write. He did not take long. He put the notebook hack in his pocket and faced the sullen group of Vietnamese who awaited a positive move. 'What is wrong with my original plan, Comrade? Why do you not believe what I have told you? I challenge you in your effrontery. State your case.'

The man who had cast doubts on Vong's group spoke up with conviction. 'You are travel-stained and weary. You have been out in the open for much longer than since the start of the operation. And anyway, 135 are not committed in this sector. You're phony! I'll bet you anything you like you're phony.'

Vong stood up and looked at him. 'You poor fool,' he said condescendingly. 'I'll tell you if I'm phony. I'll go back with you and meet both your next senior military and political commanders. How about that?' He moved over to the centre of the group. 'I'll go with you now. In exchange for me, will you or one of your men go with my group? That will tell whether you are intent on making this an issue or not. Whether it is I who am phony or you.'

The man demurred: he was obviously taken aback by this turn of events. Vong gazed at him with loathing. 'I'll go back with you. Don't bother to give us anyone in return. You're wrong. Crazily wrong. Once this is sorted out, I will demand your severe punishment.' He turned to his own men. 'I'll be back in base tomorrow. I'll join you there. I'll go back with these people. I am bit tired. I am sure you can take my pack for me. I'll just take my pistol,' and he gave them a look which turned their blood cold but again they knew better than to argue.

Vong turned back to the Vietnamese soldiers. 'Come then. Get a move on. We've wasted enough time as it is. Get a move on, I said, blast your horrible eyes.'

The remnants of Vong's group watched their leader go, each with a lump in his throat. Vong's particular friend shook his head in disbelief then rasped out, 'If he can do this for us, we can do our best for him. Whatever the cost, we will catch up the rest of them tonight and reach Bouam Long just as early as we can tomorrow. We are living on borrowed time in this neck of the woods.'

Vong was weary unto death but the last thing, or almost the last thing, on earth he would have done was to show it. On the way back to the NVA forward base camp he made the patrol spend a lot of their time by leaving the main ridge wherever there were signs of a re-entrant below them on the pretext of looking for tracks of the alleged Ban Ban gang, and finding none. He was so insistent that they look everywhere that, before they knew it, they were benighted, so had to stay where they were.

On the morning of 19 March, Rance flew in the Pilatus Porter from Wattay to Long Cheng where the plane refuelled before taking a circuitous route north of the Plain of Jars before turning east, then south. Mango was also in the plane. Rance knew he must be a CIA man but did not know that he was Head of Station who would not normally expose himself to the risks of that particular journey. For his part, Mango was in no doubt who Rance was. Wisely they only talked pleasantries.

Mango was invaluable in sponsoring Rance through Long Cheng. General Vang Pao's orders were strict: no one he himself had not personally sponsored, except certain Americans, could go to Bouam Long. In his haste, General Etam had neglected to put a priority on his passenger list message and the signal, sent routine, arrived after the plane had taken off on its third and final lap to the enclave.

It was not until around 9 o'clock on the morning of the 19th that Vong and the Vietnamese patrol reached the base camp near the saddle to the north of point 7247. By then the man who had doubted him was thoroughly cowed. Once Vong had met the commanders, he demanded a meal, saying he was famished and that he would only talk after he had eaten. It took a valuable hour to prepare it and an equally valuable half hour to eat it and relax with a cigarette afterwards. By that time the doubting man had regained his confidence and, taking his superiors to one side, had told them of his suspicions. Vong was then closely cross-examined. He reckoned if he kept himself awake until noon, he had succeeded and the rest of his team would get to Bouam Long without further harassment. To the very end, he was painstaking as ever, not taking his luck for granted.

By noon the senior Vietnamese commander was almost convinced that Vong was a phony. Vong sensed his moment. 'Then send a message to higher formation. Send this,' and he took from his pocket the message he had written the previous day. As they started to read it, Vong turned to the political man and said, 'Don't ever believe your Lords and Masters, believe your own eyes,' and before the man could react, he quietly took his weapon, shot and killed the political man and, equally calmly and deliberately, took his own life. It was the way he had always planned: the setting could not have been better contrived.

When the immediate fuss had died down and the military commander had dealt with the two corpses, he once more studied the message. It was a strange and unsettling communication. It was addressed to Nga Sô Lửu at Office 95 and read, 'I kidnapped Tâ Tran Quán, brought him to Ban Ban and drugged him, the stupid, misguided dolt I met trying to re-establish his identity. I hope he suffered by my having convinced him he was a doctor. As for Mana Varamit, I let him escape. He will be repaid for his treachery. I brought your foolish soldiers on a successful wild-goose chase. As for me, rather than fall into your hands, I have chosen my moment. You will have yours chosen for you. A devotee of the rain drop.'

After they had landed at Bouam Long, Rance and Mango reported in to the Garrison Commander who told them that there was no more news since the message yesterday. The group was expected at any time. Patrols had been sent out to escort them in and to protect them if necessary. Mango took Rance to one side and told him that no debriefing of a certain Thai – *must be Mana Varamit* – would be allowed until he had been taken back to Thailand. The man was an unknown quantity as far as the intelligence boys were concerned and a certain amount of feedback could be got from Vong and Tâ Tran Quán. Rance answered in a noncommittal fashion, not letting on that the latter would not appear.

There was a shout from outside. 'Here they are, here they are.' Mango and Rance let the Garrison Commander go ahead to meet them. The group came into view, one man on a stretcher being closely watched by another, and the remainder trailing along behind. Even from that distance, it was obvious that they were ineffably weary. They seemed not to take any notice of the Garrison Commander as he went up to them. The escort commander blurted out, 'We're three short, we've been trailed but not followed since yesterday.'

Orders were given for the escort to bring the man on the stretcher over to the plane and the Garrison Commander beckoned to Mango and Rance to join him. They noticed a worried look on his face. 'There have been casualties,' he told them.

On the stretcher, Mana had been looking around him in utter disbelief. *Why aren't the comrades welcoming me back? Surely, surely I am not in the midst of the wrong lot?* His stretcher had been put on the ground and, as Mana lay on it considering his next move, his eyes fell on Rance. Rance saw him at the same time. *So that blasted Englishman is behind this?* At that same moment, Mana noticed Rance's ring and, in blind rage, jumped up, shouting loudly, 'So you've still got it. I'll kill you for this, kill you with my bare hands,' and, forgetting his own badly swollen ankle, made a desperate lunge at the Englishman. The executioner saw Mana leap into the air and, as he landed within striking distance of Rance, tripped him up. Mana fell heavily on his injured foot, overbalanced and fell to the ground with a scream, badly bumping his head on a stone. He lay there, confused and seething, once more badly disorientated and mentally out of kilter.

The executioner said to them, 'The quicker you can get his man back out of here, the better. I've just about had enough of him and the whole crazy business. When can we leave?' He bent down and hoicked Mana roughly onto the stretcher. 'Stay there, you fool,' he said harshly to the gibbering man. 'We'll take you back to where you belong.'

Mango took charge of the situation and told the Garrison Commander to take Mana away under a strong guard, give him something to eat and be ready to move not later than twenty minutes. Turning to Rance, he told him it would be unwise to travel back on the same plane as Mana and that he would have to wait for the milk-run on Thursday. As they led Mana away under escort, the American was already fixing details of restraints on the way back.

Mana's parting shot at Rance was, 'If I am going to be expendable, so are you.'

Nga Sô Lưu waited impatiently as the search fizzled out. He had had news of the mystery of the crazed man, the Political Commissar's tragic death and the enigmatic message. He realised that his leaning towards Bouam Long was still more based on a hunch than any hard and fast evidence. The death of the message sender was, at least, something he could justify his insistence in mounting the operation. The finger of scorn had not been pointed at him but more than one crazed suicide was needed to justify the effort expended. It was certainly not the work of just one man. The perpetrators had vanished into thin air. The doctors' report on the three men was the only optimistic point there was: Tâ Tran Quán was suffering from nothing worse than a mental breakdown caused by worry. He needed rest and was to be left alone for a month when he should be completely fit again. If he had any friends, it would be well worthwhile getting them to meet up. As for the others, the CO and the Political Commissar had obviously been duped as well as doped and the Deputy was only a case of mild nervous tension exacerbated by intense but localised worry. Nga Sô Lưu would get his inquisitors to prepare a detailed report, maybe in a week's time.

Until then … he picked up Thong's report. Clever ferreting, that. He would call him up in a day or two to see Comrade Tâ. But he was worried about that extraordinary ring-swallowing act. Was his mind ever so slightly unhinged, even then? Probably was, so it wasn't so surprising that he had suffered a mental breakdown recently.

He once more read the Vietnamese rendering, not the Thai version, of Mana Varamit's report, which was plain and straightforward, except the allusion to the four days. That did not make sense. He could not have been referring to the recent four-day chase. How could he? Nga Sô Lưu then called for the report Mana had sent, not the translation, and for a Thai translator. It could be that the solution to the mystery lay there.

The translator reported in and Nga Sô Lưu went straight to

the point. 'Translate this part, will you?' he said, pointing to the offending references. The translator studied it carefully.

'I don't believe that the translation of 'day' is correct. I believe a Lao translator prepared this report, not a native Thai speaker. I see how the critical word, *ven*, has taken a meaning of 'day' which is more usually rendered by '*van*' and *wan* in Thai. *Ven*, meaning a day, has a different, shorter, *e* from the other *ven*, which has a longer *e*.'

'And what does that mean, Comrade,' asked Nga Sô Lựu, impatient at the man's pedantry.

'"Four rings", Comrade, not "four days". I hope that helps you.'

The Political Commissar thanked him and dismissed him. He himself sat silently in his chair. The coincidence, always presuming that the military man was correct and he could not have made a mistake, surely? The coincidence of Tâ Tran Quán swallowing a ring was one that needed more than normal careful thought and even more careful handling. If that was a code name for four people, who were they? Just suppose, was it just possible though far from likely, but just suppose that Tâ Tran Quán was one Ring, then who were the other three? No, the thought was too fantastic to contemplate, and yet … and yet …

He could not afford to be wrong. He would not only be the laughing stock of the Party but would also do himself irreparable harm. He would try and find out more about it, checking leads, following clues and using Tâ as his henchman. He would double check everything that Tâ did and, if his blackest and worst fears were realised, he would try and manoeuvre a conference where he would expose each and every one of the four – at one fell swoop. They might even make him Secretary-General of the Party. Wait until the take over: it was not so long for the almost magical thirty-year target. Get it done in Vientiane. A pity he could not involved that vacuous Englishman, that expendable self-satisfied, imperialist lackey …

He made up his mind with savage intensity.

6

January-March 1975: On the surface, 1975 was ushered in as traditionally normal with national leaders uttering pious platitudes about it being a time to take stock or to turn a new leaf or to redouble revolutionary efforts or whatever the national theme happened to be. To a casual observer nothing much had changed from before. But changes, some not yet due and others overdue, were certainly in the air. Yet, as the Indo-China war entered its thirtieth year, there was a sense of expectancy and urgency in some quarters, resignation and lethargy in others, with almost everywhere a feeling that this thirtieth year, come what may, come something would.

Communists may be inefficient but they can be doggedly thorough. After the Ban Ban findings proved inconclusive and neither that incident nor the killings in the jungle follow-up had been properly explained, confirmation of Nga Sô Lựu's nagging suspicion of a counter-revolutionary group calling itself the Four Rings had remained as elusive as ever. The Politburo had in no way suggested that Lựu had neglected his duty or any reasonable precaution although there had been a hint that he might have over-reacted. He had, therefore, kept his Four Rings fear to himself, angry beyond belief that the initiative had been wrested from him by unseen hands and unknown heads. Mana Varamit's disappearance was still a mystery, as indeed was Tâ Tran Quán's reappearance, but efforts to find the Thai, dead or alive, inside Laos or, perish the thought, abroad, simply had to be made. There were so many other aspects of their revolutionary struggle in Laos that he could well have done without this business. Even monitoring Tâ Tran Quán's progress would take much effort as he was loth to take anybody else into his confidence ... yet. So, while those unfortunates in and around Ban Ban who had defaulted through ignorance or inefficiency were being duly chastised, he bent his mind how best to extend his inquiries, furtively and obscurely, far and wide, into both zones, knowing full well that those who organise such activities do so months, if not years, in advance of any operation and at a safe distance from the scene of action. He had drawn up a highly confidential letter addressed personally to individual cadres making each one search his mind and let him know of anyone, of cadre rank, who had ever contacted a foreigner, even for a few minutes, without any other comrade being present or, if one were, not being able to hear what was being said. He had added a note to his draft to the effect that this information, sent and accepted in confidence, was needed the better to react to the expected change in the political situation which was certain to demand an even greater sensitivity that before. He had also drafted another letter which required relevant local agents to recheck their records of movements within Laos of foreigners, Asians included, to see if any insignificant fact had escaped them. This would take some time as the list embraced such people as domestic servants, watchmen of embassies, telephone operators, sub-agents in bars and brothels, not forgetting the man who monitored movements at the Phou Si Hotel at Luang Prabang, and Air America along with Continental Airways.

The Black-eyed Butcher had then called in his confidential secretary and shown him the two drafts. After reading them, he turned to Lưu and asked if the Soviet bloc and the Chinese were to be included amongst those targeted.

'Send our Soviet comrades a copy of each directive. I'll draft a covering letter asking for their cooperation. Don't bother about our Chinese comrades. Thank you for mentioning them. I'll exclude them from the Asians who have to be checked.'

'This will take some time and the rainy season is not far off. By when do you want these reports, including 'nil returns', to reach Office 95?'

'By the last day of 1975. And ask people to start from,' he paused as he thought of Mana's and Tâ's fateful misfortune on Skyline Ridge, '18 November, 1972.'

After dismissing his secretary, he concentrated on how best to run Mana to earth if he was still alive, as, in the heart of his heart, he felt he was.

In the American military hospital in Utapao, southern Thailand, situated alongside the Joint Casualty Resolution Centre – to resolve, hence the odd name, the fate of missing US servicemen – and adjacent to the same large complex at Sattahip where the USAF had its B-52s, F-111s and U-2s, the brain surgeon looked down at his patient, Mana Varamit, pleased with what he saw. It was a New Year social call more than a medical check up. Considerable therapeutic treatment had been administered over the past nine months, sympathetically applied, skilfully handled and sensibly controlled. The surgeon had a job to do in the unfamiliarly named centre where, in a macabre fashion, the grisly remains of the few sad unidentified American corpses, only forty-five in two years from the Indo-China war, were analysed to see if they could be identified. And now, looking down on a smiling Mana, the brain surgeon recalled when he had been brought in. An unusual case, he had been informed at the outset of his task of rehabilitation: an agent on the run from Communist-held Laos, suffering from loss of memory as the result of a head injury who, hopefully, held the key to many sensitive and unsolved matters were he normal. That the man had suffered physical hardship was obvious from even a cursory glance: sore feet, scratched arms, insect bites and physically weak with an emaciated frame, let alone a villainous scowl, disjointed speech and hostile attitude. Two constraints had been placed on the surgeon, one of complete secrecy and the other of the most careful screening before anyone was allowed to visit or even guard him. The surgeon, a Thai trained in USA, understood the need for such precautions so had not questioned them nor did he inquire too closely into the background of his patient. He had given instructions that first day and gone back to his office where the man who had escorted the sick man from Vientiane was waiting for him.

'I have ordered complete rest, sedation, light diet and some medication to build him up. Watch and ward must be unobtrusive and visitors as infrequent as possible. I will watch him closely. It is far too early to give any opinion on his chances of recovery.

Don't worry, though. I'll keep you posted as I gather you're most interested in him.'

Ed Murray, the other man, nodded his assent. Listed in the US embassy in Bangkok as a Cultural Attaché, he was one of the select group of men who already had full knowledge of the case. He had a difficult and delicate mission which needed the surgeon's permission to be fulfilled. 'Sure, Doc, I understand. Right now I and my colleagues wish to express our thanks for the trouble you're taking in this case and sincerely hope you will have success. I would like to ask you a couple of questions if you don't mind. Can you spare the time?'

'Go ahead. I understand that you have more than a passing interest in my patient.'

'Can you see yourself using psychiatric methods during the cure you'll be prescribing?'

'Most probably yes but the depth, frequency and severity I'll be applying are unknown factors at the moment.'

'Sure, sure. During this stage will you be giving any sort of drug like, for instance, Pentothal, to help him lose his inhibitions?'

The surgeon eyed his visitor narrowly. 'I won't commit myself in that sphere either. I have yet to discover what part of the brain has been affected. Maybe yes, maybe no. Why?'

'Because if you do, I have been tasked to request you see a man of, shall we say, security choice who could be properly briefed rather than a medical man who might be a security risk. I'm referring to the man you'll need to help you administer the drug.'

'On the face of it, yes, but don't rush me. I'll let you know when I'm ready.'

That had been nine months previously: at first the surgeon had found his charge recalcitrant. Most war-wounded Americans were flown back to the States so the hospital at Utapao was not ideally equipped to handle really complicated cases. But the brain surgeon persevered. During the first session of therapeutic treatment, the surgeon had been startled by the extent of knowledge revealed by his patient. Much of what he had blurted out during their talks, with his volubility induced by Pentothal even though Ed Murray was not present at that session, did not make sense. It was as though Mana was talking in code: the hints, inferences, gestures were of such intensity that only a similarly placed initiate could comprehend their meanings. The surgeon had then decided to call the man from the embassy. He rang through to Bangkok and was re-established contact. The Cultural Attaché had been warned that Mana's recovery would be slow. 'I find it strange that one name he had uttered seems to be that of an Englishman, somebody named Rance. Does that ring any bell with you?'

'Why yes, Doctor, actually it does. The fellow he's referring to is the British Defence Attaché up in Vientiane. I've heard a lot about this guy although I've not met him,' he dissembled, 'but I do know it so happens that he and Mana have met before. This man Rance used to run the British Army's Jungle Warfare School down in Malaysia and visited Thailand once or twice. Do you advise a meeting if it can be arranged?'

The upshot was that a meeting was planned. It had been on the cards for some time that the Americans would invite the Vientiane attaché corps, less Communist country representatives, to Sattahip to the Joint Casualty Resolution Centre so that they could understand the American effort to resolve the fate of missing US servicemen and use that knowledge in an effort, however forlorn, to influence friends of the Hanoi government, if not the North Vietnamese themselves, as to the sincerity of American purpose in trying to locate and recover their war dead and their prisoners in Vietnamese hands. An invitation, at short notice, was extended to the attaché corps to visit the Centre, flying there and back the same day. The British, Australian, French, Filipino, Thai and Khmer Attachés accepted, the remainder declined.

At the same time as this was being arranged, Mango had had a message from Head of Station Bangkok to contact his British counterpart and have a meeting with him and Rance. Only outline points were mentioned. Accordingly, Mango and Gordon Parks, who had frequent and regular contact, fixed up a threesome. Mango was glad anything to do with Mana was to be conducted well away from Laos. His first meeting with General Etam after Mana's snatch had been frigid to say the least of it. Rance had already been alerted by Colonel Gurganus of the trip south so presumed it was something to do with this visit that the meeting had been called. Mango gave details: first the background, then the present situation.

'Your one-time student, Major Mana Varamit, now undergoing treatment in Bangkok, has been talking about you.' He glanced at Rance who remained impassive. 'It seems that he's been put under sedation and then some psychiatric drugs administered which have resulted in your name being uttered. Would you be willing to talk to him and try to help him unravel his hang-up?'

There was a pause, quite a long one, as Rance's mind flashed back to Mana's state when they had met in Bouam Long. The Englishman had been deeply troubled by Vong's non-arrival and Mana's unbalanced animal fury. He felt no worry about reprisals, only an overwhelming sadness at the endless futility of man's hatred of man. He was reminded of the way ants fight to the death when two lots of them met, predators both. Standing with Olympian stature above them, they were so small and insignificant yet so terribly engrossed with each others' destruction, even at that tiny, insignificant level. As for men ... He had been allowed in at the initial debriefing of the escort commander and had followed the course of events, adding details in his mind's eye from his own experiences. He particularly liked the professional standard of jungle lore displayed on their way back. Vong would have made an excellent instructor at the Jungle Warfare School. He sincerely hoped Tâ Tran Quán had managed his re-infiltration successfully and safely but he was not optimistic. As for Vong, the escort commander firmly believed he was dead, but, with no proof, confirmation was impossible. He, Rance, would probably never know what really did happen. The concern he had felt then flickered momentarily on his face and did not pass unnoticed by Mango and Parks.

Rance came back to the present and cleared his throat. 'Sure. Of course I would. I only hope I can be adequate.'

'Well, there'll be a Thai brain surgeon there and a representative of my push to help guide the conversation and you if necessary.'

It was arranged that Rance would go with the visiting

Attachés and pretend to be under the weather during the lunch break. The other Attachés would be taken on a more general tour of the establishment while Rance would be offered a place to rest until the plane was due to return. If he hadn't finished with Mana, they'd keep him overnight and fly him back the next day. His absence could easily be explained to the others and his departure from Vientiane would be accounted for without any pretext.

Rance thought for a moment. 'I can slip a toothbrush into my pocket and get a shave down there if I have to make a night stop. Seems simple enough.'

The interview with Mana had to be stage-managed to the extent that Rance would not be visible to him to begin with. The surgeon had started his preparations around half past 12. Lunch was over by 1 o'clock and the visitors were sitting around coffee and liqueurs. Rance asked where the rest room was and, on his way over, told the conducting officer that he was feeling queasy and might ask to be excused the afternoon part of the programme. Regret was expressed and, once outside the room, met up with the man Mango had described – 'He'll call himself Ed' – and was taken to the hospital where he was ushered into Mana's private ward. The Thai surgeon, holding Mana's hand, was sitting on a chair by the bed. A hypodermic syringe, administered by an orderly, was stuck into his arm, just above the wrist. The surgeon gestured to Rance to sit on a chair on the other side of the bed. Mana's eyes were shut.

'Mana. Major Mana Varamit. Remember Lieutenant Colonel Rance? You must think of Rance ... Rance the Englishman ... Call for him ... Ask for him ... He may come this time and help you,' droned the surgeon as though he were incanting a ritual.

Mana stirred. An expression of pugnacity appeared on his face. A fraction of pressure was applied on the hypodermic needle and his expression softened. A tear welled in each eye and trickled down his cheeks. '*Tan Phan To Phou Banchakan* ...' Lieutenant Colonel, Commandant ...

Rance took his clue from the surgeon and answered softly, '*Sawadi Tan Phan Tri Mana. Sabai di, rü*'? Welcome Major Mana. How are you? 'Here I am, Lieutenant Colonel Rance, Commandant of the Jungle Warfare School. You are here as my Guiding Officer for the Thai students. You are in my office. What do you want to tell me?'

'I want to talk to you alone. Let's go into the jungle. There are too many people nearby. Le Dâng Khoã may overhear me. He wants to kill me. I saw him pick his ring up and give it to you. If you meet me in the jungle, Sergeant Major Prachan Pimparyon can guard us. He can keep Le Dâng Khoã away till we're ready for him. He also saw him give it to you.'

'Right. We can go right away. We're now at the bottom of the hill, on the road by the helicopters. The football pitch is over on our right. Do you recognise it?'

Another tear well up. 'Yes, I do. This is too open. Let's go into the jungle.'

'We'll move on. Out of the camp, along the road, up a track, out of the truck, into the jungle but it is only secondary.' Rance shot a glance at the surgeon who indicated him to keep talking. 'We've arrived at last, in thick jungle and we're off the track. The others are still re-organising after the final attack. Le Dâng Khoã is far away. Sergeant Major Prachan is guarding us. What do you want to tell me? Tell me now, Major.'

'Le Dâng Khoã gave you his ring. He is one of the four. He knows I know ... I've got to stop him ...' as the man was talking Rance's mind was fixed on that tense scene enacted on that near-calamitous occasion. *So Mana had crept back unobserved!* '... I've got to stop him and the other three. I've got to get word of them back to Office 95. I'm pressed for time.'

'Don't worry, Major. You're safe here in the jungle. No one can get you. You're safe here and now, also. You're safe everywhere. You know I'm your friend. Le Dâng Khoã gave me his ring. I'm like the other three. We know each other. We're friends. I still have it. Le Dâng Khoã hasn't got it any more so there's no need to kill him or Tâ Tran Quán or Thong Damdouane or Bounphong Sunthorn. Think back, think back ... You can now trust me and them. When did it start? You should never have left the wat all those long years ago. The others waited for you, five fathers, five sons. The abbot wondered where you went. He waited for you, Mana. You were taken away by someone else who didn't want you to have a ring. Didn't want you to *kha*, to kill, them like the others. Can you remember, Mana. Try, try. You're only a small boy,' and Rance hummed a popular Thai lullaby, crooning gently. He was sweating, even though the temperature was air-cooled. Mana seemed smoothed. He wept.

Grotesquely, in a feeble falsetto, he said, 'Great Teacher, why did they burn the village? I didn't understand them. Where's my father? I'm lost. And my younger brother? Dad said he'd gone away. 'With one of you I've got both, you're so alike,' he used to say. The other four boys are against me ...' and he broke off, sobbing shrilly.

The effort was tiring him. The surgeon gestured to Rance not keep to keep on much longer. Rance said, 'Mana, my child. Great Teacher is your friend. He forgives you. He is your new father, I am your new brother. We forgive you: come and be ours again.'

The surgeon held up his hand and silenced Rance. 'Sleep my child,' he crooned, 'sleep my boy. You're forgiven, you're free, you're ours once more. Sleep ... sleep ... sleep,' and he motioned to the medical orderly. The syringe was gently pressed then withdrawn. Mana's head lolled on the pillow and a swab wiped the puncture. The session was over. Rance stood up, went over to the washbasin and swilled his face with cold water. He felt whacked.

Outside in the corridor, the surgeon said, 'That was great stuff. Tremendous. Come to my office, both of you, for a coffee.' Once seated, he continued, 'Colonel, I guess you've missed your vocation. My congratulations.' Ed Murray joined in with his praise.

'Thank you, Doctor and Ed, for those kind words. Luckily for me, I've been involved with this sort of problem before with my Gurkhas. It's tiring work. What's next, after another cup of this delicious brew?' He glanced at his watch. 'Only 2.15! Seems more like midnight ...'

... Rance returned with the visitors, looking drawn enough to give credence to the earlier lie. The Cultural Attaché had thanked him and departed. Mana had slept right through the night and his cure had started from that time in a remarkable way.

Rance's visit had worked wonders ... and now, on New Year's Day, 1975, the Cultural Attaché greeted a nearly cured and sane Mana affectionately.

'Not your new year but a Farang one, nevertheless I greet you on this, for foreigners, auspicious occasion. How do you feel. Had your exercise for today, I suppose?'

'Yes, thanks. I'm feeling great. I've been thinking a lot recently. So many of my thoughts are like bad dreams but I always wake up safe and sound here. I wonder how long you'll be keeping he here for. I am quite happy, reading and the way you let me help with work in the wards is really interesting. As you know, I still get tired quite easily. I haven't had such an idle life for a long time. Can't remember when! I really like it here. It's become almost like home to me. My own home life was never one I care to remember, not that I can recall much of it clearly.'

'Well, I'm delighted to hear you are feeling so much better. I want you under my care for a little while longer. Don't fret. What I now want is for you to have enough training here so that you can have something to turn you hand to when you are finally discharged. You may have difficulty in being re-employed by the Royal Thai Army.'

Mana seemed to accept that. 'You know, one person I'd like to meet some time is a Lieutenant Colonel Rance. I met him in Malaysia. I had, I seem to remember, a most vivid dream about him wearing a ring. Seems a silly sort of dream but it conjures up vague recollections I'd like to sort out. I heard he was posted to Vientiane. When I get better and go back to Bangkok, I'd like to get in touch with him if possible. Haven't seen him since

Malaysian days. He was boss of the British jungle school. Do you know him?'

Nga Sô Lưu took the massive sheaf of papers from his secretary. It was composed of a number of separately-tied files. 'How much have you culled?' he asked.

'Comrade, I have divided various differing categories into separate files. For instance, I have put those with nothing to report in the file at the bottom of the pile. I have also made out a check sheet of our cadres which you may find useful. The top file, so marked on the cover, concerns reports about cadres who have had contact with non-Asian imperialists. The second file, those with Asian imperialists and feudalists, and so on. Each file is marked and there is a contents sheet under the cadres' check sheet. I felt that that was the least I could do to help.'

Nga Sô Lưu smiled a tired smile. 'Comrade, you are thoughtful and diligent. I think I need one more list if it's not here already. I need the record of everywhere the British Beaver aircraft has been since that sightseeing Englishman has been in Laos and where he has been with the imperialist Americans. Not that that will produce anything but it will complete our data. You can prepare one from your records?' An affirmative nod. 'Good man. I wish there were more like you, Comrade. Thank you.'

The secretary took his leave and Nga Sô Lưu settled down to a task that took him longer than he had expected. As he laboured on, then and on subsequent nights, a glow of expectancy took the place of nagging suspicion and that, in turn, was superseded by the thrill of the chase to come. His inscrutably dark, glassy eyes, blacker than a starless night, gleamed with anticipation.

Nga Sô Lưu worked his way patiently through the files, making a short list of people who particularly interested him. He started with Tâ Tran Quán on 18 November, 1972, wounded on Skyline Ridge. He then looked down the list of Rance's movements. A visit to Long Cheng. Same area! Coincidence? Rance had only been in the country for, he checked another list, three days – since the previous Wednesday evening. Hardly time. Tâ Tran Quán's time in Vientiane was only sketchily known but there could have been a time, just one day it would seem, when Tâ Tran Quán, Vong and Rance were together. Rather cleverly, he'd worked that out from an agent in the Saigon-regime pseudo-embassy. And Vong had not been seen since about the time of Mana's disappearance and Tâ Tran Quán's arrival in Ban Ban. Then there was that report from Silver City – ridiculous name – of a probable meeting of Tâ Tran Quán and Rance. Three times Tâ Tran Quán and the Englishman together. A little far-fetched at first glance but …?

He then turned his attention to Thong Damdouane. In this case it seemed unlikely that Thong had really had a chance of talking separately to a non-Asian imperialist but – once again – he did escort Rance alone to the gate of the Luang Prabang office and he sat at the back on the British aircraft on the way to Sam Neua. Rance was the military representative of the Co-Chairman, so neither occasion need be suspicious. Need be, could be: he knew enough about flying in light aircraft to know that a headset, when on internal or telephone, circuit could be heard by the others who were wearing headsets and also by the pilot. But just suppose an alteration, an unofficial modification, had been made, it would be relatively easy to talk without interfering with the pilot. He would get the military commander who flew that time to render a report on that side of the business and he'd get one of his Vientiane-based men to check if there had been any tampering with two pairs of headsets. And if there had been …

Le Dâng Khoã was a different matter: he and Mana were together at the British Army's Jungle Warfare School under Colonel Rance. Pity, in a way, those two had clashed. Certainly Rance could not have had anything to do with either of them. There was no report of Le Dâng Khoã meeting Rance anywhere alone – but wait. 'Believed sat together, briefly, during an LPF film show in the Vientiane HQ'. Then there were the other two reports from that place. One from Bounphong Sunthorn saying he believed Soth Petrasy had had a talk with Rance a few days before his own arrival from Sam Neua and also from Soth, equally inconclusive, but saying Bounphong was with Rance for a minute or two while when he, Soth, answered the telephone and Bounphong fainted, then even later for a brief moment after that 'coup manqué'. There had been a third occasion when Bounphong went around some residences on the eve of the initial arrival of LPF representatives in Vientiane on Thursday, 11 October, 1973, to gather support for welcoming them. The driver had confirmed that Bounphong had entered Rance's villa as he turned the car around in the drive. Yet another occasion was on the night of the party Rance held when it was discovered that Bounphong and Leuam were brothers. Office 95 had already had that report but the fact the Bounphong and Rance were just a bit late in coming into the house only now emerged. Nga Sô Lựu checked further but found nothing that excited his attention. An unresolved nag gnawed somewhere inside his brain but he couldn't place it.

He checked the other reports: nothing from the Soviet comrades, nothing from the bars and the brothels, nothing from … nothing? The man at the Phou Si rotunda had said he remembered Rance and Leuam in conversation one day. He hadn't mentioned it at the time as it had only occurred to him later and he had dismissed it as being of no importance. He recalled overhearing 'Great Master' being said but as Rance had told him they were going out as tourists, he had doubted it having any significance apart from referring to the Chief Bonze. Having remembered that there was something else that might, just, be of interest. After he and Leuam had come back to the hotel, the Englishman had taken a ring off his right hand, the little finger, and said, 'now that's over, I can take this off.' However, as the letter from Office 95 had been so explicitly insistent, he had forwarded the information.

So there were the names of four of the most trusted comrades, disturbing but not damning: did they have anything in common amongst themselves, other than a devotion to the Cause? And how on earth could they have anything in common with Rance? He seemed an innocuous man though obviously steeped in military colonialism with imperial tendencies. The Soviet comrades had him pretty well summed up: surface-skating, and facile after an initial impression of depth and deliberation – but, even so, a remarkable linguist and 'good with people'.

As Nga Sô Lựu considered the enormity of the situation were his suspicions ever to be proven, his thoughts went back to the name he believed Mana had been hinting at – Four Rings. Just say the four comrades he had been considering were those rings: Tâ Tran Quán was reported by the tactical military commander as swallowing a ring – was that to hide it? Rings were commonly worn by men. Was this just a code name? If not, were there four rings of the same pattern that had an esoteric bond? He felt his own little finger, stroking it as though turning a ring that was on it ... and then the nag in his mind cleared. He remembered being exasperated during one seminar he had held quite a while back when Comrade Bounphong did just that as he was doing now with his own finger. Well, well, well. And Comrade Thong over with the Chinese comrades near Route 46 on a short liaison visit? Had he behaved similarly? He'd have to find out, easy enough to. Then did the fourth comrade he was thinking about have a ring as the other three did? If Le Dâng Khoã did not have one, was the link one of his own imagination: if he did, was it pure coincidence? If only Mana had not disappeared. Vexing, not to have had any word of him yet. He had not returned to any of his old haunts. Nga Sô Lưu fought down his impatience as pieces of his jigsaw puzzle refused to fit: Mana's disappearance ... four dedicated comrades ... Rance, meddler or manipulator? ... Chief Bonze ... until he could determine any common link between them, he'd bide his time ... and what sort of ring did that damned Englishman take off his finger? It would be much too far-fetched even to think that that was the ring that Le Dâng Khoã might have worn. No, damn it, even such a travesty could never happen.

He'd also have to establish a motive, if indeed his fears proved real. He could not afford to make a mistake, it would backfire too painfully. Meanwhile, he would plan for his small cell in Vientiane, based on the LPF contingent there, to be reinforced by some of his own men. The Protocols didn't allow any increase in strength but they were way over the top already, so a few more wouldn't matter. Nothing mattered except total victory ... he ground his teeth as he contemplated the scene but he'd tell no one, no one at all, until the final exposure. He turned his attention to other matters ...

By the end of February, the surgeon treating Mana made a telephone call to a number in the US embassy in Bangkok and left a message for the Cultural Attaché that his charge was nearly, if not completely, cured and that he, the brain surgeon, wanted to carry out an experiment before he could give a definitive decision about his patient. He had to go to Bangkok for a few days sometime and he wondered if Rance could be got hold of. His patient had expressed a desire to see him and had even mentioned some dream about a ring. The experiment that the surgeon wanted to carry out was to let Mana meet Rance, talk with him and observe his reactions. Could the man taking the message please get the Cultural Attaché to arrange this? Once Rance had accepted this invitation, other details could be fixed. It would do his patient good to have a change of scenery and the Colonel had been so successful last time.

A week after the telephone call to the US embassy in Bangkok, the joint Anglo-American team that was responsible for targeting activities in sympathy with 'Operation Four Rings' met in the annex of the US embassy in Grosvenor Square, London, W 1. General Sir David Law opened proceedings by giving a resume of activities since Mana was snatched and Tâ Tran Quán restored into the Communist system. He also, for the benefit of those who might not have heard, asked Ed Murray to go through the session he had had with the surgeon, Mana and Rance at Utapao. It made a good story. Ed Murray then told the group about the Thai surgeon's latest request involving Mana and the British DA. Before any comments or ideas were asked for, Bill Hodges asked if could make an announcement that might, possibly, influence further discussion: Gordon Parks was to be posted back to London and his relief would be John Chambers. It was, in fact, a straight swap. Heads nodded with approval and the General added that Rance would be receiving notification in the near future of the Defence Intelligence Directorate's plan to extend him in post even further from the eight months already granted. October 1975 was the new date and even that was not sacrosanct.

The two Desk Officers, Maurice Burke and John Chambers, gave their opinion as to how long the South Vietnamese and the Lon Nol government troops in the Khmer Republic could withstand NVA pressure and October-November 1975 was the declared assessment. Others were more optimistic. The General then spoke on how the British government regarded the situation and, based on Rance's latest report, didn't query the timing mentioned but spoke of the lowering of RLA morale to such a point that were a sudden Communist push be made, it would be a virtual walk-over.

It was just before they broke up that the General voiced the feelings of those present. ' I only hope to goodness, Gentlemen, that we are going to gain something out of this extraordinary situation. I am loth to risk compromising either organisation, intelligence or military, but feel we simply must take advantage of any opportunity that might present itself. For that reason, I am going to write to Colonel Rance and tell that he may, if he thinks he can handle it, visit Mana. If you,' turning to Ed Murray, 'can arrange for John Chambers to be there also, so much the better. Every effort must be made to follow any lead Mana might give. We here are sensible to the constraints we have had placed on us about taking any overt action but if John and Ed's boys could help nudge some situation to our benefit, we might help Rance in his "unconscious" role.'

After the meeting, the General buttonholed John Chambers and took him to one side. 'We have only one way out. I will alert the only man I know who can help us: Charlie. Listen to this ...'

The next week's mail brought two letters for Rance. One, from General Law, briefly stated that Rance would be asked to go to Bangkok to meet Mana. If Rance felt that it was the wrong thing to do, he would have the discretion to decline. Whilst in Bangkok, he would meet up with John Chambers, Gordon Parks' relief, who would be with him during any session he might have with Mana and, as a completely separate issue, to link up with Charlie to review the general situation. As the Rance-Mana meeting was not certain, and on the need-to-know principle, it had been decided not to mention Mana to Charlie. The letter closed with a hint of what the second letter contained, namely that his time as Defence Attaché would be further extended 'in the exigencies of the service', using a word that Rance had never come across except in the context of the army and postings.

Nga Sô Lừu sighed with satisfaction, something he rarely did. Odd, he mused, that despite every precaution, check, balance and counter-check, aberrations in the system could flourish unnoticed until some totally unconnected event happened that brought them into the light. He believed that he had the Four Rings in his sights. He believed he had their motive and he also believed he had Rance's connection. He chided himself for being slow, for allowing apparent political intensity to act as a smoke screen. What had made him slower than was customary was that the two Tâ Lang men had obvious Vietnamese names, Le Dâng Khoã and Tâ Tran Quán. What he would have to do was to send a messenger to the wat at Sam Neua and see if there was, in fact, any record of their original names. He had enough time as, although he had a tenable hypothesis, he lacked both proof and convincing evidence that, indeed, the four suspects were enemies of the party, the Cause and the body politic. He foresaw a grand finale when he would arraign all four together and at the same time, to their surprise. In front of judge, jury and assembled comrades, he would expose them to the rest of the Communist world for the traitors they undoubtedly were. He would have to stage-manage it most carefully but stage-manage it he would. He even gave it a name: 'Operation Four Rings'.

Nga Sô Lừu had contacted his colleagues over in the northwest of the country and, by dint of a carefully phrased question had elicited the reply that, yes, Comrade Thong Damdouane had a ring-twiddling habit during moments of concentration. That, and what was equally damaging, yes, two pairs of headsets had been tampered with shortly before the Beaver flew to Sam Neua. So much for Comrade Thong on two counts! That had left Comrade Le Dâng Khoã, apparently ringless. He had taken out the personal and confidential files of the four men under a cloud, his cloud he thought proudly, and read them through again. In the remarks column it was noted that, although Le Dâng Khoã claimed to come from the south of Vietnam, he spoke with a northern accent: point 1. Point 2 was that the four suspects and Mana were about the same age and, if all four suspects did come from the north, wasn't it possible that, despite two being Lao and two being Vietnamese, they had some common starting point both in time and space? In Bounphong's file he'd given his birthplace as Ban Liet and, as Nga Sô Lưu had been responsible for ... it had hit him like a flash of lightening – motive!...1945, almost thirty years ago, soon after the war: the time when sap rose in his veins and loins, and the world had an exhilarating rose-red hue. He hadn't, as a young man, been in charge. Ban Liet and Sam Neua were only one raid of many. Uncle H 's directive, even if Uncle himself was absent from Hanoi at the time, was obeyed to the letter. Nga Sô Lưu remembered it word for word: *Never forget what you have been taught: 'The revolutionaries' business is destruction; terrible, complete, universal and ruthless ... and, above all, by relentless planning, remorseless opportunism and a ruthless all-pervading fear.*

At the time, he reflected, the killing in the Sam Neua wat

had been an extravagance, if only because the audience was so small, but an enjoyable extravagance to be sure. But it had been good experience. Group B, his group, had rejoined Group A, the group that had burnt Ban Liet. They had been guided there by the Thai army deserter, whom they had killed there and then. They had also taken away a lad who said his name was ... Mana. Another blinding flash ... who must have been the same Mana who was trying to reach him. Nothing then was nearly so well organised as it was now. And the abbot of that time – was he not the Chief Bonze in Luang Prabang now? Leuam, Bounphong's brother, talked about 'Great Master'. Could he and the British DA have gone together to a pre-arranged meeting? Sightseeing? H'm. He cursed himself under his breath and turned his thoughts to Rance. It had merely struck him as risible that Rance should have learnt the royal northern Luang Prabang accent. He'd come from England with some knowledge of Lao, hadn't he? He called for Rance's card from the central registry. There is was: 'Took lessons with *Tao* Inkham' who, he knew, was the King's niece. Another entry, written by his confidential secretary, made a connection even more clear: 'Observed going to the royal palace with *Tao* Inkham during the evening function held on the day of the wedding of her sister to Prince Lanouk na Champassak, on 27 February 1974'. Then a damning entry: 'Suspected of being in Bouam Long area on 19 March 1974, the time of the double-death incident in the jungle'. Nothing was proof positive yet much was undeniably suspicious.

He knew that Rance was due to leave Laos in the coming July. That was too short a time to discredit him or was it? As he was going quite soon, in the normal course of events it would save what would otherwise have been a nasty incident. Were he to stay ... and the Political Commissar allowed his imagination to dwell on a suitable method of elimination before he turned his mind back to finding Mana and dealing with the Four Rings, rubbing the heel of his hand against his temple as he sought to ignore the incessant throbbing of expectancy.

Rance was glad that Mana was better. He had been shocked at that dramatic meeting they had had in Bouam Long. It was obvious that the man was in a bad state and he had wondered if cure would ever be possible. The preparation for the raid and the part he had played in setting it up often came back into his mind. He still found it harder to be a spectator than a doer although he knew he had not much option for anything else. Gordon Parks had called him into his office in the secure part of the embassy and given him a briefing. He finished up by saying, 'There are two main points, Jason. One is that Mana's request to see you is genuine and, in that it was not suggested by the surgeon, offers him a good opportunity to gauge Mana's reactions, frame of mind, mental stability and temperament in surroundings he knows but in which he has not been in for a long time. Mana particularly mentioned a ring, dreamed he'd seen you wearing one, so play that whichever way you will. The other point is that, as you know, you will be meeting Charlie. You will have to play it by ear, obviously, as you can get no official help from anyone. However, one point that has been fed into the system is that no mention of the Four Rings and Mana or of your involvement with them is ever to be made to him. He will have been briefed that you are in no different a position from when you first met him as regards any "meddling", I might call it, is concerned. Indeed, if he is the man we are led to believe him to be, he'll know in what regard you are held by the folk you work with and, may I say it, against. You are to keep the meeting with Mana a secret from people in the embassy. Can you get down to Bangkok legitimately?'

'Hang on a mo. When does the surgeon want to bring Mana up and how easily can Charlie be got hold of? The sooner the better as far as I am concerned.'

'Any day week ending 29 March. It's the 10th today, so that means that we've got a little while to jack it up. Utapao and Charlie need only twenty-four hours' notice and, as you also may have guessed, John Chambers is standing by to come out almost any time.'

'Tell you what, Gordon. I can go on the bag run on the 26th, have our talk on the 27th and get back on the 28th, which is Good Friday. That'll raise no eyebrows. In fact, it is the turn of my clerk to go down on that run but we'll do a swap.'

'Fine, then. Leave everything to me. There should be no problem with that little lot.'

On the Wednesday afternoon, Leuam drove Rance down to Wattay with the bag. Rance was in good spirits. He felt excited at the prospect of another little jaunt down south and, somehow, he felt it was an important mission. The silent Leuam noticed his boss's good mood and wondered why.

'I've got news for you, Leuam. I am not being replaced as soon as I thought I would be.' He had had it confirmed by signal that morning and so could tell him about it. 'You've got to bear with me at least till next October. How does that affect your prophesy at the *baçi* for the last DA? It's a little more than thirty-two months for the thirty-two *phee*s. Can you get a message to your brother and the others? They'd be interested, I'm sure.'

As he left the car to go to the airport, he turned and said, 'Back on Friday. See you then.'

He flirted outrageously with the Thai Airways hostess on the flight down and she responded demurely. She felt safe with this tall, silver-haired Englishman who was old enough to be her father and Rance was in no way taken in by her fluttering eyelashes and winsome smile. 'I'm staying in Bangkok for a couple of nights. Let me take you out for a meal,' he invited, knowing full well she'd decline. She hesitated just long enough to entice him before shaking her head. *I'd like to have the best of three pinfalls with you*, he said to himself, using the wrestling jargon he'd picked up many years before in Singapore. His thoughts turned to the other Asian women who had come his way since he became enmeshed in this job – Golden Fairy, Jasmine, Kaysorn Bouapha, his language teacher in his early days who had been persuaded by the Deputy Commander-in-Chief to try and get him to compromise himself but lying nude in his bed one Sunday afternoon when he'd gone out to lunch, but particularly to Golden Fairy to whom, he admitted to himself, he'd lost his heart. The air hostess's voice broke into his thoughts as she offered him a sweet for the descent and shattered his reverie. He clicked back into focus: he was not going to Bangkok for the equivalent of a dirty weekend. He was on a job that could turn sour: would he shatter Mana or complete his cure? He'd soon know.

As normal, he was met by the embassy Security Officer and, with traffic in Bangkok heavy, they reached the embassy over an hour later. He was handed a hotel slip, New Imperial, just over the Phloen Chit road. He'd carry his own bag and stretch his legs.

At his hotel desk he was handed a message that he'd be picked up at 8 o'clock the next morning. He went to his room, had a hot shower and was sitting on his bed when the telephone rang. 'Hello. Rance here,' he announced.

A familiar voice in French answered. ''Allo Colonel. My air hostess friend told me about her passenger. I rang the Duty Officer in the British embassy and he told me where you were. Simple. Can we fix up a meeting together?'

With mixed reactions, he replied in a kindly tone, 'Mlle. Kaysorn! Long time no hear. I didn't know that you were in Bangkok.' It couldn't matter if they met: it was not near his own doorstep and he was in the mood for a tumble if the chance were to arise. 'Yes. Will you come here or shall I meet in your place?'

They decided to meet at an eating house, chosen by Kaysorn, who didn't like either of his suggestions, at 8 p.m. She was prettier than he remembered her, or was the light being kind? She talked volubly: she couldn't bear living in Vientiane and not being able to meet him. She realised that she'd been brash and he properly correct but she hadn't been herself. When asked what she did for a living, she proudly said teaching French at the French Cultural Centre. After the meal, she suggested they go to her room in Lumphini Park, in the south of the city. He happily accepted her invitation. She lived in a small bed-sitter, modest and only just not squalid.

After a bit of chat, she said I saw a friend of my brother Phoun, the barber in Vientiane who always cuts your hair, in town earlier today. Someone called Mana Varamit.'

Rance managed to hide his astonishment and asked casually, 'Mana who? I didn't catch his name properly.'

'Varamit. Mana Varamit. I hadn't seen him for quite a long time. When I last met Phoun we were only saying we neither of us had seen him since, oh, some time in 1974 – last year.'

Rance's mind reeled and, unusually for him, he fumbled for words. '1974, did you say? Where? What was he doing?'

She looked at him sharply. 'You don't know him, do you? You sound interested. Funny if the three of us knew him.'

'No,' he drawled, searching for a way out. 'Probably not the same man as I knew. I still find Thai and Lao family names muddling.'

'Well, since you ask, he was in Vientiane. Phoun and I were walking near the Morning Market and we saw him near the LPF HQ. He looked young for his age.'

Rance had by then recovered his calm and so relieved was he that he had not given anything away he took her hand and caressed it. She looked him straight in the eye and said, slowly and deliberately, switching from Lao to French, 'I'll only let you seduce me if you promise to marry me.'

It sounded so ludicrously stilted that Rance broke the tension that had sprung up by a burst of unrestrained laughter. 'Good night, Mlle. Kaysorn,' he said gravely and walked out of the room, leaving her gawping at his sudden and unexpected departure.

I'll get even with you yet, she angrily promised, muttering to herself.

The meeting with Mana, on the face of it, seemed a success. Rance wore his ring on the index finger of his left hand. Mana didn't seem to respond in any way to it, which struck Rance as a bit odd in view of what he had been told. They talked about their time in Malaysia, Rance purposely not touching on the incidents during the closing stages of the final exercise. He then switched from Thai to English and they made gentle, anodyne remarks comparing Mana's English to his Thai. Rance told Mana how he had learnt Thai when at the Jungle Warfare School and how he had never spoken to a Thai audience before.

'Have you been to Vientiane?' No, never, was the reply, he'd like to go there. Rance then asked him about his family. Mana couldn't recall when his parents had died. He only had vague recollections of the other members of his family but he thought he had one sister and maybe a younger brother. He was still a bit hazy after an accident. Hit on the head, he'd been, but he was really much better.

They had coffee and it was time to go. Without Mana seeing it, Rance transferred the ring onto the little finger of his right hand. Last to leave, he deliberately shook Mana's hand and made the *wai* salutation. A strained and worried expression momentarily registered on the Thai's face as his eyes avoided Rance's and followed the movement of the ring, hungrily.

John Chambers was vastly impressed by what he had seen and heard.

Rance had not met Charlie since his visit to Xieng Lom. For some reason he couldn't place, something didn't ring true, either because Charlie's English was perfect or because he linked the pornographic film he'd seen that night with Kaysorn lying drugged in his visitor's bedroom but as Charlie was urbane, relaxed and charming, Rance was soon at ease. They conferred in a secure room in the British embassy, Ed Murray also being present. John Chambers opened the session.

'This is an unusual meeting, Gentlemen, that we've embarked on. I believe I don't have to rehearse our common aims and aspirations. We are at a disadvantage in that, for better or for worse – and I am not saying which of the two I think it is – the British government has insisted that the rules under which she is officially represented must be scrupulously adhered to. I believe you, Ed, fully agree that, under the present circumstances, it would be folly to attempt otherwise.

'As for your country, Charlie, I don't have to tell *you* how little you need the Communists on the far bank of the Mekong or anywhere on your borders. You, Colonel Jason, are under a greater burden than are we because most of what you know is first-hand and entirely dependent on human contacts that you have so assiduously built up these last two and a half years whereas, while our knowledge may be broader owing to a wider range of sources, it is mostly second-hand and much more impersonal.

'We will, sooner or later, and I believe sooner, be in a difficult position and by that I mean it is almost certain that a Communist victory will mean a purge, lack of contacts, restrictions on movements and a host of other constraints not now encountered.

The lead up to that victory will be bloody and dangerous, certainly in Vietnam and the Khmer Republic and probably in Laos also. Anything that we can do against the Communists must be geared in accordance with our slender resources and meet four conditions: ward off the final take-over in Laos for as long as possible, allow as long a breathing space for Thailand as possible, avoid unnecessary casualties to those employed against any "opportunity targets" that present themselves and, finally, remain unattributable. There may be other minor considerations but they don't spring to mind. The $64,000 question is, quite simply, how? We are here today to try and answer that poser. Any ideas, anybody?' and three pairs of eyes were turned on Rance.

'Yes and no. Sorry, that's a damned silly answer! What I mean to say is "yes" in general terms and "no" in specifics. I can see the need for a commando-type – "Ranger" to you, Ed – operation, mounted quickly and unobtrusively by one small group of men against another small group, "inside information", to kidnap a key man or key men, rescue somebody, break in and burgle something deemed to be of vital importance – plans, codes, evidence of some sort – from a place properly guarded and/or a variation on that theme. At this stage of the game, though, it might not even be cosmetic in value. That's my "yes". My "no" is the reverse of that: no targets, no details.'

'I don't think we can do better than that, can we?' John asked after a pause to let what Rance had said sink in. The other two men shook their head. 'Charlie, have you anything you'd like to say?'

'Yes, John. We, none of us here, are not in, how shall I say it? –

big business. There are many examples of similar pitiful attempts of last-ditch stands with their even more pitiful failures. My target must be one that nobody else can deal with – and you Brits are my taskers. By that I mean it will be up to you to assess the priority and up to me to accept it or veto it. I can fix for indefinite leave of absence from my unit. Don't ask me how but I can.' He grinned engagingly. 'I must be easily contactable, discreetly placed and have as much warning as possible. As regards my team I can call on the services of men who mean nothing, politically or diplomatically, to the United States or to Great Britain. I would like to suggest I will be based over the river on Thai territory in Nong Khai so in easy reach of Vientiane and I will arrange to be contactable at twelve hours' notice through the foreman of the boatyard where the British launch is kept. As for when I will be ready – it'll take the Communists anything from one month to, say, eight to topple Saigon, so let's say I'll be ready from 1 May.'

The meeting had little more to say and anyway Rance had to go and make arrangements for the return bag. As he took his leave from John Chambers, he said, 'See you up there, John.'

John Chambers looked at Rance as he replied, shaking his hand. 'You know I'll need quite a lot of help from you in Vientiane if only because all these Asians look alike to me! It will take me a long, long time to get anywhere near your standard.'

'So you've come to report to us, have you, Leuam, at long last?' Soth Petrasy, flanked by Leuam's brother, Bounphong and Le Dâng Khoã, sat at a table the other side of which stood Leuam, looking sheepish. 'You haven't taken much notice of our previous invitation.'

Leuam shuffled his feet. 'I haven't come because I've had nothing to say. My *Colonen* only ever talks routine business – dates, times, duties, places and the like, normally with a laugh and a joke thrown in. You know he likes to walk to and from work. I'm not a great talker. I hadn't forgotten but there never seems to be anything worth reporting.'

'Why didn't you report that Colonel Rance flew away with some other Attachés, in an imperialist American aeroplane. It wasn't a full Attaché function as no true comrades were there.'

'I have no idea who or what was involved and it never occurred to me that you'd want to know anything like that. It's not the first time my Colonel has been in one of those planes. And you obviously know more about it than I do without my telling you so it wouldn't have been news, would it?'

'That's not the point,' said Soth, slightly disarmed by the frank reply. 'What have you come to see us now for?'

'Only to say that Colonel Rance has taken the bag down to Bangkok. Took it down yesterday and returns tomorrow. On the way down to Wattay he told me he was not now leaving Laos in late April-May but had had another extension. He seemed very happy. Nothing else.'

'Accepted this time. Off you go but remember what I said.'

Leuam excused himself and left. The other two men got up and, nodding to Soth, followed Leuam outside the building. A car drew up to take Le Dâng Khoã to the other side of town. Bounphong nudged Le Dâng Khoã and suggested he drop Leuam off on the way.

'In you get, Leuam,' said Le Dâng Khoã. 'How far do you want to go? If it's not out of my way, I'll take you there.'

Leuam turned and bade his brother farewell. He got into the back of the car, which struck the watching Soth as being over-familiar. The car drove off and Bounphong rejoined his senior.

'I hope Comrade Le Dâng Khoã also gives him a talking to as they go, especially as he's sitting in the back,' he grumbled. 'I can't understand his reticence.'

'Naturally shy and rather cowed,' said Bounphong. 'Always was, as well as not realising the implications of the situation. In fact, it was either Leuam or the escort sitting in the back.'

In the car Le Dâng Khoã said, softly enough for the escort and driver not to hear, 'When you see Colonel Rance tomorrow, tell him his friend Tâ Tran Quán has reached where he wanted to go, is in reasonable health and is establishing himself carefully. However, he is not out of danger – nor,' as an afterthought, 'are we … nor, for that matter, is the Colonel himself.'

As Rance flew back on the morrow, no matter how much the hostess, the same girl as on the flight down, tried to attract the attention of the man she had decided might make a good sugar daddy, she failed. He was lost in thought … *perseverance?*

7

March-June 1975: It was the unexpectedly early fall of Danang, four hundred odd kilometres north-northeast of Saigon, announced on Sunday, 30 March, 1975, that sent shivers down many a spine – chillingly for those fighting against the Communists and those who were feathering their nests like so many of the Lao hierarchy were, despairingly for the countless thousands who were fed up with the years of misery, joyfully for those Communists who had been labouring so long for victory. Conventional wisdom on both sides of the political divide saw the battle for Saigon six months later, while those who thought they controlled events and men's destinies saw the fall of Laos as 'Saigon plus two months'. It was this eight-month period that needed careful orchestrating in Laos and Nga Sô Lưu had to give detailed thought how best to direct the LPF cadres who, for the past eighteen months, had been beavering away under the surface with their subversive activities among students, the armed forces, police, minor functionaries and many others including those working for the American aid mission, USAID. He licked his lips in anticipation of tormenting the imperialists. It was also time to put another of his contingency plans into action now he had heard that the British DA had been extended in post. Maybe his Soviet comrades could lend a hand.

The new Attaché, Colonel Vladimir Gretchanine, that tall, grey-haired, the KGB official who was working in Paris when Rance was learning French with Yvonne Grambert in London, was reliable and clever: Nga Sô Lựu had learnt that the Englishman had been a target of a 'honey pot' operation set by Yvonne as ordered by Gretchanine as well as another, set by someone else, soon after his arrival in Laos.

Meanwhile, along the whole length of the two zones that divided Laos, more and more land was won back by the PL, eroding the morale of the RLA troops on the ground until, as Rance noted during his routine visits, the will to defend their homeland was almost extinguished. By the end of March almost only a smidgen of territory that the LPF had held at the time of the 1962 ceasefire was not in their hands again.

By 11 April each ministry had a member of the opposite faction as deputy and Prince Lanouk was much incensed with the PL soldier escort who was never far away from his office. It angered him each time he saw the sentry in the passage. The Minister had called Rance to meet him and Rance could see that he was worried.

'I am glad you could come this morning, *Tan Colonen*. I am most concerned about something I have recently learnt. I need your advice. There are twenty-seven Vietnamese "hit men" in the PL camp at Ban Dong Nasok, where the Neutralisation troops live. You know the one I mean – not far from the Wattay complex.' Rance said he did. 'They have only recently arrived from Hanoi. The advice I need from you is shall I try to have them exterminated or not?'

Rance, used by now though he was to so many of the unusual aspects of Lao methods, was taken aback. Before he could answer, Lanouk continued, even more surprisingly, 'I will do whatever you advise. If you advocate extermination, it must be complete, leaving none alive. Whatever you advise will have an ineradicable effect on the future of the country. I don't know what forces your embassy can arrange – I understand your Mr John Chambers might have some good ideas – but, whatever else, I am relying on you. Come round to my villa on,' he looked at a calendar, 'Monday of next week at 6 p.m. and tell me your plans.'

Rance, knowing in advance that nothing official could be done, merely told the Minister that he would see what he could do.

Rance gave Leuam his orders. 'Listen. It is time we started making plans for the future. I am going to Luang Prabang tomorrow, 16 April, for the New Year ceremonies, and returning on Friday 18. I am flying both ways, so won't be needing you. While I'm away I want you to contact your brother or Le Dâng Khoã. I am sure that you have to report my activities from time to time.' He noticed that, at that remark, his driver looked ill at ease when he glanced up at him. 'Don't *worry* about it, Leuam, but I *am* right, aren't I? Stands to reason you've got to. Well, feed them some tidbits. So pretend that you have news of me you have to impart: that I was recently invited to drinks by Lanouk na Champassak at his villa. During our talk that morning in his office, he told me that he had no intention of leaving the country and going to Paris. But, between you and me, he also said, "What I want is a sketch map of Ban Dong Nasok camp, showing where the recently arrived twenty-seven 'elder brothers' live, work, eat and sleep. I want the answers by whenever it is convenient to my two friends." Can you do that? If anyone hears you or becomes suspicious of you, drop it if you can. If you can't, though, tell those two you've heard of a mad plot – we know there are many rumours in the air so they'll believe it and you've come to get a map of the *wrong* place so that the plotter won't harm the Comrades and will go to the wrong place so be easier to defeat. Now, have you got that? Let's go through it together, slowly, once more. You must contact ...'

The journey up to Luang Prabang for the New Year of the Hare celebrations was regarded by many of the foreign diplomats and ancillary aid staffs as an unnecessary bore. The recent news depressed them and rumours of a PL 'march on Vientiane' alarmed them. The small British contingent took two embassy pool cars and drove in convoy with an armed escort organised by the Ministry of Defence. It was not so much an endearing trust in the ability of the Lao military to protect them but rather a desire of the travellers to see part of the country till than inaccessible to them that made the more adventurous opt for that mode of travel.

The celebration was an unhappy one. Nobody seemed to be enjoying it and even the procession of virgins seemed jaded. Not far from the royal palace, Rance joined a group of officials, representatives from both sides. One of the LPF was saying, 'Now there is a socialist victory in Indo-China there is no need for any more fighting.'

A member of the right-wing objected to that remark and a

heated discussion developed. They were joined by another man who Rance saw was Thong Damdouane. By now the LPF had discarded the traditional form of Lao greeting so Rance merely greeted him as 'Comrade', followed by the inevitable handshake. He and the British DA drifted away from the main group and chatted for a while, then Thong said, 'My boss is going to hold a conference, so I've come to learn, down your way in Vientiane. Nothing has been mentioned to the Politburo yet but he has mentioned it to Tâ Tran Quán – could be to see if he passes it on so that you get to know of it. He says he wants to discuss policy matters during the next stage of developments, once certain preparations have been made. He has already sent twenty-seven of his top men down. I believe Tâ Tran Quán is also going to attend and I may be roped in: rather strange. I wonder ... we'll try and keep contact with you these processions are most traditional, don't you think, *Tan Colonen*,' in a slightly louder tone of voice as another LPF official came with possible hearing distance. 'I'm sure a man like you appreciates so we four may be there together and the rain kept off. I thought it was going to pour at one stage, important cadres of "elder brothers", might be our chance but I like the boat races better. There's a bit of cloud still ...' but Rance, left gasping trying to follow two conversations as potential eavesdroppers came and went, never did learn whether Thong referred to a real or metaphorical cloud as, from behind, they were joined by the PL military commander, the man who had flown to Sam Neua in the Beaver that time, to tell Rance how the PL were cooperating with road convoy protection measures for the return journey next day.

That evening in the palace, the atmosphere was unsettled. The procession of lights went off at half-cock and the banquet was ill-prepared. Rance met Golden Fairy's mother who seemed worried about her daughter. Rance had never written to her, more out of reticence than conviction and he asked her mother to remember him most kindly to her when she next wrote. The King's sister-in-law became upset at the mention of mail and it suddenly occurred to him that, like everywhere else, disturbing tales of post office mail tampering were worrying her. Things must be coming to a pretty pass if palace mail was being mucked around with. 'I don't want to alarm Inkham but if you were to hear that anything that was not as it should be with us here, I'm sure I could rely on you to tell her about it.'

Rance had never found the royal family so worried or forthcoming: for him it was a thoroughly depressing day with the foreign guests worried about the safety of the return convoy.

The journey back, as far as the Brits and other armchair heroes were concerned, had to be rearranged. The Beaver would make three trips, the remainder were to be put on an RLAF Dakota that had been especially laid on to cope with the problem and Rance would travel by road in one of the two otherwise empty cars. The prospect didn't perturb him particularly. It'd be a long day but should be interesting to see how the protection measures worked. In the event he only saw a sprinkling of PL soldiers mixed with RLA men.

As the convoy made its way down the final slopes into the Vientiane plain, it got hotter, dustier and more uncomfortable. There were a lot of vehicles on the road and, once the flat ground of the plain itself was reached, there emerged a kind of race as the more impatient drivers tried to overtake vehicles in front of them, both to escape the dust and to get home before dark. Rance managed to get his two cars into a side street in a small village where he ordered bowls of fish soup. By the time he and the drivers had finished that and washed some of the red cake of sweat-laden dust from their faces at a standpipe, the convoy was so far ahead that the road was dust free. Their onward journey was, however, far slower than normal as one of the vehicles developed engine trouble which the driver correctly diagnosed as a blockage in the fuel system. He had to wait until the engine had cooled down before he cleaned it and it was dark by the time they reached the outskirts of Vientiane. The same engine then hiccupped and stopped functioning so the driver freewheeled to the side of the road and, with a curse, got out and had a look under the bonnet. 'As I thought,' he announced with another curse, 'dud battery.'

Rance summed up the situation. 'You go back to the embassy garage and get the fitter out here with another vehicle, a charged battery if he has one, and a towrope,' he instructed the driver of the other vehicle. 'I'll stay here till he arrives. Oh, and warn my house boy that I'll be late for my evening meal. The telephone number is 2362.'

After the car had gone, Rance and the other driver chatted for a while then the DA said, 'It'll take an hour or so to get help. I'm so cramped. I must stretch my legs. Stay here and I'll be back soon. I won't go far and I'll certainly be in earshot so, if I'm not back by the time you're ready, give me three toots on your horn.'

He wandered away in the gloom, retracing his steps up the road. He came to a track that branched off to the left and, on the spur of the moment, followed it. There was just enough residual light from the town in the distance and the night sky to be able to pick his way without too much trouble. He saw headlights to his left, coming up the road towards his car, half a mile or so away. *Back quicker than I expected*, he thought to himself, but the car drove on and swung into the track. On an impulse he moved into the bushes on the left so the sweep of the headlights wouldn't pick him out. Instinct told him to lie flat on the ground as it passed. The occupants couldn't have seen him. He picked himself up and watched the rear lights dance and flicker through the undergrowth, then come to a halt. He heard the slam of the doors – at least two passengers, he noted – then silence. He was intrigued. It wasn't normal for any vehicle to be so far out of town after dark, although it was still early. He decided to go and investigate, if only for the hell of it. He saw a light shining in a hut. He picked out the car in the shadows and approached it cautiously. No chauffeur. He looked at the number plate: 124 CD 052. So it was the Soviet DA's car! Hoping that there wasn't a dog around to give notice of his presence by barking, he moved close enough to see who was inside the hut. There were five men sitting around an improvised table that had a hurricane lamp on it. Two were Europeans and he recognised one as Colonel Vladimir Gretchanine, tall with silver-grey hair and red face – he was not to know that the gallant Colonel, a member of the KBG, had been instrumental in getting Mme. Grambert to try and compromise him in London. The other he couldn't place but he noted him and would pick him up from John Chamber's 'Rogues Gallery'. The other he couldn't place but he noted him. John Chambers would pick him up from his 'Rogues Gallery'. The other three were Asians, wearing the drab green of the PL. They must have come from the PL camp at Ban Dong Nasok which was quite near but in the opposite direction. They had their backs to him so he moved round till he could see them. What he saw made him more inquisitive. He thought one of the men was Charlie but he was not sure as he was almost unrecognisable, with hat pulled well down over his eyes, collar turned up and a puffy face as though he had toothache. He was obviously hiding his knowledge of English, but the others? One looked like Phoun, the barber. The third man he could not place – could it just be Le Dâng Khoã? Surely not! He crept forward, painfully slowly, almost as though he were mesmerised by what he saw. He got as close as he dared and listened intently. The conversation was in bad English and muffled. Charlie must have been hiding his knowledge of English as the Soviet DA said something that obviously was not understood by the others so he repeated himself. No joy. He then behaved as many people do when what they say hasn't got over to their audience – he raised his voice. Rance heard 'dress rehearsal', which puzzled him. He knew that none of the Soviet mission spoke Lao although some did speak Chinese and Vietnamese. Time to go, so he crept away, back past the car. On the spur of the moment he let the air out of one tyre and the spare.

He reached his own vehicle, hoping against hope that the recovery car would reach them before the Soviet DA's car came back, although he could comfort himself that the deflated tyres could delay him for a while. He sat in the back, deep in thought. This was a completely new ball game. He had never thought out how it was that Charlie had been able to say so confidently that he could mount an operation, presumably he'd have to have some nefarious contacts but surely not the Soviets? Or did it mean that Charlie was playing a two-edged game, acting as a double agent? Again it was scarcely credible. Lights appeared from the direction of Vientiane and the relief car drove up. The new battery the fitter had brought did the trick and they were soon on their way – had the party in the hut seen the lights? Had they noticed the broken-down vehicle's British embassy number plate? At least it was not Rance's personal car so there might be no suspicion about who had let the air out of the tyres. But Charlie and, to an extent Phoun, worried him badly. Just suppose that Charlie had hoodwinked his foster father – just the thought of such an occurrence would probably kill the old boy. No, the more he thought of it, the more he realised that he had to play it so close to the chest no one at all should be told about who he had seen and what he had heard.

The fall of Phnom Penh, two weeks later, on 17 April, following news of the NVA thrust south from Danang, made a deep impact on many people in Vientiane. Neither side had envisaged that events would move so quickly, no one forecast the fall of Saigon before the rains, still some months off. Nevertheless, certain precautions were being made with great urgency

In Ban Dong Nasok camp on the western side of Vientiane, Comrades Le Dâng Khoã and Bounphong conferred with some recent arrivals from Office 95. In the guise of sending some of their garrison troops back for re-assignment, the AN-21 had been allowed to fly into Vientiane from Hanoi with an equivalent number of men. The Protocols specified the number of troops both sides could retain in Vientiane – not that the LPF had any scruples about not sticking to the agreed figure – and, although it was easy to bring in or take out a few at a time in the AN-2, it was a different matter flying in a larger amount, by AN-21. The body that regulated the functioning and implementation of the Accords, the 'Joint Mixed Commission', had given clearance for the flight. The LPF were scrupulous about observing certain political points. There are none more vehement than those recently converted or when fanatics regard politics with as much fervour as a religion there are certain limits which they will strive to attain and other limits beyond which they will not go. Thus it was that an unplanned influx of twenty-seven men had to be fitted, somehow, into an existing political framework – framework to some, loophole to others.

It was the arrival of these men that had been reported to Lanouk. With the inability either for accurate assessment or for reliable information, this group had been reported by the remnants of Lanouk's intelligence organisation as military advisers to help PL troops based in Vientiane take over the town in one swift action if and when an opportune moment presented itself or if not, to advise on selected assassinations. This was true for some of the group. The remainder were political cadres, reinforcements for the time when Vientiane had been fully liberated and the workload would be unusually heavy.

By then the Black-eyed Butcher had had a report back from Sam Neua. The men he had sent had seen the records in the wat, written in early April 1945, and yes, the original birth-given names of two boys from Tâ Lang had been changed to Le Dâng Khoã and Tâ Tran Quán. 'Anything else', the Political Commissar asked. 'Yes,' came a rage-engendering answer, 'we had to pay for the answer. The correct codeword to find out is "the Black-eyed Butcher".' Nga Sô Lựu ground his teeth in rage. *So that's where my cursed nickname originated.*

Among the twenty-seven men was a two-man cell sworn to secrecy by Nga Sô Lựu who were to shadow Le Dâng Khoã – a suspect even without a ring – and Bounphong Sunthorn and see what foreigners they contacted and, without causing any suspicion, to see if either had a particular tattoo mark on the inside of their little finger on their right hand: rings can be lost but tattoos, and their erased traces, cannot be kept secret. This particular tattoo mark was not easy to discern, as it happened, as the dye used was old and faded, and had stretched as the boys grew up. The colour of the skin also hampered any detection, nevertheless efforts to establish the fact were to be made. Nga Sô Lựu had told the two men half the truth during his briefing: these two men had needed an identity sign to establish themselves as members of some esoteric cult that had to be penetrated in the name of the Cause, that die-hard initiates might try to expose them to the Cause's disadvantage if the sign was still there and that secrecy was imperative, though quite why Nga Sô Lựu skilfully kept secret. He also hinted that it was a kind of test of their ability. He would ask Le Dâng Khoã and Bounphong later if they had twigged to what was happening. In the over-secretive and arcane Communist world, any piece of rubbish can be made convincing. It was these two men who were conferring with Le Dâng Khoã and Bounphong. On some excuse that their ring covered too much of the map to make it easily legible he had persuaded them to take it off, something that they did even if, inside, both felt a pang of something sinister but yet to be understood. It put them more on their guard from then on. That way the two men did see what they sought when the two suspects opened their fingers wide as they poured over street maps and lists of possible people who needed removing.

The Communist victory, consummated on 30 April by the capture of Saigon, stunned the world by its speed: speed of advance and speed of demoralisation of the South Vietnamese. Any hopes of a 'Third Vietnam' under Air Marshal Ky had evaporated and stark reality prevailed. The appalling stories emanating from Phnom Penh had already struck terror into so many hearts that rational thought was hard to come by, even though the North Vietnamese had allowed an escape corridor from Tan Son Nhut airfield for the remnants of the American embassy staff. It had to be Vientiane's turn next, come what may and come it would. Laos would never be the same again. Or would it?

In the caves of Sam Neua a high-level Politburo meeting was under way. It was tense, tenser than usual, because now it was time to take full advantage of the previous day's victory news and make urgent plans that would finalise their conquest of Laos. Then the old imperial French dream of a united Indo-China would pass to the Vietnamese based in Hanoi although the Communist leaders there wrapped it in so much polemic gobbledygook that it fooled many people. 'Saigon plus two months' had been a firm rallying call and a useful planning date but now it was openly admitted to be completely unrealistic. With so much that had to be done, total liberation of the rest of Laos by 30 June was out of the question. 12 October, the 30th anniversary of the liberation of Laos after the Second World War, was chosen as the new deadline.

It was further decided that the long-standing invitation to the King to visit Sam Neua be extended once more, as a matter of cosmetic urgency, with an announcement that it was to discuss arrangements for the coronation – '"Will you come into my parlour" said the spider to the fly,' quoted Rance to John Chambers later when that news reached them. But there and then in the caves it was not time for the hard men to show their faces: that would wait until the necessary political deadwood had been cleared away and this, despite his proposed visit to his loyal subjects in Sam Neua, meant deposing His Majesty, King Savang Vattana, the last King of Laos, still uncrowned. Comrade Nga Sô Lưu had been included among the delegates at the meeting, along with his Lao counterpart and Tâ Tran Quán. They were coming to the end of their session and the chairman was summing up.

'So, Comrades, there you have it. We will plan on our cadres in Luang Prabang and Vientiane continuing to prepare the masses for the ultimate but, naturally, in the stages we have so carefully planned and meticulously laid down. To that end, territory that has yet to be liberated, less the two neutralised towns, will be taken over starting on 11 May. That day will also see the start of the Cultural Revolution. Finally, to coordinate the Vientiane end of our activities, Comrade Nga Sô Lưu, who has been working so selflessly for the Cause for so long, will go there. I understand that Comrade Nga Sô Lưu will be taking Comrade Tâ Tran Quán with him and that, having made certain enquiries in Luang Prabang, will continue down to Vientiane with Comrade Thong Damdouane. Once there they will meet up with certain officials, including Comrades Le Dâng Khoã and Bounphong Sunthorn so that will mean four of our brightest hopes for the future will be able to combat the revolution at first hand. We also need to maintain our close liaison with our Soviet comrades – here I am particularly thinking of Comrade Vladimir Gretchanine – and when Comrade Nga Sô Lưu has laid his plans, he will convene a meeting with those I have already mentioned. We have already had one tentative, preliminary meeting in Vientiane and our next could almost be said to be a dress rehearsal for when we final and definitively make the announcement that the People's Democratic Republic of Laos is fully Communist.' He sat down to deafening applause and then asked Comrade Nga Sô Lưu if there was anything he would like to add to what had already been said.

Desiccated and deadly dull in manner, feverishly fervent as a Communist apostle, the Vietnamese representative of Office 95 shuffled his papers, looked around the assembled gathering, cleared his throat and, black eyes blacker than ever, said, 'Comrades. All of you here are fully aware of the gravity of the situation, its uniqueness and its glory. We are on the verge of complete and total socialist victory. What I am planning on is the final analysis of results that my office has managed to achieve since it was established because, once we have reached a certain stage in the revolution, we can channel our full efforts into constructing nation-building and many of our staff can be directed towards different targets. There are, as you may have guessed, a number of traitors and counter-revolutionaries lurking in the fleshpots of the den of iniquity, Vientiane. Some are even disguised as senior cadres. They represent a real and ever-present danger and must be ruthlessly rooted out.'

He waxed indignant for several minutes, giving a performance for which he was justly famed and of which he was justifiably proud. He finished up, with more applause, 'For speed and efficiency, therefore, I have decided that the plan I have outlined will be put into operation next month. The dates I have picked are, on 13 June to Luang Prabang, 15 June to Vientiane and on 21 June ... we start.'

On the evening of Sunday, 4 May, Rance had had his meal and was reading when Singha barked at a visitor's approach. The bell rang. Rance shouted to Khian An not to worry and went to open the front door. There stood Charlie, looking less smart than on previous occasions, but dressed so that he could pass muster in a crowd of locals.

'Come along in, Charlie. Had a meal? Sure? Then what can I get you to drink?' Charlie plumped for whisky which Khian An brought. If he was surprised to see Rance's visitor, he didn't show it. 'Cheers! Good luck!' and the houseboy went out of the room, leaving them alone.

'I hadn't expected you so soon, somehow. No difficulty? Before we go any further would you like to spend the night here? The guestroom is ready.' Charlie declined. 'Well, the offer's there should you change your mind. What buzzes?'

'Colonel. This situation is developing faster than I expected. I've got my men with their weapons safely on the other side of the river. I've yet to work out where we'll stay until we're needed against the twenty-seven "hit men". My men are Thai Isan, men from the northeast of Thailand, who are, in fact, first or second generation Lao, so the problem of being spotted is not quite as fraught as if I had "native" Thais with me.' Rance nodded. 'Ideally, what I would like to happen is to get them installed somewhere unobtrusive before the PL move and cut Vientiane off from the rest of the country, as I'm sure they will pretty soon. You, with your knowledge of the possibilities, may have some ideas that I've overlooked.'

Rance had been undecided whether to ask Charlie if he had had any contact with the Soviet DA but now he felt he just had to know. 'Charlie, there is something I must ask you. On my way back from the royal bun-fight on the 18th …' Charlie looked at him quizzically as Rance told him what he had seen. 'I thought I saw you, hat down over your eyes, collar up and puffy faced, with Phoun and Le Dâng Khoã. It would make me feel happier if I knew one way or the other if my eyes were deceiving me or not.'

'You are right to ask if you are worried. I would hate you to think that I was where I was for reasons unconnected with what we are both hoping to achieve. However, from the little the Soviet DA could see in the ill-lit room it is more than likely he would never recognise me again. Now, please help me out with a location,' he said, in a defensive tone of voice.

'There is a camp not far from here, one that I walk past quite often, that has been set up since Vientiane was neutralised. The last time I went that way it was empty. You might, possibly, but how I don't know, use that as a base. It used to hold a company – walked round with the boss once – so certainly you'll fit into it. Any other country I've ever been in I'd never have thought of such a solution but round here right now there seems to be so little direction from above and also local commanders have so much discretion, I quite honestly believe you'd cause no worry to anyone if you just went and squatted there. Of course, you'd always have to have a fallback position wherever you were. Think it over: don't condemn it out of hand.'

Rance got up to pour him another whisky. 'Have you got a map of the town handy?' Charlie asked. 'I didn't bring mine and I'd like to get my bearings.' A tropical storm that had been threatening to deluge the place rumbled ominously.

'Charlie, stay the night. We've lots to talk about. The impending rain storm is a reason and an excuse not to return so late. You may want to come back again and a night here now could allay suspicion that the LPF might harbour,' and he nodded towards the servants' quarters.

'Thanks, Colonel. It'll also make a pre-dawn getaway easier. Thanks for the offer.'

Rance went to fetch his town map. On his way downstairs he met Khian An on his way up to shut the windows. 'This rain has spoiled my friend's chances of getting home dry. Turn down the guestroom bed and put out a flask of hot water and the coffee things for an early morning brew – like you do for me at weekends – so that my friend can get an early start without disturbing you. I'll let him out when I go for my run. Don't wait up for us. Good night.'

They spread out the map and Rance showed Charlie where the camp he had suggested was. The rain started lashing down and they smiled at each other. 'I like it but,' and he shook his head dejectedly, 'it's a big area. I've only got fifteen men, counting myself. Also it's too far away. I think it'll have to be in Ban Dong Nasok camp itself. John Chambers told me that Lanouk had given a sketch map of it to you. If you have it handy please show it to me.'

'I'll get it. Unusually I have it upstairs, hidden away.'

'I have already made contact with some of the inmates of the camp but if only I could get information, spot-on information, where these guys live, eat, sleep and work, I'd be a much happier man. I had presumed that my target would be smaller.'

First thing next Monday morning, Rance went to see John Chambers. They had a lot to catch up with. They had taken to each other early on in their acquaintance, each recognising the other was a dedicated professional, Chambers having the advantage of having known about Rance ever since before he became an Attaché. They greeted each other warmly. Rance asked John how he was settling in. 'Fine, thanks, Jason. Make haste slowly is the rule of my game. I got a lot of help from Gordon and had that invaluable interlude in Bangkok. This country, from what little I have seen of it, nearly defies description. Can't think how you have managed to keep sane for so long, to say nothing of having found out what you have and establishing such a fantastic network. As you know, I've been following events from Day One. I'm vastly impressed.'

'Kind words, John, and I thank you for them. It has been fascinating, frustrating, rewarding and revolting. Quite where we're going to now I'm not sure. I've got a couple of matters to discuss. Can you spare the time now? Or would you like to clear any telegrams first?'

'No, they can wait. What have you for me?' Rance first reminded Chambers about his talk with Lanouk as regards the target he had described, then went on to say that Charlie had contacted him and he, Rance, had given him the sketch map of the camp he had been given by Lanouk. Now it's up to him, not us, surely?

John Chambers agreed. 'Tell me. Any news of the Four Rings?'

'The last message that I had was passed on by my driver on my return from Luang Prabang. He reported that Tâ Tran Quán had got where he was wanting to get, was in reasonable health and then my driver became nervous and I got the impression that none of us, the Four Rings and myself, are out of danger. That doesn't alter any decision we might come to or any plan we might make. What does matter is that we keep our collective noses clean.'

'Indeed so,' said Chambers and anything else he was going to say was interrupted by his secretary knocking on the door and excusing herself as she came in with a telegram. She gave it directly to the SIS man who read it. 'Fasten your seat belt, Jason.

Mana's escaped.'

Colonel Gretchanine made one of his periodic tours of the residential areas in other parts of the town. He had a habit of keeping his eyes skinned for anything unusual. As he drove slowly past one particular house, although it was by then dark, he saw two men come out, one of whom he immediately recognised as John Chambers and the other, he thought, might be the comrade he had met up with in the hut – thinner in the face – that night he mysteriously found two tyres without air in them but no puncture. And then he recalled something that had only been an unconscious memory since then: that car by the side of the road that was there on their way up but not on their way back was a British embassy car, 24 CD something. He knew John Chambers was not in it and the Colonel Rance was the only person from the British embassy who came down by convoy. He'd follow that one up *and* get equal somehow.

Escape from any 'open' institution, such as a hospital, is relatively easy. The American air base at Utapao had many Thais working on or near the premises, some as servicemen in parts of the camp where ultra tight security was not considered paramount, like sentries on outer perimeter gates as well as hospital orderlies, others as civilians, who worked, with entry permits, as servants, mechanics, drivers and cooks, while the rash of bars, massage parlours – that did an ever-thriving business despite the local camp radio's frequent pronouncements of 'You cain't get Demarb with a Blarb on your Narb' – souvenir shops and soda fountains attracted the mean, the merry and the plain unscrupulously nasty, everyone of them, of course, clothed in an aura of Thai politeness and out for a quick buck. The USAF mingled with this throng in varying degrees of density, depending on how many or how far their activities took them from the actual business of flying or maintaining aircraft.

Mana, therefore, had no problem in giving the hospital authorities the slip so confident were they that he was back to what they had supposed to be pre-accident normal. When it was discovered that he had disappeared, urgent but cautious steps were taken to try and recover him. Messages flashed, watch was kept on possible contact points and tabs kept on people he might, just, try and meet. Gloom deepened as nil report followed nil report.

As for Mana himself, isolated as he had been for so long and cocooned against news of developments, he felt he needed time to think. He had managed to get his hands on some money during his stay in hospital and had also picked up some more from the pockets of a careless orderly so he was not broke. The countryside around Utapao was pleasant. It was near the coast. There were fishing villages near the beach and the locals were used to seeing folk from many parts of Thailand. It did not take him long to find himself a pleasant young thing to shack up with and work off much of the surplus energy and frustrations that had accumulated with enforced inactivity. He stayed with her for a week then made his way to Bangkok, only one hundred and seventy-seven miles away. As he arrived there late one evening, he made some discreet enquiries and, later that night, rang the bell of a room in the area of Lumphini Park in the south of the city and was let inside by its resident, Kaysorn Bouapha.

Mana, not used to excitement or action as had been the case, was content to stay quietly in Kaysorn's room while she was away working. On the first Saturday after his arrival they had the whole day to themselves. She was a great chatterbox and he listened with half an ear until, for no apparent reason, she mentioned the British Defence Attaché in Vientiane as an example of whom she had had as a pupil.

'Such a gentleman, *Tan Colonen* Rance. I used to visit him when he was learning Lao. He was out one Sunday when I brought him some temple rubbings. He was so long coming back that I had a lie down in his guest room. Shouldn't have, really, I suppose but I had a good look round first. I mean a girl has to be ready for anything, doesn't she? Such a lovely ring I found in his bedroom dressing table drawer. Big, looked old, had *kha* written on the inside. Quite took a fancy to it. It was in a little green leather case where he keeps his studs and cuff links. There was one pair of little crossed knives in silver. Real dinky ...'

Mana only half listened after that as she banged on. *Vientiane next stop*, he decided.

8

June 1975: On 9 June the British embassy became worried when two young technicians, on loan from the British Broadcasting Corporation to Radio Laos, hired the local Flying Club Cessna aeroplane, went on a farewell trip prior to leaving Laos for Britain and did not return. Since the Americans had left, many of the flying aids on which aircraft were so dependent had ceased to be functional. The technicians had filled in a flight plan for the Vientiane Plain and Vang Vieng, the small town at its northern end. The DA and Anthony Crosland made an air search in the Beaver and, overflying Vang Vieng, saw the Cessna on the ground there. Landing in the Beaver would almost certainly mean both aircraft stuck. They flew back to Vientiane and the Ambassador ordered Jason Rance to go to Vang Vieng by road to see what was what once the all-engulfing paperwork was ready.

On Wednesday, 11 June, the AN-2 left Vientiane for Sam Neua. It had to stop and refuel at Luang Prabang, and deliver a bag of mail to the garrison. It was met by Comrade Thong Damdouane and the military commander who brought some mail for delivery to Sam Neua. On board were the two henchmen sent by Nga Sô Lựu, going back to make a detailed report. At the royal capital, the Russian pilot and crew bade farewell to the two officials, thanking them for their security arrangements and confirming that they would see them on Sunday, 15 June, on the way back. As the two henchmen shook hands, neither of them could resist letting their gaze fall on the little finger on both men's right hand.

'Why did those two look at our hands like that?' queried the military man. 'Jealous of your ring and wondering why I don't wear one, I expect,' he said, with a hint of sarcasm.

'Never tell with that lot,' answered Thong with a levity he did not feel.

The church, not far from Rance's villa, had been taken over by the new regime as a lecture hall so the remaining diplomatic community decided to hold services in people's homes instead. On Sunday, 15 June, Leuam came to take Rance to the house of an Australian who lived on the other side of town. On the way there Rance glanced out of the car window and saw the AN-2 circling before landing. He was not to know that it contained three important men: Nga Sô Lựu, Tâ Tran Quán and Thong Damdouane and it was just as well for his peace of mind that he didn't.

It was almost dark when he was driven back to his villa as he'd stayed on for a drink and a chat with the rest of the congregation – all three of them. As the car turned the last corner, he looked up past the driver and saw a figure on a bicycle leaving his house. There was something familiar about him but he was too far away to recognise. Then he was out of sight. Leuam stopped the car outside the gates, tooted on the horn and Khian An came out to let the car in.

Back in the house, Rance looked at his house boy and said, 'You look worried. Anything wrong?'

Khian An hesitated. 'I was in the back preparing your meal. My wife opened the door to a man she thought had visited you and spent a night but she wasn't sure. He said he needed something from upstairs and she told him to wait while she fetched me. I was in the lavatory so wasn't immediately available. He wasn't there when I reached the door and I saw him as he went through the side gate and get on a bike, just before you blew your horn.'

'Never mind. *Bor pen nyang.* I'm sure he took nothing,' said Rance, going upstairs to change into something comfortable. On an impulse he had a good look round. On examining his stud box he found that his ring was missing.

Monday, 16 June: inside the Soviet embassy Colonel Vladimir Gretchanine interviewed a man who, despite having certain facts of an intelligence nature he could use, puzzled him. The man seemed vaguely familiar, both face and voice, although he could not place him. Many Asians looked alike to Gretchanine, that hirsute Muscovite, whose other tricky problem, alike for every diplomat, is to know whether a person who reports in with a story or a wish to defect is a nut-case or genuine. This man had reported to the Soviet embassy earlier in the day, obviously anxious to make contact with a third party and only using the Soviets as a go-between.

'You tell me your name is Mana Varamit?' The Soviet Attaché spoke English well but gutturally. 'And you want to contact a certain comrade named Nga Sô Lựu who is near Sam Neua?'

'Yes, that's correct. I went looking for him but I didn't find him.'

'And you say you are a Thai national and have recently come across from Thailand?'

'Yes. I've told you that already. Didn't you understand? I have an urgent message for Comrade Nga Sô Lựu. I was on my way trying to find him when something happened.'

'What happened? You lost your way or you became ill or what?'

'Yes. Both. But I do know that Comrade Nga Sô Lựu is expecting me. Can you get a message to him for me, please? I want to see him urgently.'

'Why come here? Why not go to the embassy of the Democratic Republic of Vietnam? Surely they are much more likely to help you with one of their nationals than we can? I do not understand why you should come to see me.'

Mana looked at the man, shook his head and tried again to explain his point. 'It's like I was trying to say earlier on. I was in the area of the British Attaché's house. I wanted to get something out of his house that would convince the comrade of the truth of what I wanted to tell him. As I was leaving the area on a bicycle, I turned and saw Colonel Rance in his car. He saw me. I was afraid he would alert some of his men and try to look for me. I had tried to find the Vietnamese embassy but didn't succeed and anyway I felt it far less of a risk to come here. No one would suspect I'd come here. I'll be no embarrassment to anyone and I'll leave you alone as soon as I've cleared myself with Comrade Nga Sô Lựu.

I'm happy to wait for you to contact him.' He smiled disarmingly. 'You see, I believe I lost my memory but I have some vague recollection of a Russian doctor trying to help me. Comrade Lưu is expecting me. Won't you help me?'

Vladimir Gretchanine knew that Comrade Lưu was, by then, in Ban Dong Nasok camp. It would be easy enough to check up without bothering Moscow. He had had nut-cases to deal with before but there was something in this instance that might be worthwhile following up. Besides which, hadn't he mentioned the British DA? He'd play along with him. 'Right you are. As you seem so keen on it, I'll arrange for you to be my guest ...' He broke off. 'Tell me, have you recently suffered from toothache and had a swollen face?' Mana shook his head. 'No? Well, as I was saying, be my guest but only until I've tried to contact that comrade of yours. Where does the British DA come into this? That's what I can't yet get.'

'Oh. Don't you see? He had the fourth ring. Comrade Lưu will understand.'

That same day a large preparatory conference was taking place in Ban Dong Nasok camp. It was an important meeting, chaired by Comrade Nga Sô Lưu, who impressed the others by his cold tenacity of purpose, his obvious inner strength and his mere presence, let alone those black baleful eyes. He had given his audience a résumé of how he envisaged the main conference to be held on Friday, 20 June, when he had an especially important announcement to make. It was pointless making it now because some of the comrades involved were not yet present. Security was paramount – there were still, it was believed, counter-revolutionaries and imperialists at work. It was against them he had had his hand-picked defence squad of twenty-seven men sent down earlier. They also had other tasks to do in connection with the revolution. Defence and protection were of particular importance and he would make a detailed reconnaissance of the conference venue next day. He thanked them for their devotion to duty and chillingly reminded them that vigilance could never be relaxed: 'enemies are everywhere,' he told them.

On Tuesday, 17 June, Rance went to the Ministry of Defence to try and seek an interview with the senior man there, the Deputy Minister, a man he had met many times already. It was virtually useless trying to arrange any meeting by phone as there seemed no system whereby anybody could fix an appointment on behalf of anyone else and even if such an appointment was made, there was no guarantee it would take place. Rance waited half an hour for the Deputy to arrive but found him less than normally cooperative when they started talking. What Rance, and a great many other people, had yet to understand was that in the Communist world even the most mundane and trivial of decisions needs a high level of consensus before it can be made. A person acting on his or her own always courted danger.

In the present affair, the decision to release the two men stuck in Vang Vieng would have to be taken by the Politburo after it had been fully analysed by the local worthies, each man jack of them scared out of his wits lest the least spark of initiative be construed by some other zealot as being counter-revolutionary or whatever the 'in' catchword was. In a world riddled by suspicion, even that with no trace of suspicion attached to it is viewed suspiciously because it is unsuspicious. So it was that even had the hapless Deputy Minister wanted to help, he would have been unable to. Instead he stalled, muttering platitudes and looking embarrassed, with Rance making no progress. After a fruitless fifteen minutes, Rance was told that if he wanted to try his luck and go to Vang Vieng, he would have to pursue the normal channels. Rance gravely thanked the harassed Lao, left him and went to the office where road permits were issued, expecting and finding nothing but bureaucratic dreariness. There were two men, supposedly one policeman from each side, and some armed sentries. They were polite, offering him a seat, and interested in him as a person but totally unconcerned with his request for a permit, a *laisser passer* to Vang Vieng. Eventually he managed to get them to laugh and then they went off for their meal. Rance said he'd wait because he was working on the orders of the Ambassador and had been to have a chat with the Deputy Minister of Defence.

He kept his temper and his patience, and eventually, hours later, got what he wanted from the full-bellied bureaucrats for himself, his driver and his car.

Comrade Nga Sô Lựu declined to see the Soviet official until 10 o'clock on the morning of the 18th. The Russian had given no details but had merely said that he had news that could be of importance. 'What is it?' the Vietnamese asked, once they were seated.

'A man calling himself Mana Varamit' – Nga Sô Lựu sucked

his breath with surprise at the name – 'came to call on me. He seemed to think that you wanted to meet him. He gave me the impression of being entirely rational but of having had some emotional disturbance some time or other which still gives him memory problems.'

Nga Sô Lựu collected his thoughts as Vladimir Gretchanine was talking. After his initial surprise, his face remained impassive as his mind raced. 'Had he anything specific for me?' he queried. 'I know exactly who you mean and it is true I badly want to see him. It is really a question of how I handle him and when.'

'Comrade. His message was to the effect that Colonel Rance, the British Defence Attaché in case you didn't know, has the fourth ring.'

Nga Sô Lựu nodded tortoise-slow and appreciatively. 'Thank you, Comrade. I am indeed grateful to you. I was half expecting something along those lines. It makes more sense to me now than it would had it come from any other source. To take full advantage of your news I must make careful plans. May I request you to tell Mana Varamit that you have met me, that indeed I am happy to meet him and have a long talk, that he is back with us again, that he's better and that I will meet him just as soon as I can in the next day or so.' He broke off. 'I request you bring him here, yes, I want you also, at 1800 hours on 20 June, that's Friday, the day after tomorrow. Here. You need not tell him that until shortly before the time. Can do? Can you keep him till then? Great will be our rewards because, in our case, I believe you would also like to get the edge on the British *Colonen*.'

The Russian looked surprised. 'Yes, I can keep Mana until

then, keep him quiet somehow, and I'd also like to pay off a few scores with that overbearingly rude Englishman. As this is, shall we say, rather personal, let us not make it official? Not yet, at any rate. I think you are indispensable in helping me with my dress rehearsal, probably more than even you can appreciate at the moment.'

That evening a message was sent to the LPF HQ in Vang Vieng. It warned that the British Defence Attaché was being sent up Route 13 by his Ambassador to meet the two Englishmen in custody there on 20 June. Under no circumstances was he to be allowed to see them. He was to be told that permission was expected on 20 June so he should report to the HQ in Ban Dong Nasok the day after, 21 June. An escort for the journey back up to Vang Vieng would be arranged.

In drafting the message Nga Sô Lựu reckoned that Rance would find nothing strange in this request and that no suspicions would be aroused. By getting Rance to visit his camp without a fixed time would make no difference to his planned schedule in order to bring his exposure of the Four Rings, the four traitors, even more conclusively into the open now that Mana had so providentially shown up. He had debated whether to see Mana before his conference or not and had decided that, for presentational purposes, he would arraign the Four Rings with every scrap of evidence that he had and then, as they squirmed to try and get free, he would produce Mana – who would be listening in to the entire proceedings out of sight – as a prime witness and a star performer. 'Operation Four Rings' would be a total success: nothing could prevent it now.

He had also decided how he would carry out the conference. The main building in the camp had been a school long before it had been decided to put some temporary huts and tents around it to make it the base of the Neutralisation Forces of the LPF. It was in the centre of the camp, which would have an increased guard on it. In the main hall of the building was a stage. He would sit at a table in the centre of the stage with his secretary and have a further two tables, the one to his left with four senior cadres and the Four Rings on his right. His special group of twenty-seven picked men would be seated on chairs facing the stage in a semi-circle, to be guard and jury to the terrible indictments that he would bring against the four counter-revolutionary traitors. He would not breathe a word about his plan to anyone. He would need to keep Le Dâng Khoã in the dark but that would be easy enough. He would arrange for the Russian to bring Mana along and be shown into the building from a rear door after, the time decreed for the meeting to begin, with Mana ready to be brought out from behind the stage when called. He dismissed Rance from his mind entirely as far as this operation was concerned. Once Rance's car was away in the Liberated Zone he would arrange for something 'permanent' to happen to it and to him. He turned him mind back to other, and more pressing, problems.

Next morning, 19 June, at 8 'clock, he sent for Le Dâng Khoã. 'Comrade. Come in and sit down. You are responsible for security in this camp. Let us discuss what arrangements you have made for tomorrow night. What have you done so far? Let me have a full briefing. Leave nothing out. I want to hear everything.'

'Certainly, Comrade. The hall will have been checked to ensure no unauthorised persons have access. The camp security will, as far as the perimeter and gate protection are concerned, be as normal. There will be ten men in the guardroom, one section of seven men patrolling the perimeter and one section in reserve as stand-by in their sleeping quarters. As far as guarding the hall is concerned, I am detailing the group you yourself designated from Sam Neua. That is about the sum of it. Have you any comments or suggestions, Comrade?'

Nga Sô Lựu mulled this over, then said, 'Fine, but I want the entire squad of twenty-seven men inside the hall because much of what I have to say is not concerned with immediate local security and covers our future political work. I want them to hear what I have to say from start to finish so you must find need extra men to guard the building during the session.'

'Comrade. This will, of course, be done but I must have your clearance and written authority for all twenty-seven men to be present. As far as I am aware, some of them are not ranking cadres or even party members. My orders on this are specific. I will only allow them in if you so insist and order me in writing.'

Nga Sô Lựu stared at Le Dâng Khoã with an expression of disgust and disdain, black eyes flashing glassily. *Insolent pup*, he inwardly fumed, glancing unconsciously at Le Dâng Khoã's right hand. *Fancy daring to put me in my place*. The mood passed and, with only a trace of hesitation, said, 'Of course, Comrade. You are correct. I was about to say that. Can you arrange that to your satisfaction? Good. If there are insufficient men for the extra guard duties you will, naturally, call on our other resources, won't you?

Now, our own seating arrangements. I wish for three tables to be placed on the stage, one in the centre where I and my secretary will sit, and the other two to left and right of it. I am arranging for representatives from my office in Sam Neua, our forces in Luang Prabang and Vientiane on both of the other tables. I would like you, along with Comrades Tâ Tran Quán, Thong Damdouane and Bounphong Sunthorn, on the right of me.'

If Le Dâng Khoã had any reservations about the seating arrangements, he kept them to himself. 'Right, Comrade. I fully understand what you require. I have no more questions so if you'll excuse me, I'll go and made some special passes for the guard that will be responsible for the security of the conference hall.'

Le Dâng Khoã, although he hadn't let on to Nga Sô Lựu, was deeply suspicious of the seating arrangements. Two points had struck him as unorthodox: one that the group of men who had been billed more as security men than anything else from Office 95 were to be part and parcel of the main proceedings and the other was that the four of them who had perfectly adequate protocol placings were to be together on one table. Frankly, it stank. The glance towards his hand hadn't gone unnoticed. There had to be something else that he needed to take into account. He thought back. There was only one telephone in the camp and there was a radio link with Sam Neua and other stations. There was also the Guard Commander's report book. During the course of the day he would find out if there was anything that could help him determine what the danger was and where it lay.

He waited until Nga Sô Lựu had gone back to the hut he used as an office, outside which stood one of the men from Sam

Neua as sentry. He went over to the guardroom and asked for the register. There, amongst others, was 124 CD 052, the Soviet diplomatic number, and a Colonel Vladimir Gretchanine had been written down as passenger. That was unusual. Foreign cars, even those of the fraternal bloc, seldom came into Ban Dong Nasok camp. Wasn't that why they had met outside that one inconclusive night? He turned back and went into the telephone room. Most Communist organisations only boasted one telephone and it was easy to keep tabs on who wanted to contact whom and what was said. On his way over, he passed the main building and, on an impulse, made his way into the little room behind the stage. It had always been empty but now a table and two chairs had been put there. He sat down in one of the chairs, head in hands, pondering deeply. He heard a fatigue party moving about in the main part of the building. Some men climbed up onto the stage and started talking. They were easily audible and Le Dâng Khoã recognised the voices of the Sam Neua lot and also Nga Sô Lưu's secretary who said, 'You've put the chairs and the table into the room at the back, have you? Good. I'll go and lock the door myself from the inside and you,' obviously detailing one of the men, 'make sure the outer door is locked from now on until our meeting. Here's the key. It's unlocked now. Go and get some oil and put some on the lock. Comrade Nga Sô Lưu does not want it to squeak during the conference.'

Le Dâng Khoã got up and quietly left by the outside door, quickly testing it and noticing that it did, in fact, make some noise. He went over to the telephone operator. 'Just want to check if Comrade Soth Petrasy rang through yesterday. Can I see your list?'

The operator handed it over without question. Sure enough, at 1700 hours on the 16th, a call for the Black-eyed Butcher had come from the Soviet embassy. 'No, he didn't. Obviously he himself found what he was looking for.' He gave the list back. So the Soviets wanted Nga Sô Lưu on the 16th and came over to see him on the 18th. Must have come when he was over at the other side of the camp. And what of the radio? The operator was a young lad who held all cadres in awe. At a guess but speaking firmly, he asked, 'Have you had any confirmation of the message Comrade Nga Sô Lưu got you to send yesterday?'

'I don't think confirmation was required,' he answered dubiously. 'I'd better make sure,' and opened a cupboard where copies of messages were sent. He flipped through a file. 'Here you are. I presume this is the one you're referring to as there weren't any others.'

Le Dâng Khoã quickly ran though it and found nothing suspicious. 'You're right. Well done.' He smiled. 'That's why none has come. I'll remind the Comrade that no confirmation was requested. Thank you.'

He left the radio room, nodding at the sentry, who was also one of the recent influx. He sensed that he had two advantages: one that Nga Sô Lưu would not recognise any of the new guard he'd be getting and the other that nothing would be done to alarm him until the comrade was ready. And he was sure that that would not be until 20 June.

One of the problems facing Charlie was how best could he get quick enough warning to take advantage of any situation that could make his job easier. He had had information about the meeting on 20 June but, despite his having been able to infiltrate the staff of the camp, it had not yet been possible to move his men there. He had had a meeting with one of the comrades who had some how got to know him during this period of uncertainty and restlessness. The hut he'd had his second meeting with a member of the camp was not far from Ban Dong Nasok. He had been just a little surprised when the Russian DA had turned up that first time but he had gathered that, in Bangkok, the Russians never thought they were achieving anything unless there was a great deal of mystery and an equally great deal of secrecy.

Charlie had pondered for a long time just what line to take when he had first been given this mission of neutralising, if not eliminating the twenty-seven NVA 'hit men'. He had the wherewithal to masquerade as government troops or as PL. The speed of the PL advance had made him concentrate on the PL aspect and he had already done a lot of homework on various personalities in the LPF hierarchy to be able to talk authoritatively enough to be accepted as one of them and his intelligence work had given him sufficient background data he needed to make himself and his men seem genuine. He also knew that, by and large, the administrative side of the LPF was sufficiently weak for any rapid checking, especially during this present period of flux. He had posed as one of the left-wing Neutralists from somewhere up north in far Phong Saly province who had brought his men down on a training mission to Sayabouri province and then had been given orders, probably garbled as it was turning out, to go to

Vientiane. He had come down the river by boat but the necessary paperwork had gone astray. He was hoping that the tenuous link he had fixed, Phoun through Leuam, thence to a comrade in the HQ by the Morning Market and finally to a comrade in the other camp would prove solid enough to last him out. Their presence had been accepted without query and the line that Charlie had put across was that he was an ardent nationalist and a Vietnamese-hater, had something against the Communists that burnt inside him. If and when an opportunity came, the comrade would infiltrate him into the camp. He would then, and only then, be able to make his plan, obviously on the tenuous basis of chance. It wouldn't have been possible anywhere else in Asia but where else in Asia was there another Laos? He would pick his moment, take his chance and hope that by then he could formalise getaway plans. He was just a little worried by Colonel Rance who was either deep and devious or shallow and stupid: whichever was the case, he was glad that the Englishman had nothing to do with anything that really mattered. Charlie was his own master.

Late on the evening of Thursday, 19 June, Phoun and the other man who had infiltrated, rode into their temporary camp on bicycles, with orders for the whole squad to proceed, as soon as possible, to the LPF camp.

Well after dark that night Le Dâng Khoã met Charlie's group at the main entrance of Ban Dong Nasok camp. He welcomed them in a manner that would not cause the Guard Commander any suspicion. This was not difficult; odd packets of men dressed in PL uniform were constantly coming and going, acting as police or escorts for important people or merely on patrol. Copying the Chinese army, none of the PL wore any badges of rank or regimental distinguishing marks so it was impossible to tell what unit a person did belong to. Although the Neutralisation Forces had been stationed in Vientiane for twenty months, there was a constant trickle of changes so new faces were a commonplace. Charlie's contacts in the world of intelligence had allowed him to be prepared with the necessary documentation so, unless any nasty situation blew up, he and his group should easily escape attention. He had studied, in detail, the camp plan that Rance had provided so had a good knowledge of its layout. There was a hut in the far corner from the main entrance. Le Dâng Khoã led the group over to it and told them to sort themselves out. He took Charlie to one side for a briefing.

'This corner of the camp is less crowded than the other parts. Tomorrow evening is the critical time for action. There is to be the meeting we have long talked about. It will take place in the old school building. I'll show you when we get a chance. I'll leave the details for you to work out but it won't, I'm afraid, be as straightforward as I'd have liked. I suspect our Russian friend will be coming despite assertions to the contrary. Whether he'll be alone or not is uncertain. There is some plan to hide him in the room at the back of the stage – him and one other, I suspect, because a table and two chairs have been put there without my being supposed to know although I am in charge of the security details. There's something afoot. But about the room. I'll show you the obvious things such as the light fuses. You have explosives with you? I'm concerned about the blowing up of the place. It's not the messiness you'll understand but myself and three like-minded men are to sit at one table on the stage and a man you may yet to have heard about, Comrade Nga Sô Lưu, known as the Black-eyed Butcher, probably the most senior and influential cadre along with certainly a secretary and possibly another senior Lao cadre. Their arrival from Sam Neua has made me most uncomfortable. On the other side of the stage from where I'll be is another table with another lot, probably four, of senior cadres. I'd be more than happy for that lot to go but I wouldn't want us four to go with them. I'm sure you understand that.'

Charlie said he did then asked, 'Will the twenty-seven "hit men" be at the meeting and, if so, will they be carrying their weapons with them?'

'Yes, both. I'm afraid they will so your task will be that much harder.'

Charlie nodded. 'I'll have a good look around tonight and again when it's light early tomorrow. Rather than explosions, too chancy, I'll concentrate on shooting them, which is less chancy. In my mind's eye I can see the easiest solution to be I and my men hiding in the room behind the stage and when I judge the best moment – quite how I'm not yet sure – I'll switch the fuse off. Immediately you four leave your chairs and move almost faster than you've ever moved before to the back of the stage and get into the room. Just as soon as you're in, I'll move my men out onto the stage and do what I have to. Of course I can't guarantee killing or even maiming all of them in the dark but Phoun and I will work something out. That will leave you four to get away, so I'll also be looking for a place for my getaway somewhere at the back. I haven't checked yet but on the sketch map I have been given a gate is shown. Locked on not, I don't yet know. I'll only be able to check on that, though, when people are concentrating on the security of the meeting. Can you detail my group to be responsible for the gate sector of the perimeter? I'd like to be undisturbed while I'm leaving through it. I may not have a key for any lock but I do have some strong wire cutters.'

'I am sure I can fix it. I'll confirm that later.'

Friday, 20 June, dawned fine. The British Defence Attaché's paperwork was at last ready. Leuam drove round early to collect Rance who had packed an overnight bag, as a precaution. He also carried his passport, his Attaché's identity card and the *laisser passer* for the journey to Vang Vieng. Leuam had his own separate documentation and the vehicle's various bits of paperwork so that even the most regulation-bound and bureaucratically-minded functionary would not cavil but be appeased. They set off up Route 13, Khian An anxiously watching them go. Traffic was light and they reached the first barrier in good time. It opened as they approached it, no doubt impressed by the flag fluttering in front of the big white car. Troops manning the barrier paid him little attention, which struck Rance as odd but everything today was a gamble. It was the day Le Dâng Khoã had warned him about and he had told Charlie to be especially careful. He was worried about the disappearance of the ring – it just could not have been Mana, surely? – and certainly not Charlie. But neither man could have any idea that he, Jason Rance, had it nor, even if somehow they did have knowledge, where he kept it. He had never mentioned it to Khian An, certainly, but Leuam knew he had it. *Talisman or incubus?* How would Leuam react on learning it had been stolen? He was worried about the relationship between Leuam and Bounphong, even though they were brothers. He had yet to place Phoun in the chain between Charlie and Le Dâng Khoã. Could it just conceivably be coincidence? Could it be that Phoun was playing a deeper game than he, Rance, had been led to believe? If Phoun were a PL agent, was he safe in Charlie's group? If not, was it to be expected that Phoun would have been in the hut that night? But he was still not certain sure about Charlie. Had it not been for Le Dâng Khoã's presence he would be even more worried but, as it was, nothing was sure. What was Leuam's real relationship with Phoun? Did it really matter and, whether it did or didn't, what could he do about it? He teased these thoughts around in his mind. The road led over a small hill and, just beyond the ridge, the PL manned a large barrier which had a notice written in big letters, Liberation Zone. The car crawled to a stop. In front were a few lorries and a couple of taxis. When their turn came, the sentry stood in front of their car and another armed man came and beckoned Leuam out and to follow him up the bank to an office. Rance sat still, waiting. A third armed man came and opened the back door. He saw the overnight bag and searched it thoroughly. Rance kept quiet and the man ordered him, in halting French, to follow him. They went up the steps together and, after having seen Leuam's face look forlornly at the *laisser passer*, Rance realised that the document he had so sedulously acquired, had not been accepted. The unexpected comment about it was that, as it had been issued in Vientiane which was not yet in the Liberated Zone, it had no currency outside Vientiane.

When Rance remonstrated and quietly pointed out that one of the signatories had actually written Lao Patriotic Front under his name it still made no difference: Vientiane was not in the Liberated Zone therefore nothing it produced could be valid. Rance had just begun to give up hope when he changed tack. He congratulated them on their soldierly appearance and said that he presumed they realised that he was the Attaché for all Laos, not for one side or the other, and that he had been to Sam Neua and met So-and-So, none of which had any bearing on the actual problem of being allowed through the barrier into the Liberated Zone. However, it must have convinced whoever was empowered to give the order to raise the barrier because the 'laisser passer' was countersigned, returned and Rance was allowed to continue on his journey – a whole hour later.

Comrade Nga Sô Lưu was busy that Friday morning, 20 June. He had once more rehearsed his points for the conference that evening. He had checked with Le Dâng Khoã that the security arrangements with the reinforced guard were in order. He had walked round the camp, had the new security guard pointed out to him from a distance and had once again been to the scene of the evening's conference. He had been shown the small room at the back of the stage. He had tested the door to see if it squeaked and had expressed himself satisfied. Now he was in his office with his secretary. He felt a deep thrill inside him which he could scarcely contain. Tonight, at long last, he would reveal the treachery of those four so-called comrades and then, to put matters right, he would deal with the Englishman. 'I know we have our hands full for today but there is another problem we must give our attention to. The Englishman, Colonel Rance, has been meddling too much. I have asked him to come to the camp tomorrow but I'd like confirmation that he has gone to Vang Vieng to meet those two other meddling Englishmen. Will you make sure that, whatever happens, he does not turn up tonight. Just to make absolutely sure he does not come here,' and he turned to one of his bodyguards, 'you, Comrade, in case you didn't hear what I just said, are responsible that the British Defence Attaché, in his car 24 CD 050, does not enter this camp tonight.'

The bodyguard acknowledged the order and took a step to the rear.

Nga Sô Lựu continued talking to his secretary. 'After he gets to Vang Vieng today, he'll be kept there long enough to make it impossible to get back during our conference.'

In the Soviet embassy, Vladimir Gretchanine was talking with Mana Varamit. The Russian was intrigued with what the Thai had to say and Nga Sô Lựu's reaction. He was not so concerned with Mana's background, which he could find out about later, but with what Mana had to say about Rance. Gretchanine had, like so many other Communist cadres, been particularly busy with more pressing business now that the programme for complete Communist domination of Laos had to be speeded up, so he had paid less attention to Mana that otherwise he would have. Now he was trying to pump him.

'What were you saying about a ring?' he asked when they

were having a chat over a cup of coffee after their midday meal that same Friday. 'You haven't yet told me anything that can really justify wasting so much of my time on you. Ring? That sort of stuff is more for women, not men. You're not one of those Thad Luang tarts like we thought the Colonel was?'

There was something about Mana that intrigued yet repelled him. The Russians were never much good at handling Asians and Vladimir Gretchanine was no exception. His hectoring tone annoyed Mana who, as a Thai, felt rudeness was the one fault that could never be forgiven and, also as a Thai, could keep his emotions so bottled up that he personified the 'inscrutable oriental'. Mana was not going to tell this coarse man anything that would put at risk his pent-up emotions. He knew that once he started talking it would be all or nothing. With a sudden spurt of anger, he pulled the stolen ring out of his pocket and gave it to the Russian. 'Put in on and show it to Comrade Nga Sô Lựu when we meet him this evening. That will make sure you'll learn everything. Don't let's talk about it till then. I can't bear the thought of having to say everything twice over.'

Rance's car drove round a bend and there was a village, the last one before Vang Vieng and one from which a feeder road led away into the hills to the northeast, towards Meo territory. The road junction was in the middle of the village and, in the middle of the road, was a rough booth that had not been there before and a crowd of some fifty locals milling around a couple of LPF officials, one of whom turned at the sound of the car. He held out his hand in a gesture that meant halt. Rance told Leuam to stop the car short of the booth, got out and went to see what the hold-up was. He wanted to stretch his legs and Leuam could have a break.

There was an air of disquiet among the small crowd. They looked at the Englishman as he came up to them and then some looked away again. Rance gave the PL his *laisser passer* to examine and asked if he could drive on.

'No.'

'Are you in charge here?'

The man looked at him, unsmilingly. 'We two are both the same,' and turned away.

Rance went into the booth and showed the other man, the elder of the two, his documents. The man glanced at them. 'Don't mean a thing to me,' he said. 'None of you can move on from here. You can't, they can't,' and he indicated the crowd around him.

'I've been allowed this far,' Rance ventured. 'I have to go to Vang Vieng and meet two Englishmen who are there. I have seen the officials concerned and have their permission to go and see them. How long are you going to keep me waiting here?'

The senior cadre, with one eyebrow cocked higher than the other, had taken off his uniform shirt and Rance was intrigued beyond measure to see a star of Tonkin tattooed on his shoulder. A memory stirred. *After the war in 1945 looking for Vietminh with the Japanese – that man hiding in the ditch … wanting to shoot us up from the rear.* The British Defence Attaché, feeling hot, took off his hat and stared at the man.

The functionary looked at Rance and his malevolent stare

became even darker. 'I remember you but you probably don't remember me. You, many years ago, ordered some Japanese feudalist soldiers to piss on me. You had three puppet soldiers with you. You bound me and led me away. The French lumps of *merde* tortured me but I managed to escape. The man's voice grew thick with rage. 'I've a good mind to bind you and piss on you, here and now. If you don't get out of here within five minutes that is what I'll do. Get out of my sight here and now and stay out.'

To Rance here was a prime example of the world's most dangerous man, the over-educated idiot whose education outruns his common sense the day he learns how to sign his name. He was probably working under some sort of orders and Rance wondered if it could be connected with a rumour he had recently heard of NVA troop movements in the vicinity directed against alleged Meo rebels. There was no option but to return to Vientiane. It was a pity he had been unable to penetrate up the road as far as Vang Vieng but he realised that there was so much in Communist bureaucracy that militated against the right hand ever knowing what the left hand was doing, it would have been a wonder had it worked out as hoped for. He walked back to his car, got in and ordered Leuam to turn round and drive back. It was still early and he was in no particular hurry. If he got the chance he'd stop and give someone a lift. Might conceivably learn something of interest. One never knew …

'There is no sign of this Englishman. What do you think has happened?' The Deputy Commander of Vang Vieng camp asked the Commander. 'Do you recommend we try and contact Ban

Dong Nasok Camp?'

'No, leave it till tomorrow. They are much too busy to bother about him and anyway the troop movement in the area will have slowed him down.'

In Ban Dong Nasok the Four Rings were talking together. Bounphong Sunthorn and Soth Petrasy had come across from their office near the Morning Market. This was the first occasion all four Rings had been together for a long time. Le Dâng Khoã looked casually around and, seeing nobody else, said, 'We are now in a critical situation. Nga Sô Lựu suspects us and I fear he will take some dramatic action this evening. It is just possible that he will delay doing whatever he has in mind because he has been referring to a "dress rehearsal". However you may, almost undoubtedly will, experience some shooting tonight. Play it completely orthodoxly. Remember – nothing is sure until it has happened or proved to have happened. For our own safety, keep separate until we meet naturally and normally. Before we go, I must say that I am delighted that Tâ Tran Quán is well and among us again. And also there is one favourable omen: remember that the Great Master said "right not left". Our table tonight is on the right of Nga Sô Lựu, not the left. As for the rest of what he said, who would have thought that the English *Colonen* would have found out about us as he did? And been the help to us he has? It's the greatest shame he can't extract us from our predicament tonight. No Mana: no Rance. It's up to us – now or in another thirty years' time, despite what His Holiness read into the divinations. But one thing is certain sure: only with that

Black-eyed Butcher out of the way will we pertain as prophesied. If *only* the English *Colonen* could come to our rescue. If it does come to a choice between him and us, it will have to be him, come what may.'

They dispersed and Le Dâng Khoã went in search of Charlie. It was late afternoon, overcast and a monsoon downpour looked imminent. The senior cadres of the LPF carried umbrellas and, as a few spots of rain spattered down, he put his own up. It was not made of cloth but of oiled fibre that made more noise when rained on than did the cloth type. He reached the guardroom and went inside. 'What orders have you had, Comrade?' he asked the Guard Commander. 'I want to check and confirm everyone is ready and talking with the same voice.'

'I have orders to expect a diplomatic car in at around six thirty. Its number is,' and he turned to the ledger by the window. 'Bother, some rain has splashed the entry. Is it 124 CD 050 or 124 CD 052? Whichever it is, that's the only one.'

* The diplomatic plates of the Soviet and British embassy vehicles were as given in the text.

Le Dâng Khoã nodded sagely. 'Yes, that'll be the one,' he said and turned away, making for the hut where Charlie's men were. Under the umbrella he was just another pair of legs wearing green. He passed some men he recognised as Charlie's, already on duty in the vicinity of the main building. He continued until he was about thirty metres from Charlie's hut when he saw another figure nearing the hut from the other direction. As the other man lifted his umbrella he saw Nga Sô Lựu and paused momentarily before moving on. Le Dâng Khoã's heart missed a beat. *Act normally*, he told himself, as he also made for the hut. About ten metres from it, he saw Nga Sô Lưu open the door, look inside and heard him say something he couldn't catch as the rain was, by now, noisy on his umbrella. As Le Dâng Khoã reached the door, Nga Sô Lưu turned round, faced him and said, 'Don't waste your time here. I've checked it,' and, almost as though he meant to say something else, changed his mind and stalked off in the direction from which he had come. He probably did not hear Le Dâng Khoã's 'No matter, Comrade. Just a routine check.'

Once the senior cadre was out of sight, Le Dâng Khoã opened the door and looked inside. There were Charlie and Phoun. He looked quizzically at Charlie who was looking bemused. 'What's up?' the Vietnamese asked.

'I am baffled. The man who looked in here a moment ago said, "You're earlier than I expected. When," and I did not catch the name, "comes, go and take your seat in the room behind the stage. I'll call you."'

The storm that hit Vientiane in the late afternoon spread down from the hills to the north and northwest and made Rance's drive back slower than he had reckoned on. The road quickly lost any semblance of dust and turned into red mud that bespattered the car. The rain washed some of it off but the number plate stayed patchily mud-streaked. Leuam stopped the car a couple of times to wipe the windscreen and it was then that he was approached by the odd person to give them a lift and this he had willingly done, chatting with them and finding them friendly. When he reached the barrier into the Neutralised Zone, he was waved down and checked. Leuam was just about to start up and drive on when a man came hurrying down the steps from the guard tent and beckoned Rance to open the door for him. This Rance did and the man got in, turned to the Englishman with a smile and said, 'I liked the way you spoke this morning. You said you were here representing your country and not taking sides.'

Rance looked at the man and said, indeed, that was correct but surely he hadn't come out into the rain only to tell him that?

'No, but I'd be most grateful if you take me to Ban Dong Nasok camp. The rain has delayed me. Can you get me there by 6 o'clock? Don't mind, do you?'

Rance looked at his watch. 'No problem. Glad to be of assistance. Away we go, Leuam and turn right near KM 5. We'll take the short cut up the track that leads straight to the camp and that should get us there by,' he made a calculation, 'around 6 o'clock.' He turned to his companion and continued, 'if we were to go round the long way, we'd only get in by about half past and you'd be late.'

They drove off and, just as it was getting dark in the gloom of the overcast evening, reached the camp. The sentry looked as the dirty number plate, making out the 24 of the CD followed by 050, behind the red mud. The passenger opened the window and shouted out, 'It's all right, Comrade. I am the senior cadre in the main check point on Route 13.'

The sentry opened the barrier and, as the car drew level with him, put his head through the window and said, 'Drive round to the left of the main building.' He then turned to Rance and said,

'Go in by the back door and wait till you are called for. That's what the comrade said.' He withdrew his head and beckoned the car on. Rance wondered who was to call him and why.

The cadre leant forward to Leuam and gave instructions as how best to go where directed. The lights of the car flashed against the window of the building as it neared, then swung away to the left as the cadre said, 'Here we are. Halt, will you? I'll get out and go by foot from here. I really appreciated the lift, *Tan Colonen*. Great help. Would have been in a fix if it had not been for you.'

He got out and walked away. Rance hesitated. The situation intrigued him but something was wrong somewhere. He told Leuam to switch off the engine and his lights. He got out and saw the door. He went up to it and opened it. There, to his intense surprise, was Charlie with several armed men. As he entered, Charlie whipped round and gave a little yelp of surprise when he saw who it was. He put his hand to his lips and went up to him. 'Go away. Get out of here. You're in mortal danger,' he hissed in desperation. He looked outside and saw the car. 'Continue round the block and leave. Drive as quickly as possible. For God's sake go,' and he turned the astonished Rance around and gave him a shove. Rance went to the car, pulled the door to, gave Leuam instructions and they drove off. Rance leant forward, thankful he'd memorised the plan of the camp. He directed Leuam and in a short time they were at the guardroom. Again the Guard Commander waved his down. 'That was quick, Comrade. Dirty night, this. Back to the embassy? Long live Lao-Soviet friendship,' and waved them on.

Inside the hall, the delegates ready for the meeting. The twenty-seven 'hit men' sat in the body of the hall near the stage in a semicircle. The senior cadres had taken their places at the three tables on the stage and, even as Nga Sô Lựu was shuffling his papers, a car drove past, making the hall brighter and casting shadows. Nga Sô Lựu permitted himself a little smile of triumph: *it's working out well*, he thought, *although they have come separately*. He had planned to give the main lecture first and then turn and rend those four traitors. Melodramatically he withdrew his pistol from its holster and put it on the table, checking once again that it was loaded as he did. He moved the safety catch to the fire position. The audience was armed but, except for him, none of the men on the stage carried weapons. He stood up, cleared his throat and started. 'Comrades. Welcome. There is serious business tonight. During the evolvement of our Glorious Revolution ...'

The Soviet car, driven by Vladimir Gretchanine with Mana in the front seat, passed Rance's car about five minutes from the camp. The rain was still heavy and the lights of both cars obscured the other's passengers' view. At the gate the car was flagged down. The sentry came out into the rain, stooped below the barrier and beckoned the driver to lower the window. 'What do you want?' he asked in halting French. 'No one is allowed here. You must go away.'

Vladimir Gretchanine remonstrated. 'Don't be so foolish, Comrade. I have already received clearance from Comrade Nga Sô Lựu. I came to the camp on 18 June, two days ago. Look at my number plate and check your records. Hurry up, my man, I'm a bit late as it is.' He turned to Mana. 'You tell him from your window. Bloody apes. None of you can ever do anything right.'

Mana said nothing and waited until the sentry returned from checking the records in the guardroom. 'What's wrong, Comrade?' Mana asked.

'Been a balls up somewhere. We've just let a car in with a European and a Lao. Sorry, you can't go into the camp although the number's OK, 124 CD 052, like the last car's, except that its final number was 050 but as my records are smudged I believe that one and not this. Stay here. I'll go and ask the Guard Commander.'

Mana translated that to the Soviet Colonel who cursed and swore but other than break the barrier or open it himself, there was not much he could do about taking the car in. Grumbling madly, he opened the door of the car and got out, a tall, heavily-built, silver-haired man with blue eyes. 'Come on, then, Mana. Let's walk it. Nga Sô Lựu said something about going round to the back of the main building. I'll contact him and let you know. I'll go in and ask him what the hell this is about.'

The Guard Commander joined them and the three men splashed their way towards the building. Charlie's men on guard met them twenty metres away and challenged them. 'Go to hell, you bloody Wogs,' retorted the Soviet, thoroughly uncomfortable in the wet. 'I'm going in there whatever you may urge to the contrary,' and he indicated the closed door of the conference room.

'Comrade Guard Commander, go back to your duty in the guardroom,' said the senior man of Charlie's group. To the Russian, 'You cannot go in there. I order you to leave the camp immediately. Get out!'

With another oath, the Russian moved forward, taking not the slightest notice, this time for the main door, Mana following. The senior man acted swiftly and decisively to stop him from going inside. In one deft movement, he moved forward and kicked him hard in the back on the knees. Vladimir Gretchanine fell down heavily, getting plastered in mud. His temper snapped and he started threshing about, cursing hideously. By then Charlie and Phoun had reached the main door. Charlie saw what to do. 'Phoun. Go back now. Off with the main switch when you hear me shout or any firing'

Inside the conference room, Nga Sô Lựu's rhetoric and his obvious cold-blooded sincerity of purpose, let alone his deep-set black eyes with their glassy stare, had fully engaged the attention of the audience. The Four Rings, being on the side of the building nearest the door became aware of a rumpus before the others did. Le Dâng Khoã, in his capacity of being responsible for camp security, should have made an effort to find out what was happening but, in the belief that any initiative he took should be nicely balanced between prudent official reaction and his own survival, maintained a discreet silence. It was one of those nasty situations where whatever he did, he would probably be wrong. He gently nudged his neighbour, Thong Damdouane, who, turning, saw the sweat on Le Dâng Khoã's upper lip. Some of the twenty-seven 'hit men' also heard the noise and started fidgeting, looking towards the door. Their inattention was suddenly noticed by Nga Sô Lựu who stopped abruptly in mid-sentence, cocking his head from side to side like an indignant hen. In a sudden hush there was an unmistakable English expletive.

'What on earth's that noise?' he snapped as he looked at the door with fiendish intensity. 'This is completely unforgivable. I won't stand for this sort of thing under any circumstances.' He took a step forward, lifted the pistol off the table, quivering tensely, and gave Le Dâng Khoã a villainous glance of concentrated hatred. 'Comrades! Be fully alert. Be ready to take any action necessary but do *nothing* until I order you to.'

His voice was raised to a shrill bark of barely-suppressed emotion. The 'hit men' fondled their weapons, waiting for action. Hadn't they been warned that Vientiane was a dangerous place? Luckily they were ready for anything – and anybody. One or two of them fixed their gazes on Le Dâng Khoã, wondering, as the Comrade in charge of security, how his system had broken down. Tension mounted. The noise grew louder and more confused.

Charlie was taken aback as any by the turn of events and, in the drizzle and confusion, found it hard to take in what was happening and who was involved. He saw the mud-bespattered Russian was on the point of opening the door. Once inside he would spoil everything and ruin Charlie's plan so he had to be stopped. Charlie reached him before he could grasp the door handle and hit him really hard, on the side of the head, with the butt of his weapon. The Russian staggered and, in trying to regain his balance, caught hold of the door handle with his left hand, turning it, so the door swung open, into the room. He put his right hand around the lintel. 'Muck me about?' he snarled. Everyone inside saw him clearly and made ready to repel this new and still unexplained danger. Some of the cadres had risen to their feet, hands clutching weapons, crouched in an exaggerated pose, their eyes flicking from door to leader to door, waiting for the sign that would launch them into action.

Those sitting at the two side tables were gazing horrified at what they saw, and what Nga Sô Lựu also saw, and understood, as those on the nearer table understood but were helpless to do anything about. There, on the little finger of the tall, slumping European who had mouthed that English expletive, was a ring, their ring. The three who wore rings instinctively covered their own hands as though by so doing they could ward off inevitable disaster. Why had the Englishman tried to thrust himself on them so grotesquely, so out of character? They then, almost as one man, glancing at the Political Commissar whose eyes were riveted on that pink hand that pawed the lintel, almost caressingly with epicene stroking. And, in that moment, the Four Rings knew with sickening clarity that the senior Vietnamese cadre knew ... as he raised his pistol. *I'll get that cursed Englishman, scum that he is. If ever a man was expendable ...* he thought savagely, almost beside himself with rage and the desire for revenge for the months of frustration and fretting. Then a head came round the door, a European with blue eyes, staring, fixed, frantic and malevolent, his grey hair streaked with blood. At that very moment the hard edge of Charlie's rigid right hand struck him on the brachial plexus nerve bundle at the base of the neck. The Russian went limp and slumped. Simultaneously Nga Sô Lựu aimed between those maddened eyes, squeezed the trigger and killed the intruder with a single shot, exulting as he did so that he had got rid of one enemy, a fool and an interfering meddler. Now he would get rid of the others.

The Russian crashed forward – and, as Princess Golden Fairy had prophesied so long ago, 'died a savage death' – and Charlie saw a new Nga Sô Lựu, flushed and snarling, turn towards the table between him and the door and draw a bead on Le Dâng Khoã. Charlie fired. Nga Sô Lựu took the bullet between his coal-black eyes and his shot went madly wide, hitting Mana who had appeared in the doorway, standing over the dead Russian. Mana staggered back with a shriek and fell at Charlie's feet. The lights went out and pandemonium ensued as the rest of Charlie's team opened fire at the twenty-seven 'hit men', who, seeing nothing and not knowing what to do, blundered about, bumping into each other and firing at imaginary enemies they could not see, making the already unmanageable confusion into a nightmare of chaos. The guards and sentries from the other parts of the camp came doubling up to the conference hall to do battle with any renegades left alive. In the dark Mana made a supreme effort to rise and wrest Charlie's weapon from him. Charlie turned back and finished Mana off with one bullet, never realising that the man he had killed was his own look-alike but unseen-since-babyhood elder brother.

Charlie dashed back to the rear of the hall, called his men off the stage and switched the lights on. Firing ceased. His men gathered behind him, he stepped onto the stage. In a commanding voice he shouted for calm at the moment that Le Dâng Khoã, arms waving for silence, quickly moved back onto the stage to join him. Wounded men moaned and struggled to rise.

'Quiet! Silence! This meeting has to be cancelled,' shouted Le Dâng Khoã. He had been joined by the other three Rings who loudly approved that decision.

Eventually order prevailed. Without waiting for the normal Communist practice of convening some sort of meeting, Charlie took the law into his own hands. 'I will arrange to evacuate the body of this Russian and dispose of it properly. You', he pointed to senior unwounded 'hit man', make arrangements for gathering the dead and the wounded, taking them to hospital and immediately informing the Politburo.'

He turned to his own squad. 'Lift him up and carry him to the guardroom. If his own car is not there I'll think again. Hurry. The quicker we get him away, the safer for everyone here.'

They lugged the body to the front of the camp and, yes, there was the car. Charlie felt in the dead man's pockets and produced the ignition key. Put him in the front seat and I'll drive,' he said. 'Three of the squad sit in the back, the rest find your way over the river to Nong Khai. Once there wait for me.'

Before Charlie drove the Soviet DA's car away, Le Dâng Khoã, who had been following close behind, took the ring off the corpse's finger, wiped it on his trousers and put it on his own hand. Charlie and he waved farewell to each other and the Thai drove away to Thad Luang where, in a piece of delicious and unintended irony, he parked the car in front of the shacks where the quarrelling and vicious catamites lived. Dousing the lights, he and one of his men shifted the corpse over into the driver's seat, quietly shut the door and left on foot.

Epilogue

June 1975 – January 1976 Despite the incident at Ban Dong Nasok camp, about which, despite many rumours, no firm details ever emerged, life continued normally – or what passed for normal. Rance met John Chambers on 23 June and told him of the strange way he had been allowed into the camp and so unceremoniously turned out. He also reported to the Ambassador and told him of his failure to reach Vang Vieng. The two men were, in fact, released some days later, none the worse for wear but ponging a bit as washing facilities had been limited. They confirmed that the Beaver would have been impounded had it been so foolhardy as to have attempted a landing.

The British Defence Attaché asked for a meeting with the Defence Minister and, once in his office, told him what little he knew, apologising for not having been as helpful as he would have liked to have been. In fact, Lanouk already knew what had happened and Rance found him more jovial than he had expected to find him.

'*Colonen* Rance, you have failed neither your country nor mine. You have tried harder than was your due and, in a most impressive way, managed to keep your name unsoiled. You have my personal and the country's thanks. Not only were a number of those twenty-seven men I was worried about killed and wounded, the remainder have flown back to Sam Neua.'

One day in early July Rance was walking back to his villa when he was overtaken by someone riding on a bicycle who, as he was passing, said, 'I'll come round and see you tomorrow after dark.'

Rance looked up and recognised Phoun. Next day he ordered Leuam to be on hand after work until Phoun came, just in case he could be of any use. Phoun came at 8 o'clock. Rance welcomed him in, took him upstairs and offered him a drink and waited.

'You surprised us that night when you so unexpectedly turned up,' he said. 'Why did you come?'

'I was asked to give a lift to a cadre from the check point up Route 13 to the camp. The sentry on the gate told me to go where I did. I, for my part, was never more surprised to see you all crouched there. What happened after I'd gone?'

'So you really have no idea?' Phoun asked in astonishment. 'Apparently someone had killed the Soviet DA who had also unexpectedly arrived and was killed himself. Charlie had to kill the man who came with the European and who was trying to kill him, Charlie. No, Charlie didn't know who the man was. Many of the men inside the hall had been killed or wounded. Our group safely escaped across the Mekong that same night. I came back to meet my wife but found a PL guard on my house so I am going back over the river tonight. I have met Le Dâng Khoã who gave me a message for you: "The four of us you know are safe and bless you for your help and stubborn dedication to a cause not your own, that he had taken possession of a ring that the Russian had been wearing when he had been shot by Nga Sô Lựu'" – a name that meant nothing to Rance – "and that the traitor Mana Varamit was dead. Tell the English Colonel that his path is now his own," were his words and I hope that means more to you than it does to me.'

And Rance remembered Leuam's thirty-two-month prophecy, his thirty-two *phee* body souls were now placated. Mana's death was a blessing in disguise. *Did Charlie ever recognise his brother?* he wondered. *From what Phoun says it seems not.*

In London, Lieutenant General Sir David Law KCB, CBE, DSO, MC, Head of Defence Intelligence, wound up a meeting, called to close the activities concerning 'Operation Four Rings'. He was in sombre mood. '... so there you have it, Gentlemen. It was a forlorn hope at the best of times. It was a bold step on our part and, for all the good it's done, we might never have bothered. However, it has taught us a great lesson that we here in Britain disregard at our peril. It is not for me, on the eve of my retirement, to be glib and say that until the government and the people realise that the Welfare State and the Permissive Society are no substitute for a faith, a cause or a purpose, Communism of one sort of another will continue trying to devour others until it implodes and burns itself out. But no one will listen – it's too hard work! However, what I want to say is that until we take ourselves seriously, and our methods seriously and plan seriously and react seriously and try to maintain the initiative, until then the desperate, last-minute, hit-and-miss attempts that we decided to use as a substitute for long-term planning are our only recourse:

under these circumstances I believe we have done better than any of us could ever have imagined. If we take the Indo-China case book and extrapolate the northwest European one from it, we could well be wiser, if not sadder, but better prepared than we are now.

'Certainly, what reports we have had over the years from the DA indicate that Laos, the Laotians, to say nothing of so many other countries and people, have yet to find the happy medium of how to live in dignity: too much or too little and always too late.

'So, that's it. Just for your interest, I told Colonel Rance when I briefed him that I'd put him in for the OBE if he got the King crowned! I was being flippant when I said it but the fellow has done just as much as, if not more than, any Town Clerk or Pop Singer who will appear in the Honours List. So I've put his name in. Even though his days of service will be over, tone and tint, I hope he will have something to remember his time there.'

In the Cabinet Office in Whitehall, representatives from the Cabinet Office itself, the Treasury, the Foreign and Commonwealth Office, the Ministry of Defence and the Secret Intelligence Service met to consider and make recommendations about Britain's role as Co-Chairman of the 1954 and 1962 Geneva Accords for Indo-China and Laos respectively, in the light of the worsening financial situation in and the diminishing credibility of the United Kingdom as a Great Power. It was not a topic to inspire confidence, some of the participants feeling that it was an infringement of their valuable time when they had other and more pressing tasks to do.

The last meeting had been held in November 1974, a year

prior to this one, and, even without reading the minutes, it had become blindingly obvious that no more British aid would be given to Laos unless for humanitarian reasons and then only in the direst of emergencies.

There was hardly any comment when it was formally agreed to cease giving aid, including payment to the Foreign Exchange Operating Fund, which would have to be disbanded as soon as the Co-Chairmanship had formally been dispensed with. Sir James Redfeather, KCMG, the Mandarin who normally chaired such meetings, had recently retired and in his place was a much younger man, nearing forty, called Jeremy Coulson. He was summing up: '… so, Gentlemen, as our interests always have been tenuous, as was our influence nugatory and presence unwanted, this is a fitting and timely end to our involvement in Indo-China in general and Laos in particular.

'I wonder if we ever have a Defence Attaché in Laos. If we did then we must withdraw him and close his office. I cannot for the life of me see what he was wasting good taxpayers' money for. Those military gentlemen are, I believe, an expensive luxury who can never possibly achieve anything. What sort of fellow did you put out to grass there? Some "pear-shaped has-been" probably who could not be placed anywhere less useful.'

No wonder Britain is 'going to the dogs' thought both military and intelligence representatives, not bothering to answer the pompous and ignorant man chairing the meeting. Better to keep quiet and let the others know their real feelings by their frigid reaction.

Six weeks after the thirtieth anniversary of the Independence of Laos, celebrations were held in great style on 23 October 1975, when the country was officially united as one, and there was an important announcement: it was to the effect that, by request of the people, the King had been deposed and the country renamed the Lao People's Democratic Republic and that the new government would be headed by a president – *Tan* Souvannouvong, once known as the Red Prince. It would be ruled by a Politburo of dedicated cadres who had been working for such a regime as this for just over thirty years, most of the time from the fastness of Sam Neua, combating the imperialist Americans, feudalist Thais, reactionary, right-wing elements of their own countrymen but always buoyed up by the fraternal support of the comrades of the Union of Soviet Socialist Republics and the People's Republic of China. There would be a formal appearance of the Politburo at the President's Residence, the old feudal royal palace, in Vientiane on 5 December. Representatives of the diplomatic community would be invited to attend.

In London the FCO gave formal recognition on the same day that the new President and the Politburo showed themselves to the world. From half past 6 onwards, that Friday evening, on the lawn in front of the large building, so recently done-up for coronation ceremonies and celebrations, waiting for the new rulers to show themselves, there was a mixture of ill-mannered levity from the representatives of the puppet states, Cuba being particularly ill-served, and the Soviets. The Chinese were quieter. The non-communist representatives were Rance, a new American, the French and the Thai, the rest having gone.

The new national flag, red and blue with a white circle in the middle, was everywhere in profusion. Shortly before 8 p.m. all heads were turned to the top of the steps leading down from the main door and, at 8 p.m. exactly, lights were turned on, revealing, for the first time in public, the new men. The lighting was such that they looked like death heads but, as they descended the steps, the illusion gave way to reality – a bunch of pallid-featured, humourless fanatics. The guests had been drawn up in correct pecking order and, in their turn, they reached Rance who, by then, was doyen of the Attaché corps, so stood at the right of the other Attachés.

The new leaders passed by, the President in front, each man inclining his head slightly at each guest. As a sop to credibility, one of the old regime remained as an adviser, Souvanna Phouma, the one-time Neutralist Prime Minister. As he passed Rance, almost as though there stood the last remaining vestige of the life he had once known and worked hard for, he came forward and shook the Englishman's hand, giving him a long, sad look with troubled eyes, then, with the ghost of a smile, passed wordlessly on. And the last four men who passed by, the youngest and most recently joined members of the Politburo, came near enough to shake hands with Rance, who, in the semi darkness, felt that each one wore a ring on the little finger of his right hand. A smile of thanks was just visible on their lips as they passed by.

January 1976. London: But there was something for Jason to remember his time in Laos as Lieutenant General (retired) Sir David Law KCB, CBE, DSO, MC found out when, towards the end of January, he received an invitation to the wedding of Colonel Jason Percival Vere Rance, OBE and Miss Inkham Hatsady, with Major Xutiati Xuto as Best Man. As Sir David told his wife, 'That will make "a fifth ring with a golden belle".'

Laos, 2005: The caves at Sam Neua were no longer even a tourist attraction but, nevertheless, an unusual party was being held. There was an elderly Englishman and his still pert and pretty Lao wife, younger than her husband but still burdened by years. They were being fêted by four elderly Lao gentlemen.

'It is sixty years since cataclysmic events started and thirty since the upheaval that changed not only the way the country was governed but the flag, the national anthem, the currency and even the postage stamps,' one of the four was saying, playing, as he did with a large ring on the little finger of his right hand.

'I left the country feeling sad to a degree I never thought I could have done when I first set foot in it,' said the Englishman. 'I found the Lao people so pleasant and understanding but utterly lost at the way events outside their control were taking place.' He rubbed his bald pate reflectively.

'Yes,' joined in his wife. 'I thought I never could come back here but Jason persuaded me, just for the very last time. And I am so glad to find the place unchanged yet changed in so many ways.'

'Pray explain yourself, dear lady,' said another of the four gentlemen.

'It is difficult to express it properly,' she answered, smiling as delectably as ever she had.

'I'll stick my neck out and try for her,' said her husband. 'The

Lao have a wonderful way of managing their affairs at a practical level, that is the level below what the politicians talk about, that has hardly changed over the centuries.' He looked round at the four Lao gentlemen and saw that each was nodding his head and smiling. 'My wife is, I think, trying to say that matters have almost returned to what they were before the upheaval thirty years ago that started thirty years before that. Much has been lost but much has been gained so the equilibrium has been maintained.'

'Jason, you are correct as usual,' said his wife, looking at him adoringly.

The spokesman of the four said, 'Let me have the last word before we have a last cup of tea and move off. Phannyana Maha Thera, when abbot of Sam Neua and later as Chief Bonze of Laos in Luang Prabang, were he here today, could not have put it any better. He would also have said that any political virus, like the Communists espoused, would have diseased seeds that only produced crooked timber and genuine, satisfying and clean religious thought has to win through to the end.'

Heads nodded in agreement. As goodbyes were being said, one of the four said, 'It is all a question of Perseverance,' which the one-time Princess Golden Fairy corrected, 'Not "it" but "he", my Jason Percival Vere Rance …'

Read more in the Jason Rance series of historical military fiction set in Southeast Asia. Based on historical fact and the author's personal knowledge, the series comprises, in order, *Operation Black Rose*, *Operation Janus*, *Operation Blind Spot*, *Operation Stealth* and *Operation Four Rings*. The author, a retired Gurkha colonel, draws on real characters and events he witnessed across various theatres of war.

Volume 1: Operation Black Rose

In 1938 Malaya, Japanese intelligence officers and pro-Independence Indians conspire to test their suspicions about British intelligence officer Philip Rance by attempting to burgle his office. The plot is foiled by Rance's teenage son, Jason, who must move to England to escape revenge. Singapore and Malaya fall to the Japanese and captured Indian POWs are enlisted in the anti-British 'Indian National Army' under Subhas Chandra Bose. All four burglars are involved. The young Jason Rance now serves in a Gurkha battalion and he finds himself involved against all four renegades who try to kill him.

Volume 2: Operation Janus

Chinese taxi-girls dance with off-duty British military personnel at the Yam Yam nightclub and listen out for loose talk, which they feed back to their Communist handlers. It is 1950s Malaya and the country is in the throes of the Malayan Emergency. As the British do battle with Communist terrorists hiding deep in the jungle, one British officer, a Communist sympathizer, is spirited away to the jungle Communist HQ, Chin Peng, the leader of the Malayan Communist Party, gloats at what he hopes will be a major propaganda victory. Jason Rance, is despatched with five Gurkhas to hunt Hinlea down and the chase through pathless jungle becomes a race against time and a contest of deadly jungle warfare skills.

Volume 3: Operation Blind Spot

After years of jungle service, Jason Rance, a maverick Chinese-speaking British major of Gurkhas has one final chance of qualifying for promotion to lieutenant colonel. During a covert operation on the Thai–Malayan border, Rance meets a Chinese schoolboy friend from jungle-operation days and together they must pit Malaya's orang asli, or indigenous people, against Chin Peng and the Malayan Communists, now hiding in south Thailand, trying to rescue two stranded wartime Gurkhas as they do. Rance is further tasked to command Borneo's Border Scouts during the Borneo Confontation. Rance and his Gurkhas lead raids over the border into Indonesia and Rance becomes a personal target for the Indonesian military.

Volume 4: Operation Stealth

In post-WWII Laos, Vietnamese communists secretly commence to infiltrate the kingdom. They are countered by four dedicated Lao 'moles' who try to thwart these aims. Gurkha Colonel Jason Rance is unwittingly dragged into a confrontation between one of the Lao moles and a Thai spy and the mole gives him a ring as a reward for saving his life. During his appointment in Laos as military attaché, Rance becomes a target of the KGB and of the Vietnamese communists, and is sought by the remaining three Lao moles because of the ring in his possession. *Operation Stealth* is followed by *Operation Four Rings*.